Pearl

Books by Lauraine Snelling

A SECRET REFUGE

Daughter of Twin Oaks   Sisters of the Confederacy
The Long Way Home

DAKOTAH TREASURES

Ruby   Opal
Pearl   Amethyst

DAUGHTERS OF BLESSING

A Promise for Ellie
Sophie's Dilemma
A Touch of Grace
Rebecca's Reward

RED RIVER OF THE NORTH

An Untamed Land   The Reapers' Song
A New Day Rising   Tender Mercies
A Land to Call Home   Blessing in Disguise

RETURN TO RED RIVER

A Dream to Follow   Believing the Dream
More Than a Dream

Pearl

LAURAINE SNELLING

BETHANYHOUSE
MINNEAPOLIS, MINNESOTA

Published by Bethany House Publishers
11400 Hampshire Avenue South
Bloomington, Minnesota 55438

Bethany House Publishers is a division of
Baker Publishing Group, Grand Rapids, Michigan.

Printed in the United States of America

ISBN   978-0-7642-2221-4

Library of Congress Cataloging-in-Publication Data
Snelling, Lauraine.
    Pearl / by Lauraine Snelling.
       p.   cm. — (Dakotah treasures ; 2)
    ISBN 0-7642-2221-X (pbk.)
    1. Women pioneers—Fiction. 2. Medora (N.D.)—Fiction. I. Title.
PS3569.N39P43   2004
813'.54—dc22

                                              2003027327

Dedication

Pearl is dedicated to all the daughters God has given me, not to replace Marie but to make her absence easier.

LAURAINE SNELLING is an award-winning author of over forty books, fiction and nonfiction, for adults and young adults. Besides writing books and articles, she teaches at writers' conferences across the country. She and her husband, Wayne, have two grown sons and two dogs and make their home in California.

Acknowledgments

Historical societies are great research places for historical writers, and for this new series I thank the North Dakota Historical Society at Bismarck and Diane Rogness, the curator at the Chateau de Mores in Medora, for information and early pictures, of which there are few, of Little Missouri. Doug and Mary at the Western Edge Bookstore in Medora added bits and pieces to this series and directed me to the most helpful books and maps.

I am blessed with the most able and helpful assistant in Cecile, who has learned she is part brainstormer, part editor, part encourager, and part researcher. When she came to work for me, she didn't realize she would lose sleep over the characters in these books.

Thanks to husband Wayne for becoming more expert in the care and feeding of a writer under deadline and for the research, reading, and remembering he contributed. It sure helps to be married to a man who can pull historical dates out of his mind without looking them up and who enjoys being a partner of this writing life of ours.

My editor, Sharon Asmus, and all the staff at Bethany House Publishers did their usual fine work, for which I am extremely grateful. I waited a long time for an agent, and Deidre Knight has helped make my writing life both simpler and more diverse. Thanks, all of you.

CHAPTER ONE

Chicago, early March 1883

Once a teacher, always a teacher.

Pearl Hossfuss stared at the line she'd written in her most perfect script. *That is the story of my life, the rest of my life for however long it may be.* Was that a sigh of despair or acceptance she felt working its way up from her toes?

"Miss Pearl, your father said you are late for supper." The maid stood in the doorway, a quick glance over her shoulder giving the impression she would rather be anywhere than where she was at the moment.

"Thank you, Marlene. I'm sorry you had to come searching for me." Pearl corked her inkwell and stood, tucking her hair into the gentle wave that, along with the high-necked waist, covered the scar on her neck. She glanced in the mirror as she passed the oak-framed oval mirror. No sense in not being perfectly groomed. She'd been sent back to her room more than once to repair an imperfection.

She touched the cameo at the neckline, her talisman, the last gift from her mother. Would her father even remember that today, March fifth, was the tenth anniversary of her mother's death? Not that he would say anything, of course.

She made her way down the curved and carved staircase, the gas-lit chandelier on the landing dispelling the gloom of a gray day. The light reflecting off the Venetian crystals was a sight that never failed to lift her spirits.

"I'm sorry I'm late. I was studying for tomorrow." She made her way to the chair at her stepmother's left hand, where she had sat ever since Amalia joined the Hossfuss family a year after Pearl's mother died. Her father had at least paid tribute to the strictures of society regarding the year of mourning.

The way he snapped his napkin and laid it across his lap told her he would have more to say later on the subject of her tardiness. Muttonchop whiskers, two shades darker than his sandy hair, bristled. Gold-rimmed glasses perched low on a nose as regal as a Greek god's.

Eleven-year-old Jorge Bronson Hossfuss Jr., a miniature of his father, sans glasses, in appearance only, glanced at her from lowered eyes, one twitching in a wink. If it weren't for the antics of Jorge, life in the Hossfuss mansion would be far more sober.

"Let us pray." Mr. Hossfuss, the name still called him by his wife, bowed his head and began without waiting to make sure everyone did the same. He just expected it.

"I Jesu navn . . ."

The Norwegian words flowed around the table, a daily reminder of their heritage, a heritage that Jorge Bronson Hossfuss Sr. had capitalized on as a way to the wealth that built a warehouse, office buildings, and as Pearl recently discovered, some of the tenements where her pupils lived, as well as the Hossfuss estate on Lakeshore Drive.

Pearl brought her thoughts back in time to join the others in the amen. Was that why her father allowed her to teach at the settlement house? As a way of atonement for his investments? Or, as she had suspected more than once, was it because teaching was the only permissible position for his elder daughter who refused to become a leader in the society where his new wife thrived? After nine years of marriage, Amalia was not new, but Pearl always thought of her that way.

"Thank you," she responded as the maid set a gilt-edged flat bowl centered on a matching gilt-edged plate in front of her. Fish ball soup tonight. Inga, direct from the old country, cooked all manner of meals but was truly in her element when she could serve true Norwegian fare.

"How was school today?" her father asked his son.

"All right. I made an A on that composition about the wreck

of the *HF,* thanks to the information you gave me."

Mr. Hossfuss shook his head. The *HF,* standing for Hoss Fuss, had been one of his ships, veteran of many Atlantic crossings, but had sunk in a freak storm on Lake Michigan.

"And you, Pearl, have you a good report also?" His mandatory question asked, he nodded to the maid to remove his soup dish.

"Yes." But she made no effort to continue. He never bothered to listen.

"Mrs. Smithson said that she'd heard your headmistress saying what a superb teacher you are." Amalia patted her mouth with her napkin. "I know that makes your father very proud of you."

Pearl knew no such thing. Once, back when she was his princess, she had thought that, but no longer. He did his duty by her—he would never bear to have someone say he had shirked his duty—but with that taken care of, he relegated her to things past.

Wishing she were up in the nursery with the younger children, Pearl finished her dinner, waited for her father and stepmother to adjourn to the parlor for their evening together, then she and Jorge headed for the second floor in the west wing, the floor devoted to children.

"Did you see the stage since I remade it for Arnet and Anna?"

"No. When did you finish?"

"Last night."

"So they will be able to give their first performance for Father's birthday?"

"Right on schedule. He'll have to believe you had a hand in the script."

"No one will tell him." She'd already made sure of that. All the credit would go to Arnet and Anna who, while they were ten months apart, looked more alike than many twins.

"Do you think Father will like our surprise?"

He better. "Of course he will. After all, it's about when he came to America. How many times has he told you the story?"

Jorge grinned. "I can't count that high."

Jealousy was one of the seven deadly sins, and Pearl had to

fight it off on a regular basis. On one hand she rejoiced for her younger brothers and sister, but on the other, if only her father would grace her with the smiles she remembered from before, then . . . But it was always *before*. Before life had changed in an instant. Accidents happened. That's why they were called accidents.

"Are you having your class do a play this year?" Jorge asked.

"I'd like to." Ignoring the memory of the extra long hours she'd put in to make the play a success, she thought only to the faces of her pupils, the smiles, the excited jabbering, the fear overcome. Could she manage to create such a production again, or had her children last year been especially gifted?

"I'll help you."

She turned to her brother. "*Tusen takk* and more."

He sketched a bow. "You have no idea what it will cost you."

Her laugh made his smile widen.

— ❧ —

That night as she prepared for bed, Pearl opened her Bible to Psalm 91, one of her favorites. She recited it aloud as she loosened her corset, sliding the bone-ridged garment down so she could step out of it. She hung it in the chifforobe, lifting her dressing gown off the hook at the same time. "'He that dwelleth in the secret place of the most High shall abide under the shadow of the Almighty. I will say of the Lord, He is my refuge and my fortress: my God; in him will I trust. Surely he shall deliver thee from the snare of the fowler, and from the noisome pestilence. He shall cover thee with his feathers, and under his wings thou shalt trust: his truth shall be thy shield and buckler.'" She turned the pages to verses fourteen and sixteen, her latest verses to consign to memory. She read one verse aloud, reciting it again as she sat to brush her hair the required one hundred strokes. Dark like honey, left in the hive over winter, that glinted fire when sparked by sunlight, the strands rippled down her back. She could call one of the maids to come brush it for her, but she knew they were busy cleaning up from supper. The pitcher of water, still warm for her to wash her face, was a luxury. Bathing in the bathroom was also a luxury, but there was something special about the privacy of her own room. And besides, this was the time she used to spend with her mother, a sacred hour just before bedtime, when Anna asked about her day, told her stories of when she was little after coming from Norway, and always, the most delicious, brushed her hair. And allowed her daughter to brush hers. Ah, the rippling gold of her mother's hair. Pearl's had never held the sheen and silkiness of her mother's.

She stared at the face in the slightly wavy mirror. She knew she looked like her mother—straight nose, full lips, and eyebrows with a tendency to arch, both in question or amusement. Except for the side she kept turned from the light. Always there was an *except*. But her mother had been a beauty, so why didn't the similar features do the same for her daughter?

Was it the touch of her father's square chin? His wider brow? The tiny gap between her two front teeth? Beauty was in the eyes of the beholder, or so the old saying went. And her eyes always saw only the almost, the not quite.

She folded back the covers and stroked her hand over the warmed sheets. Marlene had been busy with the warming pan, a long-handled round pan filled with coals that she stroked between the sheets. Settled with two pillows propped behind her so she could read, Pearl opened her book, carefully placing the leather bookmark beyond where she was reading. Nothing gave her more pleasure than a good book. Even though she'd read Jane Austen's *Sense and Sensibility* before, she lost herself in the story, finally turning off the gaslight when her eyes grew too heavy to stay open. In the darkness of her room she watched the branches outside her window dance in the wind. As a child they'd frightened her, but now they'd become old friends.

"Lord, what is to become of me? Am I to remain here in my father's house, doing his bidding for the rest of my life? Is there not another place for me? Perhaps even a husband? I hate to sound like a whining woman, but I'm nearly twenty-three, an old maid in everyone's eyes. Is that your will for me?" She paused, a heaviness settling on her chest. A sigh sent it scurrying. "I surely do hope not, pray not. Have I been remiss lately in saying how I love you? Forgive me for being so wrapped up in my own concerns. I do love you. I honor you and praise your most holy name. Amen." She turned on her side and tucked the quilts up about her shoulders.

Sometime later, she woke from a dream of traveling on a train. *I wonder where I was going.*

CHAPTER TWO

Pearl stared across her fifth-grade class at the settlement house. Half of them belonged at home in bed if their coughing and runny noses were any indication. But they were at least warm here and had a hot meal at noon.

"Miss Hossfuss, I gotta go," one of the boys said.

"You may be excused." She gave him an arched eyebrow look. "But come straight back." She refrained from adding "this time," but he knew. One more trip to the principal, and he would be out on the streets.

No one with even a lick of brains wanted to be out on the sleety streets of Chicago. The wind seared skin and sucked the juice out of one, leaving a person reeling. And yesterday had been the first fine taste of spring.

"All right class, since we cannot go outside for recess, we will play a game in here. Now count off by twos." She pointed to the girl on the far left side of the room. "Start with you, Sadie."

Sighs and groans accompanied the numbering as the sides took shape. Letting them choose took far too long and always left the last one standing feeling as though no one liked him, or her, as the case may be.

"You're here with us," someone called when the boy re-entered the room.

"All right now, form up behind the line. We're going to do a relay. The person at the head of the line runs to the front of the room, grabs an eraser off the blackboard, and runs back, handing it off to the next runner. The first team to finish wins."

"What is our prize?" Several children asked at the same time.

Pearl kept a jar of peppermint candies for such a time as this. She reached down in the drawer and set the jar on her desk. "The winning team each gets two pieces, the other team one." As soon as the cheers quieted, she counted, "One, two. . . ." and paused. They groaned. "I forgot to tell you that you cannot cross the line until the runner ahead of you does." She pointed to the line she'd painted on the worn floorboards. When they nodded, she began again, "One, two, three, go."

Yelling and jumping as they cheered their teammates on did more to warm kids up than the actual running. The teams were neck and neck when they hit the tenth and last person. The last two runners, the two weakest class members, grabbed their erasers and scrambled to keep their footing as they headed for the blackboard.

Pearl stood at the side to judge fairly. The blue team won by such a slight margin that she shook her head. "I declare a tie." Now she hoped she had forty pieces of candy in the jar. "You two can each count out how many pieces?"

They scrunched their faces.

"Ah . . . ten," one boy said. His team groaned, but no one shouted out the answer. They'd all learned a hard lesson one game when someone shouted the answer and their team went without the treat. Keeping to her decision had been one of Pearl's more difficult moments.

"Think again, Ean. Two for each person on your team."

"I know." A girl on the other team nearly burst her skin with excitement.

"Now write down your answer." Pearl pointed at a piece of paper and pencil on the edge of her desk.

As the girl wrote her answer, Ean's grin lit his face, like a gas jet flaring.

Pearl held up her hand as if stopping traffic. She checked the girl's writing, nodded, and turned to nod at Ean.

"Twenty," he said triumphantly.

"Very good." Pearl poured the red-and-white striped candy pieces from the jar onto a napkin. "Count them out."

With everyone sucking on peppermint candies, she motioned them to sit on the floor in front of her closer to the radiators where it was warmer. As soon as they were settled, she opened the book she'd been reading a chapter at a time. *Oliver Twist* took off on another adventure with his gang, each child sitting spellbound as Pearl read to the class.

When the dismissal bell rang, Pearl closed the book. "Now remember that we have a test tomorrow in arithmetic, and you must all be ready to recite your poem." Knowing that few of them had more than a candle or lamp for light in the evenings, she hesitated to give homework assignments during the long winter nights. Not that many of the parents paid much attention to the assignments she did give.

If half of her fifth-grade class returned in the fall, she'd be surprised. Too many families needed the older children to be out working, especially those with no fathers.

Three children stayed after the bell to help her clean the classroom, chatting and laughing as they washed the blackboard, swept the floor, and banged the chalk out of the erasers on the lee side of the building.

"Miss Hossfuss, are we going to do a play this year?" one of the girls asked. Her brother had been in Pearl's class the year before.

"I believe we will start work on it next week. What fairy tale do you think we should do?" Nothing like a snap decision.

"*Cinderella.*"

"I want *Snow White and the Seven Dwarfs,* and I get to be a dwarf."

Pearl wasn't up to making a decision at that point. She wasn't even sure she was up to all the work it would take to put on a play.

"You need to hurry home now before it gets dark. Thank you for your help." Pearl waved them out the door, took her outer things from the cupboard and, coat over her arm, shut the door to her classroom behind her. She'd think about it overnight and if she felt up to it she'd put the play story to a vote in class tomorrow.

Pearl stood on the steps for a few moments, feeling like the children must. She'd rather be here than at home.

"Miss Pearl!" A male voice broke into her thoughts. Of course, her stepmother had sent their family carriage for her.

"I could have taken the trolley." While she knew there was no sense in taking out her ire on one of the servants, nevertheless, she failed to keep the grumble from her voice.

"Now, you know the missus. I picked up the children too and will go back for the mister." He tucked a robe about her lap and smiled up at her. "You wouldn't be wanting me to be out of a job, now, would you?" The wind had whipped his cheeks red, but his smile took the sting from her thoughts.

I should be grateful, Pearl reminded herself. But the self scolding did not brighten her mood.

An air of suppressed excitement met her at the door. Two maids were tittering in the hall when she entered but broke off and hurried about their duties as if she were the head housekeeper.

Jorge Jr. met her on the stairs. "You must wear your newest frock to dinner. Mother said so."

"Why?"

He shrugged. "I think we are having company."

"But nothing was said at breakfast." They reached the landing of the second floor.

"I know. I think it is someone important Father is bringing home."

"Oh, brother. I thought to take a long bath and go to bed early."

"Are you sick?" He peered up at her, concern darkening his blue eyes.

Sick of . . . no, you agreed you would find things to be thankful for, remember? "Just tired."

"I think you better look your best." He didn't add anything further, but Pearl could without effort. *Or Father will be angry.* And no one in the household wanted to make Father angry.

"Hurry, Miss Pearl, I'll run the bath for you," said Marlene, one of the family servants, meeting her in the hallway.

"Thank you, Marlene. Please use the lavender bath salts. Perhaps the steam will make me feel better."

"Are you ill?"

"No, just droopy."

"You'll catch your death from all those settlement children. You mark my words," Marlene commented as she rushed to run the bath.

Jorge snorted under his breath and rolled his eyes. "If she had her way, none of us would leave the house. Life is too dangerous out there." He mimicked Marlene's voice perfectly.

"You need to think of a life in the theater. You're already better than Barrymore." Pearl stopped in her doorway. "Will you be dining in the dining room?"

"No!" Delight danced in his eyes. "I am relegated to the nursery where I shall—"

"Master Jorge, come here this instant!" Marlene's voice echoed down the hallway.

"Oh no, I forgot to get Herman out of the bathtub." He hotfooted it down the hall, his chuckle floating out behind him.

Pearl shook her head as she shut her door. Herman was a turtle, and every once in a while, Jorge took him from his sandy box and let him loose in the bathtub for a real swim. Obviously he'd forgotten to put him back in his swampy home. Marlene didn't care for turtles or any other creepy-crawly creatures. All of which were beloved by the younger children.

Pearl could take them or leave them. As she undressed and donned her wrapper, she thought again of her students. *I could take Herman in for a few days. They most likely have never seen a live turtle.* Rats like Arnet's Peabody they saw in abundance. Most likely not spotted white, however.

After her bath she returned to her room to find her new aqua dress with the slightly darker overskirt and matching shawl hanging on the chifforobe door. Lace the same color filled in the heart-shaped bodice, while intricate beading and stitching covered the required high collar. A lovely frock for a command performance, no less.

She rang for Marlene when she was ready to have her corset tied, but Bernadette, her mother's maid, appeared instead.

"Ah, is there some secret going on that I'm unaware of?"

"No, miss. I am to do your hair also." Bernadette had a reputation for creating elaborate hairdos, and on Amalia, they always looked lovely.

"I don't wear my hair—" She *oof*ed as the corset drove all the air from her lungs. "And I don't go anywhere laced this tight."

Bernadette loosened the strings only a hint.

"More, or I will not leave this room."

"But, Miss Pearl, you—"

"Miss Pearl nothing. If I cannot breathe, I will faint on the stairs, and then what kind of scene would we have?"

The tsking from behind her clearly stated the maid's opinion, but she did as requested. Barely.

Pearl sucked in three-quarters of a breath and rolled her eyes. "I am not a slave or a horse being trotted out for inspection, and I insist on knowing what this is all about." She shook her head at Bernadette's pointing to the padded bench in front of her dressing table. "Not until you tell me what you know. And I know you know something, because the two parlormaids were tittering when I came home and hustled out without speaking. Jorge told me there is company for supper."

"If I tell you, you'll let me do your hair and won't let on you know?"

"Bernadette, I am far from stupid, and all this extra fussing has to alert me to something. Even Father would understand that. Just tell me so we can get this charade over with."

"I don't know who the guest—"meeting Pearl's direct gaze in the mirror, Bernadette backtracked—"er, man is, but Madame Amalia told me what you were to wear and that I was to fix your hair. That is all I know. Cross my heart." She loosed the knot of hair that Pearl had pinned high on her head to keep it out of the water.

"I think a feather here would be nice." She fashioned a mound of hair on top of Pearl's head.

"It has to cover the scar. You know that."

"I will sweep it down on the sides then and up to fall in ringlets down the back."

"I despise ringlets."

"I could braid a string of pearls . . ." As she talked around a mouthful of hairpins, Bernadette's hands were busy with the hair, roping it one way, twisting another.

"No, that won't work either. I look like some . . . some debutante or something. You know I like simple things."

"Ah, but simple is often plain, and you are anything but plain."

"Flattery will get you nowhere. Just finish, or I will be late, and then all your work will be for naught because my head will roll."

Within minutes Bernadette held the dress high over Pearl's head and dropped it into place without stirring a hair, a feat that always elicited Pearl's amazement. While the maid buttoned all the tiny buttons up the back, Pearl smoothed a hand down the front.

This was a far cry from her everyday wear in the schoolroom, that was for sure.

"Now." Bernadette spritzed one of Amalia's perfumes at Pearl's chest and wrists, pressed a lacy handkerchief into her hand, and shooed her out the door. "I will clean up in here."

Her father checked his watch as she entered through the arched doorway, an act that immediately set Pearl's teeth on edge. She was not late. In fact, she was a few minutes early. She'd checked the ornately carved clock in the hallway to be sure. They always ate at seven.

"Good evening, Father, Amalia." If one was to play a role, one must do it well, including perfect diction and posture. She smiled at the nondescript man standing beside her father and extended her hand, palm down and limp.

"Mr. Longstreet, I would like you to meet my elder daughter, Pearl Hossfuss."

"I am pleased to meet you, Miss Hossfuss. Your father has spoken of you most highly."

Pearl almost sent her father a look of astonishment but covered with a slight cough behind the handkerchief. A fan would have been a delightful touch. "Thank you." *It's a shame he has never mentioned you to any of us.*

"Mr. Longstreet is new to our company and to Chicago. I thought perhaps you would give him a guided tour on Sunday after church."

"Really." Her gaze flashed to her stepmother. Amalia shrugged but only with one shoulder and almost imperceptibly.

Amalia might not have had any advance warning either

unless Mr. Hossfuss had sent a message home by one of his office runners.

Mr. Longstreet bowed over her hand.

He did know how to do that right. Pearl smiled an acknowledgment, as if she did this every day. Her years of watching and loving every stage play that came to town often paid off in unexpected ways.

"Supper is served, madam," Mr. French, head butler, announced from the doorway.

When her father extended his bent arm to his wife, Mr. Longstreet did the same for Pearl. She placed her left hand on his sleeve lightly, as she had seen an actress do on stage and read in countless books. Memories of practice lessons at Mrs. Eldridge's Finishing School for Young Ladies returned. She'd thought such affectations a waste of time even back then. A good book was far more worthy of discussion than the list of topics one was allowed to introduce in polite society during the meal.

She was grateful she'd not had to play this part often, one good thing that had come of the scar on her neck. Her father believed her less than perfect appearance would offend some of the people in the society he would like to have conquered. While he had made a fortune, that alone did not qualify one for the *crème de la crème* of Chicago society.

Pearl allowed herself to be seated by the butler, nodding her thanks over her shoulder and making sure her parents did not see the slightly raised eyebrow.

"You are most welcome, miss."

"Tell me about yourself, Mr. Longstreet," Pearl suggested over the cheesy corn chowder, a perfect soup for such a miserable night. She would have preferred a larger bowl of the chowder with crusty Swedish rye bread up in either her own room or the nursery or the kitchen. Anywhere but here, where the strictures around her waist would make taking more than a few mouthfuls of any course impossible.

"I . . . ah . . . work for your father, and I moved to Chicago from Duluth, Minnesota." He took another spoonful of chowder and wiped his mouth with the napkin.

Pearl did not believe she was a snob, but the worn look of the cuff nearest her, the shiny elbows, and the slightly limp collar of his shirt told her no one was looking after his clothing. They were definitely not the sartorial caliber of most of her father's friends. She wrinkled her nose at the slightly musty odor that emanated from him, as if both he and his clothing needed an airing or a bath.

"Duluth is quite a bit colder than Chicago, is it not?" The weather was always a safe topic.

"Not really."

She waited for him to say more, but when he returned to his soup, she did likewise.

When their soup plates were replaced by the salads, she caught her father's glowering look and dug around for another question.

"What kind of books do you like to read?"

He crumpled his napkin. "I . . . ah . . . I'm sorry to say I-I haven't read much."

Doesn't read much. How distressing. "Oh." *Music, everyone loves music.* "Have you been able to attend any concerts since you came here?"

"Ah . . ." He shook his head. "No."

"Have you joined a church?" Rule number three of Mrs. Eldridge's list for polite conversation. Do not discuss religion.

"No, not yet." He turned slightly to see her better. "You see, I have five children, and between home and my new position in your father's company, I have little time for anything else."

"I see. Well, once you settle in, perhaps you would like to join us at First Lutheran. Your children would love the Sunday school there."

"Thank you. I will keep that in mind."

They finished the roast pork main course with decidedly desultory conversation among the four of them. While waiting for dessert, Mr. Hossfuss spoke up resolutely.

"I thought that perhaps, if the weather improves, you would show our guest your favorite parts of our city on Sunday afternoon, after he joins us for dinner, of course." His smile notified Pearl that this was more than just a suggestion, and that if he had anything to say about it, the weather would be balmy.

But that's when I prepare for my week's lessons. Pearl bit back a retort and smiled, just barely, but it was a smile. She could feel her cheeks move. "Why, certainly. If Mr. Longstreet can find the time, that is."

"Oh yes, that would be most agreeable."

I sincerely doubt that. So far we have absolutely nothing in common, and I shall have to talk myself hoarse.

"Good, that is arranged then," her father said. "Ah, Inga has outdone herself with her dried-peach upside down cake."

Even Father can't keep the conversation going. Pearl tried to catch Amalia's gaze, but her stepmother was whispering something to the butler.

What a bizarre evening, what a waste of her best gown. Getting comfortable in her nightdress and reading in her cozy room sounded infinitely better than dragging through dessert. Surely their boring guest would leave right after supper unless, of course, her father invited him for a cigar, and then they'd have coffee again. Could she feign a headache, something she'd never done in her life?

Who was this man, and why was he here?

CHAPTER THREE

He never mentioned his wife, only five children.

Pearl sat straight up in bed at the thought. Here she'd been almost asleep, and this thought grabbed her like someone reaching from the bushes and snatching her hand.

Surely her father hadn't—no, of course not. He'd never pushed a suitor on her, in fact he'd seemed content that she helped with the other children and accompanied Amalia on her missions of mercy, as she called them. Amalia took to heart the Bible's admonition to care for the poor and downtrodden. He'd also seemed pleased—or was it relieved?—when she started teaching at the settlement school.

Or had he ever even cared?

I know he loved me at one time. I can remember him bragging about his little girl. When I was the only one he had.

"Far, Far!" Pearl ran to her father when he came through the door.

"How's my datter today? Were you a good girl?"

"Yes." Her blond, near to white, hair haloed around her face. "I am always good."

"And your mor, she would agree?"

"Yes. Ah . . ." She tipped her head to the side and gave her father an extra-wide smile. "Mostly."

"Should I go ask her?"

With a very brief nod, Pearl ducked her chin, and her fore-finger found its way to her lower lip. She no longer sucked her thumb, but the fingertip to the lip sufficed. "I didn't want to take my bath after playing in the dirt." The words were spoken into the finger and all run together.

"Ah, I see. And then what happened? You look all shiny clean now."

"Mor said she would say I was bad, and . . ." Here her blue eyes found his again, and she whispered, "I don't ever want to be a bad girl."

He picked her up in his arms. "You will never be a bad girl, naughty sometimes but never bad." He kissed her cheek and stood her back on the floor, taking her hand in his. "Now let's go find Mor and have supper. Oh." He stopped and dug in his breast pocket. "I found this today. Do you think you could take care of it for me?" He handed her a lemon drop.

"*Mange takk.*" She popped it in her mouth and skipped beside him, sucking all the while.

"Mr. Hossfuss, you are going to spoil that child." Anna's smile made her husband laugh.

And that wasn't just one day, but the pattern for most of the days.

Pearl could still taste the lemon drop when she remembered. All before that one day. The day of the accident. After that . . .

She jerked herself back to the present, finding her fingers tracing the scar.

She plumped her pillow and lay back down. Only at night did the memories trap her, only at night when she had no defenses.

— ⁂ —

Getting ready for school in the morning, she made a decision. No play this year. Not that it had been an annual thing. Last year had been the first, but still, she'd been seriously considering it. But there just wasn't time before school was dismissed for the summer, although if she had her way, there would be no summer without regular classes. These children were too far behind already. So what special thing could they do instead? Wishing for Bernadette's facile fingers to do her hair, she instead pinned the usual sweep in place to cover the scar and bundled the mass into a crocheted snood. She checked her appearance in the mirror, satisfied that nothing was amiss, and picked up her satchel with all her supplies for school. While descending the stairs, her mind worried at the puzzle.

"Your father had an early meeting," the maid said in response to her questioning look. The table seemed empty without him sitting at the head, glasses on the end of his nose as he memorized the newspaper. Keeping up on all the news and politics was one of the traits he claimed helped him build his empire. One thing was for sure, once a fact entered his head, it never left.

Pearl laid her napkin in her lap, said grace, and took her first sip of coffee, one of her favorite rituals of the day. Tea was for later. Coffee started the day. If she'd known she'd be eating alone, she'd have moved to the sunroom, one of her favorite places in the Hossfuss mansion.

Jorge Jr. slid into his seat, his smile lighting the room. "I thought you might be gone. Father left early, eh?"

"You're just the person I need to see."

"Really?" He checked his reach for the platter of rolls.

"I've decided it is too late to do a play this year, and besides, this class takes longer to learn things than last year's, so now I need an idea of something for them to look forward to." *For me too, as the case may be.*

"I'll have to think about that."

The maid brought in Pearl's plate of soft-boiled eggs, bacon, and one piece of toast. "Here you go, miss."

"Thank you." Pearl watched the new maid replace her father's napkin in the silver napkin ring. "Mr. Hossfuss wants a clean napkin with every meal," she instructed.

"Oh, sorry."

"The rest of us don't care."

"I see. Is there anything else I can bring you?"

"Not at the moment. Jorge?"

"Inga is already preparing my plate." He propped his elbows on the table, another indication the master of the house was absent.

"You're going to forget one day and . . ."

"No I won't. Not after the last time." He rolled his eyes, munching on the roll he took from the platter in the center of the table as he talked.

Pearl ignored his manners and motioned him to pass the rolls. "Before they are all gone."

His grin made her smile back. "Cook would send out more."

"So what do you think?"

"An art project?"

"Like what?"

"A mural."

"I don't think so."

"Shame you didn't start a garden."

"*Now* you think of it."

"You could bring them here for a picnic. Inga would love to fix a picnic."

"That's a wonderful idea! We could walk over, talk about the things we see on the way, and walk back a different way."

"What if you took the cable car? I'll bet most of them have never ridden on that." He dug into the pancakes, two eggs, and bacon set before him.

"Here's warm syrup." The maid set the pitcher at his elbow. "Would you like your chocolate now?"

"Yes, with half coffee, please."

"Sacrilege." Pearl murmured the words for his ears alone which made him laugh again.

"I read that some people drink theirs that way. It sounded good to me. But when I asked Cook to make croissants, she shook her head." He leaned closer. "I don't know why."

"You mispronounced the word. Perhaps that's why she looked confused and said no." Pearl corrected his pronunciation. "We'll go by Les Pain et Beurre sometime so you can hear and see."

"And taste and smell. I love the smells of a good bakery."

"Well, enjoy the rest of the rolls. I better be on my way." What would her father say to the idea of twenty or more tenement children, immigrants, and Negroes coming to picnic within their gates?

Somehow the idea made her smile. She'd talk it over with

Amalia instead of The Mister, as she sometimes referred to her father.

"For you, miss, from the missus." The maid handed her an envelope as she was about to go out the door.

"Does she need to see me before I leave?"

"No, miss. I hope your day is a blessing."

"Thank you." Pearl took a deep breath of moisture-laden air carried by the wind off Lake Michigan. Purple and white crocuses bloomed along the gravel walk.

On days like today she enjoyed her walk, much to the consternation of Marlene, who thought ladies of her station should avail themselves of the carriage. Even the short distance to the cable car.

She used to listen to those strictures, but since she began teaching at the settlement house and saw how those people lived, driving up in a carriage every day seemed ostentatious. Besides, no matter how she strove to be the perfect lady, her father never noticed, only castigated her when she didn't measure up. So what difference did it make? Not that she blatantly challenged the mores of society. After all, she wasn't stupid. Quite the contrary, as those who questioned her learned.

Entering the smoke-stained brick building, she headed for her classroom, sprinkling smiles on her way like sugar on cookies.

"My, you surely are in a cheerful mood," one of the other teachers commented.

"It's a beautiful day, and after all the rain and wind we've had, I decided I better enjoy it."

"Well, if you lived with *my* mother . . ." The sour look continued on down the hall.

Pearl shrugged. *You wouldn't recognize happiness if it tripped you.* Since the sun had a difficult time streaming in the filthy windows, Pearl unlocked the catches and raised the lower panes to let in some fresh air. Then she left to locate the janitor. She found him studying the furnace that had been on its last puff for several months.

"That bad, Mr. Polenski?"

"Worse, miss. Just a good thing spring has come, that's all I can say. What we'll do next winter..." He shook his head and rubbed his chin with one finger.

"We'll let next winter take care of itself, I'd say. Perhaps by then we can find a benefactor who will donate a new furnace."

The look he gave her told her how little he believed that kind of story.

"In the meantime, I have a favor to ask."

"If I can."

"Would you please wash the windows in my classroom, on the outside, that is. I can hardly see the sun through them."

"I suppose you mean today?"

"If you could be so kind." Pearl knew how to turn on the charm when needed. But she also knew she was a favorite of his because he rarely had to clean her classroom and she frequently brought him samples of Inga's good cooking.

"Might as well since I can't figure anything more to do for that old..."

He used a Polish word that Pearl was certain she really didn't want to translate.

"Thank you. How is Mrs. Polenski?" Pearl knew his wife had been ill for some time.

"Better, thanks to that basket you sent to us."

"How did...?" She paused. She'd been sure they had no way of knowing the baskets had been from her.

He cackled and slapped his knee. "I caught you this time. Had me a suspicion is all, but you just gave it away." His heavy Polish accent made understanding difficult at times, but his delight in her consternation was obvious.

She patted his arm. "I have pupils to see to."

Back in her classroom she put her hand in her pocket. She'd had her school skirts made specially with two square pockets on the front like those on an apron. While she often kept treats for the children, a handkerchief, or chalk and pencils, now she remembered the note from her mother.

Pulling it out, she unfolded the stiff paper.

Dearest Pearl,
    Please be ready a bit early for the symphony tonight. Your father has invited guests to come to our house first

and we'll all go together. You might want to wear the new gown you'll find hanging in your room. Love, Amalia

A note. She didn't want to see me face to face. Something is going on. Pearl read the missive again. Here she'd been hoping to find a way out of attending the symphony tonight. It always lasted so long, and she had to get up for school in the morning, not languish around drinking tea like many of her acquaintances. As if it made any difference what she pleased.

Perhaps if her father were feeling expansive, he would be pleased with her idea to bring her class to her home for a picnic. Perhaps not. Perhaps she would not bother to ask him in advance. Telling him afterward or waiting until he heard and accosted her might suffice.

She put the thoughts out of her mind, smiled and waved at Mr. Polenski through the first sparkling window, and went outside to bring in her pupils to begin their morning. When she stepped outside to find Sadie covered in blood, she had an idea this would be a less than perfect day. "What happened?"

"Nothing. Her nose just started bleeding," one of the students informed her.

"Here, pinch your nose." She took Sadie by the hand and led her into the classroom.

Things got more less than perfect as the day progressed, including a fight on the playground, a pencil lost or stolen, and another nosebleed for Sadie. By the end of the day, the last thing Pearl wanted to do was dress and go to the symphony, even if they were playing Strauss.

— ❦ —

Trailing a gloved hand down the banister some hours later, clothed and bejeweled again by Bernadette's artistic hand, she made her way to the gathering with only moments to spare. Her father, resplendent in frock coat with tails, greeted people as they entered the parlor.

"Ah, here you are, my dear." He took her hand and tucked it into the crook of his arm.

Pearl shook her head, enough to set the rope of pearls looped across her forehead to swishing, not that it took much. She fought the desire to brush them away. She'd never liked wearing elaborate hairdos or fancy ball gowns. After all, as the saying went, one cannot make a silk purse out of a sow's ear.

"Mr. Longstreet is so looking forward to seeing you again." Her father leaned close enough to whisper. "You made such an impression on him, you know."

I know of no such thing. And what about the impression he made on me? One of extreme boredom.

But her father had his hand on hers as if he sensed she might be inclined to bolt. Not that she'd ever given him such an idea.

"Good evening, Miss Hossfuss." Sidney Longstreet bowed as if his back were made of steel bars.

"Good evening." Perhaps before he had been terribly shy or tired. Surely tonight will be better.

She reminded herself of that hope later, when she nearly choked swallowing a yawn. While the music was lovely, an evening of Strauss had a tendency to put her to sleep. Like her partner.

After the first intermission, all she could think of was going home.

Mr. Longstreet tried valiantly to stay awake, his head jerking upward like a giant puppeteer pulled viciously on a string. Pearl could feel nothing but pity for the poor man. He should be home with his children. He still had not mentioned a wife. Ergo he had no wife, was looking for a wife to care for all his children, or her father thought she would be a candidate for that exalted position. Without mentioning the idea to her of course. As if that might be of some importance in the scheme of things.

"I-I'm sorry," her escort murmured after the applause at the end of the concert woke him up.

"Do not feel embarrassed. I had a terrible time staying awake myself. Lovely music but restful might be a good description. You were not the only one." She'd heard snoring from someone behind her.

"Nevertheless, I must make this up to you." He stood, and she followed him out to the aisle.

"May I come calling Sunday afternoon?" he asked.

Have we already progressed to that? Please, what can I be doing Sunday afternoon that will be a viable excuse in Father's eyes. Nothing came to mind. For one with so facile a brain, it seemed to be slumbering from the music also.

They made their way out to the line of carriages drawn up in the street.

"Will you be attending church with us?" Jorge Hossfuss nailed his poor clerk with a smile.

Pearl smiled her acknowledgment. She was trapped with nowhere to go.

— ✴ —

The next afternoon she hurried home from school so that she could have some time with her stepmother. As soon as they were seated in the sunroom with their tea poured, she leaped in, before someone came to disturb them.

"Father sees Mr. Longstreet as a suitable marriage partner for me, doesn't he?"

"You came to that conclusion with remarkable astuteness."

"That is neither a yes nor a no."

Amalia set her cup in its saucer and placed them on the marble-topped table in front of the wicker sofa they shared. She stared out the wide window to the walled garden where daffodils were just showing their golden trumpets.

Pearl waited, carefully disguising her impatience by sipping her tea.

"Your father has pretty much left you to your own whims in the past, providing all the schooling you desired, tolerating your antipathy to society, allowing you to teach at the settlement house."

Pearl looked over her teacup. "I have been useful."

"Yes, and a model of decorum, on the outside at least. I think if you were not devoting yourself to those poor children, you would be most unhappy."

"So very true. But the fact that I love those children does not mean I would be content rearing Mr. Longstreet's five. He and I have absolutely nothing in common. Art, literature, music—he has no interest in those. What interests he has other than working for my father, I have no idea." Pearl leaned forward. "Dull is the only word that fits the man. He might have a mind for numbers. He must have, or he would not last in his employment, but . . ." Pearl closed her eyes. "What would we talk about?"

"You would most likely be so busy caring for house and children, you would not have time or energy for evening discussions."

"Are you saying there would be no servants?"

"No, I'm sure your allowance would cover at least one or two. I believe your father will provide a suitable house for you."

"So I'm to be sold off with house and help?"

Amalia turned and took Pearl's hands. "It would not be so bad. Many a young woman has married with and for a lot less."

"But what about affection? Caring? Is that not important?"

"That can come."

Pearl tipped her head back and stared at the ceiling. "And you agree with this?"

"There have been no other suitors."

"I know. Did I frighten them away by my tongue, or was it this?" She laid a finger against the scar.

"If it were me, I would do as my father wished."

But you are not me, and besides, you did not answer my question. "I see. Is that what you did?"

"Remember, you will make of the marriage what you will. Men are malleable. And some more so than others."

Pearl poured herself more tea, added two lumps and milk. At this moment, straight tea was more than she could abide.

Silence reigned while they sipped.

Pearl gathered her courage, cloaked in years of hurt. She touched her scar. "I think Far stopped loving me because of this."

Amalia took in a deep breath and released it on a sigh. "Although he seems more formal with you, it is not for lack of love. It's just that he is a man who finds it easier to show affection to young children than to a grown daughter."

Pearl thought on Amalia's words. Somehow she had a hard time believing them.

CHAPTER FOUR

Little Missouri, mid-March 1883

No wonder the Bible said to look forward and not back.

Ruby Torvald imagined herself falling facedown in the dirt, with everyone standing around laughing at her. That's the way she felt much of the time, as though she were on the verge of tripping and the fall would not be lovely.

"Ruby?" Opal, her ten-year-old sister, called from the kitchen.

Ruby rubbed her forehead. Sometimes she wished she could just change her name. Ruby here and Ruby there and, Ruby, I need you to . . . and, Ruby, do you know where . . . If she could only have a few minutes to herself before she was so tired the words or numbers blurred on the page before her. Why were things in such a muddle—no matter how hard she tried? Take Rand Harrison, for instance. She wished someone would take Mr. Harrison and haul him far away. Every time he came to town, something went wrong. That man got far too much pleasure out of laughing, and always at her expense. On top of that, Captain McHenry hadn't written for months. Had something happened to him down in Indian country? Face it, life in Little Missouri, Dakotah Territory, was not what she'd hoped it would be.

"Ruby?" The cry grew more plaintive.

"Why can't you come here," Ruby muttered as she pushed her chair back from the table in the dining room where she'd been working on the ledger that always seemed to get further behind rather than caught up. Shouting at Opal would be entirely unladylike. Sometimes she wished ladylike behavior had not been drilled into her ever since she could walk, even before then, most likely. She straight-armed the swinging door into the kitchen of Dove House, the hotel deeded to her by her deceased father, ready to speak more than gently to her young sister, Opal.

"What in the world happened to you?" Ruby clapped both hands over her mouth to stifle the scream or the giggles—she wasn't sure which.

"Cat was chasing a mouse and they surprised me and I dropped the egg basket and then Cat caught the mouse and I tried to catch her to put both of them outside and I slipped in the eggs and banged the table and the flour tipped over and fell on me and—Can you please help me? Every time I move, I spread the mess out farther."

Ruby did her best to hide her laughter. She got a pan and dipped warm water out of the reservoir for washing, took a rag from the rod behind the cast-iron cookstove, and stared at the girl in front of her. A smear of egg on her face, egg and flour streaked her apron and congealed on her shoes. Flour turned her strawberry braids to pink and her dark skirt to gray in places.

"I'm sorry."

"Opal, this is not your fault. Blame Cat. *Uff ða*, what a mess." Ruby patted her sister's shoulder and then dusted off her hands. "You know, the best thing might be to take your clothes off right here and wash up in the pantry. I'm afraid we are going to have to wash your hair too."

"Can't we just brush it out? I hate to wash my hair."

"But egg yolk is good for making beautiful hair."

"With flour?"

Ruby rolled her lips together and shook her head. Talk about pathetic.

"My land, Opal, what happened to you?" Milly, the youngest of the hotel maids, stopped in the doorway from the second floor where she'd been cleaning rooms. Her mouth and eyes were matching O's, her head continuing to wag as she came closer.

Ruby took the wrung-out rag and dusted off the worst of the mess. "Milly, please get the broom to sweep this up while Opal washes off in the pantry. We'll pour the water in the hip bath, so we can wash her hair too."

Opal groaned but walked gingerly so as not to dislodge any more flour goop.

An insistent meow came from the door to the storeroom.

"You can just stay there. This is all your fault." Opal stopped at the pantry door and glanced back at Ruby, who was filling a bucket with water from the boiler simmering on the back of the stove.

As Opal moved into the pantry, Ruby turned to Milly. "Before you finish sweeping, would you please drag in the hip bath? I should have done that first."

"Sure." Milly propped the broom against the table. "What a mess. I bet there's a good story here." She glanced at Opal for confirmation. Opal was known to take something that happened and turn it into knee-slapping laughter when she told it later to her friends. Ruby knew her little sister would do the same with this episode after she recovered from embarrassment and from the misery of having her hair washed.

As soon as the hip bath was in place, Ruby poured the buckets of water into the tin tub. "As I mentioned, egg is really good for washing hair."

Opal kept her eyes down as she checked the temperature of the water. "Could use some cold."

"Think I'll scrape some of that yolk off the floor and—"

"Ruby, you're not funny."

"Come on, this isn't the end of the world, you know."

Opal grumbled something as she pulled her waist over her head, sneezing from the flour.

Ruby brought in more water, keeping one bucket back to rinse with. "I brought some of the rose soap that Cimarron made last summer." She handed the bar to Opal, along with a cloth for washing. "You want me to do your hair?"

"Please." Opal untied the bows and grimaced at the egg dripping from the ribbon. "Ugh."

"Drop it in the tub." After running her fingers through the strands to loosen the braids, Ruby filled a dipper with warm water and sluiced it over Opal's head. "Come on, work it through." After soaping and rinsing again, Ruby searched the strands for any remaining batter and worked a chunk of flour loose from one side. She rinsed the section again. "There, I think we got it all."

They could hear Cat yowling in the storeroom now. While she had started out wild as the bobcat they'd caught trying to get into the chicken house, Cat now figured that a lap was the best place to nap and tidbits should be forthcoming whenever anyone cooked.

"She probably thinks someone is mixing cake or something." Opal soaped her washcloth. "Silly cat. Why does she have to play with a mouse like that?"

"You used to play with your food."

"Ru-by."

Ruby leaned against the counter and tucked a strand of golden hair back in the crocheted snood she'd bundled her hair into that morning. While she'd planned to braid the mass later, she hadn't found the time, not an unusual situation for the owner of Dove House, a three-story hotel located in Little Missouri and the inheritance the two sisters had received from their father, Per Torvald. Once known for its saloon and the girls who entertained there, Dove House now served meals and rented rooms for longer than a night. Within the last few months more hunters and cattlemen used the so-called town for a camp base, and Dove House had gone from a fingernail operation to having a full storeroom and bedrooms occupied more often than not.

"Ruby."

"I'll bring you a towel." Ruby opened the door. "And clean clothes."

Opal blew a mound of bubbles off the palm of her hand. No matter how hard she fought against a bath and hair wash, as usual, she stayed in as long as possible.

"Two."

"Two?"

"Two towels."

Ruby rolled her eyes. "We'll see." Since laundry had to be hung on the lines outside till frozen and then brought in board stiff to thaw and finish drying on the lines in the storeroom, keeping clean clothes and napkins on the tables took far more time and effort than in the warmer months. While Ruby was tempted to let up on her standards, so far she'd withstood, even though it required one of the girls to do laundry and ironing full time.

Daisy Whitaker, another of the girls—once called soiled doves—who Ruby had promised her father to take care of, returned the cooling flatiron to the stove and attached the handle to the next one. "I'll be glad when we find someone else to do this. Never thought I'd be saying I'd rather clean."

"I know what you mean." Ruby shook her head. "Estelle sure didn't last long, did she?"

"She was a good worker, though, for the time she was here." Daisy kneaded the small of her back and rotated her shoulders. "Did Charlie get back yet?"

"Haven't seen him."

Milly looked up from where she was scrubbing egg and flour from the painted floor. "He was out skinning that deer, last I saw him."

I wish Charlie would recognize love when he saw it. Ruby had realized months ago that Daisy was sweet on Charlie, former bartender and now man-of-everything, but since his eye seemed to be on Cimarron, another of the doves, there was a stalemate all around. Sometimes she feared anarchy would break out.

"You going to look for more help?" Daisy asked.

"I have an ad in the Dickinson paper and a note posted in each of the rooms here. Do you have any other suggestions?"

Both Milly and Daisy shrugged and shook their heads before returning to their duties.

Cat yowled again, more insistently, so Ruby crossed to open the door. "Serves you right, making a mess like that." Cat, tail stick-straight in the air but for a crook at the end, stalked in with nary a glance in her direction.

Daisy chuckled her way back to the ironing board in the storage room. Milly wrung her rag out in the bucket of water and went back to mopping up the mess.

Ruby took the towels back to the pantry. "Here, one for your hair and one for the rest of you. Make sure you hang them up behind the stove to dry."

"Put on my same undergarments?"

"No, I'll go get you clean clothes." *Why didn't I ask one of the others to do that? At this rate, I'll never get the bookwork caught up.* She mounted the stairs as quickly as she could and still remain lady-like, no leaping three at a time like Opal still did in spite of repeated admonitions. The higher she climbed, the colder the air became. Since they kept the door closed to the third floor stair-way, the bedrooms of the help frequently had frost on the inside of the windows. While she gathered up clothing for her little sis-ter, Ruby realized anew how much Opal had grown since they came to Little Missouri a little less than a year ago. The clothes the Brandons, the family she worked for in New York, had sent with them when they came to Dakotah Territory were either too short, too tight, or too worn. Hems had been let down and then faced, seams let out, and even gussets added in the sides, all thanks to Cimarron's nimble fingers with a needle.

Ruby thought of the treadle sewing machine she had seen last time she shopped in Dickinson, the closest town of any size. While she'd read about them and seen one in operation when they lived back in New York, she'd never desired to own one like she did now. Still thinking on the things they needed but managed to get along without, she descended to the warmer regions and handed Opal her clothes.

"Is someone else going to use the bath water?" Opal, now dried and wrapped in her towels, shivered in the draft from the long window. Floor to ceiling cupboards buried the walls on both sides of the narrow pantry.

Ruby made a face. "I forgot to offer." She returned to the kitchen. "Milly, you want to take a bath?"

"It's not Saturday."

"I know, but we can add more hot water."

Milly wrung her cloth for a final time and wiped up the last of the scrub water. "No, might catch my death that way. If you ask me, you and Opal take far too many baths as it is. Not good for you. 'Specially not in the winter."

Ruby just shook her head and leaned into the storeroom to get pretty much the same answer from Daisy who, mouth round in her oval face, nearly dropped the flatiron in shock.

"Don't say I didn't ask. We'll use the water tomorrow to scrub the cardroom floor. If we could only train those men to either hit the spittoons or chew outside." Her shudder came from her stomach.

Daisy brought the flatiron in for another exchange. "Sure smells good in here." After setting the cool iron back on the stove, she peeked in the oven, inhaling as she held the door open. "Gingerbread. I don't think anything can smell better."

"Better than apple pie?" Milly came back in from dumping the water in a slop bucket on the back porch.

"Bread's best." Ruby eyed the five loaves on the table, covered by clean dishcloths. "As long as you have your head in the oven, press on the top and see if it's done."

Instead Daisy took a length of broomstraw they kept in a jar on the shelf behind the stove and stuck it in the middle of the cake. "Nothing on it." She lifted the stove lid and tossed the straw in the fire. Using the potholders kept on the warming shelf, she pulled the pan from the oven and sat it on a wooden rack on the table to cool. "Tonight we can serve it with either whipped cream or applesauce. Or both."

At the beatific smile on Daisy's face, Ruby chuckled. Whipped cream had been scarce for the months Johnson's cow had been dry. Since she calved a couple of weeks earlier, they'd been churning butter, whipping cream, and letting some sour to serve on pancakes or use for sour-cream cookies.

"Now I won't have to take a bath for Easter, huh, Ruby?" Opal continued to dry her hair in front of the stove.

"You wish. Easter is still ten days away. Would you like me to finish brushing and braiding your hair?"

"Please." Opal handed her the brush and pulled a stool out from under the well-used oak table.

Ruby started at the bottom and brushed all the tangles out, working her way up through the thick hair. "Mm, you smell like roses."

"Better than egg and flour." Opal turned to look up at her sister. "Are you going to bake kolaches like at the Brandons'?"

"I think not. They take too much time." Ruby shrugged at the look on her sister's face. "Sorry. Maybe next year."

Milly stopped peeling potatoes to ask, "Whatever is that?"

"Braided bread with colored eggs nested in it. I think it is a Russian tradition."

"What's Russian?"

Opal adopted her teacher attitude. "You use a sweet dough." She'd been working with Milly and Daisy, teaching them to read during the summer until Ruby took over the schooling when the hotel business slowed down for the winter. "Russia is a huge country in Eastern Europe. Guess we need to study geography too."

"You can find a world map in that last box of books Mrs. Brandon sent us." Ruby had been a governess at the Brandon home in New York before she and Opal came west at their father's bidding nearly a year before. Often when she allowed herself to think back, she felt sadness push down on her shoulders. Life had been so much easier then.

Milly, bone slender no matter how much Ruby tried to feed her up, let out a sigh. "I'll never learn it all."

"But you and Daisy can both read good now and do your sums," Opal said.

"*Well*, not good." Ruby always tried to correct Opal's grammar and manners. After all, some standards were necessary, even on the frontier. As Bestemor always said, "*It's how you behave when you're alone that says who you really are.*"

"Oh yes. Read *well*."

"Your penmanship has improved too. You've both learned a lot." Ruby started at Opal's forehead and fingered out three sections to begin French braiding.

Daisy brought back another sadiron to the stove, unhooked the wooden handle, and attached it to a hot iron. "I heard my name. What did I do now." She leaned over and inhaled gingerbread flavor. "I think we've all been working so hard we should have a cup of coffee and a piece of that gingerbread."

"Before supper?" Ruby braided a ribbon into the end of a braid and tied it off with a knot and a bow. She shook her head at the pleading looks on all three faces. "Oh, all right, but cut the pieces small. Who knows how many we will have here for supper."

"There's only two guests."

"So far."

"But it's getting toward dusk. Belle said she'd be back to practice." Milly glanced out the window. "It's snowing again, and here I thought spring had finally took over."

Belle had been the madam in the days before Ruby stepped in at her father's dying request and took over Dove House, long before Ruby even knew what kind of situation she and her little sister were getting into.

Just the mention of Belle's name brought something to mind that Ruby mulled over more and more often of late, sometimes even keeping her awake at night when her body was so exhausted it screamed for rest. Strange things like something missing and showing up later, never where it was supposed to be. The townsfolk, even though they knew the real situation by now, still looking at her like she'd become one of the doves instead of changing their lives around. She was sure money had been missing more than once. Was it all Belle, or should she be watching all of the others to catch the culprit?

"Sometimes I think spring will never come," Daisy grumbled. "We'll be stuck in winter forever."

"Me too." Ruby caught herself sighing along with Daisy. Would ten days be enough time to perfect the Easter music for the girls to sing? The irony of three soiled doves singing at a worship service in a former saloon, resurrected as a dining room, made her smile inside. What would the fair citizens of Little Misery think anyway? She caught back her snort at the word *fair*. Ha. If they came at all.

CHAPTER FIVE

"Every year at Easter we all got new clothes." Opal sighed nine days later. "I really miss the Brandons."

"Brand-new?" Milly wore envy like a petticoat, mostly hidden but peeking out at times.

"Well, usually Alicia, the Brandons' eldest daughter and two years older than me, hadn't worn them much before I got them."

"Like that blue coat you got hanging in your room?"

"Um-hm. Matching shoes and hat too. Along with the dress." Opal smiled, a dreamy smile that spoke of good memories.

"Well, I never. Like in a picture book. Bet you was sad to come out here."

"Yes, but I wanted to meet my papa."

Milly's snort suggested perhaps Opal had not made the best choice. After all, Milly had been the maid when Dove House had a less than savory reputation. Not that Opal had had anything to say about the matter.

"I ain't . . . er . . . never had . . ." Milly flinched as she corrected her own English before someone else could do it for her.

"Good." Opal grinned back, her approbation making Milly's smile even wider.

"Never had a new dress for Easter, or any time, until Cimarron sewed this for me." She fingered the folds in her dark serge skirt. "And now I have two new skirts and another waist. Ruby ripped my old things up, said they was—were almost too

44

patched for rags. Patches on patches they wa—were." She rolled
her eyes heavenward. "Land sakes, tryin' to talk right is harder'n,
well, about anything I ever done before."

"Did."

"Oh!" She stamped her foot but gently, as if to make a point
and make Opal laugh at the same time. "See, what did I tell
you?"

Everyone liked to make Opal laugh.

Opal leaned closer and dropped her voice. "Ruby's got a surprise for you."

"Opal?"

At Ruby's call the two stepped apart and stopped giggling.

Ruby came through the door from the dining room, humming under her breath. "All right you two, what are you up to
now?"

"W-why? Nothing." Opal donned her most innocent expression, an act of supreme expertise.

"Oh really?" Ruby turned her head slightly to the side, a sure
sign she didn't really believe her younger sister. The way Opal
was growing, she wouldn't be called little sister much longer.

"Have you seen Belle?"

Both the girls shook their heads.

"The others are ready to practice, and she promised she'd
play the piano." Ruby made a tsking sound through clamped
teeth. Belle could always be counted on to play dance hall and
drinking music. But hymns? Anything to cause friction. Could
nothing go right this day?

The sound of scraping boots at the back door caught their
attention, and with a blast of cold air, Belle sailed into the room,
snowflakes dusting the shoulders of her black wool shawl.

"So is everyone ready?" The feather on her green felt hat
dipped over one eye. With a twitch of a hand, she settled the
upper drape over her full skirt.

That's new, Ruby thought, trying to remember if she'd seen
the outfit before. *Why is it Belle can afford new clothes when the rest
of us sew our own or make do with what we already have? I better ask
Charlie if she's been skimming off the card take again. Surely she
wouldn't. She promised me to deal fairly and keep only a third of the*

winnings. Ha! Only if she felt I wouldn't check. But what about the missing money?

The argument in Ruby's head seemed to go on continually. No matter how hard she tried to subdue or ignore the inner discussions, any confrontation, especially those with Belle, set her head to clamoring. She often wondered why Belle stayed on at Dove House. Although why not? She obviously made enough money running the cardroom to buy the things she desired. Her room and board were cheap, and unless she volunteered like she had for the Sunday music, she had no further responsibilities. Unlike the rest of them who worked from before the world even thought of dawn to well after dark.

"The others are waiting for *you*." Ruby emphasized the word, waiting in the hope that Belle would get the hint.

"I won't change then." Belle, amber eyes lined with kohl, lips red as raspberries, and with the hauteur of a foreign royalty, entered the dining room, even the door staying open longer, as if timid about wrinkling her skirt.

She better wear something less ... less ... Ruby struggled for the proper word. *Flamboyant, provocative, brazen. Why didn't I reprimand her for her tardiness? Bring her to task for her rudeness?*

Why don't I do a lot of things?

Because I get tired of being Mother Superior or headmistress. The bickering, the lack of enough help, my stars, how can I complain about having so many guests? We need more help.

Some days one needed ... She paused in her mental ruminations and castigations to listen to the lovely harmony coming from the dining room.

"Don't they sing pretty?" Milly paused in bringing ironed linens from the storeroom where Daisy spent most of her time with a flatiron and its cousin the ironing board. Table linens were stored in a cupboard off the dining room and bed linens at the end of the second-floor hall. Charlie had built the cupboards last fall, much to everyone's delight. Especially Cat who liked nothing better than sleeping on a stack of starched tablecloths or pillowcases, if anyone made the mistake of leaving a cupboard door open. Cat took her job as mouse hunter seriously and had become such an adept hunter that news to stay away from Dove House must have spread about the local mouse population.

"Why didn't you sing with them?"

Milly shook her head. "Can't carry a tune in a rain barrel."

"Who told you that? I've heard you humming when you work, and you do just fine."

"Really?"

It was always amazing to Ruby how a bit of encouragement and a smile could change Milly from a washed-out mouse to a glowing marigold.

"Ah, Milly, why didn't I think of encouraging you sooner? I'm sorry."

"Maybe next time. Opal, now, she can sing like the meadowlarks in the summer."

Ruby listened more closely. All the voices blended so perfectly, one would think they'd been singing together for years instead of days. Perhaps the girls had. It was so seldom she thought of them as "the girls" any longer. In the year since she'd inherited the hotel, many things had changed, most importantly, the lives of the women who'd once been known as soiled doves and who now worked with and for her, more as friends than hired help. Until someone caused a ruckus, and as she'd slowly learned, the culprit was more often than not, Belle.

"No, no." Belle bellowed as the piano stopped midnote. "Cimarron, pick it up on the second beat. You're coming in too soon."

"I thought I counted it."

"Let's take it from the beginning again. Opal, honey, take a deep breath and let that high note soar." The piano picked up again with Belle counting, "One, two, and . . ."

"Up from the grave he arose. . . ."

They'd have lovely music, the rolls were baked and ready to reheat in the morning, invitations had gone out to everyone in Little Missouri and the surrounding area, the dining room gleamed from all the scrubbing, Charlie would read the Scriptures, and Opal had carefully printed fifteen copies of the hymns they would sing. They had no preacher, but there would be worship and celebration of Christ's victory over death.

Ruby deliberately kept her mind on today. Thinking back to former Easters, in real churches with real families, brought nothing but a desire to throw herself across her bed and let the tears flow.

"Ruby Signe Torvald, forget the pity production and be grateful for what you have. After all, God wants a cheerful heart. He says that's better than medicine. So think of things to be thankful for." She pulled another pan of sweet rolls from the oven. "I am thankful for this kitchen, the wood for the fire, the food we have, for enough guests to pay the bills and then some. And that all of us now have beds to sleep in, no more pallets on the floor." The last made her smile. Who'd have thought that a wooden bed frame strung with ropes in a woven pattern, then padded with pallets, made a comfortable bed? Thanks to Charlie's and Cimarron's good hunting of duck and geese, she and Opal now had a feather bed on top of the pallet. What luxury. Having removed the rolls to cool on the table, she now spread a thin frosting on top.

Tomorrow was Easter, and it would bring the first worship service to be held in Little Missouri. Held in a former saloon, with music sung by women who'd turned from their former ways and now believed the message they sang.

Now if only a congregation will come.

— ❦ —

Morning dawned between capricious snowflakes, adding to the two-inch new blanket of white. A chinook wind the last few days had melted all but the drifts and banks around the buildings. The drip off icicles had sung a merry tune, but were now shut off again by the hand of winter.

Ruby entered the kitchen, tying her apron as she came. The smell of coffee had floated up the stairs and hastened her ablutions.

"Christ is risen, Charlie."

"He is risen, indeed." His mustache twitched at the look on her face. "I was raised proper, Miss Ruby, even if I don't always show it."

"Would that all of us showed our caring as often as you. I thought I told you to take it easy this morning, that I'd start the coffee."

"Ah, couldn't sleep any longer. Those sweet rolls were calling my name."

Ruby rubbed her hands in the heat of the stove. "I thought spring had come."

"It did, but winter had to bluster one more time. It's about blowed out. You watch, the sun will send it packing."

"I hope so. None of the ranchers will come in if a blizzard is blowing." She popped a plate with two rolls on it into the oven, then brought a pan of cornmeal mush in from the storage room to slice for frying.

"Charlie, you have a new shirt."

"Thanks to Cimarron. That woman is a whiz with a needle."

"Most assuredly. Would you please slice the ham?"

"Already finished. I'll get it for you." He returned from the pantry with a pan of sliced ham.

Ruby folded a dish towel and opened the oven door to take out the rolls. "Sit, and we'll have our coffee."

By the time they'd cooked breakfast, served the hotel guests, moved the table into the cardroom, and lined up the chairs, time caught up with them.

They all fled to their rooms to change. Ruby snagged Opal before she escaped.

"You have to rebraid your hair."

"Ah, Ruby . . ."

"Get the brush." Ruby fixed her cameo pin to the high neck of her lace-trimmed waist. She'd thought of wearing her deep red traveling outfit with the lace inset in the upper bodice. She kept it carefully brushed and covered by a sheet, the matching hat stored in her trunk. Charlie had warned her early on that it was too fancy for the likes of Little Missouri, that folks might take her for one of the fancy women instead of the naïve girl she used to be. Of course, according to Charlie, she still had a lot to learn of life on the frontier, but now she knew much of a life she'd never even dreamed.

With her lower lip protruding, Opal handed her the brush, at the same time finger combing out her hair. "But we gotta hurry, Ruby. You said so."

"I know." Ruby quickly brushed and braided Opal's waist-length strawberry hair, looped the two braids together, and tied them with a plaid bow.

"There, you look lovely."

"Not like the others." Opal dodged away and out the door.

"Now what does that mean?" Ruby checked her reflection in the mirror, tucked another strand of fine hair back in her chignon, and followed Opal down the stairs. She could hear the others still dressing.

Charlie, bowtie freshly tied and a black wool vest over the new white shirt, looked every bit the gentleman he claimed not to be. His freshly trimmed walrus mustache set off the razor shine of just shaven cheeks. Charlie would never be considered handsome by anyone's standards, but the smile that twinkled in his dark eyes created friends wherever he went.

"You're looking mighty lovely, Miss Ruby. I'm thinking this Easter will be something more special than usual."

"Thank you, Charlie. Do you think anyone will come?"

"Don't you be worryin'. I know Rand is coming. He said he'd be playing his guitar, and he always lives up to his word."

Ruby contained her snort, an action that the mention of Rand always brought forth. Why was it that everyone else thought so highly of the man when she always wanted to whack him in the kneecaps, send him out to play with his cows, catch him dribbling on his chin, anything to take the edge off his perfection? And to think he'd had the gall to ask her to marry him, without courtship, or even a hint of his intentions. And then he had acted affronted when she'd told him exactly what she thought of his proposal. To top it all off, ever since then, he'd acted like nothing ever happened.

What unmitigated gall!

The bell tinkled over the front door.

Ruby made sure a smile lifted the corners of her mouth before she pushed open the swinging door of the kitchen and entered the polished dining room, now set up for church.

Rand Harrison, hat pulled low against the wind, sheepskin coat darkened on the shoulders by snowmelt, and carrying his guitar case, blew through the front door. He set his Stetson on a nearby table, hung his coat on the hall tree, and laid his case on a table to lift out his guitar.

"Mornin' Miss Torvald. Blustery day out there."

"Happy Easter, Mr. Harrison. Thank you for coming."

"Happy Easter, Mr. Harrison." With the lilt in Opal's voice, even Ruby could hear the difference in the greeting.

Opal gazed up at him with something close to hero worship. After all, he owned horses, horses that could be ridden. "Is Mr. Beans coming?"

"My men are putting the horses up at the livery in case the weather turns nasty. Hate for them to stand out in a wind like this. Mrs. Robertson and her family are almost here."

Ah, good. There will be someone here besides the residents of Dove House.

"Rand, how good to see you." Belle's gravelly voice came from behind Ruby, along with the greetings from the rest of the Dove House staff.

As soon as Ruby turned to ask Cimarron a question she clapped a hand to her throat and felt her smile slipping. "You can't wear th-those . . ." Her voice squeezed to a squeak.

CHAPTER SIX

All she could see was bosoms.

Ruby quickly turned her back on the women as she struggled for something to say.

"My, ladies, don't you look lovely." Rand might well have tipped his hat, had it not been resting on a table in the rear.

I'm going to . . . Killing him was not appropriate, but even the thought was immensely satisfying. Instead she sucked in a breath, turned back to the girls, and said in her most gentle and strangled voice, "Oh my, I . . . uh, I . . . perhaps you, I mean, I believe you might want to return upstairs and change your, uh, ah . . ."—she tried again—"garments."

"But, Ruby, you said to wear your best clothes, and these are their best," Opal hissed under her breath. She stared at her older sister, at the same time clenching and opening her fists at her sides.

"I-I'm sorry I was not more clear." Ruby rubbed her hands on the sides of her skirt. "I . . ."

"She means, wear your good wool skirts and those downright lovely waists that Cimarron sewed for everyone." Charlie stepped in between Ruby and the wounded faces before him. He dropped his voice. "You look lovely, all of you. It's just, well, you know."

"I shoulda known better." Belle glared at no one in particular, spun on her heel, and like a mother duck led her brood from whence they came.

Ruby stared after them. *How could you be so thoughtless,* she scolded herself. *Of course they would wear their best dresses, those brighter than butterfly dresses that scream out their former occupation. You know you wanted to wear your brick red traveling dress when you visited the townspeople, and only Charlie's adamant advice kept you from that mistake.*

But why do you let those old biddies here in town who won't even talk to each other dictate what goes on here at Dove House? Who made them more perfect than us? She rubbed the spot between her eyebrows that was beginning to ache.

"Sorry, miss, I shoulda seen that coming," Charlie said in an undertone.

"That was not kind." Opal slit her eyes. "And you tell me we must always be kind."

"I know." Ruby sighed and shot Charlie a pleading look. "But I just want the other women to like them."

"How can they like them when they don't come to visit? Mrs. Robertson likes us and them too. And she's nicer'n anyone in town."

Ruby sighed again. "What do I do? All I wanted was for us all to have a happy Easter." Was that compassion she saw in Rand's gaze? No, it couldn't be. He must be laughing inside even if he has better manners than to show it. Why couldn't he have come later?

"Nothing now." Charlie glanced to the door at the tinkle of the bell. Mr. and Mrs. Paddock, who owned the livery, closed the door behind them and shook the traces of snow off their clothing.

Charlie strode across the room, greeting the newcomers and inviting them to sit wherever they wanted. Church would be starting in just a few minutes.

"You going to sing with me?" Rand asked Opal.

"Uh-huh. We all sound real pretty." Opal put special emphasis on *all*.

Ruby laid a hand on Opal's shoulder, hoping to calm her sister.

"Well, we do." Opal's look showed pure frustration.

"Come on, help me tune this to the piano." Rand pointed at the keys. "Hit a low E."

Wishing she could be assured that Opal wouldn't spill any more of the family secrets, Ruby turned instead to greet her guests and breathed a prayer of gratitude when all the girls returned in total decorum.

Cold blew through the room with every subsequent tinkle of the bell, blowing away her fears that no one would come. When the seats filled up, they brought more chairs out of the cardroom.

Ruby turned as the opening chords of "Christ the Lord Is Risen Today" rolled from the piano, joined by the melody plucked from guitar strings. The guests quieted, the bell tinkled with the last of the worshipers, and hands shaking, Ruby made her way to the front of the room.

When the song finished, she stood and smiled. "Welcome to our first church service here in Little Missouri, and a blessed Easter to you all. Thank you, Opal, for the copies of our hymns for today." Ruby held her papers up. "Do you all have copies of our songs? I know we have to share." When no one raised a hand, she turned to Belle and nodded.

Daisy, Cimarron, and Opal took their places, Belle hit the beginning chords of "Up From the Grave," and one by one the congregation joined the singers, gaining in volume as rusty pipes cleared and the music swelled.

They sang all four verses. Ruby could hardly believe her ears at the harmonies that surrounded her. Bass, baritone, tenor, alto, and even a strong soprano, the melody flowed on a river of beauty. After the third hymn, Charlie stood, the Bible open on his broad hand.

"Today we are reading from the Gospel of Luke."

As he read the Passion story, Ruby fought to keep from crying. *Christ died on that cross for me.* She could hear sniffing from other parts of the room. Charlie read beautifully, another of his hidden talents.

He closed the Bible. "Let us pray in the words Christ gave us. Our Father..."

People joined in softly at first, as if still locked in the story he read, then gaining as the beloved words rolled on.

"And now I give you the Easter greeting my mother always said. Christ is risen."

He nodded for their response, and a few answered, "He is risen indeed."

"All right, not bad for a start, but let's try that again. Christ is risen." He paused.

"He is risen indeed."

After a moment of silence he continued, "The Lord bless us and keep us all the days of our lives."

The amen came almost in unison.

"Much better. We do indeed thank you all for coming. The coffee is hot, so make yourselves comfortable. We will be serving sweet rolls in just a minute or two. Our Easter gift from us at Dove House to all of you."

"You sang wonderfully," Ruby said to the girls in the kitchen.

"You didn't think we could do it, did ya?" Belle paused on her way up the back stairs. "And we didn't have to change clothes. Don't pay no nevermind to those biddies."

Leave it to Belle to get her digs in. "I'm sorry, Belle. I—"

"We're ready, Miss Ruby," Charlie said.

"Of course." Ruby led out with a tray of cups, followed by Charlie with the coffeepot. Cimarron brought out the cream and sugar, and Milly assisted Daisy with the platters of rolls. Opal handed out spoons and napkins.

"That was a right nice service," Mrs. Robertson said when Ruby handed her a cup. "We've been needing religion out here, that's for sure. Sister, you sit yourself down right there and wait your turn." She gave the order without even looking over her shoulder, just chatting with Ruby like they were old friends.

Ruby rolled her lips together to keep from smiling. Another mother with eyes in the back of her head.

"And Mary, that's enough of that. Why, thank you, Charlie. A cuppa is just what we all need. I've heard tell that those rolls made here at Dove House are worth driving halfway across Dakotah Territory, let alone to town on a spittin' morning." She smiled at the puzzlement on Ruby's face. "Snow was spittin', that's all. Last skirmish before spring really takes over."

"I was afraid no one would come, with bad weather and all." Ruby handed each of the five girls a cup. "There's hot chocolate for you in the kitchen, if you'd rather."

"Really?" The next to the youngest daughter looked to her mother, who nodded. "I surely do want some."

"Opal will bring out a pitcher." Ruby smiled once more and continued her way around the room. The cowboys had congregated in the back, as if afraid to mix with the so-called townsfolk. The two sodbuster families, as the newcomers were called, acted like they were chained together, and while the staff of the hotel served everyone, the lack of conversation was evident even to the most unobservant.

"Good morning, Mrs. McGeeney," Ruby said with a smile. "Blessed Easter."

Mrs. McGeeney turned her back as if studying the hang of the curtains.

Ruby moved on to meet the others. "Glad you all could come. Happy Easter." Refusing to allow herself to look back over her shoulder, she kept on smiling and welcoming the visitors to Dove House. Being gracious and polite was paramount to being a lady.

Milly was anything but subtle. "Ruby, how come that woman," she said, nodding toward Mrs. McGeeney, "is so rude to you? You didn't do nothin' wrong."

"I know, but, well, perhaps she had a bad morning." Ruby tried to keep the venom she felt out of her voice. Here she was trying to do something good for the town, and this was the thanks she got. The snub made her want to accidentally spill the coffee in the woman's lap. But rude didn't begin to describe the cruel comment about Cimarron that Mrs. McGeeney had murmured slightly under her voice but just loud enough that Ruby overheard. She was sure she was meant to hear.

Had the woman heard nothing of the Bible reading? Wasn't the fact that Jesus died such a terrible death because He loved them a good reason to at least be *kind* to one another, even if loving was beyond the possibility of the moment?

Were all their efforts a waste of time?

"Don't you worry none, Miss Ruby," Charlie whispered as he returned to the kitchen to refill his coffeepot.

Ruby tried not to. She smiled at Opal talking with two of the Robertson girls. When Opal took their hands and led them through the kitchen door, Ruby figured Cat was about to receive extra attention. And Cat never minded extra love and pats. But her attention kept returning to the glowering Mrs. McGeeney.

Heap burning coals of kindness upon her head. The thought floated through her mind like a wisp of fog off the river. The idea held no appeal for her, but Ruby took the plate of rolls and bent in front of Mrs. McGeeney. "Would you like another roll?" *Please, Lord, what can I say or do here?* She sat down in the chair next to the rigid-backed woman. "Isn't it amazing how many people are here? Have you met Mrs. Hanson and her sister yet? You know, they live downriver, closer to the Triple Seven spread."

"Those ranchers are gonna run them sodbusters off. You wait and see. We don't want no fences around here."

"Surely there is enough land around here for everyone." *Why didn't I think of something else?* She tried to catch Charlie's eye. When that failed, she leaned slightly closer to the woman. "I am hoping that we can continue to have Sunday services here. If there is anything that you can suggest. . . ?" She smiled and stood. "I thought that since you have lived here from almost the beginning, you would be a good person to ask." She smiled again, in spite of the tightness of her jaw, and took her serving platter back to the kitchen for refills, since no one seemed to be moving on. Talking to a wall would have been as rewarding.

She looked again to the group of sodbusters and stopped when one of the women put a hand on her arm. "Yes?"

"I just want to thank you for inviting us. The service was real nice, and the music sounded like a little bit of heaven. Made me so homesick I near to busted right out crying."

"Thank you. I'm hoping we can meet like this more regularly."

"Me too. One place we lived, everyone brought something for dinner for after church. We met in different homes, but you got such a lovely place here."

"Thank you. I'll be right back with more rolls." *Well, doesn't that beat all, as Cimarron would say.* Ruby set her plate down on the kitchen table. Just one more pan, and the rolls would be all gone.

"Coffee will be ready in a couple of minutes." Daisy, dark hair wisping around her oval face, added two more chunks of wood to the firebox and set the round lid back in place. "I never dreamed we'd have so many here."

"Me either. And here I was afraid no one would come. You all sang so beautifully. Mrs. Hanson said the music was like a little piece of heaven."

"Now wasn't that nice of her?"

Go ahead and ask. What can it hurt? Ruby stepped closer to Daisy and whispered, "What does Mrs. McGeeney have against us?

"Well, it's what we used to be. I mean us girls, not you and Opal."

"But that's over and—"

"Her husband used to . . . you know." Daisy studied her fingernail. "Well, let's say he didn't come to Dove House just to drink and play cards."

"Oh. So no matter what we do, she isn't going to forget that? Like it was your fault that her man . . ."

Daisy nodded. "Most women feel that way."

"Didn't any of them hear the message this morning?"

"I did. And I know my sins are forgiven, that Jesus died for me."

Ruby ignored the burning at the back of her eyes and hugged Daisy close. "I'm sorry I was so abrupt this morning. I just want those women to forget what used to be and see all of you for the new women that you are. All of us women need to work together to make this a better place for everyone to live."

"You're doing just that." Daisy patted her arm. "Don't let that Mrs. McGeeney bother you none. We don't."

"Thank you." Ruby transferred more rolls to her plate. "Good thing we made a huge pot of ham and beans for dinner. We might have more guests than I thought we would."

Between the altercation with Belle and Mrs. McGeeney's attitude, Ruby still had a sour feeling by the end of the day, and to top it off, Rand had been so nice that she was sure something was brewing—and all she wanted was a lovely Easter for all.

— ❧ —

"Cat sure is getting fat," Opal announced the next morning.

"Perhaps you are feeding her too much." Ruby looked up from the letter she was writing to the Brandons, who, though she had not seen them for a year, seemed like family, especially since she had no other.

"Ah, it ain't that Cat is just getting fat." Charlie flinched and ducked behind his coffee cup.

Opal's eyes widened and her brow wrinkled. "She isn't sick, is she? Oh, please don't let her die."

Charlie shook his head, sending Cimarron a pleading glance.

Cimarron's laugh made Opal look more hopeful. "No, honey-bun, Cat isn't going to die, but she is going to have kittens."

"But how . . . ?" Opal stared from Cimarron, who wet her lips, to Charlie, who managed to hide his entire face behind his coffee mug, to Cat, who butted against Opal's stomach for the stroking to continue.

"I think I better get at stripping those beds." Cimarron winked at Ruby as she left the room.

"Got to get at that ironing." Daisy hefted her flatiron off the stove and headed for the storeroom, where her ironing board had taken up permanent residence.

"Kittens." Opal breathed the word like a prayer.

"We sure do need more firewood." Charlie took his jacket and exited out the back door.

Milly, who'd been visiting the outhouse during all the discussion, had to flatten herself against the wall to keep from being run over.

"What's the matter with him?" She flinched as the door slammed in her face.

"Cimarron said Cat is about to have kittens, and Opal said 'How,' and everyone left." Ruby wrote a few more words on her letter.

"Don't s'pose you've ever seen kittens born?" Milly asked.

Ruby glanced at Opal. "No."

"You mean there are real live kittens inside of Cat?" The awe on Opal's face made Ruby smile. While she'd never seen anything born, she did understand the principle of the thing. She rolled her lips together to keep from smiling. No wonder everyone left. They didn't want to be subjected to Opal's endless and perceptive questions.

"But, Ruby, how will they . . ."

"I guess we'll have to wait and see."

"But . . ."

"If you are lucky, perhaps Cat will share her grand event with you."

"When?"

"Cats usually go off by themselves to have their kittens." Milly said. "They like small dark places with soft stuff. Most of the ones I know had their kittens up in the barn where no one could find them until the mother brought them out."

"But we don't have a barn."

"So she'll find somewhere else. Cats have been having kittens for a long time."

"Not our Cat. How will she know what to do?"

"Ah." Milly looked to Ruby, who shrugged helplessly. "I guess they just know how." A smile broke forth. "Guess God just gave them that kind of know-how when He made cats."

"Very good, Milly." Ruby hid a sigh of relief.

"Did God give dogs and people know-how too?"

Ruby quickly set her empty coffee cup in the pan of hot soapy water on the cooler end of the stove. "Opal, you do the dishes while Milly sweeps out the dining room, and I'll knead the bread. Looks like we'll need to make a trip to Dickinson before long, so I better start the shopping list too." She stared out the window for far too brief a moment. A chinook wind had moved in during the night, and all the world was a'glitter.

"When we doing lessons?" Opal gently set Cat on the floor. "Now you be careful, you hear?" Cat answered with a purr and arched her back to rub against Opal's skirt. Opal stroked from her head to the tip of her tail. "You sure are one beautiful cat."

"We'll do lessons after dinner cleanup. I've been thinking we should talk with some of the new folks and see about starting a real school here in Little Missouri."

Opal straightened up. "Who would teach us? You?"

"I could, but perhaps it is time to look for a real teacher."

Charlie dumped a load of wood in the box by the stove.

"What do you think, Charlie, about a school here?"

"You better be talkin' to those who have children. You think there are enough?"

"I don't know about now, but the way things are going, there might be more by fall." *One thing I know for sure, I don't have time to teach and run Dove House too. I don't have time to do half what I need to do as it is.* Ruby scattered flour on the table and dumped out the rising bread dough. Kneading bread was always a good thinking time. Where could they have a school?

CHAPTER SEVEN

Chicago, one week after Easter

"The shipment arrived today."

"Pearl, that is wonderful. Libraries always need new books and especially that school. It seems to me that libraries should be built where people need them the most, not where they look the best." Amalia laid down the paper she'd been studying, an application for one of the grants which the Hossfuss Company gave away at her instigation and approval.

"What is that one for?"

"The new women's hospital is in terrible need of an operating room. We have helped Dr. Morganstern before. If I had my way, we would help her a lot more, but this would take pretty much all the money I am allowed."

"So the question is, do we put it all on this concern and not help so many others who are just as needy?"

"Yes. However, the cost of things like your books for the school are so minimal, don't feel you have to hesitate to do things like that."

"Thank you. Can I get you some tea?"

Pearl had always loved her father's study. She savored the big cherrywood desk where she used to hide in the knee cubby, the book-lined shelves, the smell of leather bindings synonymous with her father's attention as he used to hold her in his arms and point out different books he wanted her to read. She'd been reading by five, thanks to his encouragement.

"Far, listen." Hair in ringlets tied with a blue bow, she popped up, book in hand. "I can read."

He picked her up, put her on his lap, and laid the book on the desktop. She opened the beginning McGuffey's Reader and read the first lines. "The dog. The dog ran."

"See?" She looked over her shoulder to catch his nod and the smile that warmed his eyes, eyes that glittered lake blue when he was pleased, like now, or became storm-tossed gray when he was upset.

"She has been working so hard." Anna, gently rocking the buggy where baby Micah lay gurgling and cooing, said with a smile for her precocious daughter.

"See, I can read this too." Pearl marked the line with a fingertip and read across, then the next one.

"I believe a princess like this needs a present. What would you like, Princess Pearl?"

Pearl scrunched her eyes to think better. If she said a doll, he would buy her one, but she had plenty of dolls, and while they were good for lining up to play school, she wanted something else, something far more important. "I want to go to school."

"But you are so little."

"I'm big, and I can read." She turned imploring eyes on her father, to catch a teasing light in his eyes. She patted his cheek with her right hand. "Please?"

"My dear Anna, is there any school who would take a minx like this?"

"I'm certain we can find one." Her gentle words always bore the Norwegian accent of one born in the old country but who had learned the English language too. Pearl always knew that if she were a princess, her mother was the queen.

She threw her arms around her father's neck, squeezing him tight, inhaling the scent of good pipe tobacco, shaving soap, and the faint underlay of the sea.

She'd been a year or two younger than the others in her new school, but she quickly caught up. Until the accident.

"Where have you been?" Amalia asked gently.

"Back to when I was little and his princess."

"When your mother was still alive?"

"And before the babies died. It took my mother years to recover from that double loss. And then Jorge was born, and she never regained her health." Pearl spoke in that dream voice of seeing both worlds, the then and the now, and not being part of either.

"The accident was my fault, you know." Her fingertips found the scar in unconscious protection.

"Tell me what you remember."

"Not a lot. Just that I was about six years old and trying to help with something. I reached for the pan. It tipped and poured boiling water on my neck and shoulder."

"Your father blames himself."

Pearl jerked fully back to the now. "Why?"

"He feels he should have kept you away from the stove."

"I've always felt he blamed me. He grew so distant."

"Guilt does strange things to one. He does love you, but I think he finds it difficult to show his affection for you. He's so proper, you know."

Pearl stared at Amalia. "Why have we not had this discussion before?"

"We haven't had much conversation through the years."

Because I didn't trust you. You weren't my mother. "I'm sorry." *Sorry for all those years of turning away.*

"I am too. I was the adult, and I should have known how to help you."

But you were off doing your good deeds, and I wanted no part of anything you did. Or he did. Not true. "I would do anything to know for sure my father loves me."

— ✁ —

She thought back to that conversation several evenings later when the entire family was gathered in the parlor for one of their rare times when both father and mother were at home at the same time.

Each of the children reported on their schoolwork and what they'd learned. Father gave Anna, named after his first wife, a hug and a kiss, shook hands with Arnet and patted his shoulder, gave Jorge Jr. a well done and slipped him a packet of something, coins most likely. Anna recited from *Hiawatha* and for that received a coin and another kiss.

Pearl felt as though she was part of the wallpaper or perhaps an aunt come to visit. She watched as the four of them laughed at something Far said, her fingertips stroking her jawline.

"I have something I'd like to read," Amalia said, taking a letter from her pocket.

"Good. Read on." Jorge Sr. settled back in his chair, Anna on his knee.

> Dear Mr. and Mrs. Hossfuss,
> I want to take this opportunity to express my gratitude and the future gratitude of all our pupils for the wonderful boxes of books you donated to our library. I know that Miss Pearl Hossfuss had a hand in this, and I want to thank her also. Helping to shape the minds of these young boys and girls will make more differences in their future lives than we can begin to dream of. Your generous sharing of the rewards God has given you for your hard work and astute business sense will be marked by results other than here on earth. I must thank you also for the many lads you have employed from our schools.
> Sincerely,
> Mrs. George Burnham, headmistress

Mr. Hossfuss nodded. He looked directly at Pearl. "Well done." Her heart warmed at his words, and she smiled back. A real compliment. But when his gaze slipped to her neck, she kept her hands in her lap with a spurt of resentment. Why did he always check to see if the scar was showing?

Or was it as much a reflex action on his part as her smoothing her collars always higher? This thought brought forth an uncomfortable sensation, one that made her palm itch. Too many contradictory things to think about.

At least he'd not condemned her for her school donations, not that he ever had. Would that this ugly duckling could become a swan or a princess.

CHAPTER EIGHT

Dakotah Territory

Another dead cow.

Rand Harrison always knew there would be losses due to winter and predators, but he hated it just the same. Didn't seem to bother the big ranchers much, but then that was the difference between running thousands of head instead of hundreds, and running your own stock rather than managing for some big shot back east. But all in all, his herd had fared pretty well by the looks of the cows about to calf. Since they'd put up hay last summer for the bull, he'd done well too.

Rand leaned on his saddle horn, staring out across the Little Missouri River Valley. April, 1883. He'd been here five years now, and what did he have to show for the long hours and the investment of every dime he had? Besides a beginning cow herd multiplied by four, he had feeder steers ready to ship in the fall, a snug log cabin, four permanent hands, possibly five, a herd bull, thirty head of horses, a pole barn, and a corral—not bad for a southern ex-soldier.

One of these days he ought to make a formal claim on the homeplace—he'd named it the Double H Ranch—before some sodbuster came in and took it away from him. He'd heard tales of that happening. But he'd have to go to Dickinson to make his claim. He tipped his hat back so the sun could reach his face.

Snowmelt had frothing full creeks feeding the river, sending it roaring through the canyons. The grass hardly waited for the snow to melt back, showing green shoots right at the verge. After the last snowfall on Easter Sunday, the chinook returned in force, and spring took over the badlands, with buttercups glowing golden orange against the receding snow.

Rand stepped out of his stirrup and leaned over to pull the new leaves off the dandelions that were already near to blooming. Beans, his chief cook and all-around ranch hand, would welcome some fresh greens to throw in the stewpot. Beans had come out of the Civil War with Rand, ready to head west and find a new life. Shame they, meaning Beans and his other hands, had set him to thinking about getting a wife. He'd been perfectly happy with things as they were until they put that thought in his head.

And then she'd turned him down.

But as his sister had reminded him, women liked to be courted. And if he was honest, springing a request on that unsuspecting young woman had been about as foolish as roping an ornery longhorn cow with a string.

But her shock rankled like a burr dug into his socks. Except a person could dig a burr out and throw it away, a far easier chore than digging out the sight of flashing blue eyes, a slightly turned-up nose, and hair the gold of a Kansas wheat field ready for harvest. One thing for certain, she had no trouble speaking her mind and making her ideas real clear.

Marrying him was not even a consideration.

So why did the thought of her plague him like a sore tooth? He remounted and nudged Buck on down the gully to the riverbed and back to the ranch. They wouldn't know the actual count of the herd until branding time, but things were looking good. Now if the weather held through calving—freak storms were really hard on the newborns—and if the rains came when needed, and if—There were far too many ifs in ranching, but there wasn't anything he'd rather be doing the rest of his life.

Other than sharing his homeplace with a lovely blond woman rather than smelly old Beans. Did his future wife have to be that particular blonde, or would another woman do?

He stopped at the edge of the meadow, studying his herd of horses grazing in the fetlock-deep grass. Didn't look like old Bay, a mare he'd caught wild and gentled, had taken again. He'd bred her to a paint stud from the Triple Seven Ranch, hoping to get a paint colt. She was slab-sided instead of nicely rounded like a mare about to foal. He'd known she was getting up there in years but had hoped for one more foal out of her. She threw good colts.

He rode nearer the herd, all of them still skittish after not being handled all winter. Like other ranchers he turned most of his horses loose in the fall to let them fend for themselves, rounding them up again in the spring, keeping only two or three horses pastured near home. He always kept Buck on the homeplace. He'd become more than just a good horse. He was a friend.

"So, you thinking what I'm thinking, fella? That old mare just might make a certain young girl very happy and would keep her safe too."

Buck snorted as if he understood.

The next thought remained just that. Perhaps that might make the older sister happy too. If he and the boys built a pole fence around that area behind the hotel and a pole shed by fall, what could be her argument?

— ❧ —

"You're what?" Ruby stood on the top step of the porch, so Rand had to look up to her, not much but enough to make him want to take a step backward.

He didn't.

"As I said, I have an elderly mare who would be a great horse for Opal. My boys and I will fence this area off." He waved at the field behind Dove House. "It should be enough pasture." He paused, wondering why she wasn't more pleased with the idea. "I know how bad Opal wants to ride, and this old horse is so wise, she's perfect for a beginning rider."

"But . . ."

Flummoxing Ruby set his lips to smiling, but he camouflaged that by rubbing his mouth with one leather-gloved finger.

"Opal would have to carry water to her and sometimes ride her out for extra pasture if things dry up some." He nodded to the buckboard where Beans and Joe waited patiently. "I thought of getting barbed wire but didn't want to wait for it to come from Dickinson."

"Mr. Harrison, why?"

He could tell she was frustrated by the color staining her cheeks. She looked too pale from the winter anyway. Needed to get out in the sun some. "Guess, if you like, I could bring you in a horse too. I mean, if you are worried about Opal riding alone. Got a right pretty little filly" *For a right pretty filly*. He wisely kept the finish of the thought to himself.

"Mr. Harrison, I-I cannot afford a horse at this time."

"Hey, Mr. Harrison!" Opal came charging around the corner of the porch and leaped to the ground, her pigtails bouncing higher than her head. "Can I pet Buck?"

"You can ride him if you like."

"Really?" Her gaze pleaded permission from her sister like a pup smelling a steak bone.

"You have to be careful."

"Ru-by." This said with a touch of impatience. "I am always careful." She grinned. "Well, mostly." She stopped in front of the buckskin and waited for him to sniff up her arm, her shoulder, and her hair. His puff of breath in her face made her giggle. She stroked his cheeks and rubbed under his forelock.

Rand watched Ruby watching Opal. Talk about visible love, love written so plainly on her face that even a dolt would recognize it. He felt the need to grab his chest for the pang that pierced his heart.

"What are you building with all the poles?" Opal directed her question to the two men on the seat of the buckboard.

Ruby closed her eyes for a second. When she opened them, she flashed an indecipherable look to Rand. "They're going to build a fence around our field."

"To keep Johnson's cow out of our garden?"

"That too." Rand agreed.

"What?"

"Mr. Harrison has a horse that he thinks you might like to have."

Opal's eyes widened, her mouth dropping open. As if afraid to believe it, she squeaked, "Really?"

"But you have to promise to take good care of her." Rand tried to look stern and only halfway succeeded before he caught a hug head on as Opal threw herself at him.

"Oh, Mr. Harrison, you are the best, the most . . ." Opal leaned back enough to gaze up into his face. "I get a real live horse of my own." The awe in her voice and face made him shift slightly back.

"Your sister agreed."

Opal threw herself at Ruby, leaving Rand feeling something, he wasn't sure what. Bereft perhaps? He'd not been hugged like that since he'd said good-bye to his sister's children the summer before when he went to Ohio to buy his bull. There was surely something to be said about being hugged by a little girl with adoration in her eyes.

Or by her big sister.

Rand cleared his throat. "All right if we begin the fencing?"

"Yes, and thank you." Ruby paused for a heartbeat. "Could we repay you a small bit with supper here at Dove House?"

"That you may surely do. Beans, there, might take a lesson or two." Rand touched the brim of his hat. "Thank you. If you want to ride now, Opal, I'll give you a boost."

"Guess I'll have to ask Charlie to bring the mounting block back out." Ruby smiled to the men. "I'll see you for supper then."

"How far back does your property go?"

She shrugged. "You'll have to ask Charlie. Seems he said we have two acres, or it could be more than that."

"Beyond that cottonwood tree?"

"Yes, but those shacks back there aren't ours."

"Good enough. Where is Charlie, by the way?" Rand tipped his hat back slightly.

"On his way to Dickinson."

"Wish I'd known. He could have gotten us some barbed wire."

"I thought cattlemen didn't believe in barbed wire."

"We don't, but this isn't exactly the open range."

"You should have made that clear to Johnson's cow last summer." The arch of her brow told Rand she was teasing. Sure beat being razored by the edge of her tongue.

He boosted Opal into his saddle. "You can ride without the stirrups?"

She nodded, her eyes shining. "And I neck-rein him, right?"

"Just ride around the field out here where we can keep an

eye on you. Get the feel of riding again."

"Yes, sir." She gathered her reins in one hand and evened them up. "Thank you."

"You are most welcome." He patted Buck's shoulder. Captain McHenry had taught her well.

"Thank you, Mr. Harrison, you have given her the dream of her life," Ruby said quietly.

"I'm serious about a mount for you also."

"I think we'll do with one horse, at least for a while. Give us time to get used to having a big animal like that." Ruby watched as Opal leaned forward to pat Buck's shoulder, the sun picking out the gold tints in her strawberry hair.

"You can be real proud of her."

"Oh, I am. She's all the close family I have left."

"She reminds me of my little sister. How she loved to ride. Fearless as could be too." He shook his head. "And now she has a little girl of her own. Hard to believe how fast time goes by." He slapped his gloves against his thigh. "Guess I better get on out there and help with the fencing. I'll see you later." He smiled up at her. Leaning against the porch post, she was pretty as any picture he'd ever seen.

Maybe he'd bring in that filly after all, and the three of them could go riding. She sure had seemed to enjoy herself with Captain McHenry.

Now why did that thought make him set his feet down like he was stomping grasshoppers?

CHAPTER NINE

Now why'd he go and do that? Ruby frowned.

"You all right?" Milly paused to look where Ruby was staring.

"Of course." Ruby glanced across the field.

"He's a right nice feller, wouldn't you say?"

Not usually, but today . . . Ruby mumbled something under her breath that she hoped sounded like an agreement and returned to the kitchen. Seeing that Daisy had the trays ready with sandwiches, cookies, hard-boiled eggs, and coffee for selling during the train stop, she went back to the door. "You better go tell Opal the train should be in pretty soon."

Taking care of the train passengers was one of Opal's and Milly's main chores and was a source of regular income for the hotel. Because of the good food, more than one guest had chosen to stay over in Little Missouri rather than go east to Dickinson or west to Beach. Not that many stopped in Little "Misery" without a definite purpose, like hunting for game or for land.

The train whistled, the girls hurried out to get themselves set up, and for a few minutes peace reigned in the kitchen. Ruby had just poured herself a cup of coffee and sat down to finish writing that letter to the Brandons when a shriek from the second floor brought Daisy in from the ironing and Ruby off her chair, leaving a spreading ink blot on her paper.

"What now?"

"That's Belle, and something sure upset her this time." Daisy followed right behind Ruby as they flew up the stairs.

The cuss words flying from Belle's lips would do a stevedore proud, but they burned Ruby's ears. *What now? What is she going to try to blame on me or charge me for this time?* Ruby didn't bother to knock, just pushed open the door. "What's—?"

"Cat! That's what! Look, there in my drawer."

Ruby looked to where Belle pointed. Daisy knelt in front of the half-open drawer.

"Would you look at that?" Daisy whispered, a stark contrast to Belle's bellow.

Cat lay on her side in the froth of lacy unmentionables, two still-damp kittens nuzzling her belly.

"Wait until Opal sees this."

"She ruined my things!"

Ruby turned to the fuming Belle. "I distinctly remember reminding everyone to close drawers and boxes. Charlie told me to, and now I really know why." She joined Daisy on her knees.

"She's about to have another," Daisy whispered.

"How do you know?"

"Look at her. She's straining to push it out."

"How many will she have?"

"Three, four—seen up to six."

"And Opal's going to want to keep every one of them."

"Cats are at a premium here. Not too many around. Coyotes think they're prime pickin's. Saw one carried off by a hawk once. 'Course that hawk didn't last long after it took some of the chickens too. My ma waited right inside the hen house with a shotgun. Nailed that ol' hawk with one blast."

"Never mind telling your stories now," Belle ordered. "Get that cat out of my things."

"You can't move her now. It'll get her all upset. You want her to leave her babies?"

"I-I . . ."

Ruby looked over her shoulder to see Belle caught in a quandary.

"But she's ruinin' my . . ." Another string of swear words blued the room.

"She hasn't ruined anything!" Daisy rose to her feet and

advanced on Belle, shaking her finger all the while. "I will wash your underthings as soon as we are able to move her. If you'd have kept your door and your drawers closed like you were warned to, this wouldn't have happened."

"I . . . ah." Belle took two steps back.

"And since this is all your own fault, I will come up with something that you owe me for all the extra laundry, you hear?"

Ruby's hands itched to applaud. She turned her focus back to Cat, who was now cleaning up the new baby. The first two looked to be gray like their mother, but the third one was possibly orange and white.

Ruby stared at the kittens. "Their eyes are shut."

"They don't open for ten days to two weeks, but don't you worry none. See, they already know how to nurse."

Ruby watched as one tiny paw rubbed against the swollen side of the nipple the kitten had latched on to. "They are so tiny."

"Soon they'll be tumbling around, playing. There's nothing more fun than to play with them then. We need to fix her a box behind the stove. Cats like a dark place where they can feel safe. Otherwise she'll move her kittens to somewhere else."

Listen to her chatter. Daisy, the silent one. Come to think of it, both she and Milly talk more now than they ever did.

"Ruby!" The call came from the kitchen below. Opal and Milly had returned.

Ruby stood and, with a pat on Daisy's shoulder, headed for the door. "Is it all right if I let the girls come up to see the kittens?"

"Why not." Belle rubbed her forehead and leaned over to check something about her eye in the mirror. "You'd turn my room into a nursery if I let you."

Ruby left her muttering and made her way down the back stairs. She'd not even noticed that the train pulled out. Somehow seeing Belle caught in a quandary for a change was highly refreshing; in fact, she couldn't quit smiling. And like Daisy said, it was Belle's own fault.

"Ruby, we're going to have—What? What's happened?"

Ruby kept her finger to her lips, quieting her boisterous sister. "Cat is having her kittens."

"Where?"

"In Belle's dresser where her drawers are kept."

Opal's mouth dropped open, and she clapped both hands over her face to stifle an outburst of giggles. Milly did the same. The two girls looked at each other and giggled harder.

"Shush. You want Belle to hear you?" Ruby kept her voice to a whisper with difficulty. The urge to join the revelry made her suck in a deep breath and roll her lips together. She straightened her shoulders, anything to keep from busting a gusset.

"You go on up. But be quiet so you don't disturb Cat." Let alone Belle, who somehow failed to see the humor in all this. *Lord, forgive me for laughing at someone else's expense, but...* She choked back another spurt of laughter and returned to the kitchen. As usual, the tray was now empty but for the cream and sugar, stirring spoons, and the money box Charlie had carved out of a pine burl. While it looked more like a round bowl with a lid, they all called it the money box.

Just as Ruby lifted the lid and removed the money, she heard the bell over the front door announce visitors. She dropped the coins into her apron pocket and headed on through the swinging door into the dining room.

Four obviously wealthy men waited for her at the counter, which had formerly been the bar of the saloon. Charlie had removed the stools and the shelves that held liquor bottles on the wall behind it, leaving the gilt-framed mirror. She and the girls had spent hours polishing the red-oak bar to its present sheen, buffing out nicks and scuffs. Turning the dining room respectable had been a fierce undertaking, but against all odds Ruby and her crew had accomplished the transformation.

"Welcome to Dove House. How may I help you?"

"Four rooms, *s'il vous plait.*" The shortest of the four stepped forward and raised four fingers.

"Will that be for one night or. . . ?"

He turned to the man studying the room and asked, *"Combien de nuits?"*

"Je ne sais pas," the man answered. *"Deux ou trois. Ce n'est pas important."*

Ruby debated. *Should I tell them I speak French?*

She wrote out the cost while the two conversed back and forth. While her bestemor had always said eavesdroppers heard no good about themselves, this eavesdropper was feeling steam arise and hopefully exit by her ears before it blew the top of her head off.

She glanced up to see the man called Enrique watching her. "The marquis says you have a lovely place here, and he is looking forward to our stay."

Of course she knew that was not was he said. She couldn't resist. *"Peut-être vous préféreriez une ferme avec les vaches, monsieur?"* ("Perhaps you would prefer a farm with cows, sir?")

The marquis laughed, gave her a gallant bow, and said, *"Enchanté de faire votre connaissance, mademoiselle."* A smile tilted the ends of his handlebar mustache. His dark eyes danced. "You and your country are filled with surprises."

"Merci." Ruby smiled back.

"I do prefer your hotel. And you serve dinner here?" The marquis nodded to the dining area.

"Yes, at twelve, and supper is at six."

"Ah yes, supper, and so early."

"Here on the frontier many retire at dark." Even though the smile that lifted the corners of his waxed mustache seemed a bit condescending, Ruby let it go by. New York people were often like that, let alone the French. She could see him playing the villain in a melodrama very easily, twirling his mustache and laughing sardonically at the heroine's distress.

"If you will sign here, I have four rooms available, as you requested."

"I will wait here until Enrique has the rooms made up."

"Pardon me, sir, but the rooms are made up. We wash the sheets after every guest, and you will find neither bugs nor dirt in your rooms." She knew her words sounded clipped and formal, but had he set out to offend her, he could not have done so more. "Right this way."

But only the older man, with a trunk on either shoulder, followed her up the stairs.

"Do you have more baggage to bring up?" *Other than the offensive man downstairs?*

He rattled something back to her in French but so fast she could barely follow.

"I see." *I don't care how fine a man your marquis is, and I don't care if he is used to staying at the Biltmore, he . . .* Ruby caught herself before she spoke her thoughts. *Don't be a ninny. He didn't single you out for disrespect. He's like that all the time.*

"I can use your kitchen to prepare monsieur's coffee?"

"I will have coffee sent in to them as soon as I go down."

"*Non, non.* He very particular about his coffee."

Ruby kept her hands unclamped and off her hips. "By all means."

"And the . . . ah . . . facilities?"

"Out back or a chamber pot." Ruby left the room before she said any more. Shame she hadn't tripled the price for the rooms, instead of just doubling it.

"Take coffee in to the gentlemen, will you please, Cimarron?" Ruby set a plate on the tray and arranged molasses cookies on it.

"Of course. You want I should make fresh?"

"No, I think not. Simple is what we serve, and simple is what they'll get. If they don't like it, they can go down the street to Mrs. McGeeney's. Her greasy stew ought to sit real well."

She glanced up to see Cimarron watching her carefully.

"Are you all right?" Cimarron asked.

"Of course I'm all right. Why?"

"You're muttering to yourself. I see our guests are of the wealthy kind. I could bake a pie for supper. Everyone likes that."

Ruby leaned her backside against the table. "Enrique is the servant. Marquis de Mores . . . or rather Antoine Amedee Marie Vincent . . ." She closed her eyes trying to remember. "Oh yes, it's Antoine Amedee Marie Vincent Amat Manca de Vallombrosa, but he said we can call him Marquis de Mores." She caught herself rolling her eyes. *Ruby Torvald, what on earth is the matter with you? Instead of being grateful for four rooms taken, at a premium no less and who knows for how long, you are acting like a spoiled child. You have dealt with the wealthy before. Remember Mrs. Adames, emphasis on the last syllable. She was so impossible, she made even Mrs. Brandon groan.* She stopped her musings to see Cimarron staring at her, one eyebrow arched.

Ruby picked up the tray. "You're right. I'll take this out and behave myself."

"I didn't say a word."

"You didn't need to. You have an extremely expressive eyebrow." She turned and pushed the swinging door open with her backside, something niggling at the back of her mind. Where had she heard of the Marquis before? Had she seen his picture in the paper back in New York?

"Here you are, gentlemen." She set the tray on the table next to them, poured the coffee, and set a cup on a saucer in front of each. "Cream? Sugar?" Lastly she placed the plate of cookies in the exact center of the table. "Can I get you anything else?" She waited, but when they nodded their dismissal, she did exactly that. Left.

Cimarron was rolling out pie crust when she reentered the kitchen. "What's going on upstairs?" she asked.

"Why?"

"All the giggling and shushing."

"Oh, I thought you meant—Oh, my goodness. Daisy, Milly, and Opal are in Belle's room admiring the kittens."

"Cat had her kittens?" Cimarron gave the dough another lick with her rolling pin. "How many?"

"Three so far." Ruby headed for the stairway. "I'll go see if we have more."

She met Opal coming down.

"Ruby, Cat has four kittens. I saw one get born." The awe in her voice earned a hug from her sister.

"How's Belle?"

Opal turned and continued back up the stairs with Ruby.

"She huffs about the mess, but she pulled up a chair and has been watching along with the rest of us."

"And Cat doesn't mind?"

"Not yet. Daisy says she might later. When will Charlie be back?"

"Tomorrow, since he wasn't on today's train." *I wonder what's keeping him?* Charlie always returned the next day. "I'll have him build a box for the kittens."

"Good." Together they entered the now cat nursery.

"If those stains ever come out, I'll be shocked." Belle, cigarillo in hand and smoke graying the room, muttered before taking another puff.

"Keep the door closed. We have guests, very wealthy guests,

from France, no less." Ruby knelt next to Daisy. "You think that's all?"

"Most likely."

"You going to name them?" Milly, sitting cross-legged next to Daisy, asked.

"Maybe we can each name one." Opal stroked Cat with a gentle finger. "Your babies are beautiful, just like you." She turned to Ruby. "You suppose she's hungry? I could go get her some milk."

"No, leave her be. She'll come down when she's ready." Daisy got to her feet. "S'pose I better get back to the ironing, and I know we better be getting supper ready. Belle, guess that leaves you in charge of the cat watch."

Belle shook her head. "I got to take my nap so I can be bright and in a winning streak for tonight." She looked up at Ruby. "Did you triple the room rate like I told you to do when rich travelers arrive?"

Now it was Ruby's turn to shake her head. "No, but I did double it, plus a little extra."

"When are you going to learn?" Belle paused for a smoke. "But that's better'n nothing. They'll leave more on the table tonight."

Ruby returned to the kitchen to find Enrique and Cimarron nose to nose.

"This is my kitchen, and if I allow you to use it, you will stay out of the way when we are busy. Your marquis can—"

Ruby took a step forward.

"Oh, but mademoiselle, I will teach you . . ." He paused at the narrowing of her eyes. "You will teach me to share with you, and we will both be the richer."

Cimarron's shoulders relaxed a trifle.

"Anyone with glorious hair like yours . . ." He kissed the tips of his fingers and threw it into the air.

Ruby never thought to see Cimarron simper, but she came close.

— ❧ —

When Charlie came home from Dickinson the next day, Opal met him at the door with the news, told so fast all her words ran together into one very long one. "And so, will you build a box to put behind the stove with a lid on it for Cat so she won't go hide her kittens somewhere else?"

"Sure. How many did she have?"

"Four."

"Four. That's a good number." When the girl tore back upstairs, he greeted Ruby. "Sorry I'm late."

She waited for him to give an explanation, but when he didn't, she just nodded. The man had a right to his privacy, the same as anyone else.

"I see Opal is dancing on the ceiling."

"With permanent stars in her eyes. She wondered if maybe we would each like one."

"Five cats *is* a few too many."

"I know. We have guests, the Marquis de Mores and his entourage."

"I take it you aren't too pleased about something."

"Charlie." She stared at him, slowly shaking her head. "How do you figure things out so quickly?"

"Bartenders tend to learn to read people, that's all. And your tone of voice said as much and more."

"Oh. Well, we'll see how it goes. Thanks in advance for making the box."

Four tables were occupied for supper, and Cimarron's buttermilk pie brought accolades even from *the Frenchman,* as Opal had dubbed him.

Ruby returned to the kitchen feeling somewhat mollified and reassured only to find Cimarron and Enrique once again staring daggers at each other.

She started to say something, shook her head, and returned to the dining room with one sentence thrown over her shoulder. "You two figure some way to get along."

— ⁂ —

That night Ruby searched her Bible for verses to help her be able to overlook the extra man in her kitchen. *"A soft answer turneth away wrath."* No help, the wrath was hers. *"Whatsoever ye would that men should do, so ye even so to them."* She closed her eyes on that one. *"Love one another as I have loved you."* She kept her finger in the page and thought back to the day. So topsy-turvy, laughing one minute and wanting to choke someone the next. Pulled one way and pushed another. *Father, I want all people who walk through our doors to feel welcome, to feel as if they have come home and can be both comforted and comfortable here. This is your house, and we are your children, all of us. Please, please help me. Forgive me for my impatience and for being so quick tempered. And thank you for the kittens. Babies are such a special gift.* She reread the last verse again. *"Love one another as I have loved you."* I suppose you mean Belle too. A soft sigh. *Thank you again.*

When she blew out the lamp, she could see the wisp of smoke in the moonlight streaming a square unto the floor. With the window open again for the first time since winter, she could even smell spring. She closed her eyes, thankfulness and a new resolve swelling in her heart.

CHAPTER TEN

Dear Miss Torvald,
Please forgive the great length of time since my last letter. I find it impossible to write when we are on patrol, and
that has been almost constant these last weeks. The Apache
are not biddable as the Sioux of the northern tribes. They
do not believe they should be confined to the reservation.
A more warlike group of people I have never known.

I cannot begin to tell you how much I treasure your
letters. Two of them were waiting for me when I returned
to the fort. Mail here is hit and miss, with emphasis on the
latter. I'm glad to hear that Cimarron has put that terrible
act behind her and is more herself. And Belle, well, Belle
will be Belle and always taking care of Belle before all else.
It sounds like this winter has been relatively good for your
hotel business. To think you have been in Little Missouri a
year is unimaginable. How I wish I were there to help you
all celebrate. You will have a celebration, won't you?

Ruby paused in the reading. Celebration, anniversary, she'd
not given such a thing even a thought. It wasn't like the whole
town—more accurately, the other inhabitants of the village—
would rejoice with them. If they celebrated, it would have to be
a private party for the hotel family. Now that was something else.
Some family. Belle screeching about Cat. Milly mooning over the
young private, Adam Stone, who'd left with the military when

they vacated the cantonment. Cimarron snapping at Daisy over trivial matters. She herself wanting to strangle them all at times. Some family. Even Charlie had gotten up on the wrong side of the bed some of the short days and long nights of winter. And Belle, she'd caught her skimming again. She'd have to watch more closely, but what really rankled was that somehow Belle had turned it into Ruby's fault. "I just made a mistake," Belle had said, "and you act like it was deliberate." Why did everything have to be a confrontation with Belle? Why couldn't the woman be trusted?

Surely there was a better way to handle the cardroom—or perhaps she should close it all together. What a thought. Could she afford it?

Ruby was certain she had sugarcoated the local miscreants in the last letter. But then the captain knew the foibles of Little Missouri far better than she.

She returned to the letter.

You would be amazed at the difference in the land here compared to the badlands. Both have such stark beauty, but here there is more desert, with giant saguaro cacti's arms reaching to the sky. Cacti is the plural of cactus, another of the many lessons I've learned here. One learns to stay away from the jumping cholla, a form of cactus that seems to throw its spines. The spines appear soft from a distance, but we are always digging them out of our horses' legs if they venture too close. Denizens of the desert are fascinating. You would be delighted to see the long eyelashes of the jack rabbits. These rabbits are huge compared to the cottontails of Dakotah. They look almost like a dog when they stretch out in a full run. Please tell Opal that there are wild burros here that can be easily tamed once caught. One of the young recruits has made a pet of one, but of course everyone teases him unmercifully. Some of the older campaigners say donkey is as good as deer to eat, but when you are hungry enough, even rattlesnake tastes good.

Ruby felt her throat tighten. The thought of eating snake made her want to heave. Had he been that hungry?

Now that I have most likely offended all your sensibilities, I will finish. I am hoping and dreaming that someday I will return to Dakotah Territory and reacquaint myself with the friends I have made there. Since you have taught the girls to write, perhaps you could encourage them to write letters to some of my soldiers here. Many never hear from anyone at home, and letters mean so much. Thank you for making me one of those most envied. May our good Lord guide and keep you.

Captain Jeremiah McHenry, U.S. ARMY.

Ruby placed the letter on the table. *What a wonderful man*. She had enjoyed his company—rides to the river with Opal, quiet conversations on the porch. *A good friend. So unlike Mr. Harr*—

"Ruby, come quick." Opal burst through the swinging door so hard it slammed back against the wall.

"Now what?"

"You've got to see this."

Ruby tucked the letter in her apron pocket. She'd read it to the others later. Following Opal, who was now tiptoeing and making shushing motions into the pantry, she saw Cat lying in her box, three kittens nursing, the sun making their fur shimmer. Finding the limp form of the fourth kitten pushed away from the others had been a shock, and many tears had followed—not all of them Opal's. But now these three days later, Opal had recovered from the death and was once again savoring the miracle of the new lives.

"Aren't they pretty?"

Cat had not liked the box behind the stove, and was constantly trying to move the kittens. She once moved one of her kittens into a linen drawer before they caught her and put it back.

The first time Opal caught sight of Cat carrying a kitten in her mouth, she had let out a shriek that brought them all running.

"She's killing the kittens. Cat is killing her kittens."

Charlie had burst through the door first. "Opal, where, what?"

"There." Opal stood in place, pointing at Cat who'd started up the stairs.

Charlie picked up Cat with one hand and the kitten with the

other. "No, she just wants some privacy. Think I'll try moving her box into the pantry."

"Opal, you scared me out of three Sundays." Cimarron leaned against the doorframe to the stores and ironing room, fanning herself to restoration.

"Sorry. I was scared to touch her for fear she'd kill it."

"That's how cats carry their kittens. It's not like she can walk with one in her paws." Daisy plunked a flatiron on the stove. "You come help me iron the napkins, get your mind on something else."

After that, Cat seemed to settle into contented motherhood.

As they now stood in the pantry admiring the new mother with her babies, Ruby laid an arm around Opal's shoulders and squeezed. "I'm going out to Mrs. Robertson's. You want to come along?"

"How are you getting there?"

"Charlie's driving us in Rand's buckboard."

"Sure, I'll go. Can Milly come too?"

"No, I got something else to do," Milly put in quickly.

"What?"

Ruby looked over to see Milly turn fourteen shades of red. No need to ask. She only blushed like that when something involved Private Adam Stone, even to writing letters. "Now Opal . . ."

Opal looked up at her sister, disgust splashed all over her face. "I'd rather go with you any day than . . ." Opal returned to the pantry to sink down by the box and stroke Cat.

"We'll be leaving in just a few minutes, so you better wash your face and put on a clean apron."

The sigh that came made Ruby smile. One day Opal would understand how Milly felt, but she hoped that day would be a long time coming.

Meadowlarks showered the earth with their golden tones as they flew up ahead of the team. A crow announced their coming, and another answered. Charlie kept the team at a trot where the track permitted and kept them pulling where the mud in a gully tried to trap the wheels.

Ruby was glad he'd volunteered to drive. She figured she

could do it herself but now realized there was more to it than met the eye.

A basket at her feet contained a burnt-sugar cake and a still warm loaf of bread.

She took off her straw hat and let the sun warm her face. If only she could have invited the others to come along and see, hear, and feel spring. The sun, the birdsongs, the breeze lifting the tendrils of hair that insisted on curling about her face, the perfume.

"Charlie, what smells so good?"

He inhaled, expanding his lungs to stretch his shirt. "Ah, that's just green shoots of grass growing and leaves a'poppin' and the sweet smell of good dirt as it comes to life again."

"And you, my dear friend, are a poet."

"Naw, Miss Ruby, I can't rhyme nothing."

"You see through artist's eyes though."

"What are artist's eyes?" Opal leaned on the board that pretended to be the back of the seat, made of another board.

"People who see the beauty in the ordinary."

"You think this"—Opal swept a hand wide to encompass all they could see—"is ordinary?"

"What do you see?"

"Well, the sky goes on forever, and those white cotton clouds make the blue even bluer, and the green, it hurts your eyes it is so pretty."

"See, you got 'em too." Charlie tipped the brim of his bowler hat farther back on his head. "That's what's good about hard winters."

Ruby and Opal shared a mystified look and shrugged in perfect unity.

"Sure, Charlie, we loved the hard winter. Near to froze my nose." Opal let out a shout of laughter that set the crow to scolding. "I am a poet. Froze and nose."

"Please, sir, explain yourself."

"It's easy, the colder and darker and longer the winter lasts, the more you dream of and look forward to and finally yell, 'It's spring, by cracky.' Some folks even been known to go dancing on the hills. Not me, you understand, but some poet types."

Opal giggled, making Ruby chuckle. That made Charlie

snort, which made Opal burst out in her contagious laugh, catching them all and setting the crow to flight, his caw sounding like a scolding for their noising up the prairie.

As they drove, Charlie pointed out Chimney Butte off to the west, the cows in the creek bottom, and the deer trail down to the river.

"You sure see lots," Opal said.

"All in the training. Another year out here, and you'll be surprised how much you've learned."

"Maybe Mr. Rand will soon bring in that horse he promised, and then I can ride up here all the time."

"Maybe you'll be riding around Little Missouri and grateful for that," her sister chimed in.

"Ahh, Ruby."

"Ahh, nothing. First you learn to ride really well, then we'll see. And besides, his name is Mr. Harrison."

"See that smoke up there?" Charlie pointed over the next rise.

"Yep."

"Yes," Ruby corrected.

Opal sighed.

"That's where the Robertsons live."

"We're almost there."

"Oh, Ruby, I heard more about the marquis," Charlie said. "He already owns that land across the river, and he's planning on building a house up on the south butte."

"Well, I'll be switched."

"Ruby, you sound more like the girls all the time," Charlie said, pulling up to the Robertsons' house.

The Robertson girls were as excited to have company as Opal was in being there and as Ruby was in being away from the hotel.

"You all come right on in. Charlie, Mr. Robertson's out in the barn. I'll put the coffeepot on, and we'll just have ourselves a right good visit."

The girls took Opal out to see the new chicks and the baby pigs, the older girls laughing and one carrying the youngest.

"You have such lovely daughters."

"Thank you. My husband and I, we know we are indeed

blessed. Speaking of blessed, that Easter service, that made my soul feel real good. I've sorely missed having a place of worship, and while God sometimes even speaks on the wind out here, there's something about a group of people worshiping together. No wonder the Bible tells us not to neglect gathering together like that." While Mrs. Robertson talked, she stoked up the fire, filled the coffeepot with water, and measured out her ground coffee. Once the pot was set on the hotter front of the stove, she came and sat down at the table with Ruby. "My land, what a pleasure to have your company."

"Thank you. And thank you for making the girls feel like members of the family when you came to the service. Some of the others treat them as servants or far worse. That makes me so mad, I could—"

"Me too. The Lord says to forgive and forget, and I don't have the energy to carry around a load of holier than thou. Just too heavy."

Ruby smiled. "I never heard it put just that way before, but you said it right."

"So, child, how are you settlin' in to life in Little Missouri? You've made some mighty big changes in a short time."

"I came this close to leaving." Ruby held thumb and forefinger about half an inch apart. "More than once."

"But God wouldn't let you go?"

"Actually it was Opal who kept me here. She reminded me of my promise to Far."

"And what was that?"

"He made me promise to take care of the girls. Well, I had no idea who or what he meant by that, but he was close to dying, and I'd have promised him anything."

"Ah, lass, God knew how they needed you, how the whole town, if you can call it that, needed someone like you." Mrs. Robertson patted Ruby's folded hands. "Much as I love this land and my family, I needed you too. I didn't have the gumption to take on those wives, but then I didn't have to watch my husband visit Dove House neither. Drinkin' or playin' cards aren't as bad as the other . . ." She gave a shudder. "No, we need to get together to worship."

"We need to get together to get a school going too. That's the other thing I wanted to talk with you about."

"A school, you say." Mrs. Robertson nodded while adding, "But of course. Are there enough children in the area yet?"

Ruby counted them off. "And probably more will be here sooner than we think, if what Marquis de Mores wants comes to pass."

"The what of what?"

"He's from France, and according to what Belle and Charlie have heard the marquis and his men discussing, he wants to build a slaughterhouse and ship meat back east in ice-cooled railroad cars. The man has big dreams, and it sounds like he has the money or at least the backing to make those dreams happen."

"Where's he going to get the cattle?"

"He plans to buy cattle back east or from Texas, bring them out here to range, then slaughter and ship the carcasses east. He's been out talking to ranchers and inspecting the land on the other side of the river. It seems he already bought or is buying land from the railroad."

"He hasn't been here yet."

"He's staying at Dove House. He's got to get people out here to build all that, and if the men bring their families, we'll need a school."

"And they'll need houses too. All that might just put Little Missouri on the map."

"If I write a letter to the superintendent of schools and we hire a teacher, will you send your girls in for school?"

Mrs. Robertson got up to pour the coffee. "On all but the worst days. They can ride on in. Where will the school be?"

"That's a good question. I thought maybe we could start at the hotel, but that won't be easy."

"We could have a schoolhouse raising, like a barn or house raising. Perhaps the army would lend a hand."

"What do you mean by a barn raising?"

"Well, you get the material there, then all the men get together and build it all in one day. The women provide lots of good food, and the children run around and make themselves useful or just play together. The young folks make calf eyes at each other, and the men try to outdo each other—a real community kind of time. Always amazes me what all can happen when a group of people get together."

One of the girls came running in, and Mrs. Robertson sent her back out to call the men for coffee.

"How can I help?" Ruby asked.

"You can put those cookies out on a plate. If I'd known you were coming, I'd have made something special."

"I have a burnt-sugar cake in the basket." Ruby pulled the basket out from beside her feet. "We got to talking so fast, I forgot to give it to you. There's some bread in there too." She handed the basket to Mrs. Robertson.

"Well, how about that. I'll just whip up some cream to go on that cake, and we'll have ourselves a party."

By the time they had to leave, Ruby felt that she'd made a real friend. Opal chattered all the way back to town about the girls and the things they did. And Charlie whistled a tuneless tune that Ruby had come to realize meant he had enjoyed himself right well.

Dusk blued the landscape by the time they drove back into town. Supper was finished and the girls had already cleaned up.

"They staked out the *abattoir*," Cimarron announced.

"Who and what?" Opal stared at Cimarron like she'd gone loco.

"The marquis and the men with him. Abattoir is French for slaughterhouse."

"Mighty fancy word for such a place." Charlie looked in the oven. "Didn't you save us any supper?"

"We almost ran out of food. Three more rooms are taken. I can make you sandwiches if you like." Daisy snatched a quick breath. "They plan to start building as soon as the supplies can get here. And . . ." She paused for a heartbeat. "They're even going to build a brick plant because we have such excellent kaolin."

Opal turned first to Ruby who shrugged, then to Charlie, who shrugged, and finally to Daisy, who looked like the cat that swallowed the cream. "What is that?"

"Clay. Really good clay, not only for making bricks but for making dishes and such too."

"Things really are going to change here." Cimarron stopped slicing bread for a moment. "You wait and see."

"Well, I have a letter to write, and then I'll help set more bread."

"The marquis would like water for a bath." Enrique stopped in the doorway.

"I warned that you was supposed to ask earlier in the day." Charlie sounded a bit surly.

"That's all right, Charlie. I figured he'd want some, so I heated extra. We just gotta hoist that boiler back up to hotten up." Daisy smiled back at Ruby's approving nod.

Later, after writing the letter to the Territory Superintendent of Education and sealing the envelope, Ruby thought back to the evening. Cimarron sat mending, Milly helped Daisy with the ironing, Belle and Charlie ran the cardroom—they could have set a third table—and Opal took over preparing the sourdough starter for the morning's pancakes. The girls had handled things without her and Charlie there, had managed new guests, a full house for supper, and had come up smiling.

And she'd had a day away. She started up the stairs when a man's shouting stopped her. Should she go to the cardroom or stay away? She continued on up to bed, hoping Charlie would be able to calm things down or throw the man out, if necessary. Ruby hated to have anything broken, be it bones or furniture. She ignored the voice in her head that said she should check. Sometimes *should* was one of her most hated words.

CHAPTER ELEVEN

"He's here!" Opal slammed out the kitchen door to the back porch. "Hey, Mr. Harrison."

"Hey yourself." Rand swung off Buck and flipped his reins over the hitching rail. "Bet you thought I was never coming."

"Nah." She grinned at him. "Well, maybe, but you built that whole fence, so I thought sure you wouldn't waste all that time."

"You're right. I wouldn't. Just had some chores needing doing at the ranch. This here is Bay. She's on the old side, but she'll be good to you."

Opal stood in front of the horse and let Bay sniff her hands and up her arms. When Bay seemed to approve, Opal raised her hand slowly and rubbed the horse's cheek, then down her neck.

"You really are a beauty. You know your name? It's pretty simple—Bay."

"I thought that you two ought to get acquainted some before you ride her. Why don't you take her out in the field and lead her around, help her to know her new home."

"Thank you, sir. I'll take good care of her."

Rand watched as Opal led Bay up to the gate, slid back the bars, and took the mare into the field. Then she carefully slid the three rails back in place, and the two set off across the grass. Rand nodded. *She passed her first test, the bars of the gate. She's a thinker, not one to just run off and make mistakes. Ruby has done well by her.*

"Thank you, Mr. Harrison. You have no idea how happy you have made one little girl." Ruby strolled down the steps and across to the hitching rail. She and Rand walked together out to the field.

Hope I've made her older sister happy some too. Rand looked over his shoulder to the woman standing beside him. Her voluminous white apron wore stains from the cooking she had left to come see what was going on. Flour smudged one cheek. Sun glinted off her hair, so carefully tucked into a bun at the base of her head. She smelled like cinnamon and something sweet. He inhaled again. His arm felt her nearness, sensing without eyes. Funny how he could feel her presence without seeing or hearing her.

"Hey, Opal, I see you got your horse." Cimarron trotted from the porch to the fence to his other side. "Mr. Rand, you done brought a smile to her face, that's for sure. She's talked of nothing else ever since you started the fence."

"Old Bay needs a good home. She hasn't foaled for the past two years, and she's getting kind of old to be out on the range. Besides, every young girl who wants a horse should have one."

"I always had horses to ride. Used to beat my brothers when we raced. My Pa said it weren't ladylike, but I didn't care."

"You want me to bring in another?"

"Would you really?"

"If I thought any of you wanted to ride with Opal, I would." He turned to Ruby. "Would you like to go riding with her? It'll take some of the worry away if you did."

"Mr. Harrison, while that is such a generous offer, we don't have saddles or bridles. Well, Opal has a bridle from her birthday, but . . ."

He watched her worry her lower lip. *Now, Harrison you done went too far and made her uncomfortable. You ought to have figured out by now that she doesn't cotton to handouts and, sure enough, that's why she's backin' off.*

"I'd love to ride again. Make me remember the better days," Cimarron said wistfully.

Ruby glanced over at Cimarron and caught a hint of the pain the woman had suffered at the hands of those two men and most likely a whole life gone wrong.

"If you would like to bring us another horse to use for the summer, we'd be most appreciative," Ruby said.

"Really?" Both Cimarron and Rand spoke at the same time.

"I said so, didn't I?"

Well, I'll be hornswaggled. "Good, I got an old gelding too. He isn't as pretty as Bay, but he's dependable."

Opal and her horse stopped in front of the three spectators. "Ruby, isn't she beautiful?"

Cimarron reached out and stroked Bay's neck. "Needs a good brushing to get out some of that loose hair."

"Brought you a brush and curry over in my saddlebags. You ever ridden bareback?" he asked Opal.

"No, sir. But I can learn."

"Best way to ride." Cimarron rubbed Bay's furry ears. "Gives you good balance. That's the way most of the Indians ride, maybe with a blanket. Won't be long before you can swing up on her, but for now use these fence rails." Cimarron motioned to the rails they leaned against.

Rand bent over and slid between the rails. "Come on, I'll give you a boost. Bay will stand if you drop her reins. That's called ground tied. And she's trained to neck-reining like most horses around here." He cupped his hands and nodded to Opal. "Here you go. Hang on to her mane."

With one smooth motion, Opal sat astride Bay's back, her grin wider than the sun. She leaned forward to pat the horse's shoulder.

"How's it feel?" Rand smiled up at her.

"Good." Opal wiggled her feet. She tried to straighten her skirt. "I should go put on my divided skirt. It would work better." She glanced at Ruby, down at the hole in her stocking at knee level, and over to Cimarron, who chuckled.

"I could spend half my time mending your stockings, Opal. Good thing summer is coming, and we can all go barefoot again."

Ruby groaned. "Keeping you in clothes is getting worse all the time. You're growing faster than the weeds in Charlie's garden."

"I snagged the stockings on a tree branch."

"Tree branch?" Ruby's eyebrows matched her tone. "Do I want to know why you were up in a tree?"

"Well, ah . . ." Opal sighed. "I was up in that big cottonwood down by the river. The robins are building a nest there, and I wanted to see if they'd laid any eggs yet."

Cimarron didn't bother to hide her snort.

Rand stood on the offside of Bay, watching Ruby's reaction from under his hat brim. He schooled his mouth to hold a straight line, in spite of a mustache that threatened to twitch.

"So were there eggs in the nest?" Cimarron asked.

"I-I . . ." Opal glanced over at Ruby and made a scrunched-up face. "That's when the branch broke, and I snagged—" She stopped at the audible intake of her sister's breath.

"How about I lead for a bit, so you can get your balance?" Rand didn't dare look at Ruby, knowing for sure the horror she'd be feeling. But, Opal hadn't fallen, not far at least. Of course, young ladies shouldn't be climbing trees like that, but life out here on the prairie didn't bear the manners and frills of city life. Opal would do well here with her courage and sense of adventure. "Now hang on to her mane and let your body relax so you move with her." As he spoke, he watched Opal's grin grow wider.

They ambled around the pasture, and as she relaxed her grip on the hank of black mane, he walked Bay in circles, turns, and figure eights.

He glanced over to the gate to see Ruby and Cimarron talking as they watched the horse and rider. When Cimarron laughed, he figured things were settled down somewhat and it might be safe to go back.

"How you feelin' up there?" he asked Opal.

"Ah, like I could ride forever."

He nodded. "Yeah, ridin's like that. When you ride the high buttes, it's like you can see forever, all the world laid out in rumples and valleys, greenin' up, the sky so blue you can taste it."

"Sure different from where we came from."

"Me too. How about we pick up the pace a mite, and see how you sit to a trot. Best way is to lean back some, stay loose. If you clamp your legs tight, it offsets your balance. You ready?"

"Sure."

Rand clucked to the horse, jogged a couple of steps, and Bay came right along with him. He caught a glance of Opal out of his eye, jiggling to the left, centering, and off to the right before she caught on and did as he'd said. Her stuttering giggle brought him back to a walk.

"That's fun."

"I know. You go ahead now and take the reins. Keep her to a walk for a while." He stopped and watched as Opal gathered her reins. "When you squeeze your legs, that's telling her to go forward. Don't go flappin' your reins. Let your legs do your talkin'."

Bay stood, her head slightly down, like she was taking a well-earned snooze. Opal nudged her. Nothing happened.

"Come on, Bay."

"Rein her to the left and dig in your heels. She's feeling a mite on the lazy side."

Opal did as instructed, and the mare moved off.

Rand watched a moment longer, then ambled over to the fence.

Ruby was watching Opal carefully. "What happens if she falls off?"

"She gets back on."

"Mr. Harrison, that's my little sister you are referring to, not one of your cowhands."

"She'll make a good cowhand if she keeps on goin' like she is."

"I think not."

"You never know. Not the most ladylike of aspirations, but it's good, honest work, and there's lots of it."

"I'd go on a cattle drive, if I could." Cimarron rested her chin on her stacked hands that clutched the fence post. "Herdin' cows ain't like servin' customers. Never seen a dishonest cow. Nor one deliberately mean, lessen you get between her and her calf. Any dumb fool does that deserves to get stomped on."

"Yeah, well, come brandin' time, you can come out and argue with those long-horned mamas who resent us with every hair on their hide."

"Not me. I'll leave that part to you cowboys who don't mind being dragged through the dirt. I'll bring out the beans and biscuits."

Rand watched Ruby's face. "Opal learns quick, Miss Torvald.

Don't go worryin' about her so much."

"Mister Harrison, Opal is my only living relative, and it is my duty to worry about her."

Rand watched her flounce past Charlie, who was digging manure into the garden, answer something he asked her, and stomp, as much as a lady like her would allow a stomp, up the porch steps and into the hotel.

"You sure can get her dander up, Mister Rand." Cimarron emphasized the mister. She and Rand had been on a first-name basis for some time.

"Not like I mean to. I was just offerin' some good advice." Rand tipped his hat back. *And here I thought we were gettin' along pretty good for a change.*

— ❧ —

That evening, after a fine supper in the dining room, Rand joined the other men in the cardroom.

"Rand Harrison," he said by way of introduction when he sat down at the table with Belle and three men he'd not met before.

"Marquis de Mores," said the man with dark eyes and waxed mustache tips.

"Fulbright of New York," said another. "I heard you own a spread south of here."

"Small one, only seven hundred head." He shook his head at the offered cigar. "No thanks." He glanced at the man on his left.

"William Van Driesche," he said with a nod.

"All right, boys, what'll it be?" Belle shuffled the cards, riffling them back into a perfect stack between her cupped hands.

"Five-card draw." The Frenchman's accent lay heavy on the air. He bit the tip off his cigar and spit it off to the side.

Rand caught a quick look of censure from Belle. With her foot, she shoved the spittoon closer, the act a remonstrance in itself. *Ah, he's gotten on the wrong side of Belle. Wonder what brought this on?*

"Mind if I join ya?" Jake Maunders barely paused in pulling out the chair between Rand and de Mores. Rand got a faceful of the odor that made de Mores flinch.

The evening went downhill from there. When the three visitors to town periodically tried to discuss what Rand assumed to be de Mores's dreams for the area, Jake interrupted with loud, increasingly rude comments.

Rand quietly pulled in his rather consistent winnings, earning dirty digs from the odoriferous man beside him.

After losing yet again, Maunders pushed back his chair and half stood. Rand raised an eyebrow, and glanced in his direction as a hint to Belle. Her minuscule nod told him she realized what was about to happen.

"You're cheatin'!" Jake leaned on his arms over the edge of the table.

"*Pardonnez-moi?*" The French words came softly but were underlaid with steel.

"Jake, sit down and behave yourself. You know no one cheats at my table." Belle went on gathering the cards to shuffle again. De Mores had won the hand.

"You're in cahoots with him. I ain't won a hand in three nights." Spittle dotted the tabletop.

Rand leaned back, arms loosely crossed. Silence, but for Jake's heavy panting, filled even the corners of the room.

"Sorry for the interruption." Charlie appeared from the next room, picked Maunders up by the collar and, with another hand at his belt, quickstepped the now swearing man from the room. The bell jingled as he opened the door and tossed the bellowing drunk out onto the dirt street.

"I'm sorry, gentlemen. I should have called for Charlie sooner."

"It is not your fault, *madame*. Please to continue the deal." The marquis nodded toward Rand. "And please see if you can keep all the good cards out of his hand."

The other two men chuckled, and one blew three perfect smoke rings. "How many cows did you say you have, Harrison?" the marquis asked.

"Cows or cattle?"

"Cattle."

"Seven hundred head."

"And, when my abattoir is operational, will you sell me your steers?"

"Abattoir?"

"Slaughterhouse, monsieur. It will be, how you say, operational by next summer."

"Where are you building this?"

"Right across the river. That flat meadow, it now belongs to me. I will be buying steers from Minnesota and Texas to be delivered this summer and fattened until next."

"I see."

"I will offer market prices, and there will be no loss for shrinkage in shipping with beeves shipped in ice-cooled cars."

Belle dealt the final round. "Ready, gentlemen?"

The men picked up their cards as if having never dropped such an amazing bit of news.

The marquis studied his cards and glanced over at Rand. "It is not a dream, monsieur. The town will be named Medora, after my wife. Building will begin as soon as materials arrive by train."

"You gonna wish you had plenty more cows, Rand. This man means business." Belle blew smoke out the side of her mouth, waving her cigarillo like a baton. "You mark my words, Little Missouri is in for some big changes."

"Pass." Rand folded his hand and laid the cards on the table.

The marquis won the pot, which brought a satisfied smile to his dark eyes and groans from his friends.

"Thanks for the entertainment. I have a long ride home." Rand pushed his chair back. "I'll look forward to working with you."

"*Bien.*" The Frenchman dipped his head in a single nod. "What I build will bring wealth to Medora and the ranches."

"And you."

"And you also."

"Guess we'll have to see what happens."

"Oh, it will happen. Never fear."

"Good night, gentlemen." Rand stuffed his winnings in his pocket and, after bidding Belle good-night, headed for the door.

Charlie handed him his hat as he left the room. "I've been listening to him for the last couple nights. Either he is a preposterous liar, or he has the backing of men with access to great wealth. Wish I had some steers to feed out."

"You think he's on the up and up?"

"I do."

"Well, we'll see. Night, Charlie. Thanks."

Once out the door, Rand settled his hat securely on his head and headed to where Buck was still tied at the hitching rail. True to her word, Opal had fed and watered him, the bucket still half full of water.

Rand checked his cinch and swung aboard. He crossed his hands on the saddle horn and studied the hotel for a moment. He could stay here overnight, but he'd told Beans he'd be home.

Could all this be trusted? Only time would tell.

CHAPTER TWELVE

Chicago, May 1883

> Growing town in western Dakota Territory seeking teacher for all grades. Applicants must be of good moral character, preferably with teaching experience, without family encumbrances, able to relocate by the opening of school in September. Send letter of intent and list of qualifications and experience. Include return address and references.

The ad closed with the address to which applications should be sent.

Pearl Hossfuss read the advertisement for the third time. She had all the qualifications but one—family encumbrances. Would her father let her go? Would it be worth applying?

At a knock on her door, she laid the paper back on the table after folding it so the advertisement lay hidden.

"Come in." With an unconscious movement, her right hand checked to be sure the high ruching-trimmed neckline of her fine lawn waist covered the wrinkled red scar on her neck.

"Supper is served, miss." Erin, the newly hired Irish maid, bobbed her head, setting the curls that were supposed to be covered by the white mobcap to bouncing.

"I'll be right there, thank you." Pearl stopped at the mirror to make sure not a hair had escaped from the chignon bound firmly to the base of her head. Neither dimple in cheeks that once bloomed like the freshest of peaches had the temerity to show forth. Seeing herself as passable, Pearl adjusted her favorite piece of jewelry, her mother's cameo.

She shook her head at the image in the mirror. She should be smiling, happy. After all, her father was out of town on business, and the family would eat in the nursery, no formal dining room tonight. No surprise guests. None of those looks she'd been receiving since she had explained to her matchmaking father that the man he'd been bringing around was not acceptable.

Pearl made a face. As if what she thought and had expressed so gently—she still thought she had done well in not speaking the way she wanted to—was of any value in her father's eyes.

You've always done what he said, so why should he expect anything different this time? I have tried. I really have given it my all. Pearl Elaine Hossfuss has been a model daughter, on the outside at least. She repeated the words, this time aloud, then added, "I should be grateful for all the education, the freedom to teach, access to books and art and music, and a stepmother who cares deeply for me instead of treating me the way others have been known to do." Should be grateful. But wasn't. *Lord, please help me feel grateful. I have so much to be grateful for.* She waited, hoping to feel a rush of something. Dead and empty wasn't what she'd asked for.

Thank me anyway were the words that came.

Now that was an unusual thought. *A sacrifice of praise.* Where had she read that? In the Psalms? Mentally she flipped through the verses she'd memorized over the years. Memorizing had always come easy to her. "I will praise thee," King David sang and said often.

Lord, I will praise thee. I will come unto thee with singing. For thou are my God, and I am thy handmaiden. Thou, O Lord, art the keeper of my ways; thy thoughts to me art constant, thy ways—thy ways. . . .

Is all this thy way, Lord?

What a question. Now, if only she had some answers.

She fingered the ruching again and turned to look at the advertisement. Should she show Amalia? Should she just go ahead and apply? Should she accept the attentions of Sidney Longstreet?

She shuddered at the last thought. No, that one was not even a possibility.

— ❧ —

The next day Pearl and Amalia were taking tea in the library where a fire snapped and crackled in the fireplace to ward off the chill. "There are far worse problems in life than being married to a boring man," Amalia said. "I do not think Mr. Longstreet would ever be cruel to you."

Pearl sipped her tea, cupping her cold hands around the warm china. "No, I don't believe that about him. But would no conversation not be a cruelty also?"

"Perhaps he is merely shy around your father. After all, he is in Mr. Hossfuss's employ."

"Perhaps. Does Father know that you have been so candid with me?"

Amalia shook her head and gave a slight smile. "No. That is one thing you must learn. Women talk things over. Men just do and always assume they are right."

Pearl pondered her stepmother's words. "So now Father has invited Mr. Longstreet and his children to dinner after church. Why is he suddenly so interested in finding me a husband? He's left me alone for years."

Amalia laid a hand on Pearl's arm. "Your father loves you and is concerned about your future, but I fear it is a comment of mine that prompted all this."

"How could that be?"

"I mentioned not too long ago that I thought a certain young man would be a good match for you. I had no idea your father was even listening. It was just one of those musing things, you understand? I want you to be happy, and I don't believe for a minute that you were created to be an old-maid schoolteacher." She said the last words emphatically, as though she'd been thinking them long enough to truly believe them.

"I had no idea."

"I know. I have not mentioned my dreams for you because I did not want to influence yours. Ah, Pearl, I could not love you more if you had indeed been part of my body. You are the daughter of my heart, and I only want the best for you."

Pearl could feel tears burning the backs of her eyes. "Thank you." She laid her cheek against Amalia's hand. "But I thought I was most happy. I love my teaching, I love my children."

"Perhaps you could learn to love this man too. Loving his children would be easy for you. They need a mother."

"Like we needed a mother?"

"True, but I also fell in love with your father before the wedding."

"I find it hard to think of anyone falling in love with Father."

"He is an interesting man, no?"

"True."

"He is interested in many things, and his enthusiasm carries others along. He is generous, he believes in God, and he can be very amusing."

"He is also bossy, didactic, and always thinks he is right."

Amalia chuckled. "True, but there are ways to get around him if one sets her mind to that." She poured herself more tea. She glanced at Pearl out of the side of her eye.

"And I always meet him head on, don't I?"

"You have a tendency that way. You are much like him, you know."

"I see." And she did. Was Amalia using the same tactics of finesse on her that she used on Father?

"I believe Sidney Longstreet would be malleable and could become more alive in the hands of the right woman."

Pearl thought for a few moments. "Be that as it may, I do not believe I am the right woman."

"But you could become so."

Why did that hurt? Pearl closed her eyes and inhaled the scent of the few lavender seeds that Amalia always had Cook add to the steeping teapot.

Pearl did not doubt that Amalia did love her and wanted the best for her. Perhaps it was time that she started treating her like a mother, trusting her like a mother. She took a deep breath. "I have seen an ad for a teacher in the newspaper. I am thinking of writing an application." There, she'd brought it out in the open.

"I see. And where would this be?"

"A small town somewhere in Dakotah Territory."

"But that is so far away."

"I know." *Far enough that I will be out of sight, out of mind. Mr.*

Longstreet will find himself another wife, and Father will let me live my life as my own.

"Would you have run off without telling us where you were going?"

"If that is what it took, yes, but here I am telling you in the confidence that you will not tell Father. I must do that myself." She slightly lifted one shoulder. "If they were to employ me, which is most doubtful, I would want to give Father a *fait accompli*."

"I could perhaps soften the way for you."

"You would do that?"

"Ah, my dearest Pearl, I do not want you to leave Chicago, but if you must, I will do all I can to make the parting amicable. A family can remain close even across the miles of that prairie I've heard about. At least I pray to God that is so."

That night before retiring, Pearl wrote her letter of application, sealed the envelope, and dropped it off at the post office on her way to school. The die was cast.

— ❧ —

Proper children they were, their manners correct, but their clothing was in need of a woman's hand. The youngest clung to his eldest sister's hand as if fearful of being out of her sight.

Pearl greeted them each by name, Henrietta, Oswald, Betsy, Irvin, and Benjamin, pretending as if she were greeting a new class in the fall. But her smiles elicited nothing but polite nods as the five clung together. Were they as bland as their father or shy or still sad beyond measure at the loss of their mother? How long had she been gone?

Pearl remembered the ache she'd lived with for so long after her mother died. But at least she had not been forced to leave home and move to a strange city. *Who has been caring for you all? Is there an aunt or grandmother? Or only housekeepers? Nursemaids? Nannies?* If only someone would talk with her!

"Come, my brothers and sister are out in the yard. We have time to play before dinner." She glanced to their father for permission, and at his nod the five rigid soldiers followed her without a word, just glances among themselves.

"Anna and Arnet, come meet our guests," Pearl called to her siblings.

The twins bailed off the swings their father had had built for them and ran up. Jorge Jr., leaving his hoop, joined them also.

Pearl introduced them all, then suggested, "We could play goose, goose, gander if you like."

"But we have our best clothes on," Betsy, the middle child, said. "What if we get dirty?"

"Oh, I see."

"We could play jump rope. You won't get dirty that way." Anna took hold of Pearl's hand. "Unless you fall down, but I don't ever fall."

"Or we could play charades," Jorge contributed.

"I don't like charades. You always win." Arnet turned his back on his brother.

"We could show them the baby bunnies." Anna turned to Betsy. "You ever held a baby bunny?"

Betsy shook her head, eyes round. "No, never. Could we?" She looked to Henrietta, the oldest, who shrugged and picked up Benjamin, the two-year-old who had clung to her skirts after she set him down earlier.

"Why don't we all sit here on the grass in a circle, and Anna and Arnet will bring the bunnies." Pearl did as she suggested and smiled for the others to join her.

"Ooh, look," Betsy squealed in delight as Anna set a tiny white bunny with pink eyes and nose in her lap.

"You pet him like this." Anna showed proper bunny handling, cuddling one under her chin in gentle hands.

Pearl held one for little Benjamin to touch, his pudgy finger guided by his older sister's hand.

Between Anna and Arnet, they had the children laughing and giggling over the tiny creatures.

"His nose. He wiggles his nose."

"Look, she's eating grass."

"They like clover better, see?" Anna fed a clover leaf to another. The bunny nibbled it daintily, tiny nose twitching, front paws on Anna's thumb.

"How many rabbits do you have?" Henrietta asked Jorge.

"Two does and a buck, plus these five little ones. The other doe will have her babies any day now."

"The buck—we call him Homer—is the father to all the babies." Arnet set his bunny down on the grass. "If your father would let you, you could have one of these when they are older. Rabbits make good house pets. They're easier to house train than a dog or cat."

Pearl smiled at the shock on Henrietta's face.

"A rabbit in the house?"

"Sure, we kept Snowflake in the nursery until we got Homer."

"I've taken Josephine to my classroom. She was a great delight."

"Josephine?"

"She's the other doe. We leave her alone now, so we won't disturb her when her babies are due. Sometimes mother rabbits eat their young if they get upset."

Pearl wished she could clap a hand over Arnet's mouth at times like this. Horror drained Henrietta's face of all color.

"You got to be careful, you know." Arnet held a bunny up and rubbed noses with it.

"I think we better put these back with their mother. I saw the maid wave us in to dinner."

Betsy kissed one of the babies on the head and handed it back to Anna. "I'll ask Father if we can have one."

"We can tell him how to build a cage and all." Anna and Arnet walked off with their hands full of baby bunnies, and one rode in Anna's apron pocket.

"Thank you," called Oswald, the boy just older than Betsy who, up to that point, had not said a word.

Pearl stood and shook any loose grass off her skirt. "Come, let's wash up."

— ❧ —

"Thank you, Miss Hossfuss, for entertaining my children," Mr. Longstreet said as they were about to leave several hours later.

"You are most welcome."

"I . . ." He turned his hat in his hands. "I hope to see you again soon?"

If only he would look at me instead of his hat brim when he talks. Could one really make something of this man, as Amalia said?

"We are having a soiree here next Saturday, and we look forward to the pleasure of your company." Amalia flicked Pearl a glance.

A glance of what? Apology? Question? Pearl stood in the doorway with her mother and father, wishing their guests good-night and Godspeed, but feeling that it might be one of the worst nights of her life.

CHAPTER THIRTEEN

Little Missouri

"You think he's going to accomplish all that, or is he just a big dreamer?"

"Wish I knew for sure, but . . ." Charlie wagged his head, slowlike, as if it helped him think. "From what I can figure, he's got all the money he needs between his own and someone, or more than one, who owns half of New York."

"I wonder if Mr. Brandon knows any of the men you heard the marquis mention?"

"What difference would that make?"

"He'd know if this was rock truth or all hot air." Ruby cut another piece of cornbread, drizzled syrup over it, and handed it to Charlie. While the others had all stumbled on up to bed, she'd stayed down to discuss what all Charlie had heard over the last few days.

While no one at the hotel would be sorry to see Enrique leave, the money the group had spent in Little Missouri would go far toward making this a good summer. And if all this about an abattoir and all the housing and stores and building supplies and arriving cattle was indeed true, Little Missouri would become a place on the map.

"So who is going to build all this?"

"Good question. I heard de Mores has a superintendent coming in, someone to run it all, but I s'pect they'll run ads in newspapers or something. Like when there's been a gold strike, a tent city springs up overnight."

"Wish we had the money to add on to Dove House."

"With news like this, you'd have no trouble getting more money from Mr. Davis's bank in Dickinson."

"Now that I have the loan paid off and a savings account started, I hate to borrow more money." Even the thought made Ruby's stomach twist and buckle. She had the ledgers memorized by now, knew to the penny how much she spent and how much she had collected. Amazing how one could change in only a year. From a governess in a good home in New York to the hard-working proprietress of a semi-successful hotel in the wilds of the badlands.

If only her father could see her now. Would he be proud? Or would he think she should have left Dove House as a saloon with the girls bringing in the "hospitality" money? As she'd often reminded herself when these kinds of questions reared their hissing heads, it didn't matter what he thought. All that mattered was what God thought, and He seemed to approve, if the till was any indicator.

Along with her peace of mind.

"Well, tomorrow's another day. Thanks, Charlie, for all you do to make this place a success."

"You're most welcome. Things is goin' to get even better. You wait and see."

Ruby made her way up the stairs, hearing laughter from the cardroom. After Jake's drunken scene from the night before last, he'd been barred from the cardroom. Still, she'd seen several locals go in, and the three gentlemen from the East always headed there immediately after supper even though Belle didn't start dealing until eight. How Ruby wished she could have been a mouse in the corner to hear firsthand the plans for her town, now that it might really become one.

Though she could hardly call the town hers when half the original inhabitants hated her for closing down the saloon and the four women in town still wouldn't talk with the girls and had tarred Ruby with a similar brush. However, they did come to the festivities Ruby put on and seemed to enjoy themselves—and eat the free food. Ruby thought to the coming Sunday morning, their first service since Easter. Would anyone show up besides Mrs. Robertson and her family?

She turned in her Bible to the passages they would be reading and hopefully talking about. Simple verses of Jesus reminding the rich young ruler of the true commandments. And the all-time favorite, John 3:16. "For God so loved the world . . ." Sometimes she wondered if that included Little Misery the way people here acted. She had to remind herself that it was God who did the loving, hoping men would turn to Him because of it.

Father, I want Dove House to be a beacon of love and hope in this small spot in your world. I know you brought us here for a reason, and I know you don't make mistakes. Please bless our service in the morning and abide with us as we learn to abide in thee. Abide, such a lovely word. She remembered one pastor defining it as being hidden within the heart of God. Now wasn't that some picture? *Lord, it would help if we had someone versed in the Scriptures to teach and preach on Sunday mornings.*

You could help Charlie write a lesson. Clear as a bell, the thought rang in her head. *Hmm.* She tapped a forefinger on the end of her chin. One wouldn't have to say much. Would he agree? He'd volunteered to read the Scriptures. Well, maybe volunteered was stretching the truth a bit. He'd volunteered after a bit of persuasion. Well, more like pleading if she got right down to the truth. But he'd done so before. And would again in the morning.

She blew out the lamp and snuggled under her down quilt. Even though spring had been here for some time, the nights still got chilly. It was not yet time to put away the quilts.

— ✴ —

Belle started playing before the first arrivals. The front door was open, so the music poured out and floated around the town. Somehow the hymns had a bit more life here than in the more formal church Ruby remembered, but she couldn't criticize this piano player, not if she wanted to have one. At least the girls all wore their more sedate clothing, as if it had done any good at the Easter service or in the weeks since. Although Mrs. McGeeney had smiled at her, albeit frost-tinged.

Rand set his hat on the table closest to the door, along with the guitar case, and came forward to tune the instrument with the piano.

"Fine mornin', Miss Torvald."

"Yes, it is."

He tipped his head slightly to listen to the chord he'd strummed, waited for Belle to hit the note he wanted, and turned the pegs to adjust each of the strings.

Realizing she'd been studying him, Ruby felt the heat rise in her neck. Yes, he was a good-looking man, but he was still Rand Harrison, who managed to infuriate her without any visible effort on his part.

"Hey, Mr. Harrison."

"Hey yourself, Opal. How's Bay?"

"She's the best horse. She comes when I whistle now."

Ruby groaned inside. How was she ever going to help Opal become a proper young lady when everyone around encouraged such unladylike behavior? She knew Cimarron had a hand in this one.

"I don't even use two fingers no—" Opal glanced at Ruby— "*anymore*." Her freckled nose wrinkled slightly as she grinned at her sister.

Ruby glanced up to see Rand studying on her. His direct gaze caused the heat to rise again. *Ruby Signe Torvald, what on earth is the matter with you?* She squared her shoulders, straightened her skirt with a twitch, and headed for the door to greet those arriving.

At promptly ten o'clock Belle played a series of loud chords, and everyone took the hint to stand for the opening hymn. Thanks to the sheets of songs Opal had so carefully printed out, everyone was able to sing along.

"Sorry we are late," Mrs. Robertson whispered as she and her family tiptoed in.

"Welcome. We still have plenty of chairs." Ruby pointed toward the front as she handed them the song sheets.

When Charlie finished reading the Scriptures, he paused. "Anyone have anything to say about this?"

Ruby watched as several people glanced sideways at one another, shuffled their feet, and squirmed in their seats, setting the chairs to creaking.

"Think I'll read it again. 'Thou shalt love the Lord thy God with all thy heart, and with all thy soul, and with all thy strength, and with all thy mind; and thy neighbor as thyself.'" He paused again and looked out over the gathering. "Now I got to say, folks, do we live up to that?"

Ruby saw some heads nodding, others shaking.

Mrs. Robertson cleared her throat. "Those are hard words to follow." She glanced at two of her daughters who stared down at the floor. "When we can't even do so in our own homes, how can we do so to others?"

When no one else added anything, Charlie closed the Bible.

"Could you read something else? Like one of the Psalms maybe?" Mrs. Paddock from the livery asked. "It's so long since I heard Scripture read out loud."

"Any favorites?"

"Twenty-third Psalm," someone said.

"Think maybe we can all say this one together." Charlie found his place. "'The Lord is my shepherd; I shall not want. . . .'"

One by one voices chimed in, some stumbling, and others were silent, but all agreed on the amen.

He read two others, including Psalm 91, his voice mellow and rich, like coffee with plenty of cream. He strung the words together, rising and dipping as if he'd been reading Scripture aloud all his life.

Ruby caught the smile on Opal's face as she nodded her encouragement. Maybe they didn't need someone to preach. Perhaps they all just needed to hear the Word of God—aloud and together.

"Anyone here want to lead us in prayer?" Charlie asked after a long silence.

Mr. Benson, one of the newcomers, coughed and cleared his throat. "Lord God, I thank thee that we can gather together in thy name, that thou hast given us this place of refuge, these thy people who believe in thee and desire to worship together. We praise thy holy name and glorify thee. Amen."

"That was some purty," whispered Daisy, loud enough that Ruby, off to the side, could hear.

He sounded like an educated man, not a sodbuster. *When will you learn to not make judgments?* Ruby sighed. Here she chose the verses to try to get the women in town to speak to each other, and God poked a finger at her. *Lord, please, I want to honor you first and not be judging on appearances alone. Not to judge but to love as you do.*

"We'll sing 'Onward Christian Soldiers,' down at the bottom of the second page."

Belle hit the opening chords, and away they went, singing three more songs before Charlie read the benediction that Aaron spoke to the people of Israel. "'The Lord bless thee, and keep thee. . .'"

"Charlie, it does my heart good to hear you readin' like that. Thank you kindly." Mr. Robertson, his bald spot showing white since he'd taken his hat off when walking in the door, shook Charlie's hand.

Ruby joined the girls in the kitchen as they picked up the trays of cups and rolls to serve those who'd come. Cimarron used two padded potholders to grasp the hot, full coffeepot and followed the others through the door.

Ruby watched as Cimarron poured a cup for Rand, laughing at some comment he made. *That's who he should marry.* The thought brought a smile to heart and lips. Of course. He said he needed a wife, and she has all the experience of ranching that a wife for him should have. They're friends. Surely he will overlook what happened to her. After all, he went after the attackers.

"You're plotting something." Charlie stopped beside her.

"Why, Charlie, whatever do you mean?" Guilt grabbed her throat so that she had to clear it before continuing. "I just had an idea, that's all." *Should I confide in him? No, he wouldn't understand.* Ruby continued her rounds, stopping to speak with each guest.

"Those Frenchies didn't think it necessary to worship, eh?" Mrs. McGeeney's voice hinted at a snide barb.

"The marquis left early this morning. He's out scouting for something, I guess. I'm sure they'll be back for supper. Did you want to talk with the marquis?" She hoped Mrs. McGeeney got the point. Frenchies indeed.

"No, not me, but if'n half of what I heard happens, would be good for Little Misery."

Which wouldn't be so miserable if you would get along with your neighbors. Ruby hoped she kept her thoughts from showing on her face. She looked around for Opal, who, along with the Robertson girls, was nowhere in sight. She was out showing off Bay, if she knew her sister.

"Did you get the letter off to the Board of Education?" Mrs. Robertson declined a refill on her coffee. She pointed to the chair. "Can you sit and talk for a few minutes? I know you have plenty to do."

"For a bit. The girls are getting dinner ready. I doubt there'll be very many today."

"I've been thinking about the school."

"Me too." Ruby nodded when Charlie offered to pour her a cup of coffee.

"The rolls are coming up."

"You make the best sweet rolls here. I'm afraid some come for the treat rather than for the service."

"Whatever brings them in. You think the men around here would like to take turns preaching?"

"I doubt it. But Charlie did a fine job today. Who'd have thought . . ." A slow smile matched the gentle shaking of her head. "Things sure have changed."

"I know, but I keep thinking we haven't seen anything yet compared to what the marquis wants to do."

"Those of us who are already here better make sure we lay claim to our land, or we could be in real trouble."

"You mean you don't own the land where your house is?"

"No, didn't need to. Let the cattle range, and you could build a house anywhere. But we got good water, so Mr. Robertson is going to Dickinson on Monday and take care of that matter."

"I better go say good-bye to the folks who are leaving. Can you stay for dinner so we can have a real visit? Please. It's on the house."

"I'll have to ask Mr. Robertson, but you can't keep giving everything away like this. I was going to talk with you about the rolls, as it is."

Ruby fluttered her hand. "Please, pay no attention to that. If this was my house, you wouldn't say no, would you?"

"No, but I'da brought somethin' along."

Ruby shrugged and headed for the open door where the

Bensons and the Paddocks were talking. But not to one another.

"Thank you all for coming. I hope we'll see you again in two weeks."

"That you will. And thank you for hosting us again."

Ruby watched others go down the steps, one behind the other, not exchanging a word or even smile. She shook her head and turned back into the dining room. Mrs. Robertson caught her eye and cocked an eyebrow, making Ruby smile. While they hadn't spent much time together, she finally felt like she had a friend in the territory. Beyond those at Dove House.

They quickly restored the tables and chairs to the proper order, flipping the crisp white tablecloths in place. Even Belle helped instead of leaving or returning to her room, as she so often did. *What is she going to demand of me this time,* Ruby thought, then immediately castigated herself for her unchristian attitude. Love others as yourself were indeed hard words to follow.

"Hey, Rand, I hear you're bringing in another horse."

"Sure enough, Belle. You want to ride too?"

"Me? I don't think so, but Ruby hasn't had her head out of this hotel for weeks. She needs to get out and see what spring does in this country."

Ruby stopped in her headlong rush to the kitchen like she'd hit a glass wall. *I must be hearing things.* She turned in time to see Belle wink. Wink? For mercy's sake, what was going on?

"Would you go for a ride with Opal and me if I bring another horse?"

"But I don't have a saddle."

"I'll look around at the ranch. We must have an extra."

"I . . . I . . ."

"Ruby!" Opal's wail came from outside.

Ruby straight-armed the door and headed on out back, Rand hot on her heels.

Tears running down her cheeks, limping, and with dust and dirt on face and dress, Opal also wore a bloody lip.

"Are you hurt?" Ruby caught her little sister in a hug.

"Bay got stung by a bee, and when she swerved, we fell off."

Ruby tipped Opal's head back. "Your lip is bleeding. Anything else? Wait a minute—we?"

"Virginia and me."

"Where is she?"

"Hiding behind her sister. She doesn't want to get scolded."

Ruby dabbed at Opal's lip with her handkerchief.

"Ouch."

"Where's Bay?" Rand looked from the girl out to the pasture where Bay stood still, her reins tying her to the ground. Rand turned back to Opal. "Time to get back on. I'm thinkin' you better learn to ride really good yourself before riding double."

Ruby turned on Rand. "She most certainly should not get back on right now. She's hurt and dusty and—"

"Opal, you go get your horse, and I'll help you mount. Virginia, it'll be your turn as soon as Opal rides around the pasture again."

The look he gave Ruby made her shut her mouth, but her eyes flashed fire. The nerve of him. When Opal left her arms and climbed back through the fence, Ruby turned on Rand.

"How can you—"

He raised one hand, palm out, his face calm. "She has to get back on so she doesn't become afraid. Only thing really hurt is her feelings. These things happen."

"If anything . . ." She spluttered to a stop at the look in his eyes.

"Trust me. It will be all right."

A shiver danced up her spine. *Trust. Why would I trust you! Why not? Has he ever done or said anything to harm Opal? Or anyone for that matter?* Even though he drove her to distraction at times, he'd never been anything but a gentleman.

Ruby swallowed the other things she'd been about to say and walked over to the fence. Mrs. Robertson joined her.

"They had a tumble, did they?"

"Looks that way."

"My Virginia, she's only worried because she is wearing her best dress and I told her not to get dirty. Long as they aren't really hurt, no nevermind."

Ruby sucked in a breath of relief and turned to her friend. "How can you stay so calm?"

"Lots of experience. You ride horses; sometimes you fall off. You get hurt; you heal. All told, makes you a stronger person, and we need strong people out here."

Ruby watched as Opal swung aboard, listened to Rand tell her something, nodded, and nudged Bay forward to walk around the fence line. When she slid off, Virginia was boosted on and did the same.

Opal came to stand by Ruby. "It wasn't Bay's fault."

"It wasn't anyone's fault." Ruby brushed dust off Opal's shoulder. "I need to get back and make sure dinner is getting ready. Come wash up as soon as you put Bay away."

"You'll make it out here just fine," Mrs. Robertson said as they walked back to the porch.

Ruby nodded. How come she felt like she'd just been given a medal for valor?

— ≫ —

The next morning at breakfast the marquis asked to speak with her. She brought another plate of fried ham to his table and waited until he turned to her.

"How can I help you?"

"I just wanted to tell you that we are leaving on today's train. Enrique will settle our bill."

"I will have it ready for you in an hour."

"Merci. I will tell others of the fine service at your establishment. Be assured you will receive plenty of business in the months and years ahead."

"Merci. May you accomplish all you desire." She knew her French wasn't great, but his smile rewarded her efforts.

As he left Dove House, the Marquis de Mores looked over his shoulder. "I will be back."

"Go with God."

He touched the brim of his hat, his dark eyes flashing.

What would all this mean for Dove House? Ruby wished she knew.

CHAPTER FOURTEEN

"Please, please come be our mother. We need you."

Pearl woke with a start, the entreating faces of Mr. Long-street's children as clear as if they stood at the foot of her bed. She laid her hand against the thudding of her heart in an attempt to quiet herself. This was the second night of dreaming about the children. Why had they trapped her heart so? They were being cared for, one could see that.

But were they being loved?

That was the question all right. Of course their father loved them. She could see it in the way he laid his hand on a shoulder, smiled encouragement. He wasn't demonstrative, but he also wasn't abrupt or sarcastic with them. Dared she ask about them at dinner tonight when he would be a guest again?

Or would that be an encouragement?

She poured herself a glass of water from the pitcher that always sat on her bedside table. One of the many little things she took for granted.

Being in my father's house has me spoiled, and all I really wanted was for him to notice me, to pay attention to me like he does to Anna and Arnet. Some Christian you are, jealous of your little brother and sister. The Bible says clearly "Thou shalt not covet," and you most certainly do.

Why were these nocturnal sessions so clear in her mind when during the day she could look the other way so easily? She slumped back against her pillows. "I'm going to be a bear in the morning if I don't get back to sleep. Only two more weeks of school, and the picnic almost here."

You should have asked your father.

I cleared it with Amalia, and if she wanted Father to know, she could have told him.

A wide yawn cracked her jaw. *Thank you, Heavenly Father, for loving me. Help me to be the woman you planned me to be. And forgive me these trespasses of which I am so prone. Please find a willing wife for Mr. Longstreet. And if it is you who are bringing the children to my mind, please make your will clear to me.*

The maid had to touch her shoulder to wake her at rising time.

— ⚡ —

Her pupils could talk of nothing but the outing on the morrow.

"And you said we would ride the cable car?" one of them asked for the third time.

"Yes. But now we will work on our reading again."

"And we will have our dinner out in your grassy yard?"

"Yes, if it does not rain." She pointed to a child in the second row. "Sally, it is your turn to read. Please stand."

And so the day went until she felt like shooing them all out the door for an extra recess. Why hadn't she thought to do this sooner—and with former classes?

— ⚡ —

Pearl took a much-needed half hour for a lie-down after she arrived home.

Much too soon Bernadette knocked on her door and entered. "Your mother suggests you wear the claret silk gown with the fringe on the overskirt." The maid took the dress from the chifforobe and inspected it for any stains before hanging it in sight.

"Thank you." Pearl did know how to choose her own clothing. But she knew she would have chosen something more simple—and not as new.

"Part it in the middle with waves on the sides, no curls in the back," she instructed the maid as she brushed out Pearl's hair.

Bernadette sighed. "But your mother said—"

"I'm wearing the dress, but I don't want all those pins poking me in the head. I thought a velvet ribbon around either a weave or a coil."

Another sigh, this one even more expressive. The French communicated a great deal with a sigh and the fluttering of hands. "But, Miss Pearl . . ."

"If anything is said, I will take full responsibility."

A tsk or three communicated equally as well as a sigh, if not better.

Feeling more like herself and yet still acceding to parental wishes, Pearl made her way downstairs before the doorbell announced the arrival of their guest.

"Good evening, Miss Hossfuss."

"And to you, Mr. Longstreet." She motioned to the parlor. "Father is serving aperitifs, if you would care for something before supper."

"Thank you. May I say you look lovely tonight."

If only he would smile more often, why, it quite changes his features. "Thank you. This way."

"Good evening, Sidney." Jorge Hossfuss waved an expansive hand. "Have a little cider, for tonight we are celebrating."

"Yes, thank you, sir." A bit of color warmed his cheeks.

"And what might we be celebrating?" Amalia asked.

"Today I promoted Sidney to Head of Accounting."

"Congratulations," Pearl said as he escorted her into the dining room. "My father seems to have developed a great deal of respect for your abilities."

"Only because Mr. Jones moved up to a better position."

"Surely he had others he could have promoted." *For heaven's sake, man, take this as the compliment it is. My father does not promote men willy-nilly. You always have to prove yourself with him.*

The conversation turned to business, and neither Pearl nor her mother made any effort to change that. Actually Mr. Longstreet had a good many things to say. Perhaps he was becoming less shy, as her mother had suggested.

Nevertheless, she had to stifle more than one yawn. Why was it Mr. Longstreet could carry on a business conversation with her father, but when it came to social conversation with her, he could barely squeak out three words?

"I have asked your father's permission to court you," he said as he was preparing to leave.

Now Pearl could not come up with three words. "Ah."

"And he said yes."

"Umm."

"I hope you agree."

Definitely more than three words, and none of them were to her liking.

"Of course she agrees." Her father stepped into the breach. His glance at Pearl warned her against dissension.

"Good night, sir." Three words all right, but again not the three she wanted. *Lord, please find him another wife. Who do I know that might think this a good match? Other than my father.*

As the door closed behind Mr. Longstreet, her father turned to her, his voice gentle, but firm. "And you will be agreeable."

Her mind spun in a thousand directions as she nodded mutely.

— ❧ —

Pearl breathed a sigh of relief when she woke to a clear dawn. If rain had spoiled the picnic, the classroom would have been like a disturbed hive of hornets. She dressed in a serviceable wool serge skirt and a white cotton waist sprigged with pink rosebuds, knowing that the embroidery and lace at the cuffs of the long sleeves would make little Esther's eyes shine in delight. The little one adored lovely things and had taken to embroidering as if born to hold a needle when Pearl taught the needlework class. She had come to life at the beautiful colors of thread.

After examining several of the millinery concoctions on her shelves, Pearl chose a deep red hat with a feather that she knew would enchant the children. If the day was anything like yesterday, she knew she should choose a hat with a broad brim, for surely her nose would freckle with this one. As if freckles were the bane of a woman's existence. Her mother, of course, would explain why that was true.

Why did men want women to look as if they were about to expire? Pale of face, tiny waisted, corseted to the point of fainting, unable to eat, let alone take a deep breath. She stopped in front of the mirror and measured her waist with her fingers. No, they didn't meet in front or back, missing by several inches. Would that her waistline would fend off Mr. Longstreet. But then, he'd seen her mostly in tightened laces, thanks to Bernadette's insistence.

"If I had my way, no woman would ever again be subjected to such torture. No corsets, no lacing, no veils so thick one can hardly see, no shoes so frail a single rock could bruise right through them, no—" She cut off the diatribe. "You, Pearl Elaine Hossfuss, are a rebel at heart."

With that she unpinned the hat and carried it downstairs to pin on just before going out the door. Her satchel waited for her there also.

She took her place at the empty dining room table, even though she much preferred the warmth and comfort of the kitchen.

"Young master will be down shortly," the maid informed her, "The missus said she will be ready to host your children when they arrive, and she is thankful for the good weather."

"As am I." Pearl fluffed her napkin and laid it across her lap. "I suppose Cook has been preparing since before daylight?"

"She baked all the cookies yesterday." The maid leaned closer and dropped her voice. "You'd think we was expecting forty guests rather than twenty." They shared a chuckle at Cook's expense. Everyone knew that running out of food would be tantamount to a mortal sin.

Half her class greeted her when she arrived at the settlement house, her normal half an hour early.

"We goin' terday? I been waitin' and waitin'."

"See, the sun is shining and no clouds."

"We'll have the picnic?"

Their eagerness splashed over her in pure joy.

Little Esther fingered the lace as Pearl knew she would. While she rarely said more than a shy "h'lo," her blue eyes shouted bursts of joy.

"All of you go play now until the bell rings."

"When we goin' ter leave?"

"At ten, as I told you yesterday." She knew they only asked for reassurance, but sometimes the repetition made her impatient.

Not today though. Today was made for her children.

"Make sure you watch out for your partners," she cautioned later after they walked the blocks and mounted the steps to the cable car. They took their places on the wooden bench seats, eyes round as teacups and giggles hidden behind their hands.

"Do you ride like this ever'day?"

"No. I'd rather walk unless the weather is bad." *Or I use the family carriage, or the sleigh in winter.*

"I would ride like this all the time."

"You can't. Don't ya see the sign? Five whole cents, a nickel. My da says feet was made for walkin'."

"You live in a house like that?" One child pointed off to a house that Pearl knew to be half the size of her father's.

"Something like that."

"You must be rich."

Pearl ignored that comment in favor of reminding the children to stay in their seats instead of dashing from side to side to see all the sights.

"Now, we will get off at the next stop and walk a couple of blocks, so you must all line up in pairs like before." She appointed the two who would be first in line and the pair to bring up the rear, and nodded to the two mothers who had come along at her request.

When they turned in the drive to her home, silence fell on the entire group as they gawked at the brick house at the end of the curved, tree-lined drive of crushed gravel with nary a weed brave enough to poke through.

"We will go around the house to the backyard, where our picnic will be set up. There's a swing and slide back there and grass to play dodge ball, jump rope, and other games." Pearl walked backward as she spoke so that all the children could hear her. "If any of you need to use the necessary, I will show you the way."

After guiding the entire group through the house to the "privy," as one called it, she realized that might be the highlight of their day. By the time each one flushed the toilet, washed hands, dried them on the towel, and oohed over the tub, she wished she could show them the entire house, but that might be asking for trouble. The bathroom they used was the one off the kitchen for the servants and not the main upstairs one.

"I'm so glad you brought them here," Amalia said after she had greeted each of their guests. "Poor little dears."

"Thank you for agreeing."

As Pearl watched the children play, her mind skipped to the next school year. Would she still be teaching at the settlement house, or would she be in a one-room schoolhouse in the wilds of Dakotah Territory, of which she knew so little? So often children from the years before would come back to see her. How she would miss them.

Even though everyone ate until they were stuffed and a few had cookies in their pockets for brothers or sisters at home, there was still food left.

"How about I fix a packet for each one, some cookies and cheese maybe?" Inga stood behind the table watching the children playing tag among the trees.

"If you would like." Pearl thought a moment. "We could put them in a basket or two and give them out once we are back at school."

When the baskets were fixed, Pearl called the children, as it was nearing time to leave. But when they lined up and she counted heads, there were only nineteen.

"Everyone, stand still please." She counted again. Nineteen. Who was missing and how long had the child been gone?

She clicked down the list of faces. Esther. Little Esther was missing. "All right children, please make a circle and all sit down so we can play another game. Mrs. Guffrey will lead you in button, button while I—"

"Go look for Esther?" one of the children asked.

"Yes, do you know where she is?"

"No, Miss Hossfuss. I just knowed she was gone."

"Why didn't you tell me?" She knelt to be on eye level.

"Thought she went to pee and be right back."

"How long ago was that?"

A shrug was her only answer.

"All right, you go join the circle and help Mrs. Guffrey. I'll go look for her." *Please, God, let her be in the house.*

She and two of the servants started on the ground floor and checked every closet and place a small child could hide. Behind the furniture, under the stairs, in the linen press. No freckle-faced Esther.

On the second floor, they did the same—looked under the beds, in the bathrooms, the chifforobes, behind screens. They checked the master bedroom, and much to Pearl's relief, she wasn't there. If her father learned some urchin had been in his things, he would have an apoplectic fit.

Pearl found the sleeping child curled up in the middle of her own bed, her cheek cushioned on one of Anna's rag dolls and a scarf with embroidered red roses wrapped around one hand.

"Ah, the poor mite. Let's just hope she don't have nits to share," one of the maids said quietly.

Pearl agreed. If only she could keep this one here for a bath, they could wash her hair, dress her in some of Anna's outgrown clothing, and let her keep that doll. How had she known this was Teacher's room? Or had that mattered?

Pearl sat on the edge of the bed and stroked the hair back from the angel's face. "Esther, you need to wake up now. It's time to go back to school."

Esther's eyelashes fluttered open, and a smile lit her entire face. "Teacher, I dreamed I went to heaven. 'Twas so nice and pretty there." She raised her arms, and Pearl leaned forward to both hug her and pick her up.

"Now we must hurry, or we'll be late."

She breathed a sigh of relief when she had all the children back on the train. Now if the servants got everything put back in order, all would be well. On the one hand she knew she should have asked Father, but on the other, he always said she should do what she could to help the poor. That was the Christian way.

Once everyone had received their packet and left the school-room, she tidied up and, picking up the now empty baskets, closed the door. How appealing the thought of a long soak in the upstairs tub, larger by far than the one the children admired.

"It went well, I take it?" the headmistress said when they met in the hall.

"Yes. I believe so." She started to tell of the lost child, then caught herself. No sense admitting to being less than perfect.

"They'll be talking of this for a long time."

"The cable car was a huge success."

"Thank you for the extra things you do for the children."

"You are most welcome, but I think it's time we have a used clothing and toy drive. Our own people need the things every bit as badly as the people who receive the mission barrels some of the churches collect."

"Would you like to organize it?"

"I suppose so." Pearl hesitated. Should she tell the headmistress about her application for another position? She mentally shook her head. Not when there was so little chance she would even hear from them. "Good night then."

She walked home, swinging a basket in either hand.

Marlene met her at the door. "Your father wants to see you in his study."

Oh, now what? And after such a perfect day too.

Pearl tapped on the study door and entered when invited. At his slight smile, she breathed a sigh of relief.

"Pearl, I expect you to be civil about the arrangements I have made with Mr. Longstreet. I am doing this for your own good, looking out for your best. This may be your only opportunity . . . You . . . I . . . ." Pearl watched his eyes glance toward her neckline. "He is a fine man, a hard worker. And he needs you."

To mother his children. Pearl took her courage in hand and gave it a good shaking. She straightened her already perfect posture. "Father, may I say something?"

"Only if it is 'yes, Father.' "

"I see." Pearl turned and rushed from the room. Why was he so impossible?

CHAPTER FIFTEEN

Minneapolis

> Carpenters, brick layers, only experienced need apply. Contact Joseph Wainwright at the Dove House in Little Missouri, Dakotah Territory.

Carl Hegland reread the ad in the *Minneapolis Tribune* for a third time. He looked down at his calloused hands. *Ja,* one would say he was experienced all right. He'd been working with hammer, saw, and level at his father's side since he was six. But did he want to go clear out on the edge of civilization to build who knew what, since the advertisement gave no further information?

On the other hand, he was always wanting to see what lay beyond the horizon.

But if he left, who would take care of his mother, the job that had brought Carl back to the city after his father died under a collapsed wall.

He studied the half thumb he had left, the top of it needing to be scratched, itching so fierce that when he closed his eyes he would have sworn on his mother's Bible that his thumb was whole.

He rubbed the fully healed flap over the knuckle on his pants. Two years and still tender. Still itched. Some things were indeed strange.

Who needed what to be built way out west like that? The only civilization there was around the railroad. 'Course now that the rail line was extending, more foolhardy souls would be moving west.

He glanced at the advertisement again, folded the paper closed, and tossed it in the woodbin. The *Minneapolis Tribune* always made starting the fire in the morning easy.

— ❧ —

"You ever give thought to moving west?" he asked his mother at supper that night.

"*Nei.*" His mor set a full plate in front of him. While she spoke some English, when it was just the two of them, they both spoke Norwegian. "Why do you ask?"

"Nothing, just thinking."

"Bread?"

"Please."

"You always have a reason for everything." She set the bread plate next to him and took her seat.

He bowed his head, said the grace he'd learned from his father, and picked up his fork. Staying here in Minneapolis, where he had a steady job and good home—and the possibility of a courtship of the Widow Wisenschraft—was much the wiser thing to do. The widow seemed to enjoy his company, and marrying someone with a solid nest egg was not a bad thing. If only his mother held the same feelings as he did. Since the two would be living together, life would be much simpler if the two women liked each other.

— ❧ —

"Hey, Hegland," his boss called about a week later. "Stop by my office before you leave."

"Ja, that I will do." Carl finished cleaning the saw and putting away his tools. He lived by the adage that one treated one's tools better than a mistress. Or, as he would say, his wife. But since he had neither, that was a moot point.

He stepped into the office and waited until his boss looked up.

"You've been a good man here, and I want to thank you for the extra work you've done."

Carl nodded. *Been?* Had he done anything to change that?

"I hate to give you this bad news, but I know a man of your caliber will have no trouble finding work elsewhere." He handed an envelope across the desk. "There's extra in there to show our appreciation." He shook his head. "It ain't my doin', Carl. Hope you understand that."

"Ja, guess that is the way things go at times." He paused. "Was it something I—"

"No, no. Nothing to do with you or your work. Just that you was the last hired on and . . ."

Carl raised a hand. "That is good. Mange takk for the good work." He turned and left, mentally shaking his head. No job and now no prospects with the lovely widow. Until, of course, he found another position.

Strange how things happened.

When he arrived home, his mother pointed to an envelope on the chest of drawers that held the linens. "That came for you today." Since her mouth puckered as if she'd sucked on a lemon, Carl had an idea she figured who the letter came from.

He washed his hands and took the envelope to sit by the windows that faced west, giving him light from the setting sun.

Dear Mr. Hegland,

I want to thank you for the good times we've had, but all along I wished for you to make your intentions clear. Since that never occurred, perhaps you were and are content with the status quo. I shall never know now. I have accepted the courtship of a gentleman I met two weeks ago. I wish you every blessing in your life and do hope you find a woman sometime who will make a good wife for you.
Sincerely,

Mrs. MaryLou Wisenschraft

He read the short missive again, feeling as though he'd just received the second of a right/left sucker punch to the midsection.

Supper passed, and he could tell his mother was dying to know what the letter said, but for some odd reason, he kept the day's two-fold calamities to himself.

That night he found himself rereading the same column in

the newspaper for how many times, he had no idea, and he still didn't know what he'd read.

How could one's life seem so well ordered and planned one day and be lower than cow flops the next?

— ❦ —

Sunday service was dry as the sawdust he'd swept up on Friday. When the pastor asked him how things were, Carl mumbled something vaguely benign and steered away from the gathering of men. While he never had a great deal to say during the discussions, today he wanted to be spared the banalities. Instead he tried to be patient standing at his mother's elbow, but when she frowned at him, he knew she'd heard the sighs he'd not tried overly hard to disguise.

"Whatever is the matter with you?" she hissed as they walked toward home.

"Nothing."

"Ja, well, that is what you say, but I can tell something is wrong."

— ❦ —

"I'm sorry, Carl, I've had to lay off some of my own carpenters lately. As soon as I have some work, I'll come find you first thing."

Carl nodded, shook the man's hand, and left. So much for *"If you ever need a job, come to me,"* which had been said more than once.

The next two shops were a repeat. No one was hiring carpenters or even unskilled laborers, not that he'd wanted that work. But when times were tough, one took what one could get.

"Can you read English?" one man asked.

"Ja, Norwegian better, but I get by."

"I'll let you know."

Ja, like when the fjords melt in January. Carl nodded and left.

When payday rolled round again, he pulled out the worn leather pouch of his father's and took out the amount he always gave his mother to run the household. *You should tell her,* he ordered himself. *She needs to know that things have changed.*

But surely I'll get something this week.

That night he stopped at the saloon where many of the construction workers gathered and left an hour later realizing he was not the only one to be let go.

Not that that helped much, if at all.

His mother was still up when he got home. "You are not seeing that widow woman anymore," she said in greeting.

Question or statement, it didn't matter. He gave his mother a noncommittal shrug.

"And you lost your job."

He raised an eyebrow. *How did you know that?*

She set a piece of dried-apple cake in front of him. "I have money saved for food. You need not worry."

He nodded. "Tusen takk." As if a thousand thanks would be enough. They would not starve and the house was paid for. Things could be worse.

— ❧ —

The next night she laid an envelope in front of him. "From Sigrid. She has fallen and broken her hip. I will go take care of her."

"What about the house here?"

"You will manage."

— ❧ —

The next morning he began preparations to head west, even though the advertisement was no longer in the paper. Talk about leaping off a cliff with no idea how far the water lay below. Or if there was any water.

CHAPTER SIXTEEN

Little Missouri

"Ruby, you gotta come see!"

"Opal, I'm busy right now," Ruby called over her shoulder, all the while her arms in soapsuds up to her elbows.

"But they might be gone then."

Ruby scraped soapsuds off her arms and wiped them on her apron. "I'm coming." *This better be good.* She let the screen door slam behind her, something she scolded the others for doing when they forgot. Had it not been for the spring on the door, half the flies in Dakotah Territory would rush right in. Along with hordes of mosquitoes.

"Where are you?"

"Over here." Opal could hiss louder than most could shout. She stood at the west end of the porch that extended on around the entire building.

An ancient cottonwood shaded the northwest corner of the building, and brush nearly hid the fence between Dove House land and that of Mr. Johnson, owner of the milk cow that so ably provided for the hotel.

Ruby started in a hurry but slowed and quieted at Opal's hand signals. What could have so entranced her little sister? Ruby crept up behind Opal and whispered, "What is it?"

"See the grouse chicks?"

Even though Opal pointed, Ruby could see nothing but stems and leaves and grasses.

"There, at the bottom of the second bush is the grouse hen. She called all her chicks to hide under her. I counted ten."

Ruby studied the light and shadows. Nothing as far as she could see. Then the hen moved her head, and one tiny bit of fluff darted out from under her.

"Ohh." Delight birthed a sigh. Standing perfectly still was no trouble. Ruby would have stopped breathing if that was what it took to keep from scaring the hen into harming her chicks or leaving with them.

Another tiny head peeked out from under the wing and chased after the other. The hen clucked and picked a morsel from the grass around her. When she stood, the grass pulsed alive with the mottled brown-and-tan babies. One could only see them when they moved, otherwise they blended perfectly into the dappled shade.

When finally the hen led her brood into the brush and out of sight, Ruby and Opal exchanged delighted smiles.

"Aren't they perfectly wonderful? Charlie told me there was a nest out there. He's been keeping an eye on it. They hatched yesterday." Opal's eyes shone her joy.

"Thank you for calling me." Ruby hugged Opal around her shoulders and tipped her head against Opal's. "We're going to have chicks of our own, I hear."

"Yup, two hens are setting." Opal stared across the back to the pasture where Bay dozed in the sun. "Can Milly and I go riding this afternoon?"

Ruby swallowed her concern. "Yes, but you have to tell me exactly where you are going and come back in time to help with supper."

"Yes, ma'am." Opal leaped off the porch.

"And help Millie get the laundry off the line."

— ❧ —

Later that day, after the noon meal was finished and the dining room was cleaned up again, Charlie went back out to continue spading the garden, Opal and Milly went riding, and the others went about their usual chores. Daisy returned to ironing after a morning of washing, and Cimarron finished kneading the bread a second time before going down in the cellar to clean out the winter grime.

Ruby looked up from her bookkeeping and letter writing when the bell dinged over the front door. The man looked to have been on the trail for some time or mauled by a wild animal. One sleeve of his coat hung by only the underside, his hat was tattered as if chewed around the brim. A bushy beard covered his lower face and met up with head hair at about eye level.

The breeze from the open door blew an extremely ripe odor ahead of him.

"Can I help you, sir?" Ruby rose, closing her account book at the same time, although the odds of someone with that appearance being able to read were pretty low.

"Ye sure can." He stared around the room, then slightly shook his head. "This be Dove House, right?"

"Yes, it is. Are you looking for a room?"

"Ye might could say that. Where's Belle?"

"I'm not sure." Ruby crossed to stand behind the counter, now polished to a permanent high sheen. When he leaned on it, dust formed a pattern around his elbow. Ruby breathed in through her mouth, his odor worse than unpleasant.

"A bath will be extra."

"I'm sure of that." The man looked around. "Per off with Belle?"

"No." Feeling a frisson of anxiety track up her spine, Ruby refrained from telling him who she was and what happened to her father. The man had obviously been gone for more than a year.

She pushed the guest book across the counter. "Can you sign your name, please?"

"Name's Jed Black. I kin make my mark."

Ruby wrote in his name, told him a price double the normal in the hopes he would go away, and kept from sighing when he made his mark.

"I'll show you to your room." She led the way upstairs, feeling his eyes on every portion of her anatomy. Her backside felt as if branded by a poker. She kept her spine straight and slit her eyes. Where were all the others when she needed them? She should have gone for Charlie. She should have turned this Jed Black away.

She pushed open the door to room eight and, after a glance inside to make sure all was right, started to step back, only to meet solid flesh. A strong arm pulled her tight against him, and his brushy face nuzzled her neck.

"Let me go." Her hiss would have done a snake proud.

"Hot little thing, ain'tcha." His other arm manacled her chest. "Ol' Per done found a good-un in you." He hauled her toward the bed, groping her all the while.

Ruby kicked at his legs and clawed his hands. "Let me go." Her voice rose to a shriek.

He clamped a hand across her mouth, and she bit him so hard she could taste the metallic of blood. She knew it wasn't hers.

"You. . . ." His string of obscenities burned her ears.

Now she knew what was meant by seeing red. One heel connected solidly with his shin, and he grunted. *Good. That ought to slow you down!*

But nothing seemed to stop him as he ripped at her bodice, tearing her apron from the shoulder straps.

Fear tasted worse than the blood.

"I allus loved a fighter."

Since he'd loosed her hand when ripping her clothing, Ruby scratched at his face, her fingers tangling in his beard, so she yanked even harder, fury giving her strength beyond what she knew.

He threw her on the bed and himself on top of her. "We's gonna have us some real fun."

The stench of him made her gag. "Help! Somebody hel—!"

He slammed his hand across her mouth again, and again she locked her teeth on his finger. He swore and drew back enough to strike her across the face.

Her head rang from the impact, and she felt her body go limp. *God, save me! Where are you when I need you the most?*

"That's better." He laughed, a deep chuckle that said he was enjoying himself.

Ruby kicked and squirmed, but he seemed oblivious to any strikes she made. *Stop fighting*, the voice seemed to echo in her head. She forced herself to relax, and he removed his hand from her mouth.

"That's good."

She screamed for help again, and this time, over his heavy breathing and her thundering heart, she could hear someone pounding up the stairs. *Oh, God, don't let it be Opal.*

With a roar Charlie grabbed the man and threw him against the wall, shattering the nightstand with pitcher and bowl.

"You all right?"

"Yes." Tears coursed down her cheeks now that she could breathe. She sat up and screamed, "Charlie!"

Charlie spun in time to catch a sledgehammer fist against his shoulder that sent him reeling into the doorframe.

Ruby scrambled off the other side of the bed, at the same time searching the room for something to use as a weapon. Only the kerosene lamp on the chest along the wall came to mind. While the two men circled, she edged behind the bed, removed the chimney, and quick as a snakebite slammed the base of the lamp against the back of the monster's head. He paused, took a step, and crashed to the floor.

"Did I kill him?"

"I doubt it. No such luck." Charlie leaned against the doorframe, chest heaving, trying to catch his breath. "You're bleedin'."

"No, he is. I bit his finger. Twice." She grabbed the hem of her apron to wipe any blood away, then flinched at the touch of it. Tenderly, she felt the side of her face, already swelling from the impact of his hand. She knew if she said the words she was thinking, Charlie would be so shocked he might quit breathing.

The man on the floor groaned.

Charlie reached down, grabbed him by the shoulders, and dragged him the rest of the way out the door.

"I'll help you." Ruby ignored the pain in her face and grabbed hold of the man's arm. At the top of the stairs they looked at each other.

"We can't just roll him down the stairs."

"Why not?" Charlie gave a heave, and Jed Black skidded and rolled on down, coming to a limp bundle at the bottom. He lay there long enough for them to slowly make their way halfway down the stairs before he groaned and shook his head. He raised halfway up on his arms, shook his head again, and when he spied Charlie, his face broke into a smile.

"Well, if it ain't ol' Charlie. You pack some powerful punch. Why, it been more'n a year, maybe two, since you throwed ol' Jed out in the street."

"You goin' to behave?"

"What'd I do wrong? Me and that new girl, we was just havin' a bit a' fun."

Ruby wanted to throw him out the front door herself. "Fun! You tried to kill me!"

"And she ain't no girl." Charlie stood at the ready in case Jed reared up again.

Jed stared at Ruby, obviously having trouble focusing. "She's a purty one, all right. Real feisty too." He stared down at his finger, still dripping blood.

"You goin' to behave?"

"Yep. You got a drink? Sure would help some."

"We do not serve liquor at Dove House."

Jed stared at Charlie. "What'd she say?" He dug a finger in one ear.

"No booze, no girls, no entertainment."

"But Per—"

"My father died just over a year ago."

"Your father?" The hair parted so she could see pure shock in his deep-set eyes.

Charlie leaned forward. "Yes, and now you may take your carcass on outside and—"

"But I want a room and a bath. She said I could." Black now sounded like a little boy with his toys taken away. "I need a bath." He scrubbed at his face, started to rise, then sat down on the stairs. "Ohh, whatever hit me?" He rubbed the back of his head.

"The base of a kerosene lamp."

He sniffed his fingers. "That's what stinks—kerosene. Why'd you go and hit me like that?"

Ruby stared at Charlie and shook her head. Was this the same man who attacked her upstairs? Who nearly scared the life right out of her? She raised her hand to her aching cheek. Yes, the same man, and he . . . She caught herself before she began spewing her thoughts out and drowning him in them.

"We was just havin' us some fun."

That did it.

"Fun! Fun! You might have been having fun, but I abhor your kind of fun. If that was the way you treated the other girls, I wish some bear had mauled you a time or two and then told *you* that he was just having fun." Carrying deadly venom, her words bumped into each other, jumping out to lacerate and hopefully poison the man who now held his head up with shaking hands.

"Come on Jed, I think it time you be on your way." Charlie nudged the man with his foot.

"But I need a bed and a bath."

"Not here, you don't." Ruby's eyes narrowed. "And if I never see you again, it will be far too soon."

"But . . . but . . ." Jed slowly rose to his feet, still swaying enough to need a hand on the newel post. "Cricky, but you cracked me a good one."

Ruby stepped back and shuddered as his smell moved with him. *Had I had a gun, I would have shot him. I might have killed a man. Is this something of what Cimarron felt?* She watched the man stagger to the door, and only after it closed behind him did she sink onto a chair. Her cheek hurt, her teeth hurt, her heel hurt from slamming into him, and she felt as though she'd been rolling in the mud and it might never wash off again.

"Now I know what real hate feels like."

"I hate to say this, but Jed Black is not a bad man. Well, not usually anyway."

Ruby stared at Charlie like he'd lost his wits. "How can you say that after . . . after . . . why, if you hadn't come, he'd have . . . ." She scrunched her eyes shut. "Ouch." She cupped her hand over her cheek.

"He'd been drinking some of William's rotgut. Goes crazy when he does that."

"And that excuses his behavior?"

"No. Just explains it. You ask Belle or one of the others."

"Charlie Higgins, right now I could tar you with the same brush I'd want to use on him." She spun so quickly her skirt flared, and she headed for the kitchen.

"What happened to you?" Cimarron stopped so quickly her wash bucket sloshed.

"Jed Black." Ruby dipped a cloth in the bucket of water by the stove and held it to her cheek.

"Oh my . . ." Cimarron set her bucket down. "He didn't try to. . . ?"

"Oh, he did, but Charlie pulled him off, and I bashed him with a kerosene lamp. Tell Charlie he can go clean up the kerosene. I most surely won't."

Ruby stalked from the room, stormed up the stairs to the bedroom she shared with Opal, and threw herself across the rope-strung bed. When the tears came, they threatened to never quit. Along with the questions. Had she done something to provoke the man? And the impossible rage. *Lord, I want to kill that sorry excuse of a man.*

CHAPTER SEVENTEEN

Chicago

Pearl bid her students good-bye for the final time. Little Esther gave her a hug, her eyes filling with tears.

"You the best teacher."

"Thank you." Pearl fought the burning behind her own eyes. "You learned so much this year. I am more proud of you than I can say."

"Thank you for the picnic. That was the bestest day of my whole life."

Pearl blinked and looked toward the ceiling, all the while patting the little one's back. "You keep reading this summer, so you come back to school all ready in the fall."

"We don't got no books."

"You can read those here at the school. You know where the library is." Pearl tipped the little girl's face up so she could smile into her eyes. "There are always books there. And"—she stroked back the flyaway hair—"you got a book from the relay race." All the prizes given away on play day were books, tablets, and pencils in the hopes that the children would use them during the summer. This had been another one of Pearl's gifts to the school in the name of her father. She had decided long before that one of his charities—he was known in the community as a generous man thanks to the efforts of his wife and daughter—would be the schoolchildren.

She turned the little girl toward the door. "You better run

now so your mother won't worry."

"Yes, ma'am." She took a step, then looked over her shoulder. "You'll be here when school comes again?"

"Ah." Pearl thought quickly. "As far as I know." She hadn't told a lie. At the moment she had no idea what was going to happen, but then God never did tell His people in advance. Neither did her father, though she had some strong suspicions on that score.

"Bye." Another step and a stop. "Can I come to your house again next year?"

"I don't know what all we will do next year, but you will be in the next grade, remember?"

"Yes." She didn't look happy at that thought.

"God bless." Pearl kept smiling in case Esther looked back again. But when the outer door closed, she sank down at her desk and stared around the classroom. Her mind flipped back to the evening after the picnic. Her father had been pleasant until he'd gone out in the backyard to check on his roses. He returned to the house where she and her mother were having tea in the sunroom.

"Whoever trampled the ground out there? Looks like a herd of wild horses ran through." His brushy eyebrows nearly met in the middle.

"Ah . . ." Pearl glanced to her mother for support.

"We had guests today, dear." Amalia set her teacup back in its saucer. "Would you like some tea?"

"No! You know I don't like tea, that insipid stuff. What were the ladies doing, having footraces?"

"Ah, you could say that."

"Something is rotten in Denmark," he muttered as he headed back outside.

"I better tell him." Pearl started to rise but stopped when Amalia laid a hand on her arm.

"Sometimes the less said the better."

They heard his growl before he reentered the room.

"And sometimes not." Amalia's one cocked eyebrow reminded Pearl that the two of them could handle Mr. Jorge Hossfuss, at least most of the time.

"There were children out there." He held up a small sweater.

"Yes, dear. Some of my friends do have small children."

Pearl watched the exchange, fascinated by the calm of the woman she was starting to think of as her mother versus the belligerence of her father. She sipped her tea, forcing the liquid past the lump in her throat.

When he left, she set her teacup down, a slight rattle at the joining betraying her agitation.

"I should have searched the garden better before we left."

"Mr. French should have too."

"I think I'd rather just tell him and get it over with."

"We neither lied nor did anything morally wrong. It's just that at times I save him increased agitation by not telling everything."

"Isn't that a bit dishonest? After all, he says we must always be honest and tell the truth."

"Did he ask me whose sweater that was?"

"No."

"Would you say those were friends here at the picnic?"

"Well, they weren't enemies."

"Exactly. And were we building goodwill in the community?"

"Yes, I suppose so."

"And doesn't he tell us to build goodwill in the community?"

Pearl felt a smile tugging at her cheek muscles.

— ⁂ —

The smile carried her through the dismantling of her classroom and the loading of her things into the carriage brought around at her request that morning.

"That be all, miss?" the driver asked as he settled the last basket.

"I just need to talk with Mrs. Fredricks for a moment, but if you are in a hurry, I can walk home."

"No, I'll wait. Mister will be late tonight."

Pearl returned to the now quiet building and made her way to the school office.

"I take it you are all moved out?" Mrs. Fredricks looked up from the books she was counting.

"Yes, and here is my key to the storeroom."

"You'll be back in the fall?"

"God willing." *And if I don't hear anything good from my application.* As if that could happen.

"Are you planning anything special this summer? I could always use another hand with the girls." Girls were invited to learn needlework, sewing, and cooking skills during the summer months, while the boys had the opportunity to plant and dig in the garden, learn woodwork, and repair tools. Sometimes they helped with the upkeep of the settlement house when there was money for painting and repairs. Mrs. Fredricks could make a nickel squeal.

"I-I'm not sure. Ah, things are . . . are . . ." *Here you are stuttering like a schoolchild. Tell her of your application.*

"Well, once you know, I would greatly appreciate any time you can give us." Mrs. Fredricks turned to answer a question from another teacher who had just come into the room.

Pearl waved and, after shutting the door carefully behind her, glanced up at the cross on the wall. She gave a slight bow and made her way back to the waiting carriage. Somehow it seemed that she was saying good-bye.

On the drive home she pondered the feeling. She should be exhilarated, another year was finished, her students had done well, and she had a good man who insisted on courting her, boring though he be.

Several days later her father announced there would be a small social at their home the following evening. "I have an announcement to make, and I want our closest friends to help us celebrate."

"Have you sent out invitations?"

"No. That is your province, my dear." He turned to Pearl. "I expect you to help make our guests welcome and take some of the burden off your mother's shoulders."

"I-I see." She glanced to her mother who raised her eyebrows in slight question marks also. "Do you have a list of those you'd like us to invite?"

"You know who they are." He ran off a few names from his business world, from their church, and from the other homes in their region. "And of course, Mr. Longstreet."

Pearl nodded. Of course. And here she'd thought to not include him.

PEARL

— ❧ —

The house sparkled the next evening. Extra flowers, including lilies from the hothouse, scented the rooms. Inga outdid herself in her domain, and Pearl's mother had even hired musicians.

Pearl dressed early and moved gracefully from room to room to make sure everything was perfect. She pulled a wilted blossom from one bouquet and took it to the kitchen to throw in the garbage.

"You look most lovely, Miss Pearl," said Mr. French, the head butler.

"Thank you. Is there anything else I need to see to?"

"Everything is in order. I have already ascertained that. You and your young man can enjoy the evening along with the others."

He's not my young man. Whatever gives you that idea? But Pearl kept the thoughts silent. Was there something going on here that she was unaware of?

Sidney Longstreet was the first to arrive. "Good evening, Miss Hossfuss," he said, handing the butler his hat and actually smiling.

"Welcome." She could think of nothing else to say to him. Was his reticence contagious? "It is lovely out in the gardens if you would like to walk out there."

"If you will accompany me."

"Oh, but Father said that I must see to our guests—"

"No, no, my dear," her father interrupted, "you two go smell the roses."

Pearl looked at her father, trying to figure out who had taken over his body. *My dear?* Since when had he ever called her an endearment like that? Was his eyesight going and he mistook her for her stepmother?

Longstreet took her hand and tucked it under his arm, then strode smartly for the French doors that led out to the gardens.

Sometimes being polite took more effort than others. It was all she could do to not snatch her hand back. What had come over the man? Yes, she'd agreed to allow him to court her, but this forward behavior could not be tolerated.

She cast around in her mind for some way to disentangle

herself without being rude. Nothing came. Her mind seemed filled with either holes or mush, she wasn't sure which. What it didn't do was come up with any witty or profound saying. In fact, she had no more to say than he.

They strode around the rose beds, twice, before returning to the house at her subtle influence. If one could call pulling slightly at his arm and guiding him in that direction *subtle*. Even her smile felt insipid as it tried to slide off her face and disappear in the froth of lace at her bosom.

"Ah, there you are." Her father greeted them as soon as they entered the dining room, where the long table had been pushed back up against the wall and was now covered on every inch with the offerings of Cook at her exemplary best.

"Before we begin, I have an announcement to make." Her father raised his voice to be heard over the hum of conversation and musical background. Amid a few hushes, they all became quiet, faces turned expectantly to Mr. Hossfuss.

"Tonight I have the privilege of announcing the engagement of my daughter, Pearl Elaine, to a fine gentleman, Mr. Sidney Longstreet." He nodded toward the young couple and began applauding.

Pearl could not get her breath. Her throat convulsed, her hands shook. Had not Mr. Longstreet covered her hand with his own, she would have pulled away and clasped her own behind her back.

"Look pleased," her mother whispered from behind her.

At the prompt Pearl assumed a smile, or at least she hoped it was a smile. She shook hands with those who came up to offer their congratulations, all the while smiling by rote, in spite of her mind gone numb.

She could not eat a bite of food on the plate her now fiancé brought her. When he turned to fix something for himself, she set her plate behind a flower arrangement and bolted for the library, where the tray of aperitifs still waited to be put away. Pouring herself a glass of sherry, she took a gulp and then coughed at the unaccustomed heat she could feel all the way to her stomach. She drank the rest neat, then shuddered. Whatever did people see in that? Eyeing the amber liquid in the other cut-glass and stoppered bottles, she thought to try something else, but someone entering the room stopped her.

"Here you are."

"Mother, did you know?" Like a naughty child she wanted to stuff the evidence of her misdeeds out of sight.

"No, he did not tell me either. But you must have realized that sooner or later—"

"Yes, and I would have chosen later, far later." Pearl fought the urge to raise her voice and scream her frustrations. "Most assuredly far later and hopefully never at all."

"You and I will discuss this in the morning, but for now, you must return to the gathering, and if you have any sense, which I know you do, you will act pleased or at least polite. And accepting. Now go, before your father comes looking for you."

Somehow Pearl made it through an interminably long evening with Longstreet at her side as if stitched there. And since he was the last to leave, she could not even plead a headache and take the rear stairs to the upper floor to hide in her room.

"Thank you, Miss Hossfuss. This evening has made me a very happy man." He brought her cold fingers to his lips and kissed them, sketching a slight bow at the same time.

If Pearl did not feel so much like crying, she would have burst out laughing.

Finally he was gone, and she could escape to her bedroom and her bed. But sleep would not come. All she could think as the minutes ticked off through the interminable night was *I cannot do this. I cannot marry this man. I cannot. I cannot.* At one point she climbed from the bed and knelt beside it, forehead resting on clasped hands. *Please, Lord, if there is any way to change these circumstances, please rescue me.* Where, oh where was God when you needed Him?

— ✄ —

"You will marry Mr. Longstreet," her father announced in the morning at the breakfast table, "and you will do so before the summer is over. If I had my way, you would be married next week, but in this we will accede to your mother's wishes."

Pearl swallowed, nodded, and made her way up the stairs, her back stiff and her insides a puddle of tears.

Sometime later her mother found her sitting in front of the

window in her room, staring out at nothing.

"Ah, Pearl, it will not be so bad."

"I do not love him."

"Many women do not love their husbands before the wedding, but they learn to later. It is easy for us to love if the man shows any affection." Amalia sat on the edge of the bed.

Not me. I will not be mollified this way. A bird sang spring outside the window and flew away. *Oh, if only I could be like that bird and fly.*

"Now answer me these questions. Do you find him repulsive?"

"No, of course not." *Insipid, but not repulsive.*

"Has he been cruel to you?"

Pearl shook her head.

"Has he shown any hint of cruelty to anyone or anything?"

"No." He seems most kind, but in a distracted sort of way.

"Lazy?"

"I think not, or Father would not have promoted him."

"Will he be able to provide for you?"

"I believe so. We have not talked of such things. We have not talked of anything at all."

"Is he a Christian man?"

"He goes to church and knows the service."

"And how is he with his children?"

"He loves them." Pearl turned and tightened her jaw, along with her spine. "That is what this is all about, isn't it? Finding a mother for his children. Surely any other woman with a modicum of sense or compassion would meet his needs."

"But he has chosen you, and that is really an honor."

An honor I don't want.

Tell her you sent the application.

I can't.

Amalia nodded slightly. "Think on these things. I know you will come to the right decision."

"Do I have any choice?"

Amalia only smiled slightly and left the room.

The next day Pearl woke with a resolve. *I will talk to my father and tell him how I feel. Surely he will listen.* She spent most of the morning deciding how to present her plan, even to making two lists, one for and one against, on a sheet of paper. Only two things came up on the against side. Number one, I do not love him. Number two, Mr. Longstreet is boring beyond measure.

All the traits her mother had pointed out filled in the other list. She crinkled the paper into a ball and slammed it down in the basket.

"I have reconsidered," her father announced to his family at supper that night. "The wedding will be in two weeks. There is a house for sale, and today I purchased it for your new home. Mr. Longstreet and I will take you and your mother over there tomorrow. I believe it has plenty of room for the children and for those to come." He nodded, tucking his thumbs into his vest pockets, a sign that Pearl knew meant he was pleased with his transaction.

Talking would do no good.

He narrowed his eyes, looking her directly in the face. "And now I expect you to put away these childish meanderings and act like the daughter we have raised you to be. Obedient, grateful for your many blessings, and ready to assume the mantle God has for you. As a wife and mother, it will be your duty to love and care for this fine man and his children."

He waited.

She knew what he waited for.

When his eyebrows beetled and his jaw tightened, she forced the words past lips that first trembled, then tightened. "Yes, Father."

"Good. This will indeed be a busy two weeks if what your mother says is true about preparing for a wedding. I am sure she will carry it off with her customary grace and skill."

As soon as the meal was served, eaten, and cleared away, Pearl bolted for her room. *I am trapped. I have no choice. None at all.* She threw herself on her bed and scrunched the spread up in her fists. No choice but to obey.

CHAPTER EIGHTEEN

Little Missouri

"He sure is a nice man."

"Who is?" Ruby turned to see where Opal was pointing. The sight made her stomach roil.

"He cleaned up right good." Cimarron pinned her end of the sheet on the line. "Sometimes he came in here smelling ranker than a dead polecat."

"What's a polecat?" Opal dug down in the basket for another clothespin to hand to Ruby.

"A mean skunk." At Opal's questioning look, Cimarron laughed. "You've seen a skunk—fluffy black with a white stripe down his back and out the tail. Night critter. If'n you ain't seen one, you sure smelled one around here the other day."

"Pee-uw. I remember. Why do they call him a polecat?"

"Got no nevermind. Just do." Cimarron snapped a pillowcase to straighten it before pinning one corner over the last one of the sheet.

Ruby moved to another line and shook out another sheet. The man they'd been discussing was out in the garden helping Charlie dig in the last of the old cow manure they'd taken from the Johnsons' barn. If only she could ignore the haze of red that blurred her vision every time she looked at him. No matter how hard she tried to ignore or forget it, the attack, with its accompanying fear, set off her rage again. She pushed a clothespin down so hard it split. Muttering, she dug in her apron pocket for another. Good thing Charlie had carved so many of them during the winter.

Except for his size, one would not have recognized the man in the garden as her attacker. He made Charlie look puny. How Charlie had managed to pull him off her was beyond her. But then, how she'd been able to conk him with the lamp base surprised her still more.

Don't think about it! She glanced upward toward the robin's song that floated from the tree. The robin pair had built a nest in the cottonwood at the west side of Dove House, right above the place where the grouse had nested. Such a cheerful song the male had, and he sported a rust red breast.

Ruby picked up the now empty basket and returned to the back porch of the hotel. They'd moved the washtubs outside again and heated the wash water over an open fire to free up space on the stove.

Daisy had sheets bubbling as she stirred the caldron with a heavy stick Charlie had smoothed for just such a purpose. One at a time she lifted out a sheet, let it drain, and dumped it into a bucket to take to the tub of rinse water. Milly rinsed one, sloshing it up and down in the first rinse, then half wrung it and tossed it in the second rinse. Finally she and Opal each took an end and twisted in opposite directions to wring out as much water as possible before they hung it on the line.

With many of the rooms full, they had fewer sheets to wash than when she changed them for frequent new arrivals. Long-term guests got clean linens once a week. Belle had often commented on Ruby's washing the linens to death, but clean was clean, and that was the way her hotel would always be.

"Miss Ruby, could I have a word with you?"

The voice set her neck on fire. "Really, Mr. Black, I have nothing to say to you."

"But I have something really important to say to you." He stood, hat in hand, sun trapping fire in his brown hair.

Now, why did I have to notice that? I don't ever want to see him again, hear him again, or even think about him ever again.

"Please."

All the years of her mother's, her grandmother's, and Mrs. Brandon's training in ladylike manners joined together, and she turned to face him. Teeth clamped to keep back her flurry of words, she waited. "Well."

"I-I come to ask your forgiveness for the way I treated you."

Attacked me, you mean.

"I know you must hate me, but I got to tell you. I'm ashamed to think I did such a thing to Per's daughter—and a right fine young lady. I mean to change. I promise I'll never touch liquor again. I never made such a promise before, but if you can see your way free to forgive me, I'll work to be the kind of man worthy of your grace."

Oh, Lord, now what am I to do? She closed her eyes and fought to keep her anger at bay.

"What makes you think—" Her words hissed through clenched teeth.

"My mamma didn't raise me to be an animal. I did that all on my own. And I do plead that you will forgive me."

"All right, Mr. Black. I forgive you." *Liar. Forgiveness is more than just words, you know.* "Now, excuse me, I have work to do."

"Thank you, Miss Torvald." He placed his hat back on his head, touched the brim, and turned back toward the garden.

Oh, please, just go away. Ruby turned back toward the kitchen in time to catch Opal and Milly staring at her with saucer eyes.

Ruby shook her head, forestalling any questions, and continued on through to the kitchen, where she sank onto one of the straight-backed chairs.

Lord, how can I forgive him? She propped her head on her hands.

I forgave and forgive you.

I know, but I never . . . She rubbed her forehead. She could hear someone whistling outside. Charlie never whistled like that. His was more a tuneless sort of song. This whistle danced merrily through the air and tickled her ears. It invited her to sing along and even come on out to jig in the sunshine.

If putting her fingers in her ears were not so childish, she would have succumbed. She could hear Opal and Milly laughing. Cimarron's horselaugh rose above the others.

Shame she can't learn to laugh in a more ladylike way.

Ruby Signe Torvald, how cruel can you get? You even think such a thing, and somehow it will come out. Now you behave yourself and quit sitting here pouting.

Sometimes giving oneself a good talking to worked, and other times it didn't. Which was it to be today?

— 🐾 —

"You noticed the difference in Jed?" Belle asked one night at supper.

"He scrubbed the cardroom floor for me today." Cimarron shook her head. "Whistling all the while."

Ruby ordered her face to smile and her head to nod.

"But he never stayed around like this before. Came in, got cleaned up, played some, and headed on out again. Usually drunker 'n a skunk before he left."

Ruby tried to ignore the discussion as she scraped the last of her gravy into Cat's dish. The two remaining kittens dashed across the floor and skidded to a stop in front of the dish, pink tongues lapping at the treat.

The other kitten had gone to live with the Robertsons, much to the delight of the girls.

Ruby picked up the orange-and-white kitten and cuddled it under her chin. A rumbling purr immediately greeted her stroking fingers. Her verse that morning had reminded her to not let the root of bitterness grow. She had yet to figure out the difference between bitterness and justifiable anger. Far as she could determine, one was the extension of the other. But it always came back to the same thing. *"Be ye kind one to another, tenderhearted, forgiving one another, even as God for Christ's sake hath forgiven you."*

Sometimes memorized Bible verses came back to haunt one.

She set the kitten down and shifted the dishpan to a hotter part of the stove.

"I'll do the dishes." Milly leaped up from the table.

"No. You and Opal go for a ride or something. I'll do these." But washing dishes gave one too much time to think too.

"Hey there, Mr. Harrison."

Ruby flinched at the news. Bad enough with Mr. Black here, but now Rand Harrison also? He must have come in to play cards, since he wasn't here for supper.

"She's inside."

Ruby could tell Opal had raised her voice. Was she trying to warn her big sister?

Ruby quickly dried her hands on her apron and, with a couple of deft motions, had all the strands of loose hair tucked back in the snood she'd worn all day, removed her dirty apron, and snatched a clean one off the hook behind the stove. She just finished tying the strings when he came through the door.

"Good evening, Mr. Harrison, what a nice surprise."

Rand held his hat in his hands, the line between white and tan even more obvious now than the last time she'd seen him.

"You have any coffee left, by chance? We ran out."

"You came all this way for a cup of coffee?" She moved the pot to the front of the stove.

"Nope. Bought some over at the store. But I hoped you'd still have some left that's ready to drink."

"Have you had supper?"

He halfway shrugged.

"Is that a yes or no?"

"Too long ago to tell." He crossed the room, his spurs jingling as he moved. Taking the chair she indicated, he sat down and set his hat on the table beside him.

"Belle going to be dealing tonight?"

"Does the Little Missouri run north?" Ruby set a cup in front of him. "There's gingerbread left."

"I'll have some if you'll join me."

Ruby could feel the heat climb up her cheeks. What was the matter with her anyway? Fixing up just because Opal announced Rand's arrival and now letting that slow smile of his agitate her further. As if she wasn't agitated enough these days, with Jed around.

Not that the two were in any way similar. Other than unsettling.

She cut two pieces of gingerbread, spread applesauce over both, and set them on the table. She checked the coffeepot to make sure it was hot enough, then poured the coffee before sitting down.

"I can make you a sandwich if you like." Now where had that come from?

"No, this is plenty. Thank you." He cut a piece and put it in his mouth, eyes closing in pleasure. "Ah. Every bit as good as my mother's."

Good thing it was slightly dim, or he would have noticed the red she could feel again. "Thank you."

"You made it?"

"Yes. I do *part* of the cooking around here." Why did the man always provoke her to sound spiteful?

Or perhaps she was becoming spiteful? The thought made her set her fork down and hide behind her coffee cup.

He must have been terribly hungry or he really did enjoy the cake. "Can I get you some more?" Ruby asked.

"Ah, I hate to be a pig."

"No, just a hungry man." She brought the pan to the table, along with the bowl of applesauce.

"But you can't . . ." Opal came through the door talking over her shoulder.

"Yes, you can." Milly insisted.

"Is there more left?" Opal slid into the closest chair, eyeing the pan of fragrant cake. "Hey, Mr. Rand, you are one lucky guy."

"Really?"

"Yup. Ruby told us we had to save the rest for paying customers."

Rand glanced from sister to sister, one wide-eyed and grinning, the other glaring a dagger or two.

"Yup, guess I'm just lucky all right." He drained his coffee. "Thank you, Miss Torvald. Will there be a charge?"

"None at all." Ruby picked up the cake pan and returned it to the pantry. "Hope you win a hand or two."

Rand left the kitchen through the swinging door to the dining room, a chuckle floating over his shoulder.

Someday, Opal Torvald, I am going to get you and get you good.

— ✺ —

By Saturday Ruby had perfected the art of ignoring Jed Black. No matter that he showed up every day, helping Charlie with the garden and Daisy with the laundry, scrubbing the cardroom for Cimarron, and bringing Belle a handful of wild flowers. He also set Opal and Milly to laughing with his jokes and antics.

"How come you don't like Mr. Black?" Opal asked one night after they had blown out the lamp and lay back in bed.

"What makes you ask that?" *Lord, how do I answer this? I cannot explain the attack. She is too young. I am too young. Do any of the others know? I never told anyone. Did Charlie? Mr. Black? Did he brag to the men in the cardroom? No, then Belle would know and she would have said something—wouldn't she?*

"You treat him mean."

Ruby sighed and rolled on her side. She propped her head on one hand and closed her eyes, fighting to come up with a reasonable answer.

"Well?"

"Opal, there are some things we cannot talk about yet. When you are older you may ask me again, but in the meantime I would appreciate it if you did not mention what you have observed to anyone else. This is a private thing. Do you understand?"

"No."

"But you will do as I ask?"

"I guess, but—"

"No buts. Just know that this is important to me."

"All right, but I still think you should be nice to him. After all, he is helping all of us, and he never asks for anything."

Only the hardest thing for me to give. "I will try. Now go to sleep or we will both be so tired we'll be worthless."

"All right." Opal yawned and murmured, "I love you."

"I love you too." Ruby rolled back to lie flat, her eyes closing as she relaxed. *Lord, help me to do your will. Please, help me.*

She woke in the predawn darkness. It was Sunday morning, and they would be gathering for worship in the dining room. The choir had practiced during the week, Charlie would read the Scriptures again, and this time he would ask if anyone else had anything to say. She'd chosen the book of Acts, where the early church meetings were described. She thought to one of the verses. People joined daily because they saw how those early Christians loved one another. Wouldn't that be an amazing thing to have happen right here? In Little Missouri. At our hotel. Can we learn together? Grow together? Can we get Mrs. McGeeney and Mrs. Fitzgerald to talk to each other?

Her thoughts roved through the people she had either come to know or at least to know of. Look at what had happened right here at the hotel.

What about your heart? The thought stopped her happy dreaming. *Who all do you have to forgive?*

Ruby leaped from the bed and gasped for breath. Why did it have to keep coming back to that? She tried to be kind to everyone. *I do, Lord. I do try.*

She washed her face in the water from the pitcher, now cold from the night air. As she donned her clothes, she forced herself to think only on the food preparations ahead.

I'll think on the other later, she halfway promised. Whether to herself or her Lord, she didn't take time to ponder the difference.

After all, the people must be fed.

CHAPTER NINETEEN

Chicago

"How do I take everything I need with me?" Pearl studied her list, titled What I Will Need in the West. According to one of the articles she'd read in the newspaper, both a rifle and a pistol were highly recommended. Surely the superintendent of education did not expect her to hunt and kill her own food. Warm clothes for winter, cool clothes for summer, which is what she would experience first. While the acceptance letter said she must be in residence by August 10, she hoped there would be a place she could stay until then. After all, if she waited until August, she would be well married and unable to go. Mr. Longstreet might appear to be magnanimous in allowing his wife some freedom—after all, he'd agreed she could continue to teach if she felt that absolutely important—but she doubted he'd agree to her teaching in Dakotah Territory.

She caught herself in a snicker. She could just see bringing the subject up for discussion. That might indeed get a rise out of him.

For her badgering certainly hadn't. *Pearl Elaine Hossfuss, you should be ashamed of yourself.* She was, if she stopped to think about it for any length of time. Two days ago she'd dragged her betrothed to a soiree where the young singer was a hopeless tenor. His overbite made her think of a parrot, which was not exactly a Christian attitude. She had not known the soiree would be such a debacle, or she would not have forced either of them to attend. Her father had fallen asleep, her mother had about worn her fan out to keep from laughing. All in all a most unpleasant evening.

And Mr. Longstreet had sat through it stoically, not even recognizing the humor in it.

She sighed. That was the sad part. Had they been able to laugh together in the carriage on the way home, she might have considered changing her mind—about accepting the Dakotah position, that is.

After pacing the floor, all the while tapping the edge of her folded list on the index finger of her left hand, she stopped and glared at the figure in the mirror.

"Why can't you just be an obedient daughter and do what your father requires of you?" She spoke to herself in the mirror and leaned forward, studying the dark half moons under her eyes. Lack of sleep caused by worrying did that to one.

"God, your Word says to honor my mother and my father, but I'm afraid that in this case, my days upon this earth would not be long, and each one that I do have might seem an eternity."

Her conscience appeared to be mercifully silent.

She adjusted the ruching that was supposed to be hiding her neck. Instead, the dark upper line of the scar showed through. The neckline of the cotton dimity day dress she wore had not been starched sufficiently.

Who will starch your collars and launder your underpinnings out on the frontier?

Surely one could find someone to do it.

And who's going to pay for that service? The teacher's pay is abysmal. How am I going to pay for my room and board out of that, let alone laundry? After I use up the money I've saved, what will I do?

Wrapping her hands around her shoulders, she rocked from side to side on the padded bench in front of her dressing table. If only she could go with her father's blessing and not have to sneak off like a thief in the night.

Or at least go with her mother's.

Could she possibly talk this over with Amalia?

She fell asleep that night with prayers for God's guidance in her heart and on her lips.

— ⚜ —

"I thought we'd go shopping today for your trousseau," Amalia said at the breakfast table the next morning as she spread jam on a muffin.

Pearl nearly choked on the bite she'd just taken. She covered her mouth with her napkin and tried to cough discreetly.

"Are you all right, dear?"

Pearl shook her head. She was strangling. Was there no mercy? She coughed again.

"Erin, get Miss Pearl a cup of water."

The maid hurried back. "Here, drink this."

Pearl did so and felt she could breathe again. "Thank you." Of course, the wedding plans. How could she possibly go through the motions with Amalia when she was in such a quandary? Preparing for a wedding should be a time of great delight.

The sparkle in Amalia's eyes should be in her own. And she knew that was not so. She looked lackluster, tired, and out of sorts. The mirror had said so.

If she asked her mother the real questions raging through her mind, would it be fair? Could they discuss her feelings without Amalia talking things over with her husband?

"Pearl, are you all right?"

She shook her head, slowly, as if any more effort might cause pain. Which is exactly what was happening. "No, not really. My head aches, and I think I might be better off with a lie-down."

"Oh, my dear, I am so sorry. And here I go on like . . . well, never mind. You go lie down, and I'll send Marlene up with a cup of tea."

"Perhaps later." Pearl wiped her mouth with her napkin and slipped it back in the silver napkin ring. She started to rise but stopped when Amalia asked another question.

"Have you not been sleeping well?"

"Not really." Pearl studied her hands resting on the damask tablecloth.

"Is there anything I can do?"

The words offered in a gentle tone, liberally laced with love, brought a burning to the backs of Pearl's eyes. *How I wish you could. How I wish that a kiss would make this all better like when I was little. But now, if I tell you what is wrong . . .* "I'm sure I'll feel better after a while. Perhaps we can go tomorrow."

— ⚘ —

But in the morning, Pearl heard the most glorious news. Her father would be gone for three days. Pearl kept herself from twirling around the dining room by only the strictest internal admonitions. If anyone saw her twirling, they would want to know why she was so happy, and the only someone in the family she could trust with her secret was Jorge Jr. *If only I could talk this over with Amalia.* The thought kept nagging at her, but she refused to listen. Although right now Amalia could not go to Mr. Hossfuss, she would feel duty bound to keep Pearl from carrying through her plan for leaving.

Nothing like an idea being forced to escalate to action. Less than two weeks now before the wedding.

Pearl went in search of her younger brother.

"I think he's out in the garden," Arnet said, looking up from the puzzle he was working on.

"Thank you."

"You want me to find him for you?"

"No. That is nice of you, but I'll go find him." Arnet was so thoughtful, she knew she'd miss him. *I'm going to miss all of you dreadfully.* The thought almost sent her scurrying back to her room—almost, but not quite.

She went down the back stairs and out to the garden. "Jorge?" she called.

"Over here, in the kitchen garden," he answered.

She followed his voice to find him kneeling in the nasturtiums. "What are you doing?"

"Planting some giant beanstalk seeds."

"Oh. Like Jack and the Beanstalk?"

"Would be exciting, would it not?"

"True. But could you leave off the fairy tale and come help me for a bit?"

He rocked back on his heels, dusting his hands off on his pants. "What do you need?"

Pearl glanced around to make sure no one else was in earshot. "I need my trunk hauled down to the carriage house."

"Why?"

"Because I have to leave. I cannot marry Mr. Longstreet, and I have a new teaching position in Dakotah Territory." Her words nearly tripped over each other in her haste to procure his assistance.

"And no one can know?" he asked. Jorge did love secrets.

"No one. I will send a letter back from the train station."

"Father will be furious."

"I know. But, Jorge, I have no choice."

"Mr. Longstreet is not a bad man."

"No, but if I marry, I want a man who will talk with me, not just marry me so I can care for his children."

"They are nice children."

"Jorge, please, will you help me or not?" She felt like stamping her feet, definitely not a ladylike action.

"Of course, but you are taking a terrible chance. What if Father says no one may ever speak to you again?"

"Do you think he will do that?" Pearl closed her eyes and shook her head slowly. "I pray he doesn't. I just can't marry Mr. Longstreet, and I can't live here for the rest of my life."

Jorge stood and stuck his trowel in his back pocket. "Where is your trunk?"

"Up in the attic. It has my initials engraved on the top. You want me to help you?"

"Is it huge?"

"No. I won't take the big one. Life is more simple on the frontier." The two walked side by side toward the house.

"How do you know that?"

"I have a list of things the school board said I would need. They included that with the letter accepting me." He held the door open for her. "I'm hoping Father and Amalia will send me books and school supplies. I have a feeling there will not be much there."

She walked with him as he carried the trunk to the carriage house, where she hoped no one would notice it, then using the back stairs, she packed her things in the trunk a bit at a time. By the next afternoon, her trunk was locked.

"I'm going shopping," she told her stepmother after dinner.

"I will go with you."

"No, I know you were planning to call on Mrs. Carlson

today, and I want to spend time just browsing in the bookstore."
Amalia was not one to enjoy browsing in a bookstore.

"Tomorrow we have to finish picking out fabrics for your
trousseau. Matilda is not going to have time to finish much as it
is."

"I know. But I really don't need much, what with the three
new gowns of late." Three gowns she would not be taking with
her, as they took up far too much room. One trunk didn't leave
her a lot of room. Perhaps her mother would send those things
on later. And then again, perhaps her father would not allow it.
Please, Lord, I don't want to be disowned.

She went up to the nursery and kissed Anna and Arnet good-
bye, then made her way out to the street as if to walk to the cable
car. The man she'd hired to pick up her trunk met her at the end
of the block and delivered her and her trunk to the train station.

As Caesar had said, "The die is cast." She sniffed back tears
and paid for her ticket. *Little Missouri, here I come, only six weeks
early.*

Pearl stared out the soot-smeared window as the Chicago-
Milwaukee-St. Paul train pulled out of Chicago heading west.
She fought the tears that threatened to drown her as buildings of
her city slipped by. Leaving Chicago was not something she had
ever planned to do. Would she see her family again? Would they
even write to her?

And most of all, would they take her back if she failed at her
new life on the frontier?

She shook her head slowly as she sniffed. No, she'd never go
back, at least not as a penitent. How soon would they receive the
letter she wrote while waiting at the train station? And Mr.
Longstreet, he didn't deserve to be treated like this, but he
deserved an unwilling wife even less.

By the time the train approached St. Paul, Minnesota, where
she had to change trains, Pearl had worried herself into a bog
deeper than needed to bury the train upon which she rode. The
marriage to Sidney Longstreet sounded like an oasis in a desert.
Not that she really knew what a desert looked and felt like, but
sand she could picture, especially if it gritted like the soot that
had invaded every inch of bare skin and worked its way into the
seams of her clothing. And the smell? Surely there was some-

thing dead on the railroad car to create that putrid odor. But when she, with handkerchief-covered nose, questioned the conductor, he just shook his head.

"Sorry, miss, but sometimes that's the way it is. You might want to move farther away from the head, er, the water closet."

Stepping off the train in St. Paul, she headed for the women's necessary, wishing she could have a bath and grateful for a basin big enough to put both hands in at once. However, a handkerchief lacked a certain amount of productivity when one had to wash one's face and as much of the neck and arms as possible with it. Even so, she felt much refreshed after her ablutions and shook out the skirt of her traveling dress after brushing her shoulders. She also removed her hat and blew the cinders off the brim and the veil. Using the mirror she pinned the wisps of veil and straw back in place so that the silver feather drooped over one side of her face.

Boarding the Northern Pacific train west made her heartbeat quicken. This was the last leg of her journey. Had she made the right choice?

The prairie flowed past, sections of farms along the rivers, long stretches of grass higher than she'd ever dreamed possible. A young rider raced the train for a ways, then waved his hat as the train pulled by him.

The land undulated on forever with a blue bowl of sky that arched to a horizon so far distant that she felt she'd moved to a new world. No longer able to concentrate on the book she'd been reading, she watched the land pass.

Where were the Indians she'd read about? The cowboys, the covered wagons heading west? Were there any towns or villages?

"How much farther?" she asked the conductor after they left Dickinson on the following day. Sleep had been nonexistent.

"Not long now, miss. You can be glad we are running on time these days. Life is changing out here, you know. People coming in like a line of ants, always looking for new forage. Killed off the buffalo, drove out most of the game, cattle will soon be king. Whatever is taking you to Little Missouri? You know, many folks around here refer to that hamlet as Little Misery."

"I am to be the new schoolteacher."

"You're a schoolmarm?"

"Yes."

"Well, now, ain't that a bit of news? Goin' to have a school clear out here. Didn't think there was that many children." He started to leave. "You got a place to stay?"

"I-I don't know. I mean I'm sure the school officials have made some kind of arrangements for me."

"Well, you check with Miss Ruby Torvald at the Dove House. She's most likely the one set all this in motion. She's a real forward thinker, that one."

When the train screeched to a stop, he assisted her down the stairs. "Your trunk will be ready shortly." He turned at the greetings from two young girls.

"Hey, Mr. Larson."

"Hey yourself, Miss Opal. I brought you a guest. Miss Hoss-fuss, the new schoolmarm."

"What. . . ?" The girl seemed to catch herself. "Hello, ma'am."

"I am very pleased to meet you." Pearl smiled at the freckle-faced girl with sun-fired hair in braids tied with blue ribbons. She doubted the girl was normally shy, but she had greeted Pearl with the subdued demeanor of a new student. Her hat hung on a string down her back rather than shielding her face like it should.

The other girl almost disappeared in her spotless white apron. Both of them carried trays tied around their necks by cords. Wrapped packages of what Pearl assumed to be food filled the trays. A man with a bowler hat stood behind them with a granite coffeepot and cups. He gave her a friendly nod.

"What you got for my passengers today?" the conductor asked.

"Roast beef on fresh bread, molasses cookies, and fresh buttermilk."

Perhaps these two girls would be in her schoolroom. She watched as the three climbed the steps, then smiled at the porter who wheeled her trunk up to her.

"Where you want this, miss?"

"Ah, I guess right here until I find out where I'm going."

She turned and glanced down what she assumed was the main street of the sorry collection of buildings that must be the town. In the distance, not that anything in this town was of much distance, she saw a three-story building with a porch all around. A sign read Dove House, and it was the only building in the area that looked like someone cared about it. Curtains behind windows that sparkled in the sunlight and hitching rails on two sides. At least there was something here that appeared friendly.

She made her way across the ruts and dust, dodging a few wagons and men on horseback, then walked up the front steps and jingled her way in through the front doors.

The dining room tables wore white cloths. What a nice surprise. A carved banister led the way up walnut stairs—all in all, a very respectable place.

A young woman with honey blond hair in a snood pushed open a swinging door, a white apron covering her almost to her feet.

"Welcome to Dove House. How may I help you?"

"The conductor on the train said that I should find Miss Ruby Torvald."

"I am she."

"I am Pearl Hossfuss, and I answered an advertisement for a schoolteacher here. I needed to come early for personal reasons and—"

"My goodness, they really hired someone?"

"Yes, me."

"But this is wonderful. We are really going to have a school then."

"I believe so. Where is the school building?"

"We don't have one."

"Oh, I see. And the teacher is to live where?"

"I don't know. They haven't told me. Obviously, since they hadn't apprised me of their having hired you."

Pearl wished she had somewhere to sit down, and rather abruptly at that. Her nightmare had come true. No one knew she was coming.

CHAPTER TWENTY

Dakotah Territory

He couldn't get Ruby out of his mind.

"Hey, Rand!"

"Boss!"

He heard their voices, finally, and shook his head. Removing his hat, he wiped the sweat from his forehead with the sleeve covering his forearm, used both hands to settle his hat back on securely, and looked around to see where the voices were coming from. Or were they only in his head too?

Beans skidded his galloping horse to a stop beside Buck. "You all right?"

"Sure, why?"

"We been yellin' at you somethin' awful, and you just sat there. Began to think you was sick or somethin'."

"No, just thinkin', I guess. What was it you needed?" Rand glanced up to catch the smirk Beans wiped off his face real quicklike.

"Some help with that last bunch Joe brought in. Got a couple a cows in there that need some doctorin'. Looks like a wolf or some other critter tried to bring 'em down and failed."

Both men reined around and headed back the way Beans had come. One of the men had a rope on a belligerent cow that had deep scratches along her top line on both sides of her backbone.

Chaps, the oldest of the ranch hands, crossed his arms on the saddle horn and spat a gob of chewing tobacco off to the side. "I'm bettin' on a mountain lion, and an old one at that, 'cause he didn't bite her neck and kill her. I think she scraped him off, leastwise that's what I read."

"Looks to me like you told the tale right." Rand rode closer so he could see more clearly. "Take her down, and I'll put some salve on those scratches. At least one of them looks infected." He rode back to the house for the salve while the men put a loop around the cow's back legs and threw her to the ground. Her calf ran bawling to the other cows, as if pleading for them to come help his mother.

Rand used his knife to scrape off the pussy scab and release the infection, then smeared the salve in place. "Better keep her in the corral for a day or two, see how this goes. How bad is the other one?"

"Looks like it happened earlier. It's healin' now."

"So we got us a predator that needs to be taken care of?"

"Seems so."

"Where'd you find these?" Rand nodded to the grazing cattle.

"Out by Chimney Butte. Saw some bones too. He musta got one."

Rand tipped his hat back and stared out to the cone-shaped peak that stood out from the rounded hills in the vicinity. Layers of rock showed tan and black and terra-cotta, giving the peak a pattern of rings. "Any more cattle out there?"

"More'n likely. Thought two of us should go on out there in the mornin'."

"We got anything to use for bait?"

"Could tie out that skinny old cow over there. No calf again, and she most likely won't make it another winter."

Rand looked across the herd until he recognized the one Beans had mentioned. Her patchy coat hung from her frame, the bones looking to poke through at any movement. "Okay, bring her in. We'll take her out there tonight and stake her out. Joe and Beans, you go on back and see if you can find any mountain lion signs. If he's real old, he might just be holed up in one of those caves or clefts."

— ❧ —

Rand stared into the night, the stars so close he was sure, if he climbed to the top of the peak, he could snatch them out of the sky one by one. *Wonder if a star would be enough to win her? I'd hand it to her just so and—* He jerked his attention back to the cow tethered down below. At least she'd given up fighting the rope and was grazing as if she had not a care in the world. Not that she knew she did. Not like humans who ruminated on everything, figuring this, discarding that. He'd finally quit calling himself a stupid *idjit* and other less complimentary terms for the way he'd handled his big moment with Ruby. Of course Beans and all the others pointed out his failings with great delight—not that any of them had proposed to a woman in recent years, or at least they hadn't owned up to it.

One of the horses snorted, then another. He had one of the hands watching the horses. No need to let that old cat take out a horse when they'd tried to give it a cow. But then horses were better than a dog at warning. And horses hated mountain lion.

Come on—attack that cow. Let's get this over with so we can all get some sleep. From his place in the rocks, he had a good view of the grazing cow now that the moon had risen. Another snort. Something was near, how near was the question. He could feel the hair stand up on the back of his neck, that feeling of being watched, an age-old dread. If he listened any harder, the thumping of his heart would drown out a buffalo charge. But buffalo weren't sneaky, like a cat, especially a big cat that was hungry.

The cow threw up her head and headed out until she hit the end of the rope. The leaping cat hit the ground with only a slight rattle of gravel, but in that split second, Rand sighted and fired. He pumped a second shell into the chamber but didn't pull the trigger again. The cat somersaulted and lay sprawled in the grass three feet from the frantic bawling cow.

"That was some shot." Beans spoke from behind Rand.

"That was pure luck. Did you even see him before he leaped?"

"Nope. I had my eyes peeled, but I don't know where he come from." The two men made their way down out of the rocks and carefully approached the cat, just in case he had some life left. One swipe with those claws could cause more infection than a dressing of dung. Rand nudged the animal with the barrel of his rifle. No motion.

"Cut the cow loose before she breaks her neck. We'll never get that carcass over one of the horses, so think I'll skin it here."

"Why? Do you want the pelt?"

"For a rug, I guess. Could take the head too, but I'll leave it here for the scavengers."

"You ever tanned a mountain lion hide?"

"Nope. Just deer and beef. Oh, an antelope once." Rand knelt down and cut the cat's throat to let it bleed out. "What about you?"

Beans freed the cow. "Bear once. Let me tell you, if you want to stay warm in a Dakotah winter, go for a bear hide." The two men set about skinning the cat. "You want the paws?"

Rand checked the cat's mouth. "Poor old cat. Hardly any teeth left. No wonder he couldn't kill those cows." Rand almost felt sorry for the beast. Without teeth the big cat couldn't break the neck of its prey, which was its most effective form of killing. Leap down on an unsuspecting animal, dig in its claws for purchase, and snap the neck with its teeth and jaws.

"Think I'll keep the claws. The Indians use them for necklaces and such. Good trading."

"Let me have a couple for Opal. She'll get a real kick out of them," Rand said.

— ✧ —

"Rand Harrison, what is the matter with you, bringing a child a present like that?" Ruby had planted her hands on her hips again, seeming a natural thing where Rand was concerned.

"I thought she'd be pleased. Not every girl has a necklace of braided leather and mountain lion claws. The Indians set great store by such things."

"I do like them. Ruby, it's all right. They just caught me by surprise. All I could think of was Cat." Opal swallowed and traced one of the claws with her finger. "So big. You said he was real old?"

"Yep, couldn't hunt any longer. We did him a favor, actually. Didn't have to die of starvation. That's what happens, especially during the winter."

"And you nailed the hide to the wall of your house?"

"You want to come out and help tan it? The Indian women chew the hides to make them soft enough for dresses and shirts."

"Ugh." Opal and Ruby both stared at him with pure horror.

"I think I'm going to be sick." Opal blinked a couple of times. " 'Scuse me."

"See? Why do you do things like that?" Ruby's hiss came from clenched lips.

Rand sighed. "I don't know. Just want to let you know how things are out here, I guess." He unwrapped the reins from around the hitching rail.

"Aren't you staying for supper?"

He stopped in the act of putting his foot in the stirrup. "You want me to stay?" *Woman, I do not understand you at all.* He glanced over his shoulder at her.

Ruby combined a shrug, a half smile, and a frown. "Well, just trying to be neighborly and to thank you for all you do, like the horses and the necklace and all."

"Well, I'll be . . ." Rand flipped the reins over the rail again and patted Buck's shoulder. He tipped his hat back with one finger and watched Ruby through slit eyes. No matter what he did, it seemed to set her off, and then she'd be all nice again. How was he supposed to know what to do? "You want to go for a walk down by the river before supper?"

"Sorry, I'm needed in the kitchen."

"After supper then?"

Ruby paused, glanced back over her shoulder, and her slender shoulders lifted in a shrug. "All right, I will." Her smile hesitated like a frightened calf peeking out from behind its mother, then widened, even to reaching her eyes.

If that don't beat all. Rand studied his boot, then glanced up at the squeaking of the screen door opening. A woman he'd never seen before came out on the back porch.

Ruby smiled at the woman. "Miss Hossfuss, I'd like you to meet Rand Harrison. He has a ranch south of here on the river. Miss Hossfuss is the new schoolteacher who came west a bit early."

Rand tipped his hat. "Pleased to meet you, Miss Hossfuss. Welcome to Little Missouri."

"And you, sir."

Her voice was pleasing, as was her face. Some man would be slinging his reins around the Dove House hitching rail as soon as the word got out. She wouldn't be teaching for long.

"Supper will be ready soon. Why don't you two sit here in the shade and get acquainted."

"I would love to help if you don't mind. I've never had so much time on my hands."

"You've only been here two days. Perhaps Mr. Harrison would show you the town."

"Be right glad to, Miss Hossfuss, not that there's much to see, but the river is right pretty."

"And these hills. I've never seen anything like them."

"That's 'cause there's no place else on earth like the badlands." He held open the gate for her. "Sunset tonight will make them look like they're on fire. Fact is, some places are on fire — coal lines that have been burning for years." He happened to glance back to see Ruby staring after them with a rather perplexed look. *Hmm.* Perhaps this was the way to catch her attention. After all, she suggested he take Miss Hossfuss out for a stroll. Besides, pay her back a bit for getting in such a dither over the mountain lion claws. He'd caught Opal bragging about them to Milly. As he thought, she was pleased. But what would it take to please the older sister? Especially since everything he tried had a habit of turning and biting him on the backside.

CHAPTER TWENTY-ONE

"He *was* here."

Carl Hegland stared at the man behind the counter. "But the advertisement said to contact him in this town. Is he staying somewhere else?"

"No, he had to go back East again, but he will be back. He said if anyone asked about him, to have them stay around, because when he returns he needs builders. What is your name? I have a list going here."

"I . . . my name is Carl Hegland, and I am from Minneapolis. I thought to go to work as soon as I arrived. The paper said—"

"I know. Sorry. I think this was some kind of emergency. I'm Charlie Higgins, and I work here at Dove House. We still have a couple of rooms, but might have to ask people to double up if they keep coming west like this."

"This man. What is he building?"

"I gather they're starting with a big house, warehouses, then an abattoir, a place where they slaughter cattle for meat. The marquis, he has a whole town planned out, brought the plans with him when he came. All of it going to be built across the river on that flat spot over there. Big changes coming to Little Missouri, thanks to the railroad and the marquis."

"Is there any other work here until he returns?"

"What can you do?"

"Whatever needs to be done."

"Punch cattle?"

Carl tilted his head slightly to the side. Was this man pulling his leg? "Pardon me?"

"You know, ride a horse, round up cattle, herd cattle, brand them?"

Carl took a step backward and shook his head. "We didn't have such needs in Minneapolis, but if I have to learn them, I will."

"Lots of cows coming in, or will be, if what I hear is right."

"Don't people need houses? Where they going to put all the workers?"

"Tents, most likely, to start with. Like they did out west during the gold rush. Cities went up overnight and came down about as fast sometimes. Did you bring a bedroll?"

"You mean bedding, blankets, and such?"

"Yup."

Carl glanced down at his feet where his bag of tools rested on one side and his satchel of clothes and a couple of books took up the other. "No." *What was the matter with you, dumbhead? You should have known you'd be camping.* Calling himself all kinds of names didn't help, nor did the lack of money to buy things like that. Not that it looked as if there was a place here to buy supplies anyway. The small store across the street, if one could call the rutted and packed track a street, didn't have much more than the necessities. For one who usually planned things out to the last dot, he hadn't done a very good job this time.

"Like I said, we got some rooms here. Dollar gets you three meals and a clean bed. Better'n you get anywhere else in this town, let me tell you."

At least in Minneapolis I had a roof over my head and plenty of food. Or rather I did before Mor left. And my boss let me go. That thought still brought a fire to his belly. After all the other jobs he'd turned down because the man had assured him he always had a future with his company.

Now he had nothing but the few dollars in his pockets and hands willing to work, if only there was work.

"Are you the owner here?"

"No, Miss Ruby Torvald owns Dove House."

"I see." Carl dug in his pocket. "I'll pay for two nights if that is all right."

"That'll be two dollars. I'll show you to your room. Breakfast is—"

A door in the back of the room slammed open, and a young girl dashed through. "Charlie, can you—oh, sorry."

"What do you need?"

"Mr. Johnson's cow won't get out of the garden."

"Oh my. Excuse me, sir. Have a seat and I'll be right back. Opal, tell Milly to bring this gentleman a cup of coffee." He and the young girl headed back the way she'd come, leaving Carl to stare after them in consternation.

Carl left his bags where they were and used the time to explore, noting the cardroom. He liked to play cards, but he'd never been much of a gambler. From the look of the room and the abundance of spittoons, he'd bet the men played poker. He turned at the sound of a throat clearing.

"I brought your coffee, sir, and some cookies to last you until supper." The young girl set a cup and plate on one of the tables. "Just holler if you want more."

"Do I pay you or the gentleman?"

"Gentleman?" Her face lit, chasing the paleness with a chuckle. "Charlie ain't no gentleman. He's just Charlie."

"He followed—Opal is it?—out to chase a cow. Are there a lot of cows around here?" He sat down at her bidding.

"Not here in town. Just Mr. Johnson's and one other over to the livery. Don't know why more people don't have milk cows." She started to leave and paused. "You want cream with that? I forgot to bring it."

"No, strong and black is the way I like it." He watched her leave with a slight wave. His stomach grumbled at the misuse he'd put it through, trying to save money by going without food. The cookies disappeared faster than the coffee he'd poured into his saucer to cool. Hot and strong. Strong enough to grow hair on his chest, as his father used to say. Not that hair on his chest was something to be greatly desired.

Charlie returned, coffeepot in hand, and refilled his cup. "I'll show you up any time you're ready."

"You catch the cow?"

"Fool critter. Out lookin' for a bull if you ask me. Tore up the peas and tromped through the potatoes. Got her before she mowed down the corn. Just barely up, it was." Charlie shook his head. "Someone musta left the gate open. Don't see no fence broken."

"I see."

Carl finished off his coffee and pushed to his feet. After retrieving his bags, he followed Charlie upstairs and down to the end of the hall. The room welcomed him with braided rugs on the floor and a patchwork quilt covering the wood-framed bed. Pegs in boards along the wall would be used for hanging up clothes, not that he had that many, and a pitcher sat in a bowl on a stand in the corner.

"Mange takk, er, thank you." The room was plenty big for one man, which surprised him. He'd read of men crammed together in freezing attics, the warmth from each other preventing frostbite. But why think of such things when June had warmed the earth, bringing forth the green grasses and swatches of wild flowers he'd seen from the train.

"Mange takk works here good as anything. With a name like Torvald you can guess where her folks come from." Charlie walked over and threw up the sash to let a breeze lift the curtain panels. "Baths are extra. If you need anything, holler."

"I . . . would it be all right if I went out walking, to view the land?"

"Suit yourself. Just don't get out of sight of the river. Easy to get lost in these hills. Oh, and the river flows north here." Charlie closed the door as he left the room, leaving Carl to put away his things. He pushed his tools under the bed, hung up his clean shirts, and pulled his Bible and a copy of John Donne from the bag, along with a canteen. Tucking the books under his arm, he whistled as he went back down the stairs and out the front door. Surely there was a tree nearby that would offer its trunk for a backrest and its leaves for shade. Somehow, even though nothing had changed, a feeling of expectation lifted his spirits. Surely God brought him out here for a reason. If indeed God had been behind it all.

He managed to keep from getting lost. After all, sitting under a huge tree with bark so thick it looked like there were canyons carved into it and reading until his eyes drooped and he slept didn't allow one to stray far. What he saw of the town didn't impress him. One saloon smelled worse than it looked. He shuddered at the thought that men drank what stunk so terrible. The ramshackle buildings looked stuck together by a capricious giant out to play. Giant trolls had been the warp and woof of his childhood stories. Tales of the old country, his father called them.

Back at Dove House he inhaled the fragrances of fresh bread, baking meat, and some kind of dessert as he climbed the stairs to his room. Young women in full white aprons bustled about setting the tables, laughing and chatting. One with glorious red hair waved at him.

"Supper will be ready in about fifteen minutes."

"Thank you." He picked up the pace. Surely he had time to wash up and shave.

"You can sit anywhere you like, sir," Milly greeted him when he came back down. She smiled over her shoulder as she set a plate in front of one of the other guests.

Carl smiled an acknowledgment and took a chair at an empty table where he could watch the servers come and go. *Wonder if the owner comes in during a meal? Perhaps she has something she needs fixed or built or carved so I can stay here longer*. The tables were about half full, some by obvious drummers, making him wonder what they were selling. Several others wore the flat broad-brimmed hats he'd come to think of as cowboy or rancher garb. He'd seen enough of them on the train and, with boots and spurs, they cut an imposing figure.

"Welcome, stranger, my name is Cimarron, and I'll be bringing your supper in just a moment."

He smiled back. The one with the glorious hair. "That suits you. I am Carl Hegland from Minneapolis."

"Hope you are extra hungry. We got a lot of good food out in the kitchen."

"I am."

"Good. I'll be right back."

"Coffee, Mr. Hegland?" Charlie stopped at his table, gray granite pot in hand.

"Please. And call me Carl."

By the time he'd used a slice of bread to clean off his second plateful, Carl had watched later diners replace those in a hurry to leave. Several of the men had lit up cigars and rocked their chairs back on the rear legs. But when a young woman with sun-kissed hair entered the room, they all snapped back upright, the chair legs slamming the floor in unison. She moved from table to table, greeting the guests and bringing smiles to the faces of all the males present. Several followed her with their eyes, although she seemed blissfully unaware of any admiration. She couldn't have been more gracious if this were her private home and all present were invited guests.

"Good evening. Mr. Hegland, is it not?" Her voice held a trace of Norwegian accent, one that he would recognize any-where.

"Ja, from Minneapolis." Now why did he keep telling every-one that?

"Charlie said that you are a carpenter."

"Ja."

"There will be plenty of work for carpenters soon."

Will and *soon* weren't what he needed. *I need work now. Or at the latest two days from now.* He studied the cup in his hands, the coffee black against the pale mug. When he glanced up, she had moved on. *Mor, you would not be proud of me now. I am not only without work, I am without manners.* That must be Miss Torvald. Tomorrow I shall bring my book with me to read. Talking with these people is not what I want.

— ❧ —

Joseph Wainwright didn't return the next day nor the next. Carl met the train each day, his spirits sinking like the coins in his pocket. He wandered back to the hotel, ready to pack his things and go ask at the buildings that used to house the military if there was a spare blanket and corner to sleep in.

"Miss Torvald would like to see you," Charlie called when Carl came through the front door. "She's out back."

CHAPTER TWENTY-TWO

"I hear you are looking for work, Mr. Hegland?"

"Yes. Yes, I am. At least until Mr. Wainwright returns. The advertisement said they needed carpenters here, and so I came."

"I see. So what you really need is something for right now?"

"Ja, that is right."

"Would room and board be enough pay for you to do some work I'd like done around here?"

"Ja, that would be very good. What do you need?"

"I'm thinking of putting more beds in a couple of the larger rooms." *If only Belle would leave, I could put four beds in there.* She'd been thinking of volunteering to start the school in the cardroom. Would that be enough reason to ask Belle to move into the attic or leave or—or whatever Ruby needed to do in order to capitalize on the coming boom? Already there were several tents up in Medora, as the marquis had christened the new town with a bottle of wine smashed on a tent pole. But not everyone wanted to live in a tent.

Lumber and other building materials were coming in daily on the train. The Frenchman had not lied when he promised her there would be a new town. And soon.

She glanced up to see Mr. Hegland still standing before her, hat in his hands. "Sorry, my mind sometimes takes off on its own. So much to think about."

"Do you have the wood to build beds? I have the tools."

179

She wanted to smile at his Norwegian accent, such a welcome sound. "I'm thinking of stacking one bed on top of another, what do they call them. . . ?"

"Bunk beds? In all the rooms?"

"No, just a couple. Then I was thinking of enclosing the western porch and putting several more out there." She was also thinking of raising her prices on the single rooms. She closed her ledger and stood. "Come, let me show you what I mean, and then you can make a list for me of the materials you will need."

"So I will stay here then. But what if I get a job before I am done here?"

"Then you could finish here in your spare time. That way you would always have a place to stay. I have a feeling space is going to be at a premium soon."

As they walked around the porch, she glanced out at the garden. Jed Black, hoe in hand, was busily attacking the weeds that grew inches by the minute after a rainstorm like they'd had yesterday.

"You would want windows in the wall?"

"I'd think so."

"And a door at either end? A dividing wall in the middle? Stove?"

"Could you move that window out of the wall there and put it in the new one?"

"Ja, I can do so with that window. Finish it inside like the rest of the walls, but then your pantry will have no window."

By the time they'd completed their planning, Ruby had a new appreciation for the quiet man who chose to sit by himself in the dining room, he and his book.

"I will measure and have the list for you by tomorrow."

"You can ask Charlie about what we have on hand. I'd want you to break the list into sections, one for the addition and one for the beds."

"Ja, I will."

"I wish I could pay you too."

"Nei, this is just fine."

Ruby left him to his measuring and headed back into the hotel. Another letter to the board of education was needed. What did they expect of the local people? There was no school building here, and if she had any idea of what a boom could look like, thanks to Charlie's colorful pictures of life in a gold-mining camp, pretty soon every square inch of roofed and walled buildings would house the people building Medora. Perhaps they needed to start praying now for a mild winter.

She was about to sign her name to the letter sometime later when a voice saying "Miss Torvald?" caused her to drop a blot of ink on the paper.

"Must you sneak up on me so?" If glares could cut, Jed Black would have bled to death on the spot. Now she'd have to rewrite the entire missive. "See what you made me do?"

"Sorry, miss. I thought you heard me."

"Well, I didn't. What do you need?"

"Something more to do. I thought maybe I could dig up some beds along the front of the hotel. Put in some seeds. Flowers out there would look real nice."

"Mr. Black, I cannot pay you for all the labor you are doing around here now."

"Did I ask for pay?"

His quiet question snapped her up short like a calf at the business end of a rope.

"No, and that's something else that bothers me. People don't just work for free."

"Got nothin' better to do, and if it gives me pleasure, why let it bother you?"

Good question. With anyone else, it wouldn't bother her. She'd give them extra cookies or bushels of appreciation. But she wished Jed Black were on the other side of the Rocky Mountains, and that might not be far enough away.

And yet she'd said she forgave him.

She pulled another sheet of paper from the dwindling stack. "If that's what you want, so be it. And please, take your meals here at Dove House. You've more than earned them."

She didn't hear him leave either. How could he be here one second and gone the next?

— ❧ —

"Those are the skills of a good hunter," Charlie explained

later when she asked him. "He learned from the Indians when he lived with them."

"Oh." *Is he part Indian?* She had questions darting through her mind like small birds after a big crow. She'd watched three dive at and harass a scavenging crow one day until the big ebony bird flew away, ducking and flapping. They made her think of David and Goliath. Size might not count if speed was greater.

But she'd not been able to outrun him, and now her mind and body remembered, even though her soul said he was forgiven.

Lord, how do I do this? I keep saying I forgave him, but I cannot stand to be around him. I feel like running, and yet to the others Jed Black is . . . Oh, Lord, please, I don't even know how to pray about this anymore. I know that when you forgive, you forget, the Bible says so, but I cannot do that. I just can't.

She recopied her letter that night, signed it quickly before anyone else could interrupt, and listened with half an ear to the men playing cards.

Belle's soprano laugh played against a man's *basso profundo*. If she closed the cardroom, would Belle move on? Where would she go?

That's none of your business. You can't worry about the whole world.

No, but you promised to take care of the girls. More inner arguments, her mind was beginning to feel like a beat-up battlefield.

Thinking about Belle brought up something else. Opal seemed to have a case of hero worship for the card dealer, sticking up for her when Ruby grumbled about her, running errands, and more than once Ruby had seen her coming from Belle's room.

When Ruby returned to the kitchen, she could hear feminine voices out on the back porch. She listened for a moment, then realized Opal had Milly reading aloud. Milly even read with inflection now, as if she enjoyed not only the words but the story.

Opal, my dear little sister, you are part of a miracle here. She went to the pantry for a jar of raspberry juice, stirred in sugar, vinegar, and water. After pouring it into glasses on a tray, she added a plate of raisin sugar cookies and headed out to join them.

A western breeze lifted the tendrils of hair that had escaped her braids. She'd taken at times to braiding her hair in two plaits, then wrapping them coronet style around her head. Opal said it made her look like a queen.

She held the tray for each of them to take a glass and a cookie, then set it on a box. Cimarron and Milly each had a kitten on her lap, and Cat on Opal's lap forced her to sit still for a time by extending her claws just to the touch point any time Opal got too jiggly.

"Ruby, wait till you hear Miss Hossfuss read. She's almost as good as you." Opal stroked Cat's head.

"Thank you for the compliment." Pearl tasted the raspberry swizzle. "This is delicious, so refreshing."

Ruby glanced out toward the garden where Jed was pounding in tall poles. "What is he doing now?"

"Gettin' the beans strung up." Cimarron set her rocker to singing. "How come you don't like him?"

Ruby stopped mid-drink, then choked. The liquid went up her nose, burning like fire.

Pearl leaned over and patted her back, running her hand in smooth circles. "They say to thump someone on the back who is choking, but I find this more helpful."

"Th-thank you." Ruby cleared her throat again, being careful not to look at Cimarron. *Change the subject, anything. What can we talk about?*

"The mean hen hatched her chicks today."

Thank you, Opal, dear sister. "How many?"

"Eight. One egg didn't hatch. They sure are cute."

"Bitty puffballs." Milly leaned her head against the back of her chair. "She about pecked my arm off when I tried to look under her." She held out her arm to show the scratches. "She's a mean one, all right."

"We had a rooster that used to chase the little kids. One day he chased my older brother and he picked up a rock, threw and hit that old rooster right in the head with it." Cimarron chuckled softly.

"Did he kill it?" Opal hugged Cat close.

"Nope. Thata bird was too ornery to die. Got up, staggered around like an old drunk, then got his bearings and went off to chase some hen."

"I never saw chickens up close before I came here." Pearl

swished her drink around in the glass. "I've seen a lot of new things, that's for sure."

"Have you heard from your family?"

"No. I haven't sent them my address yet. Thought I'd wait until school starts."

Ruby glanced up to see Cimarron studying on her. A cocked eyebrow gave Ruby a pretty good idea that she would be questioned again. Was her antipathy so obvious? Either she was not the actress she thought she was or Cimarron was a far more astute judge of character than she gave her credit for. Usually Opal picked up on feelings faster than anyone.

A mosquito buzzed her arm, followed by another.

"The bugs are out." Daisy stood, cuddling the kitten still. "Think I'll go on up to bed. Thanks for the story and the refreshments." She nodded to both Milly and Ruby.

Ruby started to stand when Carl Hegland came around the corner.

"Ah, excuse me," he said. "I didn't realize anyone was out here." He backpedaled and would have disappeared, but Ruby stopped him.

"Was there something you wanted?"

"I was thinking today that I could put rockers on a couple of these chairs, and that would make sitting out here that much more pleasurable."

"What a good idea."

"Can you do that?" Opal studied one of the chairs. "I mean, that rocker has a different angle on the seat."

"Building one from the beginning would be better, but I can adapt those."

"Can I—"

"May I." Ruby automatically corrected her sister's grammar.

Opal rolled her eyes. "May I watch you? I could help maybe."

"Sure, if you want. I found some wood out behind the chicken house that might work."

"I wish we had a swing here. Remember the one we had at the Brandons', Ruby? The one on the back porch, with chains to the ceiling? You could take a book out there and read, or sometimes we played word games. Swings are a good thing."

"I could make a swing real easy," another voice interjected.

Ruby whipped her head around so fast she almost crinked it. When had Jed Black come up? And who invited him into the conversation?

She glanced over at Cimarron who was watching Jed Black. Her face wore a dreamy look, her lips curved slightly, head tipped just a bit to the side. With one finger she twirled a tendril of hair right in front of her ear.

As if her gaze drew him, Jed Black turned his head and stared back.

Ruby had to admit he was handsome when he smiled, even though she saw him through a haze.

Yes, indeed, it looked like she and Cimarron should have a serious talk—and soon.

CHAPTER TWENTY-THREE

"Pearl, is there something I can get for you?" Ruby paused at the table.

"No, thank you. Unless you can sit down and visit with me?" Pearl leaned forward. "I'm just not accustomed to dining by myself."

"Generally the help eat in the kitchen after all the guests are served, but since we are so close to being finished, I'll bring my coffee over here."

"Wonderful. And you could eat your dessert with me?"

Ruby chuckled as she took her coffeepot on to another table.

Slowly the dining room crowd thinned out, and Ruby joined Pearl, a plate with frosted spice cake in each hand. Daisy followed behind her with the coffeepot to refill Pearl's cup and pour one for Ruby.

"Now you sit there and visit for a while. We'll take care of things." Daisy answered someone else's beckon and moved off.

"I've been wanting to talk with you, but the time just flies by." Ruby took a bite of the rich cake, as did Pearl.

"My, this is good."

"Yes, it's one of Cimarron's specialties. Each of the girls is developing her own dishes and desserts. Kind of becomes a contest to see what our guests think."

"Our cook, Inga, made the best custard pie. Then she'd put whatever berries were in season on top." For a moment Pearl was transported back to Chicago. "We had strawberries, raspberries, blackberries, even currants, along with other kinds of fruit. Some from the hothouse in the winter."

"You miss home?"

"More often than I want to admit. But as my father would say, I made my bed, now I must lie in it."

"Are you unhappy here?"

"I won't be once I start teaching."

"Then why are you waiting?"

Pearl stopped in midbite. "But I—I mean, school starts in the fall. That is what my contract says."

"But you mentioned you don't have enough to do."

"True."

"So, of those who work here, Daisy and Milly have just learned to read and do sums, thanks to Opal's tutoring, and I help when I can, mostly in the winter. I would imagine there are other people around here with the same lack of education."

"But they've not sent any supplies yet."

"When it comes right down to it, what do you really need?"

"Books to read, schoolbooks, paper and pencil or slates and chalk. Some paints would be nice."

"Necessary?"

"No. But—"Pearl glanced around the now empty room— "where would we have it?"

"How about out on the back porch, as long as the weather holds?"

"I don't suppose there is any chance folks around here could all work together to build a schoolhouse?"

"Not before fall. For the time being all the workers will be busy in Medora. Once Mr. Wainwright returns, things will really roll. If you want, rather than starting school early, you could help here in the hotel."

"Doing what?"

"Cleaning, cooking, laundry, ironing, sewing, canning—we put up as much as we can for winter. Last fall our cellar was pretty full, and this year it will be overflowing if we are to feed all the people who look to be coming here."

Ruby picked up her cup and held it with both hands. "You could earn room and board that way and save on your cash."

Pearl nodded slightly, the kind of nod that said, *I'm thinking*.

"Oh, and one other thing, I have chosen to offer you room and board here at the hotel as my contribution to the school, so you needn't worry about a place to stay. With some schools, I heard the teacher moves from house to house so everyone shares in her expense."

Well, thank you, Lord. You put me here. "Thank you, I appreciate that. However, I know you could rent my room out, so if you want, I will be glad to take a room in the attic with the rest of you, if there is space."

"Would you do that?"

Pearl nodded. "I mean, you weren't planning on my arrival quite this soon, and—"

"I wasn't sure I could plan on *anyone*. The territorial offices are a bit slow in responding. Perhaps they had to make sure we were real out here before they could officially approve."

"Or that I was."

"Ruby?" The call came from the kitchen.

"I better go. One of these days we have to sit down and really talk. I have a feeling we have a lot in common." Ruby picked up both their plates. "We've found the back porch a good place for getting together. Nice to have a bit of chatting time when the day is done."

"Thank you. I'll bring my tatting." Pearl glanced up, but the man reading the book at another table had left. While they'd not been formally introduced, she knew his name. Carl Hegland. He was from Minneapolis and could make all manner of things. She took her book out of the bag she carried and settled back to read. Every once in a while the laughter from the kitchen caught her attention. At the rate she was going, that stock of books in the bottom of her trunk was dwindling quickly. Did Ruby or anyone else have any books around here to exchange?

"Now look what you did!" The cry brought Pearl to the window in the morning. Daisy, one hand on her hip, the other with finger pointed and shaking, was scolding Milly.

"I-I'm sorry." Milly leaned down and picked up one of the half-twisted sheets.

"Now we'll have to wash it all over again. Just go throw it in the boiler."

I wonder what got Daisy going this time? She'd awakened to the same scene a few days earlier. Or at least something similar. Milly shook out the sheet and dropped it back in the tub bubbling over an open fire. Pearl thought back to the modern conveniences at her father's home. The housekeeper oversaw the laundry maids who had a crank-turned washer with a wringer above, also turned by a crank. A receptacle under the tub burned coal to keep the water hot. That was one thing about her father. He liked having the most up-to-date things around him and his household. They'd been one of the first to have gaslights and running water in the house.

Pearl washed in the tepid water and dressed for the day in a sky blue cotton-lawn dress with darker blue ribbons threaded through the skirt, along the square-necked bodice, and around the high-necked lace faced with white lawn. The puffed sleeves, also ribbon edged, came to just above her elbows. She stopped to check the mirror to make sure her scar didn't show, then made her way down to the dining room.

Today she would write home and mail her letter in time to catch the eastbound train.

"Miss Hossfuss." Charlie stopped beside her table.

"Yes, Mr. Higgins."

"Just Charlie, miss. Ruby was saying that perhaps you might like to meet those of your pupils we know of before school starts. I'd be glad to take you around if you would like."

"What an excellent idea."

"Good. I'll ask Opal if she wants to go too."

"Ah, Mr. . . . ah, Charlie." She adapted at the look he gave her and lowered her voice. "Is Milly all right?"

"Far as I know, why?"

Mind your own business, Pearl. "Is there bad blood between Milly and Daisy?"

"Naa, just the peckin' order at times, that's all."

Back up in her room, she took out her writing kit and settled in the chair by the window.

My dear family,
I am hoping you still want to hear from me after the way I left home. I could see no other way, and I beg your forgiveness for sneaking off like that. I am living in Little Missouri, which is a stop on the Northern Pacific Railroad between Dickinson and Beach, west of Bismarck. I live at Dove House, which is a residential hotel owned by a wonderful young woman named Ruby Torvald. You can guess by her name that she is as Norwegian as we are. She has a younger sister named Opal.

She went on to describe some of the other people she'd met so far, carefully omitting Carl Hegland. Her reason being that she hadn't really met him or gotten to know him. After all, he was quite alone most of the time.

I am well, and I do pray that you will write back to me and give me news of home.
Your loving daughter,
Pearl

She took the envelope down with her when she went. Since there was no sign of Charlie, she stuck her letter in the mail pouch on the front of the hotel and went in search of one of the chairs on the back porch to sit and read.

After dinner she wandered into the kitchen looking for Ruby.

"She and Charlie and Mr. Hegland are out on the porch, figuring on the new addition." Daisy pointed out the back door and to the left.

"I'll wait. I don't want to be a bother." She watched as Daisy washed dishes, then set them in the rinse water. "Could I help you?"

Daisy looked over her shoulder. "Why would you?"

"I need something to do?"

"I don't know about a guest helping."

"Mr. Hegland is."

"Yeah, well . . ." Daisy shook her head. "If you want to help, you are welcome to help. And if Ruby don't think so, she'll tell me." She nodded to a stack of folded white cloths. "Use one of them flour sacks over there. Stack the dishes on the table, and we'll put them away later."

"You have something to drain these on?"

"Guess we could use the baking rack. Under there." She pointed to the lower portion of a counter.

Pearl set the rack over the reservoir and lifted the dishes from the rinse water to drain. Then she began drying them. The two fell into an easy rhythm, the clatter and swish a pleasant sound.

"Who's singing?" Pearl asked after she'd enjoyed the sound for a bit.

"Ah, that's Opal. Has a voice like an angel, she has. She's going to sing a solo on Sunday. First time she's done that. Belle's been coaching her."

"How wonderful. I hear Opal's been the schoolteacher here."

"And a good job she has done too. I couldn't read a lick, and neither could Milly. Now we both can, and I can add and subtract too. You'll be the teacher come fall?"

"Yes, but you know, we could start earlier if some of you want more help."

"You would do that?" Daisy stopped washing for a moment and looked at Pearl. "Why?"

"Why not? I have the time, and there is nothing more exciting to me than to watch people learn something new."

"Well, I'll be switched. What would we learn about?"

"Oh, read more difficult things, learn to multiply and divide, learn history, geography, science."

"Just like in a school."

"Just like."

"Someday if I get married and have children, I want them to go to school right from the first. Not be dumb like their mother."

"Oh, Daisy, you aren't dumb. You just didn't get a chance to learn these things. But the first time you got an opportunity, you took it. Now that's the sign of a smart woman."

"You don't know the half of it. Why, before Ruby came—"

Pearl was surprised when Daisy cut off her reminiscence, but she just kept on drying dishes.

Daisy took the dishpan outside and dumped the wash water on the roses, then moved the rinse water to use for washing, and carved curls of soap from the bar into the dishpan.

"You can refill this pan with clean water from the reservoir

191

to rinse with. Use the teakettle too."

Never had Pearl seen so many dishes. Never had she dried so many dishes. The servants always did those things. Sometimes she had helped in the kitchen, but she'd asked for the privilege. While setting more plates on the table, she stopped for a second in midset. What if they didn't like her as a teacher? What could she do to earn a living if her father cut off her allowance?

She put a hand to her throat, her chin. She, who had always seen her scar as a horrible disfigurement, suddenly realized there were far worse things that could happen. What would she do? Could she do the work these women seemed to take for granted?

I could always be a governess. The thought brought instant relief.

"Thanks for helping." Daisy threw out the final dishpan of water, but when Pearl lifted the rinse pan to follow her, she shook her head. "No, we will use that one for dishes tonight. When you have to haul all your water, you learn to use everything more than once."

Another lesson that showed the gulf between her life now and her former one. And here she'd thought that having only one servant if she married Mr. Longstreet would have been a hardship.

Charlie walked into the kitchen. "Sorry, I got busy. We'd best put off going out to visit till tomorrow." At the question on her face, he continued, "It's too far out to the Robertsons when we need to be here to serve supper."

"Oh." *Pearl, here's another example of your lack of knowledge.* "How far would their children have to come for school?"

"Four to five miles. They'll ride in on horseback unless the weather is real bad. Then they'll stay home."

"I see. And how many children have to come from such distances?"

"Oh, the Robertson girls, five of them, and the children that belong to those sodbusters north of town. You'll see them all Sunday when we have church here."

"At the hotel?"

"In the dining room."

"I see." She seemed to be saying that a lot lately. She certainly had a lot of seeing to do.

That night at supper Ruby stopped by her table. "I'm running out of tables. Could I bring someone to join you?"

"Why, of course. I could eat in the kitchen if you'd like."

"No, but thanks for the offer." Ruby returned in a minute with Carl Hegland in tow.

"Miss Hossfuss, I'd like you to meet Mr. Hegland. I think the two of you have a lot in common, seeing that you both love to read."

"Miss Hossfuss." Carl nodded.

"Mr. Hegland." Pearl nodded back. And that was the last the two said to each other the entire meal.

When he was finished eating, Carl stood. "Thank you for the pleasure."

She nodded again. "Tusen takk."

His eyes lit up, and a smile showed what nice teeth he had. "Ja."

Pearl watched him leave. Was he running away from her or from people in general?

CHAPTER TWENTY-FOUR

"Easy, Buck." Rand stepped out of the saddle and flipped Buck's reins over the hitching rail before knotting to the rail the lead rope of the horse he'd brought in. The saddle he'd dug out needed work, and that's what he planned to do now as he untied a roll of tanned cowhide he'd brought from the ranch, just in case.

"Hey, Mr. Harrison. You brought in another horse." Opal leaped from the top porch step and bounded out to the rail.

"No, really, oh, he must have followed me in." He enjoyed hearing Opal laugh at his jokes. Unfettered and free, her laugh sparkled its way above the trees and danced on the breeze.

"What are you going to do with that hide?"

"Repair the saddle. See, it needs new leathers for the stirrups, and the strap on the cinch looks like a mouse has been gnawing on it."

"You can fix it?"

"Sure. You want to help?"

"Do I have to chew the hide?" She kept her face without expression, poker-faced one might say, but her eyes laughed, crinkling slightly at the corners.

He knew she was referring to his comments on an earlier visit about Indian women chewing the hide to soften it. "Nope, this time we want the leather solid, not soft. In fact, if we had a sewing machine here, I'd sew strips together to make them stronger. Now, we could sew them by drilling holes with an awl, threading sinew in a bone needle, and whipstitching the sides."

"Sounds like a lot of work. Do we have to?"

"Nope, that's the kind of thing Beans does in the winter in front of the fire. He has a whole barrelful of patience."

"Not me. I don't like to sew at all. And we don't have to punch holes first." While she talked, she stroked the new horse's shoulder. "What's his name?"

"Baldy."

"Why?"

"That was his name when I got him. He's pretty old, but he's careful with his feet and not flighty, so he should do well for around here. Just don't go shooting off him, makes him shy away."

"Good to know. I'll leave my guns to home."

This time it was Rand's turn to laugh. "You know, you are one sharp kid."

"She's a young lady, Mr. Harrison, not a *kid*." Emphasis of disgust layered the last word. Unbeknownst to him, Ruby had stepped out onto the porch.

Rand wanted to roll his eyes, but he kept his face masked. "And a right good day to you too, Miss Torvald. Meet your new mount. His name is Baldy."

"Now Bay won't be so lonesome that she has to go talk with Mr. Johnson's cow."

"Horses are herd animals, as are cattle. They like company. How about we set this business up on the porch? I'll need a chunk of wood to pound these rivets home on."

"How big?" Opal asked.

"Broad enough so it won't tip over."

She scampered off to the woodpile and brought back an unsplit butt.

"That's good." Rand pulled a chair over and laid out his tools. "You want to go get the saddle off old Baldy there?"

"So, how was the roundup?" Ruby asked while they waited for Opal to return.

Rand folded the hide in three and pulled his knife out of the sheath attached to his belt. "I need a straight edge. You have a board of some kind?"

"Charlie's square. Would that be all right?" Opal said as she set the saddle down.

"He and Mr. Hegland are working on the other side of the hotel."

Rand looked up at Ruby. "Roundup went right well. Didn't lose as many to winterkill as I'd feared, and found a bunch had wandered clear over to the Circle H. Brought 'em back when we did theirs."

"That far?"

"Yep. Perhaps something spooked them. Sometimes they get driven by a heavy wind." He laid the square Opal offered on the hide. "Hold that end."

Opal clamped down on the metal as he made a cut the length of the hide.

"Right through all three thicknesses." Opal looked up, hero worship pinking her cheeks.

"You want to do the next one?"

"Sure." She took the knife, held down the square, and could barely saw through one layer, let alone three. "You made it look easy."

"Push harder and keep going. You can do one layer at a time like that, just keep working at it." He returned to the roundup. "Funniest thing, the same old cow as last year wasn't goin' to let us brand her calf. She near to hooked Joe this time. I never saw him run so fast. 'Course Chaps never helped him at all. He was laughin' so hard he near fell off his horse." He glanced up to see Ruby watching Opal, locking her hands behind her back to keep from helping her little sister. When she looked at him, he gave her a nod and a smile.

"I'll get something for us to drink."

Were her cheeks pink? Or was it just the heat?

By the time they had the saddle fixed, most everyone had gathered on the back porch, drinking lemonade, eating cookies, and then cheering Opal as she rode Baldy for the first time.

Opal walked, jogged, and loped the horse around the pasture, with Bay jogging along for a time.

"How's the saddle?" Rand asked when she returned to the mounting block Charlie had moved into place.

"I like bareback better, but it's all right. Come on, Ruby, you ride him."

"No thanks. I'm not dressed for it; besides I do not want an audience when I try riding again."

"Okay. Milly, you want to ride?"

"Oh yes." She mounted, tried to cover as much of her bare legs as possible with her skirt, and followed Opal to where she let down the bars of the gate.

Opal climbed up the second rail and swung aboard Bay, using the end of the horse's mane.

"She doesn't have a bridle." Ruby started off the porch.

"She rides all the time without a bridle." Cimarron caught her before the first step. "She and Bay are best friends. You don't need to worry."

"But . . ." Ruby clamped her arms across her chest. She watched as Bay listened to Opal sing, ears flicking back and forth. She stood by the fence, watching the other horse, and when Opal leaned forward to hug the mare, Bay turned her head and nuzzled Opal's extended hand.

"See, what did I tell you."

Ruby relaxed arms that had tightened when Opal leaned forward. "How could that happen so fast?"

"They just were meant for each other." Cimarron reached for another cookie. "I had a horse like that once. He followed me everywhere. Called him Prince."

"What happened to him?"

"I dunno. I think my pa sold him when I left home. He wasn't a good workhorse, and they needed the money." She took a bite of the cookie. "Sure was a good horse."

"You can ride Baldy any time you want." Ruby wanted to go hug Cimarron. So many things had been lost in her life. If only they could find a good man for her, one who could overlook her past.

Jed Black ambled around the corner from where he was helping Charlie and Carl. He stopped beside Cimarron and smiled down at her.

Feeling someone watching her, Ruby turned and caught Rand's gaze. Could he tell what she'd been thinking?

"You ever ridden a horse?" Cimarron asked Pearl.

"No, and I don't really care to. I mean, it isn't necessary that I learn to ride, is it?"

Ruby shook her head. "I rode for the first time last summer, and if I could do it, anyone can. As someone"—she stared pointedly at Rand—"once told me, there's a lot of places in this area you can't get to with a wagon. Horses are easier than walking."

Rand nodded. "You learned well. And now you have a horse to ride again. Perhaps you will even make it out to the ranch one day."

"Perhaps." Why was it that man could fluster her with only a look? And why did she always want to argue with him? "Think we better be getting supper started. Rand, you staying?"

"If I'm invited."

"The invitation is always open."

That man, he can drive me crazy faster than anyone I've known in all my life. Ruby slammed the cutting board down on the table and took out a knife that needed sharpening. She found the whetstone, dampened it, and was sharpening the knife when Rand walked through the door.

"Can I help you with that?"

"You think I can't even sharpen my own knife?"

Rand sighed and rolled his eyes. "I just offered to help. I'm a good knife sharpener."

"Oh. Well, all right." She handed him both knife and stone.

"You have others that need sharpening?"

"I guess." Why did she feel this conversation had more to do with something other than sharpening knives? And why couldn't she just be grateful?

While he sharpened, she went down in the cellar where it was cool for the ham. Tonight they were having fried sliced ham and would save any leftovers for breakfast.

After supper the girls would be practicing for church in the morning. Come to think of it, she hadn't seen Belle all day. She plunked the ham on the table, panting a bit since it was a whole haunch.

"Would you like me to slice that since Charlie is still working outside?"

"Please." *All right, Rand Harrison, why are you being so nice?*

"Why don't you like Jed Black?"

That did it! So much for being nice. She spun around as if to attack, saw what she could only construe as concern in his eyes, and felt herself wilt like a pulled-up flower in the sun.

None of your business was a possible answer. *I don't* another. And *what do you mean* a third. She shook her head. "I can't tell you" hadn't been on her list, but it was what she said.

"Oh. He did something to offend you?"

Please, someone, anyone, come in here and interrupt.

She'd read a line one time in a romance, *"His eyes caressed her face."* Now she knew what it meant. Her skin tingled as if he had grazed it with a fingertip.

"But . . ." Where had her breath gone? "But he apologized, and all is right now."

"I see."

She could tell he didn't. But then, she didn't either. She'd asked God to help her feel as if she forgave Jed Black, but so far—nothing.

"Well, Rand Harrison, you going to be playing tonight?" Belle stopped in the doorway to the stairs.

Never had she been more pleased to see Belle. "I didn't see you all day. Are you feeling all right?"

"Sure, I guess. Just took a long nap this afternoon is all. That way I'll be in fine form tonight, so be prepared to lose, cowboy."

"Now, Belle, you wouldn't want to keep my hard-earned money. I came more for the social time than to lose money. We're practicing tonight, correct?"

Belle nodded. "Where is everyone? Out back?"

Daisy and Cimarron came through the back door one after the other.

"Sure will be glad when the potatoes are ready. The peas are almost there."

"I'll make the biscuits tonight," Cimarron said. "Hey, Rand, you look good slicing ham. Thank you." She tied her apron back on. "The breeze is coming up. Smells like it might be rain." She gathered her hair in a rope and looped it around before pinning it back again in a bun. "There, that's better."

When had she taken it down? In time to be seen and appreciated by Jed Black?

"Cimarron." Ruby leaned close to whisper. "I need to talk with you after the practice tonight, okay?"

"Fine."

Ruby glanced up at the feel of Rand's gaze on her again. He was the last person, other than Opal, she wanted eavesdropping on that coming conversation.

"May I sit here?" Rand asked Pearl and Carl after most of the guests were seated and the meal was coming out of the kitchen.

Pearl looked up with a smile. "Of course. You have met Mr. Hegland?"

Carl looked up from pouring his coffee into the saucer to cool and greeted Rand with a nod.

"Looks like you've been busy making new beds."

"Ja, until Wainwright comes back, and I go to work for him."

"I thought he was to be back by now."

"He is late, a week late." Carl sipped from his saucer, realized the other two were not doing so, and poured the cooled coffee back into the cup. "Excuse me."

"And how are you enjoying Little Missouri, Miss Hossfuss?" Rand asked.

"It is certainly different from Chicago."

"You have plenty of cattle there too."

"In the stockyards." She glanced up at Daisy, who set plates before them. "Thank you. This looks delicious."

Rand turned to Mr. Hegland. "So, Carl, what brought you out here?"

"The advertisement said they were in need of carpenters here. I needed a job, so I came."

"I see."

When the conversation came to a dead stop, Pearl got things started again. "And you, Mr. Harrison, how is the ranching coming? I heard you had a roundup. I am not certain what that means."

"That's when we go out and bring all the cattle in to brand the calves so the owners know which is theirs. We check for health things and count the cattle. Since we have open range here, the cattle wander wherever they want."

"So you do not feed them?"

"No. There is plenty of grass for grazing and rivers to drink from."

"And in the winter?"

"The valley is protected with plenty of forage and water. That's what makes this such a perfect place for raising cattle."

The conversation lagged again. Rand watched as Carl ate his meal without looking up or saying another word. He hadn't seemed surly outside. Was he just shy?

"Mr. Hegland, I saw you reading earlier," Miss Hossfuss said. "What book are you reading?"

He looked up. "John Donne's poetry."

"He is a magnificent writer. You brought books with you?"

"Ja, three."

She waited for a moment before asking, "And they are. . . ?"

"My Bible, John Donne, and Goethe."

"I brought books with me too. You are welcome to borrow them if you want."

"Mange—er, thank you."

"I speak Norwegian. My father came from Norway when he was a boy."

Carl laid his fork and knife on the edge of his plate. "I was born here."

Rand finished his meal and laid his napkin on the table. "I enjoyed talking with you. Excuse me, please."

He passed Charlie on the way into the kitchen and said, "If she can get that man talking, more power to her."

— ❧ —

Practice went well, with Opal gaining in confidence each time she sang. The others hummed in harmony while she sang the verses and then joined her on the chorus.

"Sounds mighty good," Charlie said when they finished. "Opal, I had no idea you could sing like that."

"Me neither."

The sound of clapping came from the corner.

Ruby glanced over there to see Jed Black laying his hands back in his lap. She turned to her sister. "Do you have enough copies of our hymns, Opal?"

"I think so. We're going to use some from before. I've been collecting them at the end of the services."

"I could help copy those," Pearl said. "What time is church?"

"Ten o'clock. That gives us time to clean up after breakfast." Opal tapped the pages on the piano and lined them up even. "We have church every two weeks."

Ruby beckoned to Cimarron and led the way to the darkened kitchen. "I really need to talk with you."

"Let's go outside. With that storm coming the mosquitoes won't be so bad." They stepped out to a gusting breeze that tossed their skirts and teased their hair.

Cimarron sat down in the rocker she'd used before. "Ah, my favorite time. I have always loved storms."

Ruby pulled another chair close. How to begin. "Cimarron, you know the other day when you asked me why I don't like Jed Black?"

"Yeah."

"And one day you commented on how he has changed?"

"Umm."

"Well, the day I met him, I showed him to his room. He'd been drinking, and he attacked me."

"Oh no."

"Charlie pulled him off before he—But even though he has asked me to forgive him, and I did, I cannot like him or even want him around. All I could think of was you and . . . and . . ."

"I put that behind me."

"I know you have, and I have to tell you how much I admire you for that. How did you do it?"

Cimarron kept her chair creaking comfort. "I asked God to forgive them for me because I didn't think I ever could."

"I think it would be easier if he were gone."

"Maybe, but he sure isn't the man who used to come in here. I kinda like him. He makes me feel like I'm special, and he makes me laugh."

"He promised to never drink again, that it was the liquor that did it. You think you can believe him?"

"When God makes the changes in a person, we stay changed. Look at me, Ruby. You helped change me, but God did the real work."

Ruby sighed, lifting her face to feel the first drops of the cooling rain. "Thanks. I just didn't want you to be hurt again."

"I won't be, not by Jed Black."

Please, God, let it be so. And like Cimarron says, please forgive him for me and help me—help me to like him for Cimarron's sake.

CHAPTER TWENTY-FIVE

"Oh for mercy's sake, leave her alone."

Ruby knew it was Cimarron talking, but to whom?

"She's always dropping something or tripping or . . ." Ruby now recognized Daisy's voice.

"And that's her fault? Those are accidental, not on purpose. She's just a kid after all."

As she'd learned, eavesdropping did not always give a good report. Daisy had to be upset with Milly, seeing as that's who Daisy usually worked with, but no one tried harder than Milly. Ruby heaved a sigh. Since spring had come to put an end to the bickering of winter, the women had been getting along too well for it to last. *Guess I should expect a relapse or two.*

So what to do? Intervene or let them hash it out for themselves? Things usually blew over if left alone long enough.

"I think you owe her an apology." Cimarron's voice again.

"All right." The door slammed against the wall on opening. Daisy was not in a good mood. "That Cimarron thinks she always knows better than anyone else." The mutter continued as she grabbed the handle for the flatirons, slammed one into place, and took off for the storeroom and the never ending stack of ironing, without even acknowledging Ruby's presence.

They needed someone else to help iron—that was for sure. Ruby was amazed that she had not received a single inquiry in response to her advertisements in the spring. Well, they would just have to make do. She'd ask one of the other girls to help carry the load—or Opal, maybe. A second ironing board was on her list for Charlie to make. Perhaps Carl could get to it sooner. She was beginning to hope Mr. Wainwright never would come back.

He arrived that day on the westbound train.

"Still have a room for me, Miss Torvald?"

"You're getting the last one. Starting tomorrow I'll have two rooms with two sets of bunks in each, so four to a room. I'll be raising the single room rates then too."

"To how much?" He signed his name in the register. "I might have to go live in a tent if you go too high."

"Two dollars a day." She felt guilty even saying the rate. While she'd charged that and more to really wealthy customers, Mr. Wainwright was more like a regular.

"I'll pay that and gladly, though I'll have to set up a tent for an office until I get something built. Charlie said you have a carpenter here waiting for a job?"

"His name is Carl Hegland from Minneapolis, and he's been working here until you came back." She leaned closer to the counter and whispered, "Thanks for being late. He got the beds made for the hotel, and he and some others are closing in part of the porch for a kind of bunkhouse."

"Good idea. Which room is mine?"

"Number seven." She watched him carry his bags up the stairs. *I wonder if he is married? Perhaps he would like to meet Miss Hossfuss. Ruby Torvald, stop your matchmaking.*

Opal, Milly, and Charlie were back from serving food to those on the train, as usual with nothing left.

"You know, we've been going to build a stand over there for months and just never got around to it. Maybe now with Carl here—" He stopped when he saw Ruby shaking her head.

"You saw Mr. Wainwright get off the train, didn't you? I'm sure Mr. Hegland will start over there tomorrow or the next day."

"That's good for him and not so good for us. But Jed is doing a fine job too, and—Now don't you go getting on your high horse. That man would walk on burning coals for you."

"But—"

"But you said you forgave him. Now it's time to act like it."

"Charlie, you just don't understand."

"Maybe not, bein' as I ain't a woman, but I been beat up far worse'n you were, and life's too short to bear a grudge like that. Like the Bible says, you can't let bitterness grow."

Am I doing that? Am I really bitter toward him? Hateful? Lord, on one hand I want to love you with my whole heart like you ask, but . . . but to love the neighbor as myself is really hard to do. Not most of the time, but in this instance. How am I supposed to love a man who . . . who . . . ?

Let me love him through you. She almost turned around to look over her shoulder the voice was so clear. Let me love him through you. How would that work?

"I know you'll work it out." Charlie patted her shoulder and headed on out to where the sound of hammering and sawing announced that men were working—on her hotel and not costing her a cent.

If this was a way God was providing for her, she should indeed be thankful. And grateful. After all, she'd asked for an addition, and here she was getting it.

By fall she'd need more blankets and quilts. Right now, sheets and ticking filled with dried grass would be enough.

"Ruby, can I . . . er . . . may I and Milly go riding after dinner?" Opal asked.

"Are the rooms all clean?"

"Far as I know."

"And the garden weeded?"

"Mister Black has been doing that."

I know I should send her in to iron, but . . . "You can't be gone for hours and hours, but you haven't been fishing lately, and a mess of fish for supper sure would be good."

"Good, we'll ride up to that fishing hole the captain took us to."

"You be—"

"Ruu-by."

"All right. I won't say it. But be sure to wear your hat. Your nose is not only freckled but sunburned most of the time." She tapped her little sister on the nose. "If you want to go now, we'll manage dinner without you. There aren't too many folks here for that today."

"Good!" Opal spun out of the kitchen. "Gotta get some worms. Milly, we're goin' fishing."

Ruby found Pearl out on the back porch sitting in the rocker reading. "So did you get a chance to meet all your future pupils after church yesterday?"

"I think so. I'm amazed that there aren't more children here in town."

"I know. It's strange, but it's like only loners settled here. I have no idea what their pasts are like. They aren't really sociable, but through some of the things we've done here at the hotel, people get together. Last year we had a big Fourth of July celebration—rodeo, dance, and barbeque."

"Barbeque?"

"They roasted half a steer on a spit with a crank that turned it over coals. Mr. Harrison took care of that. The cantonment sent men to serve and clean up afterward. The dance was right out in the street here."

"And now you have worship services here."

"We also did a small party at Christmas." Ruby wished she could tell Pearl what Dove House had been before, but what if she then treated the girls like the rest of the town did?

But what if someone told her and didn't get it all right? *I hate keeping secrets!*

After a dinner that kept them all running because Charlie was working with the men on the addition and Opal and Milly were gone, Cimarron took up her mending, and Daisy returned to her ironing. Ruby sat down on the back porch with ink and paper to catch what breeze she could. She had some thinking to do.

Pearl brought her book out but seemed content to read and not visit.

Ruby set out columns of figures, added and subtracted this way and that, all to figure if she could afford to close the cardroom. She checked the takes, estimated increased income due to the new beds, figured the additional supplies needed. She reviewed her ledger. Now that she'd been keeping it for over a year, it held solid information about the financial life of the hotel.

If she had the increased income from both cardroom and extra lodgers, she could be banking a tidy sum. If, if, if.

"Is there something I can help you with?" Pearl asked, laying her book down.

"Ah, not really. Why?"

"I heard you sigh and groan. Sounded disturbing to me."

Ruby put the cork back in her ink. "I'm just trying to make some wise financial decisions regarding Dove House, and trying to see into the future to plan is not easy."

"I would assume that if all of Marquis de Mores's dreams for this area happen, you are sitting on a gold mine here."

"That *if* is the stumbling block."

"I meant it when I said I would rather have a room in the attic than take away a paying room for you."

"Thank you. We need to get some more walls built up there. Right now Opal and I share a room. Milly, Cimarron, and Daisy share another, and Charlie has his own. There is room up there for more of the same."

"Another project for Mr. Hegland?"

"Probably not. De Mores's construction superintendent arrived back today. You might meet him at supper. I'm sure he'll be taking the men away immediately."

"Not Charlie."

Ruby felt her mouth drop open. "I . . . ah . . . I sure do hope not. Guess I better ask him. The pay would be far more than he gets here." A good part of his money also came from the cardroom when it was busy enough to need a second dealer, another of those arrangements she'd made when she was forced to take over Dove House. *Of course, Far, just take care of "the girls." Such a heavy commitment you extracted from me. If I had known . . .* She didn't bother to complete the comment. When one's father is on his deathbed, what daughter wouldn't promise whatever he asked?

I need to talk all this over with Charlie. But when? He's working harder than any of us. She closed her papers in her ledger and followed the sound of hammers and saws around the corner. The outer walls were up and the window from the pantry was installed. Instead of a door at each end, there was one door to the outside and another cut through the wall of the cardroom. She stood in the doorway and watched as Mr. Hegland measured a board, Jed Black hammered one in place, and Charlie laid another board on the sawhorses. The three worked well together, with Mr. Hegland giving quiet directions.

Charlie stopped on his way out the door when he saw her. "Lookin' good, isn't it?"

"I'm amazed at the amount you've gotten done."

"That Hegland, he knows his stuff."

"When you have a few minutes, I need to talk some things over with you."

"Sure enough. How about after supper?"

"Good." She'd rather it had been right then, but she didn't want to slow progress either.

— ❦ —

Everyone ate their fill of fried fish for supper, leaving only nibbles for the cats. Cat announced her displeasure and cuffed one of her kittens when he tried to take a piece from her.

"We should have fried the heads for her." Opal stroked Cat's back.

"Charlie snagged those for his garden fast as I cut them off." Cimarron worked a fishbone to the front of her mouth and tongued it into her hand. "No matter how hard I try to get them all when I peel back the spine, there's always one. Opal, you and Milly need to go fishing more often."

"It sure is easier when we have two horses. A fish took the first worm before it hit the water. Finally put grasshoppers on, and the fish liked them too."

Ruby watched the exchange, remembering the afternoon she and Opal spent with Captain McHenry fishing in that hole. She'd never ridden so far, had never been fishing in her life, and never thought she'd have such a good time at it either. *Wonder how the captain is?* followed the memory. She didn't remember the last time she'd written him, and she hadn't prayed for his safety lately. If she was honest, she'd hardly prayed for anything beyond the hotel and what to do next. How to work it all in was another one of those deep questions to which there seemed to be no answers.

When Mr. Hegland asked to see her, she knew she wasn't going to like it.

"I'm sorry, Miss Torvald, I won't be able to finish your addition. Mr. Wainwright has hired me to work on the house."

"I knew he would."

"I thought maybe I could help here on Sundays, but I think Jed and Charlie can finish up."

"If you would help on Sundays, I would be grateful. Thank you for all you managed to accomplish."

"Ah, about the room. I can sleep for free over in Medora in a tent, but I really like it here. Could we work something out?"

"Of course." Ruby thought a minute. "If you took one of the bunk beds and paid three dollars a week, would that be fair?"

"And I work on Sundays? Ja." He nodded. "That would work."

"Good luck with your new job."

"Mange takk."

Now to find Charlie.

"The peas are ready," he announced when she found him in the garden.

"Will there be enough for canning?"

"Not this first picking, but I can't think of anything better for dinner than creamed peas and new potatoes with ham and biscuits."

"Me neither." She found a plump pod, picked it, sliced it open with her thumbnail, and plopped the peas in her mouth, closing her eyes the better to savor the delight. Peas were best eaten right out of the garden. Forget the cooking.

"You wanted to talk with me?"

"I do."

"Something wrong?" He handed her another pea pod and opened one himself.

"No, just trying to make some decisions."

She chewed the peas with a smile of gratitude. "Let's go to the cardroom. I need a table. We can shut the door there."

Once she had her ledger and papers laid out, she explained her ideas, showed him her estimations, and then leaned back while he studied on them.

When he looked up, she asked. "Well, what do you think?"

"So the key question is, do we close the cardroom?"

"And turn it into a schoolroom."

"It could be both, school during the day, cards at night." Charlie leaned back in his chair, setting the legs to screeching.

"I guess the main question I have is, what about Belle?"

"Belle will always land on her feet, just like Cat. Wouldn't surprise me if she has something else already cookin'."

"What makes you say that?" *Do you have something else going on too, Charlie?*

"Just a feelin' I have."

"What about you? If we close the cardroom, a good part of your money goes too."

"Naa, not enough to worry about. Look at me. What more do I need? Got a roof over my head, food in my belly, people I care about, money to jingle in my pocket if I want."

"How about a wife, some children, a home of your own?"

He shook his head. "I don't think so. Too ugly and too late in life."

"Ha! Daisy would marry you in a heartbeat."

"Daisy? Really?" He stared at her over templed fingertips. "Hmm."

She watched the expression float like clouds across his face. A tiny smile, a headshake, a stroking of his mustache, another smile, this time along with a bit of a grunt. "Well, I'll be."

"I thought you cared for Cimarron."

"Cimarron is a good friend, easy on the eyes, but too feisty for my blood."

Now to ask a question she knew was beyond propriety, and yet she needed to hear a man's opinion on it.

"Is it because of what happened to her?"

"Ruby Torvald, sometimes you make me wonder if you are only naïve or stupid too." He used an expletive, something he only did when frustrated beyond measure. "No. Is that clear enough for you?"

"Yes, but the way the women in this town carry on, I was getting to the point of thinking everyone thought the way they do—that because of what she used to be, no decent man would ever want her. Cimarron thinks that too." There, she got it all out.

"Well, for me, it don't matter. I can't answer for other folks.

But I know Jed Black knows of the former lives of the girls, and he don't care none either."

"He keeps looking at Cimarron."

Charlie wore a here-we-go-again pained look. "And she looks at him, and you look at Rand, and he looks at you, and—"

"I think we need to go back to the subject of the cardroom."

"I think we need to think on this a whole lot more before you make any decisions."

"All right." She stood. "Thank you, Charlie, but I have one more question."

"Are either one of us going to be embarrassed by it?"

Me, most likely. She could already feel the flush starting up her neck. "Does Rand . . . Mr. Harrison really look at me like . . . like . . ."

At his mighty guffaw she darted out of the room as if a prairie fire were licking at her heels. The way her face felt, she might well be facing a wall of fire.

CHAPTER TWENTY-SIX

"Can you hold off on shipping those beeves until the abattoir is ready?" The marquis sat across the table at Dove House from Rand one late-July night.

"I'd like to oblige, but you see, I need money to run my ranch. We need to eat, hands need to be paid." *I'm not like you, bankrolled by men backed by banks and old family money.*

"I'll be paying premium prices. That's better than you'll get after shipping them."

"I understand that. I'll have more to ship next year."

"How many head?"

"Around seven hundred. Going to ship three-fifty to four hundred this fall." Last year he'd sold a hundred head, including some of the feeders that he'd bought from a man in Kansas at the same time he'd bought his two hundred cows. Paid out every dime he could get his hands on back then. Good thing one could live real cheap out here, mostly off the land like the Indians did. Sometimes he wondered if they would be able to keep the wolf from the door. Although if a wolf came to the door, Beans would most likely stew it and tan the hide. Wolf pelt was known to be real warm in the winter.

He watched the man across the table. Something about him caught in his craw. He pushed back from the table. "Sorry we can't do business this year. We'll see about next. Good luck on Medora."

"You ever need work, you go on over and talk with my superintendent. He's looking for good men."

Rand nodded. *In a pig's eye.* He wandered on out to inspect the new addition. Once it was finished and painted, it would look like it was built at the same time as the building. Carl Hegland was indeed a good carpenter.

Maybe someday he could hire him to help with a bigger house on the ranch. And a real barn. Not that the bull needed any more shelter, but who knew what would be happening, the way changes were already coming into the territory.

"So what do you think?" Ruby stood at the railing on the porch behind him.

"I think you're one smart businesswoman, and I hope this really pays off for you."

"Thank you."

He turned to face her, catching a look of surprise. *I think you are beautiful, and I love to see you get all afire, the way you walk and wear your clothes. I hear the sound of your voice on the wind, the hint of a Norwegian accent tinged with New York.*

He watched her face turn pink at his silent stare. *Do you feel the same way I do, whatever it is I feel?*

"I-I better get back to work."

"I thought your work was done for the day."

"There's always more to do."

"Do you ever sit out here and watch the rocks turn to fire, the dusk creep in, and the stars come out one by one, pinpricks against an azure sky?"

"Th-that was beautiful."

"We live in magnificent country. Come riding with me one day. I'll show you swathes of flowers coloring the plains, critters and birds you don't see here in town, and we'll listen to the eagle scree and the prairie wren warble."

Ruby locked her hands behind her back and leaned against a porch post. "How do you see so much?"

"Riding and knowing this land is part of the life of a rancher, just like knowing when the bread is risen enough is part of yours."

"Do you ever wish for something different?"

"Not to live somewhere else. I've found my home here. But

yes, some things I want different." *I want a wife and children, and I want you to be that person.* "What about you?"

She held his gaze, then glanced away.

"See?" He came closer, pointing to the western horizon. "See how that silver rims the rocks from the setting sun behind it? You have to see it quick before it fades away. See how the sky color deepens as you look up and around to the east? How the evening star hangs in the west, so bright even against the lighter sky."

He could feel the heat of her, even without touching. It would take so little to move his hand, only an inch or less. To take her hand . . .

"Ruby?" Opal called from the back door.

"Out here." While they hadn't moved, the moment vanished like a wild thing spooked by the snap of a twig.

She turned slightly and looked up at him. "I would love to go riding with you."

Had her emphasis been on the *with you*?

"Good."

"Ruby, I—Oh, hi Mr. Harrison. I didn't know you were still here."

"Is Buck at the hitching rail?"

"Didn't look." She turned to Ruby. "Can we make taffy?"

"I don't know. Can you?"

Opal sighed, a deep sigh, a dramatic sigh, an "I'm being corrected again" sigh. *"May* we make taffy?"

"Who is we?"

"All of us. Mr. Harrison, you ever pulled taffy?"

"Not for a long time." His stretching the word long, made her giggle.

"You going to play cards?"

"Guess not. Sounds like I'll be pulling taffy."

Ruby stared at him. Even through the dark he could feel it.

"I'm thinking of closing the cardroom." The comment lay like a snake between them.

"So, why are you telling me?"

"I-I want your opinion." She clasped her arms across her chest.

"Does Belle know?"

"Not yet, and I'd appreciate your not telling her. I have to do that."

He nodded, realized she couldn't see his head move and added, "That's only fair."

"What do you think she'll do?"

"Yell and scream and threaten something or other."

"I'm going to offer her a job here."

"As a maid?"

"Ironing."

Rand snorted. "Belle don't like work like that."

"I know, but I don't know what else to do. Wish some man would come and sweep her off her feet, take her west with him or something."

Rand chuckled. "Would make it easy all right. What does Charlie say?"

"He's thinking on it too."

"So you haven't decided for sure yet?"

"Just not the how or when."

"I see."

A burst of laughter came from the kitchen, both male and female.

"Thank you for talking with me."

"You are most welcome." *If you were by some miracle to marry me, what about the hotel?*

CHAPTER TWENTY-SEVEN

I start a new job tomorrow. Carl walked on back to the new addition to make sure he had picked up all his tools. He found a screwdriver under some wood and stuck it in his back pocket. *How will they finish this without my tools?*

He ran a calloused finger over the joints in the trim around the door. While the others could pound nails, they hadn't the skill for trim. Surely there will be time in the evenings to do some of this. Could bring a lamp or two out here.

"There you are." Jed Black paused in the doorway. "You got the job?"

"Ja, start in the morning."

"You think I could get work there?"

"Go ask. They will need many kinds of workers. He will be in the cardroom, I think."

"De Mores?"

"Nei. Wainwright, the superintendent."

Carl watched as the big man ducked out the door. While the doorframe was a little higher than his head, that must be a reflex action.

Carl took one of the chairs on the back porch where he could hear laughing from the kitchen. It sounded like they were having a party in there.

He could go up to his room to read. Or sleep. He could go in and play cards, but since the marquis had come back, the stakes were too high for his blood. He could go for a walk. Restless as he felt, that might be the best idea.

He had started to rise when Opal burst through the back door.

"Hi, Mr. Hegland, you want to come help us pull taffy?"

"I thought to go for a walk."

"You could come help, then go for a walk. Daisy says the syrup is near to ready. Besides, Charlie and Mr. Harrison say men are better taffy pullers than women. What do you think?"

"I never pulled this taffy. What is it?"

"Candy. You pull it until it becomes hard. Tastes really good, but you need a lot of pullers."

Amazed that he found himself following her into the kitchen, he looked around at the laughing people. Immediately he caught Miss Hossfuss's gaze.

With a slight nod, he went to stand in the corner. Surely upstairs reading a book would be better than this.

"All right, everyone find a partner and butter your fingers. Pick up the hot candy and pull slowly and gently until it cools enough to need more. The finished candy will be cream-colored rather than this caramel look." Cimarron glanced around to make sure everyone understood.

Opal stopped in front of him. "You want to be my partner?"

"Ja, that will be good."

"Now remember, don't drop it. This is really sticky stuff." Cimarron turned in time to bump into Jed Black.

"You will be my partner?"

"I-I guess."

"He likes her," Opal whispered to Carl as she pulled their glob of sticky candy from the butter-smeared pan and started to stretch it. "Ouch, it's hot."

Butter running down his fingers, Carl took hold of the glob and pulled, looping it back to Opal when it started to sag.

"Quick." Her giggle made him smile.

"I'm glad to see you here." Ruby made her way over to them with Rand, looping their batch over as they came.

Pearl and Milly scrambled to catch theirs before it hit the floor.

"This would be a fun thing for the schoolchildren to do for

Christmas." Pearl looped the lightening strands again.

"Good. At least now we know how."

"We made taffy every winter and snow candy too." Cimarron and Jed stretched theirs a couple of feet. "You can twist this too." She looped hers back and twisted it, like wringing out sheets.

"Oh no." Daisy grabbed hers up from a quick trip to the floor.

"Just brush it off. It'll be all right."

One by one the pairs pulled and twisted and, as the candy turned light, laid their contributions on the butter-covered pan again.

"As soon as it finishes cooling, we'll whack it into smaller pieces and have us a treat." Cimarron took up the cleaver. "Remember, the slivers are the best part."

Carl found himself standing next to Pearl. She smelled good. He'd noticed that one time at the table but now even more so.

"That was fun," she said.

"Ja, thanks to Opal, I came. Good thing."

Pearl took the wet towel Cimarron handed around and wiped the sticky off her hands. "Here. By the way, I meant it when I said I have books to share if you want something new to read. I just finished *Uncle Tom's Cabin,* by Harriet Beecher Stowe. Have you read it?"

He shook his head. "But I would like to." He looked down, then at her. "That is most generous of you." *She has beautiful eyes.* He'd worked on a building for a man named Hossfuss in Chicago. Could she be related to him, and if so, what was she doing out here in Little Missouri?

Ask her. The sense prompting him sounded more insistent the third time.

"I heard you are from Chicago."

"Yes."

"I worked on a building for a Hossfuss there once."

"Really?"

He wasn't sure if that was a question or a statement. "Ja, he expected good work, used good materials, not cheap, like some I know."

My land, we are actually carrying on a conversation. Do I tell him that is my father? Do I ignore this? "Mr. Hossfuss has several buildings. Which one were you working on?"

"A warehouse down on the docks. One of my first jobs without my father."

"Your father taught you the trade?"

"Ja, he was a good craftsman."

"And your father is still in Chicago?"

"No, he died. I've been living in Minneapolis with my mor, but she went to care for her sister, so I came west."

Pearl stuffed down her apprehension. "I had a falling out with my father, so I came west too." *Ran away from home, but that doesn't sound very grown up.* "Do you like music?"

"Here's some candy." Opal held out the tray, switching the candy in her mouth to the cheek so she could talk.

"Is it good?" Pearl asked.

"Bery." She sucked and got it back in her cheek. "Very."

"So we can say our taffy pulling was a success?" Pearl picked out a piece and laid it on her tongue. "Umm."

Carl had started to turn the offering down but smiled too when the flavor hit his tongue. "Ah, good."

Conversations died as everyone sucked on their candy, but smiles grew and soon giggles.

Charlie came through the swinging door in search of hot coffee for the card players. "Looks like more fun in here." He swapped coffeepots, snagged a bite of taffy from the plate, and waggled his eyebrows as he left the room.

"Ja, I like music, especially fiddles."

Pearl turned back to him, a smile lighting her eyes. "Symphony?"

"Not heard many, but all right."

"Piano?"

"Ja, 'bout anything."

Pearl cast about for more questions, anything to keep him talking. "Do you sing?"

"In church, ja."

"You seem to have a nice voice."

"It don't scare the crows away."

She hesitated for a moment, wanting to laugh but not to hurt his feelings. But when one eyebrow cocked and his eyes twinkled, she let herself chuckle. "That is very good."

"Ja?"

How come he could communicate so much with one word? Laugh at himself, laugh with her, and continue their conversation, all with one word—ja.

How like home. She thought to how hard her father worked to fit in with the other businessmen and society. He had fought to rid himself of his accent, but still the *ja* would happen at times. Were they going to write back? Was she still a member of the family, or had they disowned her?

Where did you go? Did I say something that offended you? Carl watched her eyes, blue with clouds scudding across them.

When she returned to her smile, he breathed a sigh of relief. He liked being around a woman who helped him laugh.

"When will you start teaching?"

"We are talking about having some classes now for adults who need help with their reading and arithmetic. But for the children, we start in early September."

"Where?"

"In the cardroom."

"Not many children?"

"Not yet. Maybe ten or twelve. But more people are arriving, so we shall see. I hope we can have a schoolhouse by next year."

"Ja, if we get the supplies, we can do that."

She enjoyed listening to the sibilant *s*'s, the rhythm of his speech, but even more the tone of his voice. Rich and mellow. She'd be willing to wager that he would be a fine addition to the church choir. Now if only he would come to the practice.

I wonder if our church at home would ship us any old hymnals they have. Or perhaps—the thought made her heart leap—*take this church on as a mission.*

"Good night, Mr. Hegland. You have given me an exciting idea." And what about the school? Wouldn't some of those she knew in Chicago like to help with a frontier school?

CHAPTER TWENTY-EIGHT

August

If Ruby ever saw another empty jar, it might be sooner than she wanted. August could most appropriately be called canning and drying month. With the garden in full production and the wild fruits bursting off the branches, they made chokecherry jam, jelly, and juice; crabapple pickles, butter, and jelly; cucumber pickles and relish; canned peas; canned, dried, and pickled beans and corn; canned, jellied, jammed, and dried strawberries, raspberries, and June berries. They also canned, smoked, and dried fish, venison, rabbit, and grouse.

"We won't go hungry come winter. That's for certain," Ruby said, stretching, then retying her apron strings.

"I think we'd can a polecat if we could catch it." Cimarron stared at the jars ready to move down into the cellar as soon as Charlie finished putting up more shelves. A person could hardly turn around down there as it was.

In the fall they would move carrots, parsnips, turnips, rutabagas, and potatoes into the bins, covering some with sand to keep them fresh. They'd buy barrels of apples to store and can applesauce and apple pie mix, and make apple butter from the peelings. Anything that couldn't be used would go back into the ground out in the garden.

Cornstalks and shucks from the cobs were dried for pallets, and thanks to the abundant waterfowl, they had down and feathers to stuff in quilts, pillows, and feather beds.

"We're going to need an entire room for a linen closet pretty soon." Daisy stacked ironed pillowcases on a shelf. With the hotel full all the time now and all the new beds, due to the addition and the bunk beds, they were no longer buying sheeting and hemming their own. Ruby had found a supplier and ordered what they needed.

Late one afternoon a squad of soldiers rode into town, including Private Adam Stone. When he walked in the front door, Milly burst into tears, then threw herself into his arms. When they returned from a long walk after supper, she glowed brighter than the rising sun.

— ❧ —

"I have a surprise for you," Ruby announced the next morning. "It should come on today's train."

"What?" Opal rolled her eyes. "I know, if you told us, it wouldn't be a surprise."

Ruby tweaked her little sister's nose.

"Can we eat it?"

"Not likely."

"Good, that means we don't have to can it."

Everyone chuckled at the look of relief on Opal's face.

"Come on, honeybun, you at least get to go fishing." Cimarron dumped the bread dough out on a floured board and began kneading. "Tonight we go shoot grouse, so don't be gone too long." Now that the young were full grown, they were going to shoot the roosting grouse out of the trees. Cimarron was such a clean shot that she could get a dozen or so before the other grouse in the tree got restless and started fluttering away. Opal and Milly then picked up the dead birds, and back at the hotel, plucked the breast feathers and cleaned them before stuffing pillows or feather beds. Baked grouse had become a favorite meal at Dove House.

"Wish you'd teach me to shoot." Opal propped her chin up with both hands.

"I will if Ruby approves. I think every woman should be able to shoot as well as a man. You never know what kind of critters you might meet up with in this country. The ranchers use two rifle shots in quick succession as a call for help. Many lives have been saved that way."

Ruby continued to roll out sour-cream cookie dough. She often wondered if Cimarron wished she'd had a gun the day she was attacked. Should she let Opal learn to shoot? Should she herself learn to shoot? Did she want to learn? Not in this lifetime. But Opal did, so why should she let her feelings keep Opal from learning something she wanted? Besides, they could have been practicing without her knowledge, but Cimarron refrained. The inner argument waged back and forth. Should she, shouldn't she? It made such good sense. Opal was too little. Besides, they didn't have a gun, other than Charlie's. She looked to her little sister who was leaning forward, almost panting in her eagerness. "I'm sorry, Opal, but I just can't give you permission to shoot a gun. Not yet. How about next summer?"

Opal shrugged, a frown wrinkling her face. "How come I'm never big enough for the fun stuff, but I'm big enough to clean rooms and help can?"

"Good question. One I suspect every child since Cain and Abel has asked at one time or another," Pearl, who had agreed to help with chores for her room and board, said with a nod. "I know my brother did."

"And you too?" Opal asked.

"No, I was always the good child."

"Is it bad to want to do new things?"

"No, no, of course not. But some people are more adventurous than others."

"Am I adventurous?" Opal looked around the group who had all burst out laughing. "Does that mean yes?"

Ruby tried to stem a chuckle and had to cough on it. "Opal, dear, you were born adventuring. Bestemor could never keep up with you. Said you turned all her hair gray overnight."

"I didn't."

"Nope, but you have to admit—"

"Let's not tell any of those stories, okay? I haven't broken anything for a l-o-n-g time."

"I know." *And for that I am exceedingly grateful.* The last thing Opal had been called on the carpet for was a visit to Belle's room and the demise of a perfume bottle. The whole building had been odoriferous for a week. Belle's room still wore a fancy smell in spite of the cigarillo smoke.

"You know, when I learn to shoot, besides doing the fishing, maybe I could bag rabbits too."

"All you need for that is snares like Charlie uses. Don't waste bullets on rabbits." Daisy joined the conversation as she exchanged flatirons. She set hers on the stove and went to dip water out of the bucket. Wetting the cloth draped around her neck, she took a hot iron back to her ironing board.

"You better get your trays ready," Ruby cautioned as she retrieved change for them from the buksbom, a carved wooden box of her father's where she kept the money. Since no one had had time to build a stand over at the train stop, Milly and Opal still carried wooden trays of sandwiches, cookies, hard-boiled eggs, and cheese. Whoever could get away, usually Charlie, carried the two-gallon coffeepot.

When they returned, handed in their money, put away the trays, and washed the cups, Milly went out to dig worms for the fishing expedition. With so many of those staying at the hotel working over in Medora, dinner guests were few. Supper, however, was another string of fish. They needed to bring plenty back.

"We have to get more help." Ruby took another rack of canned carrots from the boiler. She'd thought of setting up an outdoor kitchen on the back porch, but thinking and doing usually didn't even inhabit the same house. She'd read that in the south they had summer kitchens in order to keep all the kitchen heat from making the house uncomfortable. While she needed Milly's and Opal's hands, they also needed fish. And the two girls needed to be girls once in a while. Not that fishing was a socially approved occupation for young girls, but as the months passed, Ruby's strictures for proper society had slipped. Manners yes, society, like tightly laced corsets or any corsets for that matter, no.

Pearl came in from snapping beans outside. "This finishes this picking. Are the jars ready yet?"

Ruby pointed to the lineup on the boards set over sawhorses for extra counter space.

"You want me to go ahead and fill them?"

"Might as well. Once we get them on, I think we all need a break." She took the last pan of cookies from the oven. "Cimarron, let's use that custard mix for pies for supper. Since we have to keep the stove hot anyway, might as well continue using the oven too."

"It's going to cool off. There's thunderheads north of here."

By the time they took their cold tea out on the porch, the breeze had sprung up.

"Ah, that's wonderful." Pearl fanned herself with a piece of paper.

"There some reason you wear such a high collar all the time? Seems would be mighty hot." Cimarron glanced around to make sure no men were in sight and hiked her skirt up to her knees.

"It is hot. . . ." Pearl said nothing more.

Ruby watched her, sensing the struggle going on within her friend. While she'd noticed what might be a scar or something barely peeping out above the fabric, she'd never said anything, thinking Pearl would say something when ready.

"I-I have a very disfiguring scar on my neck and down on my chest. I do my best to keep it hidden so as not to offend anyone."

"But no one would be offended here. We're your friends," Cimarron said.

Bless you, Cimarron. Ruby felt like applauding.

Pearl sniffed, then wiped her eyes with the tips of her fingers. "I-I believe that was why I never had any suitors and why my father . . ."

Ruby and the others waited for more. The rockers creaked a duet. A robin serenaded the coming storm.

Tears dripped off Pearl's chin. Cimarron dropped to her knees in front of Pearl's chair. "I didn't mean to make you cry. Some of us have a lot to hide, but you are truly beautiful, inside and out, and I think there are several men here who think that. Men in Chicago might well be dumb and blind, but out here we see things as they really are."

Pearl took a handkerchief from her apron pocket and dabbed her eyes. "Thank you."

"What brought you out here anyway?" Daisy asked. "I mean, I know to teach school, but I bet you could teach anywhere."

"I did teach in Chicago at a settlement house, the children of the tenements and immigrants."

"Did you like it?"

"Very much so. I taught fifth grade. One year we put on a play, and once we had a picnic at my father's house. I taught for four years there."

"I bet they'll miss you come fall."

"Yes." Pearl sighed. *And I'll miss them and a proper school, not one used for men playing cards at night. And compared to here, a wealth of supplies.*

Lightning flashed against the purple black clouds, and far off thunder murmured.

"I sure hope Opal and Milly are paying attention. They better be on their way home." Ruby stood at the railing, the electricity in the air standing hairs upright on her arms and head.

"Milly knows better than to be out on the plains when lightning comes." Daisy held her cool glass against her forehead.

"They could take shelter under a tree," Pearl said.

"No, never under a tree. Lightning strikes the high points. I've seen trees explode in a torch of fire."

The breeze strengthened like a young boy trying out his muscles. It tossed leaves in the air, tugged at their skirts.

"Ah, that feels wonderful." Daisy raised her arms over her head, then pulled her dress out from her body. "When the rain starts, I'm going to wash my hair."

"And my clothes." Cimarron looked down at her feet. "Don't think my feet will ever come clean again."

"I'll get the rose soap, Daisy. We'll all get clean." Ruby nearly bumped into Belle on her way into the kitchen. "Sorry."

"Are Milly and Opal back yet?" When Ruby shook her head Belle continued, "I got me a bad feelin' about this. You know where they went?"

"Yes. Up to the fishing hole Captain McHenry showed us." *Dear God, please get Milly and Opal home.*

All through the washing of hair and clothing in the drenching rain, she kept up her prayer. Should she go get Private Stone and the other soldiers to go look for them?

When it looked like the rain had settled in for a time rather than just blowing over, Ruby put on dry clothes, grabbed a shawl, for now everything felt cold, and headed out the door.

"Where are you going?"

"To get Private Stone and some others to go look for them."

"I'll go with you." Cimarron wrung her hair out and, after twisting it, pinned it on top of her head.

"Where's Charlie?"

"I don't know, but he doesn't have a horse either." The sound of hammering was drowned out by the drip and splash of the pouring rain.

They'd gotten past Mrs. McGeeney's when they heard the sound of pounding hooves splashing through the puddles.

"Ruby, have you seen Opal and Milly?" Rand Harrison skidded to a stop. "Baldy came home without a rider."

Cimarron put an arm around Ruby as she staggered at the blow.

CHAPTER TWENTY-NINE

"I heard the army's back." Rand stared at them.

"A few."

"Just in time. Go on down to the cantonment and ask for help. Tell them to go out the west side of the river. And to bring a canvas in case Milly is injured."

"I will." *Oh, God, I want to go along.* Yet Ruby knew she'd do nothing but slow them down. She and Cimarron ran down the street, bursting into the mess before anyone could say enter.

"Sir, you have to help us." Ruby panted out her message, not sure if she was crying or rain was running off her hair. She dashed the deluge to the side.

"Opal and Milly are missing. They went fishing earlier this afternoon." Cimarron tried to catch her breath.

The officer went to the door and commanded, "Four men, mount up! We're looking for Opal and Milly!" and nodded to them to continue.

"Rand just rode into town and said Baldy galloped home to the ranch."

"Milly was riding Baldy." Cimarron took up the story. "Rand's already on his way out to find them, and he said to take the west side of the river."

"Please, our Milly might be lying out there injured." Ruby finished the story.

"We'll bring them back, Miss Torvald. Don't you worry."

"Take something along for a sling."

"We will. You go on back to Dove House."

"Thank you."

They had not crossed the parade ground before four men, including Adam Stone, were galloping their horses toward the river.

"Now don't you go worrying. We gotta pray about this instead," Cimarron said.

But it's not your baby sister, Ruby wanted to scream, but instead they both trotted back to Dove House, slipping and sliding in the puddles and mud.

"Get out of those wet things," Belle said, "before you catch your death. What did they say?"

"Sent four men out. The officer didn't even wait for us to finish our story." Ruby leaned against the table to catch her breath. Half running, half walking in soaked skirts took a lot of air.

"Did Rand stop here?"

"No."

"He saw us on the street. Baldy came home to the ranch without a rider, so he rode Buck in to see who was missing. I told him Opal and Milly went to the fishing hole, so he headed on out there."

"Here. Change in the pantry." Daisy handed Ruby dry clothes and a towel.

When Ruby came back out, Belle was making coffee while Daisy dried Cimarron's hair with a towel. Ruby went to stand by the stove. She was amazed that only a short time earlier it had been so hot in here they were about to faint, and now the fire felt wonderful. *God, please take care of them.*

— ❧ —

Rand galloped on out to the river, trying to see through the rain blinding his eyes and running off his hat and down his neck. When he shouted "Opal, Milly," the wind blew the words back down his throat.

Buck slipped and stumbled, but Rand kept a firm hand on the reins to help his horse keep his footing. He slowed down to a trot.

Surely they were on the trail. Surely he'd find them any moment.

He was nearly to the fishing hole when Buck whinnied and he heard an answer. "Good son." He thumped Buck's shoulder and called, "Opal."

"Here."

How it could be so dark when it was not even dusk yet? Buck called again and Bay whinnied back.

Please, Lord, let them be all right. I gave them the horse, if something happens — no, that kind of thinking is a waste of time.

Buck saw them first and veered off to the left, then nickered as he stopped. Bay stood, her reins loose, ground tied as he had always promised Opal the horse would.

"Rand, she's hurt. Milly's hurt." Opal's wail as she knelt beside her prostrate friend cut into his heart.

Rand leaped off Buck and knelt beside the girls. "What happened?"

"We started home, but lightning struck, and at the crash Baldy reared, dumped Milly, and ran off. How'd you know to come?"

"Baldy came home to the ranch." While he talked, he felt Milly's legs and arms for breaks. "What's going on here?"

"She's been unconscious this whole time. I didn't know if I should stay or go get help or what to do." Sobs punctuated her story. "It wasn't her fault, or Baldy's fault. We should have started for home sooner when I first saw the clouds, but we were trying to get enough fish for supper, and feeding that bunch of people takes a lot of anything." She gulped. "Is she going to be all right?"

"I sure hope so. She's breathing all right. Has a knot on her head like a goose egg. Some blood but not a lot." He stripped off his shirt and laid that over the girl on the ground. "Go unsaddle Buck, and we'll cover her with his blanket. The army will be here shortly with a sling."

Opal did as he told her and spread the horse blanket over Milly.

Rand set his hat over her face so she wouldn't breathe in any more water. *God, hurry those bluebellies up. If we've ever needed the army out here, we do now. Thank you for sending back this patrol.*

Buck and Bay both whinnied, and an answering neigh sounded.

"Over here!" Rand cupped both hands around his mouth and yelled again.

Private Stone was the first one out of the saddle, even before the sergeant ordered halt.

The young man knelt beside the white-faced figure on the ground, taking both her hands in his. "Come on, Milly, honey, wake up. Please, you got to wake up."

Two other men spread a canvas next to Milly, and gently they transferred her to the sling. They spread another canvas over her, shoved two poles through the deep hems in the side, and mounted back up. "We'll take her directly to Dove House. Ride ahead and tell them to heat some rocks and blankets. Got to get her warmed up again."

Opal stood back out of the way, her hands locked around her shivering shoulders. If she was cold, how much worse off was Milly?

"You okay, Opal?" Rand put an arm around her shoulders.

"I-I will b-be."

Rand resaddled Buck, boosted Opal up on Bay, and they headed back to town, passing the patrol with a wave.

Charlie met them at the hitching post, since he was watching from the porch.

"How bad?"

"Don't know. They're bringing her in." Rand flipped his reins over the bar.

"I'll take care of the horses, and—" Charlie caught Opal as she tried to slide off and her legs buckled.

Rand picked her up and carried her into Dove House.

"Is she. . . ?" Ruby could say no more.

"She's fine, just cold and wet. The army is bringing Milly in. She's unconscious. Get blankets and heat rocks. Need plenty of coffee." He set Opal in the chair that Daisy moved over by the stove. "Get her undressed and wrapped in a blanket, then get hot liquid in her. Lace the coffee with cream and lots of sugar." He turned his back so they could strip Opal of her wet things and wrap her up.

"I'm sorry. We should have started home earlier." Opal

sobbed into Ruby's sheltering arms.

Cimarron squeezed the water out of Opal's braids and unplaited them to dry. "You did good, honeybun."

Daisy and Pearl got the supplies that Rand had ordered. They hung the blankets on chairs around the stove and put the rocks in the oven.

"How is Milly?" Belle asked Rand as she handed him one of Charlie's dry shirts.

"Wish I knew. She was breathing fine but might have got water down her lungs. Looked mighty blue, but in that light, who could tell."

"You got any whiskey?" he asked Belle.

"A flask."

"Go get it. Might help both of them. Let's cover the table with a blanket and lay her here by the stove when they come."

"Company halt!"

Belle returned with her flask as Private Stone and one other man carried the sling into the kitchen.

"Over here." Rand indicated the table.

"Is she a-alive?" Opal, now cuddled on Ruby's lap, quavered.

"Yes." They transferred her from the sling to the table, then the men stepped outside on the porch while Cimarron and Daisy undressed Milly and wrapped her in warm, dry blankets, setting the stones along beside her.

"Is she able to swallow?" Belle stopped at the end of the table.

"Don't know. Her teeth are chattering so hard . . ."

"That's a good sign." Rand turned to the sergeant. "Anyone down there with medical training?"

"I have the most, and far as I can see, you've done all the best things. Lace some coffee with honey, cream, and that what Belle has there, and spoon just a mite in. Rubbing her will help the circulation too."

"Got to get her warmed up." Cimarron rubbed Milly's legs and Daisy her arms while Rand fixed the drinks, handing one to Opal. "Just sip it. Yes, it's going to burn going down, but that's good. The first swallow will be the worst."

"Oh, ugh." Opal shuddered as the drink went down.

"Take a deep breath and drink more." Ruby held the cup.

"Never thought I'd be pushing booze on my baby sister, but if this helps . . ."

Rand looked across at her and smiled. Never had she looked more beautiful. Seeing her out in the rain had made his heart nearly stop in fear, although he was pretty sure it was not Opal who was injured.

Belle brought a spoon and tried to get some into Milly, but it only drained out the side of her mouth.

"Can't get the spoon between her teeth." Belle looked up. "Any suggestions?"

"Just keep trying. You got any more blankets?"

"Go get a down quilt out of the linen closet and a feather bed." Ruby rested her cheek on Opal's towel-wrapped head. "Pearl, would you please wrap a hot dry towel around Milly's head?"

"Of course."

Hours passed. Finally Milly quit shivering and lay still. They fixed a pallet on the floor by the back of the stove so they could prepare supper for the guests.

Adam Stone sat next to the pallet, never taking his eyes off Milly's pale face. Her lips were no longer blue, and she wasn't running a temperature. At times he stroked her hand. He was finally able to get some of the coffee past her teeth, and she swallowed without difficulty.

Opal, who sat on the other side, still blanket draped, cheered. "Come on, Milly, you got to wake up."

With people fed and the kitchen cleaned up again, Opal curled up like a kitten behind the stove, and with Cat and her kittens curled beside her, all went to sleep.

"Son, you have to go back to the cantonment." Charlie took the cup and spoon from Stone. "You don't want to get in trouble with your officer."

"Yes, sir." Adam laid a hand against Milly's cheek. "You rest now, honey. I'll be back in the morning." He stood. "You come get me if there is a change?"

"We will." Ruby patted his arm. "Thank you for being such a good friend."

"Ma'am, I'm not just her friend. I'm going to marry her as soon as I get a promotion."

"Oh. Does she know that?"

"No, but she will soon as she wakes up." He stuttered and blinked several times. "You take good care of her now, you hear—I mean, please?"

"I know what you mean." Ruby stared out the door after him. Rain was still coming down in sheets, and earlier they'd been working hard and having a good time too. Laughing and complaining about the canning. And Opal wanting to learn to shoot. Would they have heard two rifle shots in the rain? With as much noise as the storm was making, most likely not. She glanced over at Rand, who'd not taken his attention off Opal, and her, all evening. What was he thinking?

Rand leaned down and felt Opal's forehead and shook his head when he caught Ruby's questioning gaze. He felt Milly's with another headshake.

"She seems to be sleeping peacefully. I've seen men wake up a day or so later after a crack on the head and be just fine. Just have a headache for a while."

Ruby nodded. "Thank you."

But I've also seen men never wake up. He'd seen a lot more during his brief time in the war than he ever wanted to remember. *Lord, this is in your hands. We've done what we can.* Interesting how, when the chips were really down, he always turned to his heavenly Father. So why did he rely on himself when things were going well?

Ruby handed him a fresh cup of coffee. "Thank you for coming so quickly."

"'Bout ran Buck's legs off. When I saw Baldy come galloping up, stirrups banging his sides, I knew someone was in trouble." *And I thought it could have been you. That it's Milly is terrible, but had it been you, I'd never have forgiven myself.* "You have no idea how glad I was to see you in the rain."

Ruby gave him a questioning look.

"It could have been you lying on that ground."

Ruby stared into his eyes. She swallowed, the sound loud in her ears. *What are you saying, Rand? What is that I see in your eyes?* She looked down, could hardly bear his gaze. *So this is what it feels like. Captain McHenry is a good man, a good friend, but this is what I have been waiting for.*

His hand crossed the narrow divide and took hers, his thumb rubbing the back, one finger on her wrist.

Do you know what I feel? This is not a good time to say anything, but listen to my heart. Gathering her into his arms would be so easy. Her head would fit right under his chin. He could kiss her forehead with hardly a motion.

Instead he stepped back just enough that he could no longer feel her body heat drawing him closer.

"Shall I carry Opal upstairs for you?"

"If you like."

She led the way, holding a lamp high to light the steps for him, then turning back the bedcovers so he could lay his burden in bed. She spread the covers over Opal.

"Thank you."

"You are most welcome. I better go."

"Ride home tonight?"

"Yes."

"No. We will make up a pallet for you, since there isn't an empty bed in the house."

"Then I will trade off with Charlie on caring for Milly."

"You don't need to do that." Tearing her gaze from his, she led the way back downstairs again. She stopped at the linen closet to remove bedding and returned to the kitchen.

"I let Buck out in the pasture with Bay," Charlie was saying to Rand. "Your saddle is on the back porch."

"Good. Thank you."

"Still raining."

"I know. That river is going to be raging in the morning."

Ruby finished making up the pallet in the storeroom. "Good night, gentlemen. Please call me if there is any change."

"We will." Charlie nodded.

— ⁀⧖⁀ —

Milly woke when the rooster crowed.

"Hey, young'un." Charlie smiled down at her.

"Wh-who are you?" She stared around the still dim kitchen. "Where am I?"

"Oh, Lord, have mercy," he muttered. "I'm Charlie Higgins, and you are Milly. We are in the kitchen of Dove House, where you have worked for three years."

Rand watched and listened. *Lord, thank you she's alive and seems all right in body. Now, please bring back her mind.*

"W-who am I?"

CHAPTER THIRTY

"Ruby, do you have any laudanum? That will ease the head-ache." Pearl stroked Milly's forehead.

"Good thing I had Charlie get some one time." Ruby checked the back of the cupboard in the pantry. From now on she'd be keeping a flask of whiskey or brandy on hand also. It worked well to kill infection, if nothing else. She mixed two spoonfuls of the medicine with a glass of water and held it out to Milly. "Drink this. It will help."

Milly nodded and made a face after the first sip, then drank it at Ruby's nod. "I'm tired."

"I'm sure you are. You may go back up to bed if you like. Can you find your way?"

At her nod, Ruby and Pearl watched Milly start up the steps, slowly, as if each tread took great effort.

"You think her memory will come back?" Pearl tied a clean apron around her gingham dress on her way out to cut corn for canning.

"I am trusting God for this one. I don't know of anything else to do. Keep her comfortable, yes, but she is restless. What if she wanders away some night?"

"Why would she do that? This has been her home for so long, I've never heard her even mention her former life." Cimar-ron turned from scrubbing new red potatoes.

"I know. She's a private little person. I hope she remembers she loves Adam Stone. He's like a lost orphan." Ruby gave the cake batter a couple more good beats and poured it in the greased and floured cake pans.

Opal pushed through the back door and stacked her empty tray on the shelf. Daisy was right behind her, wiping her forehead with the corner of her apron.

"Someone complained because we ran out of sandwiches." Opal handed Ruby the money from her apron pocket. "I said I was sorry but he was welcome to come here for dinner any time. He didn't think I was funny." Opal snagged a cookie off the plate on the table. "How's Milly?"

"She went back up to bed. You can tell she has a bad headache just by looking at her eyes."

"I should have—"

"Opal Marie Torvald, you did your best. You can't go around feeling guilty for something that wasn't your fault." Cimarron set a pot of potatoes down on the stove with a clang. "Someone I know told me that more than once." She glanced at Ruby, who nodded back.

"After all, did you invite the lightning to strike, the storm to come?"

"No." Opal made a face. "But I sure miss her."

"We all do." Daisy took a cookie too. "Milly's one tough cookie to carry that tray, make change, and keep a smile on her face. She doesn't look real strong, but you two girls are doing a great job." She stretched, kneading her back with her fists. "Guess I better get back to my ironing."

"I'll go get the things off the line." Opal headed out the door, whistling for Bay at the same time. "You lonesome, girl?"

Ruby watched out the window as Opal got to the fence at the same time as the mare. "Those two sure got to be friends fast." Ruby marveled at that every day.

Pearl smiled wistfully. "Doesn't happen often, but like with people, sometimes you meet someone and you feel like you've known them all your life. I felt that way by the second day I was here."

"Me too." Ruby turned from the window. "I better get out there and stir that load of tablecloths. I think Milly did far more work around here than any of us gave her credit for."

— ❦ —

Before a week passed, Milly was much more like herself, even though she didn't know who she was.

"Don't you remember going fishing?" Opal asked.

"Do I know how to fish?" With the lessening of the headaches, Milly had gone back to doing the laundry after someone showed her how.

But when Rand showed up with Baldy in tow, Milly turned white and dashed into the hotel faster than a rabbit chased by a coyote.

"What's the matter?" Ruby turned from mashing the potatoes.

"That man with the horse . . ." Milly stuttered, her eyes round as teacups.

"That's Rand Harrison, a good friend of yours. And you love to ride. You and Opal rode all over the place, went fishing, strawberry picking." Ruby made sure her voice stayed even and friendly. The terror on Milly's face told how well she wasn't doing. Now that she thought about it, Milly had made a wide detour around the pasture and Bay. If she can't remember anything else, how does she know to be afraid? She'd panicked when they had another thunderstorm too, hiding under the covers when the lightning flashed.

"Hey, Milly, how ya doin'?" Rand took off his hat as he entered the kitchen. "Brought your friend back. Would have come sooner, but we been putting up hay." He glanced at Ruby when Milly backed away, shaking her head.

Ruby moved the mashed potatoes to a cooler spot on the stove. She held out her hand. "Come on, Milly, let's go see how Pearl is doing with the beets." She nodded to Rand to join them.

Even before noon, the sun was baking the land. Hammers and saws and men shouting could be heard from across the river. The frame was up on the marquis's new home on the bluff.

"My land, look at that." Cimarron pointed to the pile of lumber and building materials they'd unloaded from the train that day. Now that a siding had been finished, the engineer would back a car or two off on that before the train itself headed west.

Ruby sucked in a deep breath, remembering the day she

wanted to shoot Rand for forcing Opal to get back up on the horse after she fell off.

Milly had to do the same.

Ruby kept Milly's hand locked in her own. "Milly, dear, I'm going to ask you to do something that might be hard, but I believe it is very important."

"What?"

"We're going to walk over to the horses now so you can remember how much you love horses and love to ride."

"I-I can't."

"Sure you can. I'm right here on your other side." Rand took her other hand and wrapped it around his arm, tucked tight against his side. The smile he sent Ruby made her heart skip a beat and then pick up at double time.

"Good for you, Milly." Opal joined them, sticking a carrot in Milly's hand. "You always give Baldy a carrot. He likes them. So does Buck, so I brought him one."

Bay nickered.

"She wants one too, but I already gave her some."

Standing at the hitching rail, Rand reached out to rub Baldy's neck while Opal fussed over Buck.

Milly shivered. "I-I think I'm going to faint."

"No, you're not. We won't let you. Besides, you're not the kind who faints." Opal lifted Milly's hand to give Baldy the carrot. He whiskered her palm as he took the carrot right in the middle, with greens hanging out one side of his mouth and half the carrot the other. Twitching his upper lip, he tried to shift the carrot around.

Milly giggled, a tiny breath of sound at first but definitely laughter.

Opal laughed out loud. "You silly horse." She grabbed the green stalk and handed it back to him.

Baldy sniffed Milly's arm and shoulder, then nodded as if he approved.

"See, he likes you."

Milly leaned against Ruby, hiding her face in her shoulder. "Then why did he dump me off and run away?" Tears and sobs burst forth, and she buried her face in Ruby's chest as Ruby put both her arms around her and gathered her close. Pearl walked over from the garden to lend support.

Please, God, let the healing begin. Ruby covered her prayer in tears of joy. "Go ahead and cry it out now. Let it all out."

Opal, ever tenderhearted, left her tears on Buck's neck. "She remembers. Thank you, Jesus, she remembers."

When the crying storm passed, Milly still leaned against Ruby. "How did I get home?"

"Four men from the cantonment brought a sling out and brought you in."

"Rand came and found us when Baldy ran back to the ranch."

"What happened to all our fish?"

Pearl was the first to burst out laughing, but the others all joined in.

"Oh, Milly, here we're all worried about you remembering, and all you care about is the fish." Cimarron clasped her hands together. "You are a real trooper."

"Speaking of troopers, Opal, you want to ride Buck on down and give our good news to Private Stone?"

Opal unwrapped the reins and, flipping one over Buck's neck, grabbed the saddle horn and stirrup and swung herself aboard. "You want to come along?" she offered Milly.

Milly shook her head and clung closer to Ruby.

"You're going to ride Baldy, aren't you, darlin'?" Cimarron took Milly's hand. "You want someone to ride with you?"

"I-I don't want to ride."

"I know that, but when you fall off, you got to get back on. That's just the way it is."

"Ruby?"

"I'll walk beside you, and Cimarron lead, so Rand can walk on your other side. No way you can fall. You ready now?"

"No-o-o-o."

Rand put both hands on her waist, and with one smooth motion, she was sitting in the saddle, clenching the pommel till her fingernails made indents in the leather.

"The stirrups are just right for you, so we'll help you get your feet in." Rand did one and Ruby the other.

Fear emanated in waves from the girl on the horse. Her jaw was clamped so tight, she was sure to have cramps in it later.

Her eyes scrunched shut, one tear tracking down her cheek.

"All right, push your feet against the stirrups so you can stand up a bit."

Even though she shook her head, Milly did as told.

"Good. Now sit back down and snuggle against the back of the saddle so you feel more secure. You can move around if you like. Baldy doesn't mind." Again she did as he told her. "You can open your eyes now."

"I-I'm dizzy, and my head hurts." The whisper came somehow from between the clenched lips.

"Now we're going to walk real slow and easy, so let yourself move with the horse. You are a good rider, and your body will remember what to do." Rand continued to give her instructions in a slow, gentle manner.

Please, Lord, let him be right. If something happens now . . . Ruby kept a hand on Milly's thigh as they started up the path to the street. She could feel the girl's body gradually relax, like wax melting in a can, becoming warm and pliable. For sure there'd been enough heat applied here.

Ruby's own shoulders relaxed, and she patted Milly's knee. "You are doing just fine up there. Braver than I would be."

"I'm . . . not . . . brave."

"You sure fooled me. Real courage is when you do something you're terrified of but do it anyway. That's what you are doing."

"You sure are. If we were Indians, we would have to give you a new name. Brave Heart or She Who Fears Nothing." Rand patted Baldy's neck as he spoke.

"Or Little Badger." Cimarron turned and looked over her shoulders. "Badgers are the fiercest fighters."

Milly picked up the reins that were crossed over Baldy's neck. When they returned to the hitching rail, she dismounted and patted the horse's neck and turned to Ruby. "So when another thunderstorm comes, are you going to throw me outside to get over my fear of storms too?"

Ruby gulped, swapped a glance over the horse's back with Rand and, when Cimarron broke into a mighty laugh, did the same.

Buck and Opal loped back up and stopped to watch. "Hey, Buck, I think they've all lost their minds."

Milly turned. "I still want to know what happened to all our fish."

"We ate the ones I brought home," Opal said, "and I guess something else ate the strings you had. By the way, Private Stone asked me to tell you he is coming by tonight and hopes you will have time to go walking with him."

"Oh my." Milly put her hands to her cheeks. "I'm a mess." The bewildered look she wore when the rest of them laughed only made them laugh more.

CHAPTER THIRTY-ONE

Tomorrow would be only the second day of school, and already she was dreading it.

"Is something wrong?" Ruby turned to Pearl after supper was cleared away.

"I . . . I . . . no, it's nothing."

"You've been awfully quiet."

"I know. What do you know about the older Grady boy?"

"Nothing. The family is brand-new to the area. Just came this summer. Atticus is so much bigger than all the other children though."

"And he doesn't want to be in school."

"Oh. Can he read at all? Do arithmetic?"

"He's never spent a day in school. He doesn't know his alphabet or his numbers. I would think his family needs him out on the farm."

"Usually that's the case. Hard to get the older students to go to school at all, or for their folks to let them go." Ruby handed Pearl a cup of tea. "You look like you need a sit-down. How did the room work?" Together they stepped out on the porch and sat in the rocking chairs.

"Fine, thanks to Charlie and Mr. Hegland for the benches they made. We put Atticus at a table by himself." She leaned back and watched the color changing in the clouds above them. From pinks to oranges and reds and back to lavender. "Just sitting out here brings peace to my soul."

"I know. Maybe he won't come tomorrow."

"I should be so fortunate. And yet I feel so sorry for anyone who cannot read."

"There are a lot of people like that out here."

"Mrs. Robertson has done a good job with her girls, just as you have with Opal. And now Opal is passing her learning on. Do you know how amazing that is?"

"At the Brandons', where we came from in New York, the children always loved to play school. That's how Opal started learning to read when she was barely five. But then we had been reading together before then. We loved *David Copperfield* and *Oliver Twist*." Ruby watched a bird dipping and fluttering for insects. One of the horses nickered. A dog barked somewhere. Cat rose from her evening ablutions and came to wind herself about Ruby's skirt, becoming more insistent in her pleas.

"All right, come on up." Ruby patted her lap. Cat leaped up and, kneading Ruby's upper legs with her paws, finally settled in, her purr rivaling the saws that were now silent after the building of the day.

"I love this time of day and this time of the year. This is my second fall in Dakotah Territory, and what a difference."

"What brought you here?"

"A letter from my father telling me to bring Opal and come west for our inheritance."

"Dove House?"

"Yes, but things were a lot different then. The dining room was a saloon, gambling all over in here. And we walked into that just before he died."

"What a story."

Ruby waited, stroking Cat and looking off into the distance.

There's something more, Pearl thought as she watched. The half-grown gray kitten approached her, so she leaned down and picked it up. Snuggling the cat under her chin, she thought back to her first day of school.

Twelve pupils had filed in, led by Opal, who showed them where to sit—the smaller children in front and Atticus, along with the eldest Robertson girl and Opal, in the back.

"Welcome all of you to our first day of school here in Little

Missouri," she had said in greeting. "My name is Miss Hossfuss, and I used to teach in Chicago, Illinois. I'd like each of you to stand, tell us your name, how old you are, and how many years you've been to school. Opal, let's start with you."

"I am Opal Torvald, I am eleven years old, and I started school when I was five, so it's been six years, but we didn't have a real school last year, so only five."

"I am Edith Robertson, and I am thirteen. I went to school for five years before we moved out here. My mother has been teaching us at home."

The boy stood to his feet. "I am Atticus Grady, fifteen, and I ain't never been to school, and I'm too old to be here now." His dark brows nearly made a line above a straight nose, giving him a menacing look.

The other children followed suit down to the youngest Robertson, Ada Mae. "I am five, and my mother said I am not old enough to come, but I can already read and do sums, so she let me. I can stay, can't I, teacher?"

"We shall see. Now I am going to pass a book around, and I want each of you to read aloud so that I can get an idea of what your skills are."

"I kin shoot better'n my pa," Atticus stated.

"Atticus, in school you do not speak unless you are spoken to. In order to speak, you must ask permission by raising your hand and waiting until the teacher calls your name."

She could still feel the glower he had sent her way.

They all had eaten their dinners out on the front porch, most of them bringing their food in a lard pail. Atticus sat by himself. The two younger boys sat away from the girls.

By the end of the day she'd had a pretty good idea of where the children would fit. Having never taught all grades before and all in one room, she knew she was in for a challenging year.

Leaving thoughts of school behind, Pearl set the rocker to creaking again. Such a friendly sound.

"My father made me promise to watch out for the girls," Ruby said.

"You mean Cimarron and Daisy?"

"And Belle and Milly. But Milly wasn't really one of them."

"One of them?"

"Soiled doves."

"You mean ladies of the night?" Pearl nearly choked on the words.

"Yes, only I had no idea what Cimarron was talking about when she tried to explain the realities of life here to me. I was packing to leave when Opal reminded me of my promise. She'd already fallen in love with it here."

"I never would have guessed if you hadn't told me. What amazing changes you have made here." And no wonder the other townswomen are so standoffish. *Ah, Ruby. Dear sweet Ruby, what a life you've led.*

"I think back to what our lives would have been had we stayed in New York with the Brandons. So protected. But here, well, Opal would sum it up in one word."

"Horses?"

"That's right."

"I got my homework done." Opal pushed open the screen door. "Why are you sitting out here in the almost dark?"

"Because it is so peaceful." Ruby looked up. "See the evening star?"

"Star light, star bright, first star I see tonight. . . ." The others joined Pearl. "I wish I may, I wish I might, have the wish I wish tonight."

Pearl closed her eyes. *I wish I might have a letter from my family. Please, Lord, not just a wish but a prayer, a plea.*

"What's that sound I hear?" The rhythmic *kerchunk* had been sounding for some time.

"Oh, you missed out on the good news today." Ruby dumped Cat on the floor. "The new sewing machine came."

"Sewing machine?"

"You remember the surprise I talked about a couple weeks ago that was coming on the train, and it never did?"

"Yes, but I'd forgotten all about it." The kitten joined Cat, and they both paraded to the door, tails straight in the air.

"We set it up by the window in the storeroom—no place else to put it. Cimarron is learning how to run it. Come see it."

Two kerosene lamps stood on shelves on either side of the wooden cabinet with a black treadle apparatus underneath. With her feet, Cimarron rocked the treadle that powered the machine.

The needle flew up and down, flashing in the lamplight.

"I've never sewn anything so fast in all my life." Cimarron held up a string of two-inch squares she'd sewn, leaving space in between to cut the thread. "I can make a quilt top in an afternoon this way."

"How did you know how to work it?" Pearl leaned closer to the light, turning the seams each way to see the even stitching.

"I saw one in action one time, but never dreamed I'd get to sew on one. All that mending . . ." Cimarron shook her head and held up her fingers to the light. "See all those poke holes? No more. I'll have more time for other things because the sewing won't take so long. You need a new skirt, honeybun, and I can't wait to make it."

"You can help me with the ironing then." Daisy folded the last tablecloth for the day. "If those men would be more careful with their cigars, we'd have less mending to do. Holes in the bed sheets even. They don't be careful, they're going to burn the house down around our ears."

"Daisy, don't you go even thinking such a thing." Ruby nodded, then added, "I think it is time to put No Smoking signs in the bedrooms. If we catch someone smoking up there, they get shown the door."

"My land, are you going to hear it over this." Daisy moved the stack of folded tablecloths to the shelf. "We get any more stuff in here, there won't be room to turn around."

— ✁ —

Atticus didn't show up for school the second day. His little brother, Robert, announced that his father needed Atticus to help on the farm with busting sod.

"Then you must learn and teach him. Tell him that when winter comes and they can't work the ground, he is welcome to return."

"Yes, ma'am, but I don't think missin' school made him sad or nothin'. Atticus don't like to be cooped up."

By Thursday Pearl had figured out the patterns for the day in order to keep everyone busy. The older children worked on their own while she helped the beginners, then Opal and Edith took turns helping the little ones while Pearl taught the next level. The days passed so swiftly she hardly got around to every-one before it was time for recess, then dinner, and then dismissal.

"You got a letter, Pearl," Ruby said when school broke for dinner on Friday. "It's in on the counter."

Pearl made her way through the dining room, where only a few tables were occupied, since construction was in full swing in Medora.

The sight of Amalia's handwriting made her step lighten as she ignored the briefest wish that it was her father's handwriting she'd see. She took the envelope to the back porch where there was a modicum of silence while the children played in the front of the hotel. She broke the wax seal with her fingernail and pulled out two pages.

> My dearest Pearl,
>
> How we rejoiced to receive your letter. When you left, I implored your father to seek after you and make sure you were all right, but until you wrote, we hardly knew where to begin. Yes, in answer to your question, your father is still angry. I think mostly because he has to see Mr. Longstreet every day. As he reminded me, a contract between gentle-men is a bond, and you broke his bond. But he has not forbidden me to write to you, not that it would have done much good. He still loves you, and I do believe that one day he will be willing to forgive. In the meantime, you can be sure I will keep you informed.
>
> We are all well. The children send their love. I know Jorge Jr. must have had a hand in your departure, but other than directing laughing eyes at me when I asked, he has been a model of silence, at least in that regard.

Pearl stopped to blow her nose, unaware that she'd been cry-ing.

> If there is anything you need, you must let me know, and I will put it on the first train west. The place you are living sounds like a real adventure for you. I do hope your school is all that you desired.

She included more news about her social activities before ending.

> I pray that all is well with you, that you are in good

health, and that all is well with your soul. Please write soon and tell us about life on the frontier.

Love and blessings from your family, and most of all from your mother.

Amalia Hossfuss.

Pearl wiped eyes and nose, folded the missive, and put it in her pocket. She would read it to Ruby later, but right now it was time to call the children back to class.

When she stood, her body seemed lighter. *Thank you, Lord, for hearing my wish, my prayer. My family doesn't hate me. Oh, thank you, they don't hate me.*

— ❦ —

After church on Sunday Carl Hegland came up to Pearl. "Good morning, Miss Hossfuss."

"And to you, Mr. Hegland."

"I was wondering if you would like to go for a walk along the river this afternoon. After dinner, I mean."

"Why, I would love to. Should I bring *Uncle Tom's Cabin*?"

"If you like. Do you have John Donne? If not, we could trade."

"That will be very nice."

Rand sat with them at the dinner table, as did Jed Black, so Pearl mostly ate and listened, learning much about ranching and building. She noted that Carl Hegland was a man very content with what he did and proud of his work. As he teased Jed Black about something from the job, she also saw a pleasant sense of humor.

— ❦ —

After dinner they began their walk, quietly enjoying the warm fall day. Pearl was the first to break the companionable silence. "So what is your favorite poem in this book?" She held the John Donne volume up.

Pearl flipped to the page and began reading. "Batter my heart, three person'd God."

Carl joined in and recited it along with her. ". . . Except you enthrall me, never shall be free, nor ever chaste except you ravish me."

"Mr. Hegland, you have a wonderful voice."

"Thank you." He ducked his head slightly. "I've thought about what you said, about singing with the choir, that is. I think I would like to do that."

"I know they would love to have you." They walked on past the big cottonwood and up the riverbank, the water low now, since there'd not been rain for several weeks.

To think, I am here, walking with a man as though I've done so all my life, and we are talking about books and music. Could this be the one, this silent man, or so I thought at first?

CHAPTER THIRTY-TWO

"That's right!" Pearl smiled at the boy who had just recited the ABCs correctly.

The rest of the schoolroom clapped as Robert Brady beamed.

"I studied on them at home." He rubbed one bare foot on his other leg. "Atticus, he helped me."

How could he help you? Pearl had not seen the older brother since the first day of school, after which he didn't return.

"He made me keep tryin'."

"You tell Atticus that I have a present for him when he can recite his ABCs also. You teach them to him. All right?"

Robert, dark hair falling over his eyes, nodded so hard the hair flopped. "I will. Ma says we got to learn to read and write and do sums."

And perhaps take a bath once in a while. Pearl looked to the next child. "Are you ready, Franny?"

Franny stood, took in a deep breath, and shotgunned the letters so fast she only had to gulp once in the middle. "U, V-V..." she scrunched her eyes closed tight—"W, XYZ!"

Two more finished, one requiring some prompting from the teacher.

"Very good. We're going to work on our numbers now. Everyone begin counting together, using your fingers if you must. One." She pointed at the numeral one on the board. "Hold up one finger." She held one finger in the air. "Now two." They repeated until they were holding up ten fingers. "Good. Now one finger on each hand. How many do we have?"

"Two."

"Good. Now two fingers on one hand, one on the other." She drilled them on simple addition, then handed out the slates that had come in the box of school supplies. "Now, make a one. Now a two." She wrote on the blackboard so all could see her hand motion. "Edith, Opal, please come help the beginners. Everyone in the first three rows, draw a number two. The rest of you take out your readers and turn to page ten. Read as far as you can until I tell you to stop."

She had the beginners make rows of numbers one, two, and three on their slates, left them with the two older girls, and gathered her four middle readers together.

"Now I want you to read aloud, and we'll sound out the words you don't know."

As usual, the middle Robertson girl, Emily, read without faltering. And while Ada Mae stumbled over some words and sounded others out, for a five-year-old, she more than held her own. Pearl prompted the Jones boy several times, but once he got a word, it was his. He closed his book and gave a big sigh.

"Reading is hard work."

The others giggled, and Pearl chuckled with them. "But it's good work, and someday you'll be able to read anything—a newspaper, a book, a magazine—anything you want."

"My ma wants me to read the Bible for her. She says she can't read all of it because some words is too big."

"Some of the words are hard, that's right."

"That's why she likes to come here to church where someone reads the Bible out loud. She follows along, and she says now she can read better too."

I have to remember to tell Ruby that. Maybe if Charlie read more slowly or waited for people to find the place, those who do have Bibles, that is. What if we had a reading class on Sunday afternoons after church?

That night she asked Ruby the same question. "What do you think?"

"I think it's a wonderful idea. If you are sure you want to do it."

"I'd do anything to help people learn to read and write. Too many have never had a chance, growing up where there's no school like they do."

The two rocked in companionable silence, other than the purring of the cats on their laps.

"A year ago I never would have dreamed I'd be out here teaching a school like this. I thought I was going to be an old-maid schoolmarm in Chicago for the rest of my life."

"There's not much chance of being an old maid out here. Too many men wanting wives."

"Not that I've noticed. I mean, I know there are a lot of men, but they seem pretty content the way they are."

"Care if I join you?" Cimarron stopped near them.

"Not at all. Pull up a chair."

"You've sure kept that machine humming." Pearl stroked the cat in her lap, loving the silky fur and the vibrations of the purr.

"I have all the mending done and finished that skirt for Opal."

"You picked it up so quickly."

"Well, we had to wash the blood out of one sheet I was mending. That thing can sew right into a finger if you don't watch out." She held up her bandaged finger to prove it.

"So how's the school going?" Ruby asked Pearl.

"I've read about some teachers who have twenty or so children in a one-room school. I don't know how they do it. Why, I only have twelve, and not everyone gets a chance to read aloud every day. It is easy to let Opal and Edith help, but then they don't get enough lesson time."

"Teaching others always teaches the teacher."

"True." Pearl raised her face to the evening breeze. "I'm thinking fall is in the air. The air smells different."

"I know. First frost can be anytime, then we'll have a few weeks of the most wonderful weather—they call it Indian summer. Why, I have no idea." Cimarron stared out at the garden where the final planting of corn was ready to pick. "I told Charlie when he planted that the last time, he was gambling with the weather. This year he won. And the pumpkins will make the best pies."

"And cakes and cookies and canned, dried, and stored. We'll have squash and pumpkin all winter." Ruby stretched her arms above her head and yawned. "Makes me tired just thinking about it."

"My ma used to cut up pumpkin chunks and cook it in the stew. Rabbit and pumpkin are a good combination."

"Never thought of that. How come you never mentioned that before?"

"Never thought about it. Things coming back to me I never gave a thought to for years. Some of the things we did for Christmas. I think we need to have a real Christmas celebration this year. A Christmas tree and a program, presents . . . Got to get to making some things." Her voice wore a dreamy quality, gauzy like silk, soft and fluttery on the dying breeze.

"You didn't have Christmas here last year?" Pearl asked.

"Not much."

Pearl thought back to the tree with white candles that touched the ceiling in their parlor at home. The parties, the gifts. She wouldn't be there for Christmas this year to help hang the swags of cedar and the wreaths of pine with red bows, get down the boxes of ornaments, plan the school party.

"Then this year we start all new traditions." Pearl leaned forward, making her lap mate leap to the floor. "This will be the best Christmas Dove House ever saw."

Cimarron grinned. "It will be the only real Christmas Dove House ever saw."

— ❧ —

"Letter for you." Ruby whisked by on her way to serve another table.

Pearl left her place and retrieved the envelope from the counter to read while she finished eating. These few moments alone were a precious treat. Her father's handwriting gave her both a start and a thrill of joy. *Perhaps he sees and understands why I had to do what I did.* Her mind played with that delightful idea while her fingernail broke the wax seal, stamped with her father's company emblem.

Hope springing eternal, as the poet said, made her heart beat faster.

Pearl,

I order you to return to Chicago and carry out the marriage that I contracted for you. I know you understand the value and commitment of a bond, a bond which I agreed to in your stead. Mr. Longstreet was devastated by your unholy departure. As he assured me, he loves you with all his heart. Send us your arrival information by telegraph immediately.

Your father,

Jorge Hossfuss.

With shaking hands, Pearl refolded the paper and inserted it back in the envelope. Leaving the remainder of her meal, she strode into the kitchen, lifted the lid on the stove, and dropped the letter into the flames. It burned with a rush, blackening around the edges, catching fire in the middle, and turning into a breath of ashes.

Just like her dreams.

"You all right?" Daisy asked, concern wrinkling her brow.

"Yes. Thank you. I must get back to the schoolroom." Like a puppet on sticks, Pearl turned and marched out of the kitchen, hastily apologizing to Milly, who almost got slammed in the face by the swinging door.

That night she began a letter.

Dear Father,

I am sorry you feel like you do, but there is no chance ... —she crossed that out —*no reason ...* She crossed that out too, crunched the paper, and tossed it over her shoulder. Three tries later, she tossed the final ball over her shoulder, corked her inkwell, put away her pen and paper, and went to stand in front of the window. She knew she was fortunate to have a window in her tiny room. Some of the others up here in the cramped third floor didn't have one. Right now she wished she had taken the room below that Ruby offered her. But she hated to deprive her friend of the revenue. She thought of her room at home with the thick mattress instead of ropes and corn shuckings, space enough to hold a dance, a bathroom with running water, maids taking care of her clothes, her room, the house and garden.

What a luxurious life she had led—and had taken for granted. She rubbed her elbows with chilled hands. Yesterday felt almost like summer, tonight Daisy was predicting frost. With a full moon throwing shadows black as night and the air so nippy as to preclude their evening social on the back porch, she could well be right. Just in case, Charlie had picked the last of the corn and tomatoes. Ruby had said they'd have fried green tomatoes for dinner the next day.

That was another thing she had taken so for granted. Food for the winter. She'd never had any concern over what was in the larder or where the next meal would come from. Why, Inga would fix whatever the family ordered.

Lord, I have been so lacking in gratitude for the untold blessings you gave us. Please forgive me. She stared at the kerosene lamp flickering in a draft she didn't feel. Gaslights, a furnace, fireplaces. Newspapers to read, magazines, books, everything needed for whatever she wanted to do—paints, art paper, threads of all colors.

Lord, I know I have grieved your heart. Did I never say thank you and mean it? Thank you, Marlene. Thank you, Mother. But for what? Serving and loving. The rosebud on her tray if she asked for breakfast in bed, something she did rarely, but still, someone fixed it, made the tray lovely, carried it up the stairs, served her, and then returned to take the tray down later. And sometimes she'd hardly touched the food! *Pearl, you wastrel, and you thought you were doing such a good work by teaching at the settlement house. The lady of the manor dispensing charity.*

She sat down, opened her Bible, and read whatever page came up. Esther. Whyever Esther? But she read the story of a young woman who became the wife of a king because of her beauty.

"For such a time as this...." The phrase stopped her cold. Yes, she believed God ordered her footsteps to bring her west. But, for such a time as this? What could it mean?

She opened her Bible again and let the pages fall where they may.

"The Lord looketh on the heart."

My father doesn't love me. The thought made her catch her breath. *Mother says he loves me but just has a hard time showing it. Well, I think she is wrong. Jorge Hossfuss doesn't care about me a whit, other than as a member of his family who should do what he says.* She nodded. That was right. A hard fact but correct. He was angry right now because she caused him discomfort. Either he would forget it, or he wouldn't, but she was too far away for that to make much difference.

But my heavenly Father loves me. He says it over and over. He does. Her heart quickened. *My heavenly Father loves me just the way I am.*

Pearl fingered the scar on her neck. Something she always thought made her ugly. Would a kind and loving spirit make her beautiful? According to the Bible it did. God looks on the inner heart.

Lord, let my heart be beautiful in thy sight. She put her Bible on the stand beside the bed, undressed, and crawled under the covers. *"For such a time as this." I wonder what is coming that I've been given that verse? What will we do for Christmas? What will I do for my family here?*

CHAPTER THIRTY-THREE

Something was going on.

No one was saying anything, but something inside Ruby sensed it. Did the others know and weren't telling her? What made her think that? How she wished she knew. She leaned against the post on the porch.

Why does there have to be a killing frost before Indian summer? Another one of those questions without answers.

She stared out at the brown cornstalks, the blackened tomato and pumpkin vines. Mute testimony to the frigid nights, but now the balmy days. Ducks and geese flying south, Charlie smoking the carcasses while Daisy stuffed the feathers into quilts and feather beds. Preparing for winter, that's what this time was for.

But not this feeling, as if she'd caught an echo, a reflection, but of such a minute trace that all she was left with was this disquietude.

Restlessness. That's what it was. But why? Always back to those questions of why, what, and who?

Ruby returned to the kitchen, which she had to herself for a change. Milly was out washing linens, the *kerthunk* of the sewing machine attested to Cimarron's whereabouts, and Daisy would be at her ironing board. She could hear the hum from the classroom that said Pearl was busy instilling knowledge in the heads of her pupils. After church the families had praised Miss Hossfuss as high as the bluffs and rock formations that made up the badlands.

Sure hope they paid her, Ruby thought as she stirred the coals and put two pieces of wood in the firebox. Maybe mixing up a cake would help quiet her restlessness. While the oven heated, she got out the ingredients and began creaming the butter and sugar together with her wooden spoon. Tonight they were having fried chicken because Charlie had butchered the first of their spring-hatch roosters. With it taking four chickens to feed the guests and walk-ins, they would need far more than they had to get through the winter. By keeping the pullets, they doubled their flock.

While her hands went about adding the eggs, beating, and then adding the rest of the ingredients, her mind went back to the puzzle. Should she have a talk with Belle? When she'd had this feeling before, Belle was always somehow involved.

After testing the temperature of the oven—it felt hot enough—she slid the cake pan in and ambled into the dining room to check for mail at the counter where Charlie always laid it.

A letter addressed to the proprietor of Dove House made her lay the other things on the counter and open this one.

To Whom It May Concern. Her attention returned to the gilt letterhead. Theodore Roosevelt and a New York address. Back to the body.

> I will be arriving in Little Missouri on September 20, 1883, for an indeterminate stay. I will require lodging and meals, and though I will be hunting and camping for most of the time, I will pay you for the room. Please advise me if this is a possibility. If your hotel has no room, would you please recommend another hotel?
>
> Thank you.
> Sincerely,
> Theodore R. Roosevelt.

Recommend another place? As if anyone with a lick of sense would stay at Mrs. McGeeney's, poor fare compared to Dove House. Unless, of course, one did not mind sharing a bed with various vermin.

She sat down and shook the ink bottle, wishing she had a letterhead for Dove House. Now wouldn't that be uppity.

Dear Mr. Roosevelt,
I will hold a room for you beginning on September 20. Since our space is limited and we will be turning away paying customers, I shall have to charge you the room rate whether you are here or not.

She rubbed the end of the pen bib on her chin. Charging him if he hadn't yet arrived took a lot of nerve. But then, she'd turned enough people away that she knew how difficult it would be for him to find a room anywhere else.

Dove House is the finest establishment in Dakotah Territory west of Bismarck.

She thought about leaving out the last three words, but honesty wouldn't allow it.

Sincerely,
Miss Ruby Torvald, Proprietor

She hadn't quoted him a price, but then he had not asked.

She let the ink dry while addressing the envelope and made a note on the calendar. She had only two rooms that weren't taken by local workers. And Belle's. It was time to talk to Belle about the rate increase.

Taking all her courage in hand, she mounted the stairs. Halfway up, she remembered the cake in the oven and went to check it.

"Smells mighty good in there," Cimarron called from the storeroom. "I suppose it is for supper."

"Unless you want to bake another, which we probably should do anyway." To keep up with all these people, they needed another stove.

"I could do that." Cimarron came out of the storeroom rubbing and stretching her neck.

"Good, then let's have a piece." Anything to keep from climbing those stairs.

"My, that smells good." Milly came in with a laundry basket

full of folded sheets. She set it on a stool and rubbed her back. "That thing just gets heavier and heavier."

"Don't put so many in it." Daisy pulled a chair out from the table. "I'm going to ask Charlie to build me a high stool for ironing. Changing off would make it easier, I think."

"Good idea." Ruby handed out plates of cake with cream drizzled over the top while Cimarron poured the coffee. "What's Charlie doing?"

"He went fishing. Took the shotgun to get more ducks and geese if he can. Said he'd be back by dark. Think he plans to smoke the fish too."

"Good." Ruby told them about the letter from Mr. Roosevelt asking for a room. "So we have to keep one open starting that day."

"People writin' clear from New York for a room. If that ain't somethin'." Daisy made a tsking sound.

A burst of laughter and shouting told them school had just been dismissed.

"You better set up for Opal and Pearl." Ruby took her courage back out of her pocket and set it firmly in place. "Oh, and tell Pearl there is a letter for her."

This time she took the back stairs, since they were closer. Knocking on Belle's door, she could smell the cigarillo smoke. She knocked again and was about to turn away in relief when she heard Belle muttering. The door opened a crack.

"What do you want?"

Ruby debated. Beard the lion in her den now or come back later when she might be in a better mood? "I need to talk with you."

"Can it wait until later? I have a splitting headache."

"Can I get you something? Coffee? Food?" Only no more booze. The smell about knocked Ruby over.

"Coffee would be good. Let me get myself in order some." She shut the door.

Well, that's some deal. Ruby spun and headed back downstairs, working up a head of steam with every step. *I own this hotel, yet she treats me like her hired help. I never treat my hired help that way. What is the matter with her? You know what's the matter — she's been drinking. So how often is she like this? We never know because she never comes down except for meals, and lots of times she does that at odd hours and just picks at whatever is handy.*

She poured the cup, started up the stairs, and turned back for another. Two cups might not be enough, but better to be prepared than having to make a second trip. As if there were any chance she was going to do this again.

She tapped on the door.

"Come in."

Her hair in some kind of order, Belle sat in her chair with her feet propped on a footstool. Her feather-trimmed dressing gown left plenty of bare skin showing, as did a corset that pushed her chest up and out. Even disheveled as she was, the kohl around her eyes and her bright red lips looked freshly done.

Ruby handed Belle the one cup and set the other on the nightstand.

"Have a seat."

Ruby looked around, and the only available surface was the bed. "There?"

"Unless you want the floor." Belle blew two perfect smoke rings, her head back as if totally relaxed, the queen granting an audience. But her left eyelid twitched.

"I know you're aware of the increase in room prices." Ruby waited, hoping for an acknowledgment. Nothing. *All right, two can play at this waiting game.* "So I am here to inform you that your new room rate will be two dollars a day in accordance with the new rates."

"I think not." Cigarillo between two fingers, she sipped from the cup.

"I'm sorry, Belle, but that's the way things have to be."

Belle leaned forward. "Sorry, my eye, you've been waiting to do this all year. Now that you got a full house, you want to squeeze another dollar out of me."

"I can rent your room for double that, so I am giving you a break."

"Break, my eye! You want to drive me out, that's what. Turn my cardroom into a schoolroom for brats, so there's not enough room for the gentlemen to even move their chairs without bumping into things. You got it all. Why do you have to be so selfish and try to take what little I have? If your father could see this,

he'd roll over in his grave or come and haunt you." Tears laced
her voice. "It's my home that I helped build, and you want to
throw me out."

"Belle, I never said you had to leave, just that I'm increasing
your rent. Unless, of course, you want to come down and wait
tables with the rest of us. Daisy could use some help with the
ironing too, and there are always rooms to clean. You missed out
on all the canning."

Ruby's fingers itched to knock the smoking cigarillo right out
of Belle's hand. The smell and the smoke made her cough. Her
eyes smarted. How could Belle live like this? "You have to make
a decision, Belle." Were those tears she saw making black tracks
down Belle's face, a face that sagged in ripples down into her
neck?

"You'll be sorry for this."

"Belle, you have no idea how often I've been sorry for all
this." Ruby stood. "You have one week to make up your mind.
And within that week I will give you my decision on the cardroom."

"You . . ." The words that followed Ruby out the door burned
her ears.

Back in the kitchen she took off her apron and hung it outside to air. She felt like she needed to hang her entire self out to
air, so she went for a walk down by the river. *Lord, how you kept
me from screaming at her, I'll never know. For the first time, I could see
right through what she was doing. I have let her frighten me into doing
what she wanted, but no more. I will do what's best for Dove House and
the rest of us, and I'm counting on you to guide and keep me. You promised wisdom to those who ask, and I have pleaded to be wise.*

She sat down on a rock and gathered her skirt tight around
her bent legs, leaning her chin on her knees. *Am I to close the
cardroom, or is that something important to our male guests? If they
want to play cards, why do I need to provide a dealer or two? They could
go play down at Williams's. But they would come back drunk and possibly
tear up the place. If I close the cardroom, Belle will either have to find
another place to work or move. What is best for Dove House?*

*What did she mean when she said that I'll be sorry? What can she
do? What has she done?*

Eventually the ripple of river and whisper of trees spread

their calming peace, and she stared up the river. Two cows stood knee-deep in the water, drinking at an eddy. A little brown bird fluttered his wings, dipping and splashing, getting his daily bath. One of the cows bellowed a sound of warning or a call to her calf.

Rand would know, Ruby thought, feeling her face relax from tight jaw to some part of a smile. He'd understand cow talk, horse talk, and most likely bird talk too.

When they were walking Milly on Baldy, had she told him thank you? If it weren't for him, Milly might have died or stayed in that netherworld for who knows how long.

Rand Harrison. Was he interested in Pearl? After all, he sat at her table whenever he came for a meal. Hers and Mr. Hegland's.

Somehow the thought made her realize how hard was the rock she sat on and how much work she had to do at the hotel. Hands locked behind her back as she walked, she kept returning to the same question. What to do about Belle and the cardroom?

CHAPTER THIRTY-FOUR

"So what are you going to do?" Pearl and Ruby were sitting on the porch drinking coffee.

"I don't know, Pearl. I detest making anyone unhappy, and yet I know that something has to change. My father said, 'Take care of the girls,' and if I force Belle to leave, I'm not living up to my word. I promised."

The nights started earlier and with a bite these October days, so Ruby and Pearl wore shawls and enjoyed the steam and warmth of the hot coffee. They'd be forced inside soon, but since these end-of-the-day meetings were so pleasurable, they made them last as long as possible.

"I think—no, it's not even that I think—I have a feeling something's been going on here and that Belle is behind it." Ruby sipped her coffee, watching Pearl over the rim. Never in her life had she had a friend to talk things over with. She had considered Mrs. Brandon a friend, but she also had been her employer. Cimarron and Daisy were friends, but they also worked for her. Milly was more like a little sister, and she worked here too. Everything was so complicated. But Pearl, while she had helped out for her room and board, was a true friend.

"Belle is a strange one, that's for sure. I've not gotten to know her at all, other than to say hello and how are you. Was she always this secretive?"

"Interesting word choice. I'd not thought of her as secretive, just as keeping to her own schedule. Work at night, sleep during the day, eat when she got hungry."

"Pretty privileged if you ask me." Pearl stroked the cat in her lap with one hand and held her cup with the other. The light from the window slanted across her face, highlighting her cheekbones and shadowing her eyes.

An owl hooted, and they heard the whoosh of its mighty wings. Cat's ears flicked, and she glanced up.

"I figured since she paid her rent, she was entitled."

"And yet you caught her skimming off the take?"

"Belle always looks out for Belle, as Charlie has reminded me more than once."

"And she does no other work."

"No."

"Don't the others get jealous at times?"

"I think they have, and since I can't pay them much, I feel bad. It's just been the last few months that we've been in the black consistently. I never dreamed I'd be running a hotel, not only running but owning a hotel on the edge of, well, the frontier."

"I never dreamed I'd be teaching out here either. But these children are so eager to learn, and their parents too. Look at that group we had after church. People are hungry for knowledge."

"And the chance to be with others. Life can be really lonely out here where folks live so far apart."

"So here we are, two misfit city girls, sitting on the back porch, freezing our noses so we can be friends. I suggest we move to the kitchen or the dining room."

"Let's." The warmth from the stove met them at the door. Along with the chords Opal was practicing on the piano, the *kerthunk* of the sewing machine, Charlie's tuneless whistle as he sanded something made of wood, and the meow of a cat insisting that Milly share some of whatever she had cooking.

"What are you making?" Ruby asked.

"Syrup for popcorn balls. Charlie popped the corn, and we're going to make popcorn balls pretty soon. Thought we'd practice up to make them for the Christmas tree." Milly held up her spoon to see if the syrup had reached the thread stage yet. When it still globbed, she continued stirring.

"I think we should make taffy again. That was so good. Candy is something I miss from Chicago. Merman's makes fudge and truffles, caramels and divinity. We used to go buy a bag of hard candies that would last for a week."

Milly laughed. "Not here it wouldn't. You saw how fast that taffy disappeared. People better be buttering their hands. This syrup is threading." She turned from the stove, pan in hand, and poured it over the pan of popped corn. "Quick now."

While she stirred the syrup in, the others buttered their hands and dug in for a handful, pressing it together to form balls.

"Lay them on the cookie sheet."

"Ouch, it's hot."

"You need more butter. Protects your hands."

"What's going on? Sounds like a party in here." Opal joined the group, buttering her hands and digging into the popped corn to make a ball.

The pan quickly emptied and the mound of white balls grew.

"Will you look at that." Opal set the final ball on top. "Looks almost like a Christmas tree."

"So, now we can eat them." Milly nodded to Ruby. "You get the first one."

"Off the bottom?" Ruby reached for the one she mentioned, but Opal pushed her hand away.

"Ruby. You know better."

"But that's a little dinky one on top. I want a big one." She wiggled her eyebrows at her little sister. How often they'd heard that from Opal, about wanting a big one of whatever was being offered.

"Um, yum." The hard corn and syrup crackled as Ruby bit into it. "Milly, this is perfect. I didn't know you knew how to do this."

"We didn't have popcorn before."

"And to think I almost didn't plant any this year." Charlie's popcorn ball half disappeared in one bite. "But I'm glad I did. Feels like home when I was a kid."

The next day Opal served the popcorn balls as a treat for school.

"I never had such a good thing." Robert savored his down to the last finger lick.

"When it snows we can make snow candy," Edith Robertson said. "I'll get Ma's receipt."

Pearl thought to all the things she'd taken for granted as she grew up. *Perhaps I can bring in some of those things for these children. I need to start making a list.*

"All right, let's get back to our lessons. Upper level, I want you to describe that popcorn ball you ate. Make sure your sentences have proper grammar and spelling. Front row, sound out the word and tell me how to spell it. Middle group, write the word popcorn on your slate and see how many other words you can make from it."

When they finished that drill, Pearl set them all to reading from their McGuffey's Readers, book number one for her beginners. She gathered them around her chair over in the corner and started with Robert.

"Teacher, I brung you this." He handed her a heart carved out of wood, polished and oiled, hung on a rawhide cord.

"Robert, how beautiful. Did you make this?"

"Atticus, he helped me."

Pearl put the rawhide string over her head, and the heart nestled against her waist, glowing against the cream cotton. "I can't believe you did this for me."

" 'Cause you been so kind to us."

Pearl put her arm around him and gave him a hug. "You tell Atticus thank you for me too. And remind him that he is welcome back at school anytime."

Half an hour before time to dismiss, she announced, "From now on we are going to have story time at the end of the day."

"Ooh, goodie. I love stories," came from different parts of the room.

"If . . ." She paused and glanced around, catching each child's eyes. "If you've all done your best for the day. Fair?"

They all nodded, so she took a book off the table. "This book used to be the favorite of all for my brothers and sister. *Swiss Family Robinson* by Johann David Wyss." She pulled her chair out from behind the table, sat down, and opened the book.

"Thank you, Miss Hossfuss, that was a right good story," Franny Benson said on her way out the door. "I do love to come here."

Later, after the children were all gone and Pearl was putting the room back in order for the card players, she picked up two of the spittoons and set them in place. When she couldn't find the third one for the second table, she got down on her hands and knees to look under a bench. Reaching back in the corner, she pulled out the final spittoon only to hear the clink of metal on metal.

She pulled out a flask with *Belle* engraved in a circle on the front. Liquid swished when she shook it, so she unscrewed the top to get a whiff of strong whiskey, and not very good quality either.

"Some of Williams's rotgut, I imagine. Ruby is going to have a conniption fit."

—⚙—

"That does it." Ruby took the flask and started to pour the whiskey out but thought the better of it. "Thank you, Pearl. I wonder who all she's been sharing this with." Ruby stared at the flask. "And now I don't feel bad about laying down the law." She started for the stairs. "Oh, you have a letter. On the counter in the dining room."

"I'll be praying for you while you go. . . ." Pearl motioned toward the flask.

"Thank you."

With every step Ruby's teeth clenched harder. Belle had promised, no more booze in the cardroom, and here she had brought her own in. Her word meant nothing more than . . . than . . . She shoved open the door to the second floor and crossed to rap on Belle's door. She should be up by now, and if she isn't, or if she has a hangover, so be it. Her knuckles rapped sharply, echoing down the hall.

"Belle, I need to talk to you—now!"

"Coming. For crying out loud, can't you let a woman sleep?"

No, I can't or I won't.

Belle cracked open the door. "I—"

Ruby pushed the door open and flashed the flask in Belle's face.

Belle narrowed her eyes. "Where'd you find that? I been

missing it for a week or more." She reached for the flask, but Ruby backed away.

"In the cardroom, Belle, where you left it. In a spittoon, in fact. You know the rules, Belle. No booze in Dove House. So your week is up. You have two days to be gone from this room, and you will no longer be dealing in our cardroom. No one will be dealing in our cardroom unless some men get together on their own. Is that clear?"

"You . . ." Belle raised her hands, claws out. "You think you know everything. Why, you'll be sorry until the day you die that you did this."

"Two days, Belle, and the sooner the better."

"Your far—"

"My far is dead, and he deeded this place to Opal and me. Dove House *will* be the kind of place where we can live and hold our heads up."

"You can't make me leave."

"Oh yes, I can. Try me."

Back rigid, Ruby left the room, closing the door behind her. She heard something smash against a wall but paid no mind.

When she got to the kitchen, she collapsed in a chair at the table. *Oh, Lord, what have I done? I surely do hope this is your will and your way of making it possible for me to throw her out. Why did it have to come to this?* She rested her forehead in her hands. *I prayed that she would know your love and hear your word. She played the piano for our services as if she enjoyed it. She's been giving Opal piano lessons.*

"How'd it go?" Pearl laid a hand on her shoulder.

"She has two days to move."

"Or."

"Or I will move her out with one suitcase. The girls can divide her things."

"Her fancy dresses?"

"Whatever they want. We'll turn the rest into quilt tops or something."

"You going to inform the others?"

"Thanks. Good idea." Ruby sighed, a deep sigh of sorrow and defeat. *Sorry Far, I failed to care for all the girls. The others are no longer what they were and are a testament to their heavenly Father's grace. For that I must be grateful.*

"You can't win them all."

"I can try."

Ruby poured two cups of coffee and took them into the storeroom. "I need to tell you what's happened. . . ." She told Milly and Cimarron her decision.

— ❦ —

"Ruby, did you really do it?" Opal asked while helping to fix supper.

"I did. Now we'll see what happens."

"I'll be sad to see Belle leave. I like her."

"You tell her that, Opal. Right now I'm sure she thinks everyone hates her." Ruby looked up from the sign she was lettering. It read, Cardroom is Closed.

"You want me to go down the street?" the marquis asked at supper that night.

"You want to play cards, you may, but Belle will no longer be dealing, nor will Charlie. You must arrange the group if you want to play."

"Ah, you hope to change the way of life by cleaning up your hotel."

"We have school meeting in that room all day, and we have church in this dining room on Sundays. Liquor and gambling do not agree with the rest."

"*Oui,* mademoiselle, but you—what you say?—cut off your nose to spite your face?"

"We shall see. But there is still no liquor allowed even if you do play—in my schoolroom." She smiled, a proprietor's smile. "*Merci* and *bonsoir.*"

— ❦ —

"Where did you get the heart?" Ruby asked Pearl later as she poured their tea.

"Robert and Atticus. Isn't it lovely?" Pearl rubbed the sleek wood. "What a surprise."

"A good surprise. Was your letter a good one also?" They chose a corner of the dining room away from the kitchen door and sat down to visit.

"Not really. I told you about Sidney Longstreet, the man my father decided I should marry."

Ruby nodded.

Pearl pulled the letter from her pocket. "May I read it to you?"

"Of course."

"My dear Miss Hossfuss,

I cannot tell you how many letters I have written to you and burned rather than mailed. I must confess that when I received your letter informing me you were leaving, I was furious. After all, your father had agreed to our marriage, and I believed betrothals to be of some significance. I looked forward to the day we would be man and wife. My children looked forward to having you for their mother. You broke all of our hearts."

"How sad."

"I know, but, Ruby, I couldn't marry him. I just couldn't." Pearl returned to the letter.

"At first, I never wanted to see you again, but now that I have had time to calm down, I want to tell you how much I miss you. I still believe you are the woman God intends for me to marry, so if there is any way you can see your way clear to return to Chicago, I still hope to bring you home to be my wife and the mother of my children.

With all the love my heart can express,

I remain yours,

Sidney Longstreet"

Ruby ran her forefinger around the rim of the cup. "Would you go back?"

"No, never."

"So what will you tell him?"

"To go look elsewhere, for God did not tell me to marry Sidney Longstreet. My father did. Though some would contend that is the same as God, I will not go back. This is my home now."

"You even have a new heart for here."

"Yes." She rubbed the heart again. The face of Carl Hegland swam across her inner vision. Now what could that mean?

— ❧ —

The next afternoon when Milly rapped on Belle's door to clean her room, there was no answer. When she pushed the door open, thinking Belle asleep, she couldn't believe her eyes. She ran down the stairs, her heels thundering on the steps.

"Ruby, she's gone."

"Who's gone?"

"Belle. All her clothes, drawers open, all a mess. But she's gone. Where do you think she went?"

"I have no idea." *And I don't really care.*

"Probably went back to Deadwood." Cimarron turned from stirring the soup. "She still has friends there."

Why do I have the feeling we have not seen the last of Belle? Ruby wished she didn't have a tight knot in her middle.

CHAPTER THIRTY-FIVE

"Cut that cow out of there, and we'll hold 'em at the house overnight," Rand shouted to Chaps.

Chaps waved and sent his horse into the middle of the herd where an old cow kept seeking safety. He and his horse edged her out of the milling steers and, with a slap on the rump with his rope, sent her off toward the river.

"Three hundred fifty. That what you counted?" Rand stopped beside Beans.

"Right, Boss. Three hundred and fifty prime head of beef ready to ship to Chicago. You goin' with them?"

"Yep. Can't afford any accidental miscounts or off weighing. I won't be gone more'n a week." Rand ducked his chin into the collar of his sheepskin jacket. After a prolonged visit, Indian summer left during the night. Gray clouds scudded across the sky, now set to embers in the dying sun. November first, and he had his first real shipment of beef ready for the journey. The hundred head last year was just a warm-up.

"Beans, you take first watch, Joe, the second, and Chaps third. We'll leave at sunup." They only needed two men to trail the cattle to Little Missouri and then drive them into the railroad cars.

Certain that things were in order and the steers were settling down for the night, Rand headed back to the cabin. He un-saddled Buck and let him loose in the corral before joining the others for a supper of bubbling stew.

What he wouldn't give for a piece of Cimarron's apple pie right now. Beans was an adequate cook, but he'd never mastered pies. *I wonder if Miss Torvald has learned to make a good pie.* The thought made him shake his head. Amazing how his mind could rabbit trail back to Miss Ruby Torvald.

That afternoon he and Ruby and Opal had gone riding and had seen the badlands in all its fall finery. Sumac bushes blazed as if torched by fire. Willows and cottonwoods danced in their best yellow gowns, and the oak trees bowed in red and rust. While Ruby had been hesitant in rougher terrain, Opal, on Bay, would try anything. Good thing Bay had so much common sense and Opal had the sense to listen to her horse. If Bay refused to step on marshy ground, Opal didn't force her but let her pick her way around the periphery.

"You can be real proud of her," he told Ruby as they rode north along the river.

"I am. The way she handled the crisis with Milly. . . . Why, if I'd been caught out in a storm like that, I'd have been weeping my way into the earth or running screaming for any kind of shelter." Ruby shuddered. "I hate lightning. It scares me silly."

"I didn't think anything scared you."

"I hide some things well."

"Other than that little snake in the garden."

"I don't like surprises like mice jumping out of the cupboard at me or a snake sticking out its tongue when I thought it was a green stick. Lying in the shade like that, it could have fooled anyone."

"I heard you ran screaming into Dove House."

"Well, you know Cimarron has a tendency to exaggerate just the tiniest bit." She pulled back slightly on the reins for Baldy to stop.

"Will you look at that?" Down below the bluff they were riding, the river looked to be surrounded by gold. Green pasture bounded the gold with a herd of deer grazing the field. "Need to get out with the rifle and take one or two of them back to the ranch, hung across the back of a packhorse."

"I need to tell Mr. Roosevelt about that herd. He sure is interested in everything of the West. He wants a buffalo in the worst way. Says he'll stay until he gets one."

"Interesting man. He's out hunting with Jake Maunders, right?"

"If they don't lose the tenderfoot out there somewhere, not intentional, mind you, but—"

"How long he planning on staying?"

"No idea. He reserved the room and pays for it even when he's out camping. I heard him express an interest in the cattle business."

They turned the horses and headed on down the game trail that Opal had already gone down.

"Keep him on a tight rein and lean back in your saddle. You'll make it."

When Baldy slid a couple feet, Ruby let out a shriek and then attacked Rand when they leveled out. "You trying to get one of us killed or something?"

"Ruby—Miss Torvald." Ever since the Milly fright, he had a hard time not calling her Ruby. Miss Torvald was proper, but when you've been through something like that, the formalities should no longer matter. Ruby had been really upset that day. She could have lost both Milly and Opal.

The log breaking in the fireplace, sending up a shower of sparks, brought Rand back to the present. He'd see Ruby the next afternoon and stay overnight at the hotel if he didn't get there in time to load for the eastbound train. Perhaps he'd get a chance to talk to Mr. Roosevelt again. Anyone who could earn the respect of the likes of Jake Maunders must be quite a man.

— ❧ —

The next day the cattle drive went smoothly in spite of a brisk wind from the north. The diehard leaves were giving up and fluttering to join their fallen comrades lying in drifts beneath brush and trees. The wild song of high-flying waterfowl played against the lowing cattle and the rustle of hooves through the dried grass.

Rand could think of no place he would rather be. He swung his coiled rope at a lagging steer. "Get on up there. We got plenty to do before we sleep."

Rand and Beans had the cattle well watered and driven into

the holding corral before the train arrived. Railroad men pushed open the doors of the cattle cars, and with ropes swinging, Beans and Rand drove the steers aboard.

"Take Buck over to Opal," Rand said to Beans. "She'll take care of him while I'm gone, and if you want, you can stay at the hotel tonight."

"If they have any room. I'd just as soon head on home, if you don't mind."

"Suit yourself." Rand swung his saddlebags and bedroll over his shoulder and headed for the railcar in front of the cattle cars.

By the time they arrived in Chicago, he'd tired of watching the country pass by from the open door. At least they'd not had to endure the heat and thirst of summer, but that cold biting wind chewed right through his sheepskin jacket. He stayed with the buyer as he counted and weighed, coming to the same count of three hundred and fifty head that Rand had started out with.

Rand thanked him, collected his money, and caught the next train west. Cities had a stink his nostrils couldn't bear.

He roused when the conductor announced Dickinson and immediately swung off before the train came to a complete halt in Little Missouri.

Milly waved when, laden with her tray, she climbed the steps to the first coach car. "Hey, Rand, welcome home. We took good care of Buck."

Rand waved to Charlie and slung his gear over his shoulders. If he could talk Ruby into providing hot water for a bath to wash the city and train off him, he'd be content to pay extra. He glanced up to the bluff to see the roof on and windows in place on the Chateau, as the locals had begun to call the marquis's country home. Although how anything that big could be called less than a castle was beyond him.

"Do you know where I could find Miss Hossfuss?"

Rand stopped when he heard the question behind him. He turned to see an expensively dressed man in a gray suit talking to Charlie.

Charlie's eyes narrowed, but he answered the man. "She's teaching school over there at Dove House."

"Thank you. How long does the train remain in this station?"

The man had a Norwegian accent, which Rand recognized

from listening to Ruby. Surely this man was too old to be the jilted suitor Pearl had told them of one day at the dining table. That left . . .

Rand waited until the man caught up with him, then held out his hand. "Welcome to Little Missouri. I'm Rand Harrison, a friend of Miss Hossfuss's."

"Jorge Hossfuss, her father. And how did a cowboy like you come to be friends with my daughter?"

"We often eat at the same table in the dining room at Dove House. Especially after church on Sundays."

"I see."

"Your daughter has a fine reputation as a teacher here."

"Ja, well, she will not be here much longer."

"Sorry to hear that. If you'll excuse me . . ." Rand touched the brim of his hat and turned back the way he'd come. That man was trouble walking, and Rand needed reinforcements. He dropped his gear at the base of a cottonwood tree and headed up the hill to the Chateau, where he knew Carl would be working.

It took him longer than he expected. He should have gone for Buck. Stopped at the door to the house, he asked, "Hey, anyone here know where Carl Hegland is working today?"

"Upstairs." The man pointed to the staircase.

"Thanks." Rand mounted the stairs and stared around at the framed walls. "Carl?"

"Here." Carl Hegland, tool belt riding his hips, stepped into the hall.

Rand stepped around lumber pieces scattered on the floor.

"Rand, what brings you here?"

"Jorge Hossfuss just got off the same train I rode in on. He's plannin' on takin' Pearl home with him."

"She won't want to go."

"That's why I came for you. The two of us can handle him, unless she wants to go."

"I'll tell the boss I'm leaving for a short time."

The two men caught a ride on a wagon fording the river and trotted the short distance to Dove House. Children playing in the street spoke of recess, so Rand and Carl entered the front door as if storming the Bastille.

Raised voices drew them to the schoolroom.

"Then you came all this way for nothing." Pearl stood behind her desk, glaring at the man who had his back to them.

"Pearl Hossfuss, I order you to pack your things. Since there will not be another train until late this afternoon, you have that amount of time to pack. Or you can leave everything here, and we will replace them."

"Father, you are not listening to me. I have a job here, a contract for the year, and I am not leaving."

"Now, you listen here."

Carl and Rand strode forward in lockstep. One on either side of Jorge Hossfuss, they turned to him.

"You heard the lady, sir." Rand nodded toward Pearl.

"She does not wish to leave." Carl stepped slightly closer.

"And who do you think you are, accosting me like this?"

"These men are my friends, Father."

"You have strange friends then, one more reason why you will come home with me."

"Nei, she will remain here—with me." Carl spoke with a quiet authority that surprised Rand, let alone Mr. Hossfuss.

Rand looked to Pearl who quickly snapped her mouth shut. "True?" he mouthed.

Pearl shrugged.

Rand watched Hossfuss and Hegland square off.

"How about we teach this gentleman the Little Missouri Quickstep?" Rand took one arm and signaled for Carl to take the other.

"Let go of me, you ruffians!"

"Thank you, my friends. I think he gets the point." Pearl rolled her lips to keep from laughing. Rand could tell by the glint in her eyes.

"I need to call my students in from recess. Father, if you would like to join me for supper, that will be served at six. If you'd like—"

"I'd like nothing more than for you to come willingly, otherwise I'll—"

"You'll what?" Carl and Rand could well have rehearsed this scenario three times over, they worked so well together. They took Mr. Hossfuss's arms again and half walked, half carried him out the door.

"He'll be waiting for you outside, Miss Hossfuss," Carl said, then added under his breath, "Unless we have to throw you in the river for a cooling off?"

"You worthless young rabble, I'll see you—"

Rand leaned in toward Pearl's father. He intended to be firm but not threaten. "You'll see us nothing, Mr. Hossfuss. There is no law here in Little Missouri save what we handle ourselves, and near as I can see, we just foiled a kidnapping. Yes, sir, that's the way I see it. And I'm sure others of the town will see this the same way. Now, if you are lucky, you might find a bed at Dove House. If not, you can borrow my bedroll, for I do have a bed here." Rand stopped and looked to his comrade-in-arms. "You have anything to add, Carl?"

"Not a thing other than I have to get my worthless hide back to work. I won't need to take time off again, will I, sir?"

If Hossfuss didn't pick up on the smiling menace that fenced him on two sides, he'd have been far less astute than the two gave him credit for.

"You've not heard the end of this."

I'm sure he hasn't spluttered like this in years, Rand thought. "Good day, Mr. Hossfuss. Care to play a game of cards tonight? It's one of our few entertainments. Unless, of course, you would rather visit with your daughter." *Telling Ruby all of this will be a great story.* "See you, Carl."

"At supper."

"With Miss Hossfuss?"

"And her father, perhaps."

The two men went about their business, leaving Hossfuss fuming in the middle of the so-called Main Street.

When Rand walked up to the back door, he heard feminine laughter, the doubling-over kind. Including Pearl's.

"Thank you, Rand." Ruby met him at the door. "This story will grow more priceless with each telling. Did you really carry him out?"

"Me and Carl." He tipped his hat back with one finger. "He's not too happy. Hossfuss, I mean, not Carl. I think Carl meant what he said, Miss Hossfuss."

"What's he talking about?" Ruby turned to Pearl, whose cheeks pinked most becomingly.

"I think Carl Hegland is smitten with our Miss Hossfuss," he said in *sotto voce*.

"Oh, really?" Ruby turned to Pearl. "Whatever gave Rand that idea?"

The bell on the counter in the dining room dinged insistently.

"Do I find him a bed or not?" she hissed at Pearl.

"I have to go teach." Pearl fled the room to the tune of Ruby's and Rand's laughter.

CHAPTER THIRTY-SIX

It's well into November, and I still don't have an idea for the Christmas program. Pearl stared at her image reflected back in the window. The first snowfall of the season was on the ground, and instead of being outside walking under the streetlights of Chicago, she was here, where it was too dark to step off the porch.

And cold. The cold seeped in through the windows and curled like a snake around her ankles. She wore a shawl most of the time. And this was only November. What would January be like?

"It's awful cold," Ruby said when Pearl asked her about it. "We keep the stoves roaring, and the heat going up the stairs heats the floors above, but our bedrooms get frost on the inside of the windows. This isn't bad yet."

"I ordered a box of books for the schoolroom as my Christmas present to the children," Pearl said. "Someday when we have a school building, we'll have to use one room for a library, and all the people around could borrow books."

"What a great idea. You ought to tell the marquis about that. He's interested in whatever will make this area more hospitable to families."

"Have you seen Mr. Hegland lately?"

"Not often," Ruby said. "Why?"

"Well, he's not been to supper much of late."

"Probably working hard to finish something up at the Chateau."

Ruby didn't tell her that Carl was taking a dinner box with him to work so he could eat over there. Since Christmas was coming, there were many secrets floating in the air.

One day she had walked into the storeroom, and Cimarron let out a screech. "You can't come in here."

"Pardon me. Maybe we better make it a rule to knock on all closed doors before entering."

Her curiosity was killing her.

— ❧ —

When Ruby entered the kitchen the next evening, Pearl sat by the stove writing furiously.

"What are you working on?"

"The Christmas program. Do you know anyone who has a donkey?"

"No, not around here."

"I thought we could use live animals for the manger scene, and Mary could ride in on a donkey. I'm going to ask Atticus Grady if he'd like to be Joseph and ask Edith Robertson to be Mary. Do you know anyone who has a newborn baby?"

"No, sorry."

"You don't know much tonight, do you?"

"I know that there are more secrets flying around here than there were mosquitoes this summer. Pearl, I'm trying to figure how to get everyone involved for Christmas. Now that Belle is gone, who is going to play the piano?"

"I can play easy things."

"You better start practicing then, because you've just been hired."

Ruby spent a good part of the week getting Belle's room cleaned out, scrubbing it from ceiling to floor, and then rehanging the brushed and aired curtains.

When the room was ready, she consulted Charlie. "You think we should divide this room in two or turn it into a bunkroom?"

Charlie scratched under one of his muttonchop whiskers. "Too bad Mr. Roosevelt left. You could have let him have this room and charged a good price. Did you hear he bought cattle to graze on the Maltese Cross ranch before he left? We'll be seeing more of him, I expect."

"No, I hadn't heard, but I'm not surprised. He really took to Dakotah Territory. But that doesn't solve our problem here."

"Well, you could leave the room as is and offer it to the marquis on a permanent fee until his house is finished. When he's not here, rent it to someone else, but when he's here, it's always his."

"We'd have to charge him a lot. Seems putting four sets of bunks would bring in more money." Ruby studied the room. "It's bigger than the cardroom. Perhaps we should have school up here."

"Which brings in no money."

"You're right. Seems strange to not have Belle here."

"Well, you haven't seen the last of her, you mark my words."

"Oh, Charlie, she can't cause trouble now, can she?" Ruby rubbed her middle. Just the thought of trouble made her stomach squeeze.

So I still don't know what I am going to do with this room, but, Lord, I know you know. "I think for now we'll just rent it out at double the single-room rate and see what happens. Does that sound all right with you?"

Charlie nodded, studying the room with his eyes half closed. "You know . . ."

Ruby waited.

"You could divide off part of this room for more storage."

"We could."

Together they left the room, and Ruby closed the door. At least the place didn't reek of cigarillo smoke, booze, and cheap perfume any longer.

Descending the stairs, she could hear Pearl in the schoolroom, reading during story time. Ruby stopped, then sat down on the steps to listen. Now that winter was here again, she would make sure they read aloud in the evening. Everyone loved to be read to, and Pearl did a wonderful job.

Pearl was accomplished at so many things, even to playing the piano. As long as one didn't ask her to cook. What if she were to marry someone out here? Like Carl Hegland. Who would cook and clean and do all the things wives do?

You learned, so can she. Ruby nodded. True. But then she'd had help from the others. She rested her elbows on her knees and listened until Pearl stopped reading.

"That's all for today. Remember that tomorrow we will be working on our pictures in the afternoon."

"Yes, Miss Hossfuss." The children's voices came in unison.

"You are dismissed."

Ruby stood up as noise exploded like a puffball when stomped. Giggling, talking, walking, slamming the children flowed out the door and to the front of the hotel where a wagon waited for some, and others went to get their horses from the shed.

She watched as Rand stepped back to avoid getting run over. "Whoa, where you all going so fast?"

"Home, Mr. Harrison. School's done." Emily Robertson stopped in front of him. "You going to play your guitar for our Christmas program?"

"I guess so, if need be."

"Opal is going to sing one song all by herself."

"Opal has a lovely voice."

"My ma has a lovely voice," Emily said. "She just don't sing enough."

"True. Most of us don't sing enough."

Talk about the truth. Ruby turned into the schoolroom that no longer had to be put together and taken apart every day. Pearl had posted sheets of paper with the entire alphabet written in both printed letters and cursive, uppercase and lowercase. Another had a list of the children with boxes after their names, some now filled with gold stars. A flat board painted black was framed in light wood with a tray for the chalks and erasers.

"This finally looks like a real schoolroom," she said to Pearl.

"I know. Feels like one too. Just wish I had some drawers to put things in. They ought to send out a teacher's desk along with the supplies." She wiped the blackboard with a damp cloth. "There now." She dusted one hand against the other, shook out the cloth, and laid it over the back of her chair to dry. "Now, tell me about your day." The two walked toward the kitchen where they could hear Rand teasing Opal.

"But if you take Bay back home, she'll forget me."

"Now who could ever forget you?"

"Can't I keep her here?"

"What will you feed her when snow covers the pasture?"

"We can buy grain."

"True."

"The army bought hay. Why can't we?"

"Guess you can, but it's expensive."

"Oh."

"Will you ride her in the winter?"

"On nice days."

"Gets awful cold out there, even if the sun is shining."

"I know."

"Well, I'll take Baldy home today, and we'll talk about Bay again soon."

"Thank you."

"Hello, Miss Hossfuss, heard anything from your father?"

"Not a word. But my mother wrote to say that Mr. Longstreet is courting someone else. She saw them at a ball one night."

"So that lets you off the hook?"

"I believe so."

Ruby set out the coffee cups and knocked on the storeroom door. "Coffee's ready." She returned to pour. "They must be freezing in there if they keep the door closed all the time."

"They only close it when you are coming." Opal took a cookie off the plate. "Where's Cat?"

"I let her out a bit ago. You might go call her."

Cat met Opal at the door and stalked in as if her mistress should have been waiting at the door to let her in. She sat down in front of the fire to clean the snow out of her paws.

The bell tinkled over the front door, and Millie went to see who had arrived. She returned, her eyes wide. "It's Belle and a gentleman. She wants to talk with you."

"I see." Ruby closed her eyes for a second, then stood. "Does anyone know where Charlie is?"

They all shook their heads.

"I'll go find him." Milly grabbed her shawl off the hook by the door. "Maybe he's gone off to the Chateau."

"Fix a tray and bring it in," Ruby instructed Daisy. "And come save me if you hear me holler."

Pearl patted her shoulder as she walked past.

Belle sure had an ability to turn an otherwise good day upside down, and she hadn't said a word yet.

"Good day, Belle."

"This here is Brett Hume from Deadwood."

"I'm pleased to meet you. I'm Miss Torvald."

Ruby nodded to the man wearing a diamond ring on his little finger and another on the stickpin in his cravat. *Flashy, aren't you? Well, I may as well get this started.* "How may I help you?" Some of the frost from outside found its way into her voice.

"I come to buy Dove House." Belle leaned against the counter, her emerald green skirt showing the effects of the muddy street.

"My word, I didn't know it was for sale." Ruby decided a lighter tone might keep her from striking the woman. The gall of her to parade back in here like she already owned the place. As if she ever would.

"Anything is for sale if the price is right."

Ah, Belle, that's where you're wrong. It might be true for you but not for me. "That's one way of thinking."

Belle's eyes slit, and the mole-sized patch she'd added to her left cheek twitched. "I . . . we . . ." She glanced to the man who stood slightly behind her. "We have the money." She patted the bag on her arm.

"You want me to set this on the table over here?" Daisy held the tray in front of her, offering no smile of greeting.

"No, I don't think we'll be needing that. Thank you, anyway." Without offering her guests a place to sit down, she asked, "And how much might that be?"

"Five thousand dollars."

"Surely you jest."

"You know that's a fair price." Belle took a deep breath and cut the rancor. "That will give you and Opal a good nest egg. Like Per would have wanted."

"That is most generous of you to think of Opal and me like that."

"Free and clear you would be."

How noble. Ruby smiled, a tight smile that scarcely moved her mouth. "Five thousand." She shook her head. "You'd have to do much better than that, Belle. A man from New York offered me double that." That was not exactly the truth, but he'd said if she ever wanted to sell, let him know.

"Ten thousand dollars? Is he out of his mind?"

"Things are booming here, thanks to the Marquis de Mores. If I wanted to sell, he'd most likely be interested too."

"Eleven thousand, Miss Torvald." The man's tone was slippery, like ice slicks in the winter.

Ruby gulped inside but kept her face serene. "No, thank you."

Belle stared arrows at her. "You're making a big mistake." Her voice slithered across the ice of his.

"Twelve thousand."

Ruby could almost imagine the man's tongue flicking like that of a snake when he spoke. "Dove House is not for sale. Would you like me to say it a bit louder?" *Twelve thousand dollars! A fortune.*

"You think about that, Miss Torvald."

"Mr. Hume, I don't believe you are hearing me. Dove House is not for sale, but should I ever change my mind, I will let you know. Now if you will excuse me, I have work to do." She ushered them toward the door, opened it, and stood back for them to pass. "Good day."

"You ain't seen the end of this."

Ruby cocked her head. "Thank you for coming by." She closed the door and leaned back against it, hearing Belle's voice through the wood. If words were venom, Ruby knew she'd be dead within a matter of seconds. Taking a deep breath, she crossed the dining room and headed for the kitchen. *Lord, I certainly do hope I am doing the right thing. I know you don't want a brothel here any more than I do. I pray Belle was only blowing smoke when she said I'd be sorry.*

CHAPTER THIRTY-SEVEN

"Christmas is coming, the goose is getting fat . . ." Opal sang as she reset the tables. "Please put a penny in the old man's hat. . . ."

"You sound cheerful." Ruby brought another stack of red napkins in from the storeroom where Cimarron was hemming as fast as the machine would stitch.

"I love Christmastime. Dove House smells like Christmas this year—the pine tree, the boughs, the candles. Tonight we're stringing popcorn for the tree."

"We had Christmas here last year too."

"I know, but even food was scarce, let alone presents."

"Opal, have you been peeking?" Ruby put her hands on her hips in mock disgust.

"No! I just know things. Things I bet you wish you knew."

"I'll wait." Ruby counted the remaining napkins. They still didn't have enough red or green ones to serve everyone on Christmas Day. "Cimarron still has some hemming to do."

"She's going as fast as she can. We should have ordered more material in the first place."

"I know. It's my fault." Ruby studied her little sister. "Your skirt is too short again. You are growing faster than the thistles did this summer."

"I know. And my shoes pinch too. I didn't want to tell you, since you just bought these this fall."

"Opal, I won't let you get deformed feet because your shoes are too tight. Put them on my list for Charlie."

"You're not going?"

"No." Ruby stopped on her way back to the kitchen. "Opal, have you heard any rumors? Anything about Belle?"

"No. I thought she went to Deadwood for keeps."

Pearl entered and headed for the piano.

"Practicing again?"

"I have to. Good thing the songbook came, or we'd have had a pretty limited choice of songs."

"We'd sing without. We've done that before."

"Six days to Christmas."

"Five until the program." Pearl played through a succession of chords before starting on "Silent Night." "Come on, Opal, can you sing this one in Norwegian?" As Opal sang the melody and Pearl harmonized, Ruby just stood and listened. *"Stille natt, helige natt . . ."* Such wonder-filled words.

"How beautiful. Thank you." Ruby turned to find Jed Black standing in the doorway. Tonight not even the sight of the big man bothered her. She took it as a sign that God was helping her forgive, as He'd promised.

"Miss Torvald, could I ask you something?"

"Of course, go ahead."

"Well, kind of in private like." He shifted from one foot to the other.

Outside was too cold. The kitchen was busy with Milly popping corn for the stringing. Cimarron was in the storeroom, and the other two in here.

She motioned toward the schoolroom. "Will in here be all right?"

"Yes, a' course." He followed her into the room.

She turned, automatically putting a table between them. "Now, what is it you need?"

"I need you to give your blessing for me to ask Cimarron to marry me."

Ruby drew up slightly and blinked. "Now that catches me by surprise."

"Why? I thought everyone knew how I felt. Still not sure if she feels the same way, but guess I'll find out by askin'."

"When?"

"I thought I'd ask her come Christmas."

"No, I mean when would you want to get married?"

"Soon as she will."

"Where will you live?" *How will I get along without Cimarron?*

"Goin' to hafta build us a house, but most likely can't do that until spring."

"You giving up trapping and hunting?"

"Yep. I kinda like building, and there's a lot of it to do. You think we should build in Medora or Little Missouri? I'm thinkin' we need an acre or two."

Lord, I know we've both forgiven him, but if I give my blessing and he hurts her, how will I ever forgive myself?

"Your blessing would mean a lot to me, and I know to her too."

Ruby had a pretty good idea Cimarron was going to say yes. She had that look about her whenever Jed was around. *Please, Lord, help me say the words.* She nodded. "Yes, Mr. Black, you have my blessing." At his smile of relief, she added, "But if you ever hurt her, I'll come after you and shoot you myself."

"You wouldn't have to. I'd do it first. Thank you, Miss Torvald. And thanks to you, I live a different life now." He nodded once and, turning around, marched out of the schoolroom, his back straight, head high.

"Well, Merry Christmas, Cimarron," Ruby whispered, then gnawed her lip for a moment of thought. Now one of the girls would be safely married. She had Milly and Daisy to go. But what about Belle? Would there ever be a chance for real happiness for her? *Far, I cannot believe you meant for me to take care of Belle too. Belle takes care of Belle, before all else.*

— ❦ —

For the next three days the schoolchildren spent part of every day rehearsing for the program. They all had parts to say and would sing two songs, with everyone singing all the Christmas carols. Atticus Grady made a good Joseph as long as they didn't ask him to say anything. When Opal sang "Mary's Song," no one said a word until Ada Mae Robertson whispered. "I din't know Opal was an angel."

Opal snorted out a laugh. Edith and her sister Mary joined in, and soon they were all laughing. Opal was definitely no angel even though she sang like one.

— ❧ —

Pearl finished reading Charles Dickens's *A Christmas Carol* the day before the program.

"'God bless us everyone.'" Pearl closed the book. "I do like that story."

"Me too" came from about the room.

"Now, we'll see you all here and ready to put on your costumes by three o'clock tomorrow afternoon. Our program will start at four. There'll be roast goose supper for everyone, and then our first Christmas Eve service right here at Dove House. Any questions?" When no one said anything, she smiled. "Then class dismissed."

When the room was empty and the last one out the front door, she brought a box back to her table and sat down to sign a book for each of the children, her present, along with an orange, for each of them. She'd bought books for each of the staff and a copy of *The Iliad* and *The Odyssey* for Carl. Books were a proper gift for a woman to give a male friend. Not that she'd ever given a male friend a present before. And here she'd done three. She ordered Rand a copy of *A Tale of Two Cities* and Charlie *The Adventures of Tom Sawyer*. Ordering the books from her old bookstore in Chicago had been a thrill. She actually had *friends* to buy gifts for.

On her way to the kitchen, she stopped to admire the tree. White candles—and a water bucket beside the tree—strings of popcorn, cellophane-wrapped popcorn balls, red paper chains made by the schoolchildren, gingerbread men for all the children coming to the party, and candy canes for everyone. Never had a tree been more loved than this one. They would light it during the singing of Christmas carols.

Pearl inhaled the pine scent one more time and entered the kitchen. "Oh, look, fattigmann and sandbakkels. Where did you get the receipts?"

"From my bestemor," Ruby answered. "And Cimarron added the kranser cookies."

"I baked the shortbread." Milly put the last of the cookies into the tins with lids. "We have enough for everybody and then some."

"Some of the families are planning on bringing food for the dinner." Pearl snitched a fattigmann. "They say it's not fair for Dove House to always feed everyone."

"Like Mrs. Robertson?" Ruby looked up from icing a cookie.

"And some of the others. They sent notes with their children. I love the flavor of cardamom. Shame we don't use it more the rest of the year."

Charlie blew in through the back door. "Brrr, it's cold out there. The temperature is dropping."

"Just so we don't have a blizzard tomorrow."

"We won't."

"How do you know?" Ruby asked.

"Just doesn't feel like it. Wainwright is letting the men off early tomorrow, since it is Christmas Eve. At three."

"Good."

"A box came on the train today from a church in Chicago. You wouldn't know anything about that, now would you, Miss Pearl?"

"Oh good. Did you open it?"

"No, it's addressed to the schoolchildren of Little Missouri."

"Then we'll all open it tomorrow."

"I can't wait." Opal picked up Cat and sat down on the step-stool. "We should give you a red bow, Cat. With a bell on it. Where's Goldie and Gray Bar?"

"Sound asleep behind the stove." Milly stirred a pot on the stove. "Cocoa anyone?"

— ❧ —

The kitchen was busy long before the sun came up to glitter on fields of white. As soon as they finished breakfast, they continued preparations for the coming celebration. Ruby mentally checked down her list, trying to make sure no one was left out. Invitations had been announced in church the last two meeting times, and Charlie had made sure anyone not in attendance received a personal invite. Announcements had been made at meal times for all the men working in Medora, so if everyone came, there would be standing room only. Ruby planned to serve on long tables with everyone helping themselves.

Every time Ruby went by the tree, she inhaled the scent of pine and another burst of Opal's contagious excitement. Once she caught Pearl standing in front of the tree, tears leaking, chin quivering.

"Homesick?"

"Um-hmm." Pearl dabbed at her eyes. "I've never been away from home at Christmas before."

"The first time is the hardest." Ruby patted her arm. "I can tell you one thing. I'm really glad you are here, and I know there are lots of others who feel the same way."

"That helps. If I could know my father doesn't hate me, that would be the best Christmas present I could receive."

"Your heavenly Father doesn't, and that's far more important."

"I know. And for that I am truly grateful." She wiped her eyes again. "Well, that's enough maudlin thoughts for today. How else can I help?"

They served vegetable venison soup and sandwiches for dinner with the smell of roasting goose and stuffing permeating the entire building. Ruby set Pearl to refilling all the kerosene lamps that were set in reflective brackets on the walls. A bit of greenery and a red ribbon hung on each. As the time drew nearer, the pace frenzied. Daisy snapped at Milly, and Milly burst into tears. Ruby comforted both of them, teeth marks roughening her tongue from the effort not to yell.

"All right. Charlie, you finish carving the meat. Cimarron, you mash the potatoes. Milly, you and Opal make sure all the chairs are out. Daisy, you fix the pickles. Pearl will take charge of her children, and I will go sit down and drink my coffee."

At their hoots of laughter, she knew she'd successfully overridden that ripple. But she was serious about the cup of coffee—she needed a moment to nurse the holes in her tongue. *Please, Lord, make this go smoothly, or at least peacefully, so everyone has a wonderful time.*

By three-forty-five all the children were ready in the closed-off schoolroom. Much of the seating was taken, but Ruby had a feeling something was wrong. None of the townspeople had walked through the doors. She stepped out onto the front porch and glanced up the street to see lights in every window. The street was empty.

Charlie joined her. "They won't be coming."

"What?"

"Mrs. Robertson just whispered to me that she'd received a message to not come. There were some scurrilous things said about Dove House and what goes on here."

"What goes on here?" Ruby glanced up the street again. Johnny Nelson, the store proprietor, was coming from across the street.

"Sorry I'm late," he called. He carried a wrapped package under one arm.

"Good evening, Mr. Nelson. Happy Christmas. You made it just in time."

As Mr. Dennison entered Dove House she turned to Charlie. "What in the world are you talking about?"

"There's rumors that the women of Dove House have returned to their former occupation, you included, and therefore those who buy that load of horse manure said they won't step foot in here again."

Ruby felt a giant fist slam her in the stomach that ignited a fire within. "Do you have any doubt as to who started such a rumor?"

"No."

"As much as we've done for the families in this town, they would believe that?"

"Some folks have a tendency to believe whatever ill gossip comes about." He took her arm and they walked through the door.

We will have the best Christmas ever, and those who won't come are the ones who will miss out. Anger well disguised a wounded heart.

Pearl played the opening chords, Rand joined in with his guitar, and the doors of the classroom opened to four angels in white sheets with gold halos set precariously on their hair walking through the crowd and up the center aisle singing, "Angels we have heard on high, sweetly singing over the plains. . . ."

"Please join us," Pearl announced after the children finished the first verse and chorus. Soon the Gloria echoed around the room.

Charlie read the age-old story, and as he read, Mary and Joseph made their way to the front, while Pearl softly played the tune to "O Little Town of Bethlehem," and then everyone sang. When Mary took the stool by the manger and Joseph stood behind her, the tallest angel stepped forward. Opal looked to Pearl, who gently stroked the keys while Rand fingered the notes, and "Oh holy night, the stars are brightly shining. It is the night of our dear Savior's birth" rejoiced across the room.

When the song ended, a small voice said, "See, Opal is too an angel." Giggles swept through the room like a breeze through the cottonwood leaves.

The shepherds came and said their parts, the angels theirs, and the shepherds returned as wise men by virtue of wearing crowns instead of headcloths and carrying presents instead of staves and crooks.

The whole room surged to their feet when the final notes of "Joy to the World" faded away. The enthusiastic clapping masked eyes full of tears and throats full of joy. The children took their bows, and Ruby came to the front. She waited for everyone to sit down again. "While we'll be giving out presents later, right now there's a big box that is addressed to the school-children of Little Missouri. Charlie, would you please bring that up here so they can all help open it?"

"I'm going to need some help. Atticus, could you come with me?"

Atticus looked down at his robe and belted undergarment.

"You can move in that thing. People been doing so for ages."

The buzz of excitement made Ruby smile. When the thought of those missing came by, she swatted it away. Nothing was going to ruin this celebration for these people. Belle's little trick would backfire somehow. The fact that all these folks were here in spite of her lies told the real story. As Charlie had said, some folks were always ready to believe the worst. She also ignored any thoughts of getting even—for now.

Charlie and Atticus carried the box in and set it right in the middle of the stage area. Charlie cut open the twine and beckoned for Pearl to take over.

"I don't know any more about this than any of you, so let's see what is here." She unfolded the box flaps and motioned for the children to gather around.

Ruby stood off to the side with Daisy and Milly on either side of her, Jed and Cimarron behind. "As soon as this is finished, we'll get the food on the table as quickly as possible."

"Ooh, lookie." Books, tablets, pencils, paints, a long jump rope, two balls, maps—the bounty spread across the front as each child held and admired the treasures.

Pearl rocked back on her heels, her face beaming. "Manna from heaven."

"Merry Christmas, and 'God bless us every one.'" Ada Mae quoted Tiny Tim and threw her arms around Pearl's neck. "You the best teacher ever."

Pearl blinked back tears as she accepted the hugs of all the children. "You all go change your clothes now so we can have supper. And thank you."

Charlie stood and held his hand up to stop. "No, wait, we have one more thing."

Pearl looked to Ruby, who shrugged her lack of knowledge.

Four men trooped out, and the others waited. And waited. They heard some banging in the kitchen. "Easy now. Careful." Those in the dining room looked questions at each other. The angels caught the giggles. Pearl shushed them.

The men pushed through the swinging door carrying something so big it took all four of them. They set the golden piece of furniture down in front of Pearl, who couldn't seem to close her mouth.

"A desk?"

"You got that right. Carl Hegland, here, he made it just for you." Charlie slapped Carl on the shoulder.

Pearl could hardly catch her breath. "I . . . I can't be . . . I mean . . ."

"I think she likes it," Ada Mae said with a sagacious nod.

Pearl took a deep breath. "Thank you very much, Mr. Hegland." She ran a hand over the surface, leaned down, and pulled out the narrow flat drawer.

"For your pencils and things."

She closed that one and pulled out the deep one on the right side.

"For papers and whatever you need. You said you needed a desk."

Pearl nodded, oblivious of all the others in the room. "Thank you again. I can never say thank you enough."

"See, I told you she likes it." Ada Mae looked around when everyone started laughing, then hid her giggle behind her hands.

Ruby smiled and nodded when she caught Pearl's shiny gaze. Christmas surprises. What a treasure.

"Rand, will you start grace for us? I thought we'd sing the 'Doxology.'"

He nodded, his smile making her heart flutter just the tiniest. "Praise God from whom all blessings flow . . ." The rich harmonies from around the room sent all her resentments scurrying out the door.

The food disappeared about as fast as they set it out. They kept refilling all the platters and bowls until the people groaned.

"We'll have coffee and dessert following our service, so if we can clear the tables, we'll continue."

"When do we get presents?" a small voice asked, making everyone chuckle again. Tonight, chuckling, visiting, and laughing all came easily.

Finally the last verse was read, the last carol sung, and many lamps were blown out as the candles were lighted on the tree.

"Oh, pretty . . . beautiful . . . ohh . . ." came from around the room as the tree glimmered and shimmered in all its glory.

"I am so glad each Christmas eve, the night of Jesus' birth." Opal and Pearl sang like they'd been singing together all of their lives.

Ruby fought the tears, she truly tried, but they slipped down her cheeks in spite of her attempts. When a handkerchief appeared over her shoulder, she glanced back to see Rand smiling down at her.

She leaned back slightly and felt the warmth of his broad chest. His hand rested on her waist. Never had she realized how comforting a man's hand could be and how strong his chest. She mopped her eyes again.

Pearl gave out her presents to all the children. Every child came and picked out a candy cane and a gingerbread man, then several of the men blew out the candles on the tree before it caught fire.

"Merry Christmas, and God bless us every one," Ruby said in closing.

When everyone had gathered their things and trooped out the door, the jingling of bells from horse harnesses carried the song on out toward the hills.

Ruby said the last good-bye and closed the door, leaning her forehead against the wood, feeling Rand standing right behind her.

"Merry Christmas, Ruby."

How fine her name sounded when he said it. "Merry Christmas, Rand." She turned and laid her head against his chest.

Merry Christmas indeed.

CHAPTER THIRTY-EIGHT

"Jed, he asked me to marry him," Cimarron announced after the last of the guests had left.

"And you said?" Pearl glanced up at the man who looked down on Cimarron as if he'd reached the Holy Grail.

"She said yes." His whisper wore awe and reverence like a costly cloak. Pearl glanced over at Ruby to see her eyes shining.

Charlie cleared his throat. "Well, I say it's about time." For some strange reason, he had to clear his throat again.

"So . . ." Opal struggled to say something she obviously didn't want to. "So, does that mean you . . . you won't be here at Dove House anymore?"

"Now, why would I leave here?" Cimarron reached over and patted Opal's cheek. "We're not goin' anywhere, honeybun. I'm hoping Ruby will let us take up that other room on the top floor until we get us a house built."

"But we can't do that until spring, so . . ."

All eyes turned to Ruby, who looked to be pondering on a deep question, her eyes half closed, two frown lines between her eyebrows.

"Ruby." Opal sounded like the elder on the point of scolding for a moment.

"Well, I have to think of all the ramifications."

"What's ramifications?"

"Ramifications. All sides of the issue, how things could be

affected by this new move, things like that."

"Just say yes and get it over with." Opal gave a deep sigh.

"Opal, you are getting to be quite an actress." Pearl chuckled. "Come on, Ruby, the suspense is costing these two people a year's growth."

"I don't know, if Jed gets any bigger, he won't get through the doors as it is." Now it was Charlie's turn to quirk an eyebrow.

Pearl glanced to the tree, now sans candles. How wonderful it would be to light it again. She looked back to Ruby.

"All right." She nodded once. "The new room it is."

Applause made the tree shiver. The tree shook. The tree started to tip forward.

Opal shrieked. Charlie leaped to save the tree. Milly squeaked and scrambled to get out of the way. Gray Bar leaped from the upper branches, landed scrambling, and tore around the room looking for a way out.

Opal and Ruby burst out laughing at the same time, joined by the others, with Jed's bass nearly drowning out everyone.

"Did you see his eyes?" Opal chortled.

"Good thing he didn't land on any of us. His claws were spread wide out." Milly covered her lower face with her hands and giggled on.

"He about got your hair." Daisy, sitting in a rocking chair, patted Milly on top of her head. "Thought sure he was comin' straight for me."

"Poor kitty. Guess he thought that tree was his for climbing." Opal glanced up at Charlie. "You sure are quick when you need to be."

"Old Charlie's always been quick. Had to be around here." Rand tipped back in his chair so the back legs creaked. "Hey, Carl, why you sittin' clear back there?"

"So the cat won't attack me."

Opal rolled her eyes. "I asked him too, and he said he liked the wall. What kind of an answer is that?"

Pearl looked over her shoulder, feeling his gaze resting on her. "How did you ever get that desk done in time for Christmas?"

"Long hours, Miss Hossfuss."

Charlie turned his chair around and crossed his arms on the

back. "I say we open the presents now. It's almost Christmas day as it is."

They had cleaned up the kitchen and moved the tables and chairs back in place in the dining room so that all would be ready for breakfast. Most of the other guests had gone off to bed, and some of the marquis's workmen were still down at Williams's.

Everyone looked to Ruby.

"What? Do you think I'm the mother here?"

"Nope, but you're the boss lady."

"We should wait for morning."

"Ah." Opal looked to Charlie. "Ask her real nice."

Charlie rolled his eyes. "I don't know how to ask real nice."

Ruby stretched out the moment. "All right. We all have five minutes to bring our gifts out of hiding and get them under the tree."

Everyone ran in different directions, and the stack of presents grew. Something big in the back had a blanket thrown over it.

"All right," Ruby declared when they all assembled again, most with a cup of coffee in hand. "Opal will hand out the gifts, and we all take turns, starting with the youngest. Someone tell Opal to pick her gift out."

"That one on your right, angel singer." Pearl pointed to a package.

Opal tore off the wrapping and held up a book. "Now I have two books of my very own."

"What's the title?"

"'Black Beauty.'" She flipped open the pages. "It's about a horse! Thank you, Miss Hossfuss. I can't wait to read it."

"Now for Milly."

"Shame Adam Stone couldn't be here."

Milly blushed forty shades of red.

Opal handed her a gift. "From me."

Milly unwrapped a pair of embroidered pillowcases. "Thank you, how pretty."

"For your hope chest. Ruby says every girl needs a hope chest."

"You made these for me?" Milly laid them in her lap and traced one of the flowers.

"Took forever." Opal's sigh made for more chuckles.

As the gift pile dwindled, Ruby kept looking at the blanket-covered one in the back.

Pearl watched her. She had a sachet filled with rose petals from Milly, a hand-carved pen with two nibs from Charlie, an apron from Cimarron, and stationery from Ruby. But the most amazing gift of all was the desk. And Carl had assured her that it was hers, not the school's. How could she ever thank him enough?

He'd moved his chair closer, close enough that she could reach around and take his hand. Those hands that could call forth such beauty from wood. A gift like that was not proper. Her mother would be aghast. Her father would ask him to declare his intentions. Did he have intentions? She angled her body so she could watch him out of the corner of her eye. When she caught him watching her, heat flared up her neck. She automatically touched her fingers to the underside of her jaw. If only she was beautiful. If only . . .

"So who is that big one for?" Opal glanced around the room to see Rand nod.

"From me to you."

"For me?" Her voice squeaked in excitement.

"I found it on my trip to Chicago. Pull it out."

Opal pulled the blanket off. "A saddle! Look at that. A roping saddle."

"Rand, you can't—"

He held up a hand to stop Ruby before she really got going. "Yes, I can. Opal needs a saddle, and that cowboy needed the money. He near to gave it away."

"Thank you, Mr. Harrison."

"Now there's another gift you can give me." He looked right at Opal after a glance at Ruby. "You can call me Rand and forget the Mr. Harrison bit." He held up a hand again when Ruby started to sputter. "I know what's proper, and we all know what good manners Opal has but, well, let's just say it is time."

Pearl leaned back, her arms locked around her knees, not the most ladylike position, but here on the floor she felt closer to all of them, like they were all gathered in a half circle that signified more than friends and people who worked together. Far as she could see, Ruby's dream of a family was mighty close to being a reality in this group of friends.

And she was included. Here had nothing to do with her father. In fact, he was *persona non grata*, at least in these friends' eyes. Here she was accepted, nay, more than that. She was looked up to as the teacher. Miss Hossfuss, a badge of honor. Pearl Hossfuss, a friend with friends.

— ⚜ —

Carl watched her as she laughed and joked with all those around her. So beautiful and yet she wore a nearly transparent veil, one she hid behind as if afraid to peek out, afraid someone would look beyond that veil and not like what they see.

How did he know that? He stroked the desk he'd so lovingly crafted. For her. Always for her. Could she look at the desk and see his reflection? A reflection was always safer than the real thing.

If he reached out, he could touch her hair. Pearl Hossfuss, the daughter of one of the wealthier men in Chicago, out here in Little Misery, a land of misfits and has-beens. Of course she came to teach school, but when she tired of this, she would return to a wealthy life in Chicago.

He'd said it. *"She stays with me."* But had she heard that in the tension of the moment? What colossal nerve he had. To even dream of it. Pearl Hossfuss and Carl Hegland?

He glanced up when someone called his name.

"Thought we'd move the desk into the schoolroom, so no one spills on it in the morning." Charlie had two corners and nodded to the other end. Carl nodded and, laying the book he'd been thumbing through on his chair, helped carry the desk into the schoolroom.

Pearl followed and set the kerosene lamp on the corner of the desk. "Where the light can reach all around the room," she said, smiling.

Carl wished he could have made a fancier desk, but with the lack of time, he was lucky to have finished this one.

"I don't know how many times I've mentioned how I wanted drawers in a desk."

"Wish there were more."

"No, this is perfect. The room isn't huge, and this way I can . . ." She stared into his eyes, shadowed by the angle of the lamp. "Thank you."

"You are most welcome."

"Perhaps we can read *The Iliad* together."

"Most certainly. I won't be working such long hours now."

Was that a hint of laughter she caught in his eyes?

"I was concerned for you."

"Really?"

She nodded. "Really. I-I think we better join the others."

I'd rather not. "Of course."

CHAPTER THIRTY-NINE

Vengeance was not a sin, or was it?

Ruby tried to concentrate on her bookwork, but thoughts of ways to get even with the people of Little Missouri ate at her like maggots on rotting meat. The night before someone had attached a sign to the front door—Go Bak Wher Yu Com Frum. If she could laugh at the spelling, perhaps she could ignore it, but things were beginning to get to her, especially considering all she'd done to help clean up this town and make it fit for decent people to live here. That was the problem. They weren't decent people and didn't want to become so.

Ink dripped from her pen and blotted the page. "Of all the—" She slammed her pen down, scattering ink on the tablecloth, and stormed into the kitchen. She poured herself a cup of coffee, took a sip, and promptly spit it out. Lukewarm.

"Why can't someone at least remember to keep the coffeepot hot?"

"Because it gets too strong, and last night you were complaining about the strong coffee." Pearl laid her book in her lap.

"I was not complaining." Ruby lifted the lid and clattered it onto the next one, leaving a residue of greasy soot on the clean stove. She knew it was clean. She had sanded and blacked it the day before.

"Horsefeathers!" She glared at Pearl, expecting a remonstrance.

Pearl wisely kept her gaze on the pages in front of her, holding the book up high enough that her eyes were hidden.

Ruby shoved the wood in the stove, set the lid back in place, and pulled the coffeepot over the heating section.

"Ruby, do you—?"

"No, I don't."

Opal stopped in the doorway. "How do you know what I was going to ask?"

Ruby's sigh screamed of frustration and guilt. "I'm sorry. I— What is it you wanted?"

"I wanted to know if you know where . . ." She glanced at Pearl. "Oh, never mind," she said and left the room.

Ruby huffed and threw her hands in the air. "What is this place coming to?"

"She wanted an answer for her homework."

"Oh. And I almost got sucked into helping her out." Ruby poured her now steaming coffee and returned to the books she disliked doing in the best of times.

Please, God . . . She stopped in her prayer. How could she pray when she was so persistently angry at anything and everything?

She could hear Rand's voice. *"You're letting them win if they wreak havoc on you like this."* He was right. But he hadn't seen the sign, and she had a feeling something else had happened that Charlie took care of without letting her know. Was there more at the heart of this than Belle's insinuations and her attempts to cause dissension? After all, how were things any different here at the hotel, other than fewer people coming to church? Obviously those who needed it worst.

Sometime later, after going to bed early so nothing else could go wrong, she closed her Bible and set about her nightly prayers. *Father, forgive me please. I'm acting rather badly. All right, I'm being mean and hateful, and I really don't like me very well this way. But I can't seem to stop. I just get over it, and something else happens.*

Opal snuffled softly in her sleep.

I have so much to be grateful for, and here I am whining like a spoiled child. Thank you for caring about this place, but why do I have to forgive everyone, when they did the evil?

She heaved a big sigh and rolled on her side to feel more of Opal's warmth. *"Weeping may endure for a night, but joy cometh in the morning.*" The verse comforted her as she fell like a stone into the depths of sleep.

She woke in the wee hours to realize it was now 1884. A new year, a new beginning. What good would it bring? *It better bring a new me, for the old one is managing to offend the people I least want to offend, and those whom I would like to offend have no idea how I feel. Nor do they care. I should have sent Belle packing a long time ago.*

But I so wanted her to turn her life over to Jesus. The others have, and look what a difference it has made.

If you're the example she sees of Jesus, why would she want to? The insinuating little voice made her cringe inside.

Why would she? Oh, Lord, why would she? You say to love, and I live out hate. Forgive me, please forgive me.

She finally fell asleep again, and daylight was peeking in the window when she woke.

"Mercy, what have I done?" She threw her clothes on, bundled her hair in a snood, and tied an apron on as she hustled down the stairs.

The fragrances of frying bacon, fresh bread, and cinnamon met her halfway down. She might have slept in, but the others hadn't.

"Happy New Year!" Opal toasted her with a cup of cocoa. "Rand is here and wondered if we wanted to go riding. He brought Baldy and Bay. You could use my saddle if you like."

"We'll freeze."

"Not if we bundle up." The light in Opal's eyes was dimming.

"Of course we'll go."

"If we were in Chicago, we'd be riding in sleighs through the streets if there was enough snow." Pearl brought her coffee back into the kitchen for a refill. "You'd think the men building over in Medora would be able to stay home in such weather."

"But then they wouldn't get paid. At least they are working in a warm building. The fireplaces are in, according to Mr. Hegland." Cimarron set her tray down. "Everyone says they had enough. Have you eaten yet, Ruby?"

"No, and if I'm going riding, I better eat quickly before Opal wears out the stairs."

"Shame you don't have any britches. With long johns that would be warmer than your divided skirt."

"I thought Belle took that outfit with her."

Cimarron tried to look innocent, but laughter chinked out the edges. "Ah, she couldn't find it."

"You knew she was leaving on the sly like that?"

"You think I was going to stop her? I'd have helped her pack if I'd known."

Ruby wisely decided not to ask any more.

— ✤ —

Getting mounted, bundled like they were, took some effort, but when they rode across the frozen river, the sky arched above them was such an aching blue that it took Ruby's breath away. Snow and ice outlined each twig and branch on the cottonwood trees, and snow was plastered on the north sides of the trunk, hiding the deep crevices in the bark. A crow announced to the world that humans had invaded the territory, his raucous caw setting a flock of chickadees to flight. A covey of grouse whirred up at their approach.

"You want to go up and see the progress on the Chateau?" Rand asked.

"I'd love to. Thank you for giving us this treat."

"Head up to the house," Rand called to Opal, who was riding ahead of them. "You need to get out more," he said, turning to Ruby.

"I do, don't I?" Ruby leaned forward, the restored army saddle creaking a protest. She patted Baldy's shoulder. "You're a good horse, aren't you, old fella." Baldy's ears swiveled, one tilting forward, one back.

"He's listening to you. I swear, Buck understands everything I say." Rand wore his sheepskin jacket, leather gloves that had a gauntlet over the ends of his sleeves, his hat pulled low to shade his eyes from the brilliance of the snow.

Rand Harrison is one handsome cowboy. The thought heated Ruby's cheeks even more than the biting breeze.

They stopped the horses on the south side of the Chateau, where the main entrance would be looking out over the southern river valley.

"He has quite the view from up here, doesn't he?"

"Magnificent."

Red and ochre lines showed on the rock formations crowned with white. Drifts, so pure they shadowed blue, crowned every hillock or filled in the hollows. Chimney smoke rose slightly east of south, a thin finger that announced a homestead.

"Robertsons," Rand said, then pointed to another one slightly more south. "Mine." His looked more like a puff of gray, mostly hidden by the hills between town and his ranch. "You watch, this time next year you'll see smoke rising from houses and businesses all over that flat down there." They looked back over Little Missouri. Both chimneys of Dove House were puffing gray, as were others. Blanketed in white, Little Missouri looked almost hospitable, like a peaceful little village welcoming strangers and those who lived there as well. The United States flag added the perfect color at the west end of the street.

"Army's back, I see."

"Two days ago. They had to bivouac due to the blizzard. Their new cook has a lot to learn, so several have been over to eat."

"You heard if Adam Stone is getting out?"

"No, haven't seen him. But what do you mean—getting out?"

"Well, last time I saw him, he mentioned the army might not be the place for him."

"Can we ride up the river a ways?" Opal trotted back from circling the house. "Sure is a big place."

"They'll be able to see that red roof for miles." Rand reined Buck around. "Anyone have ice skates? We could clear a patch of snow off the river and go skating."

"That, at least, is something I know how to do."

By the time they returned to the hotel, Ruby could no longer feel her feet. When she stepped down from the stirrup, her feet refused to work.

Rand caught her as she crumpled. "Sorry, I forgot to warn you. Opal, how about taking the saddles off Baldy and Bay and tying these critters in the shed?"

He still had his arm around her. Ruby knew she should stand on her own now, but with the knives and needles slashing her feet, she knew she'd end up headfirst in a snowbank if she tried to walk. And besides, leaning on someone stronger felt mighty wonderful.

"Your feet all right now?" he whispered in her ear.

"I think so." She took a tentative step, and now her foot only burned.

He tucked her gloved hand through his crooked arm and half supported her up the shoveled path.

Charlie was just finishing sweeping off the porch, so he swept the snow off their boots also. "There's a young man inside wants to see you."

"Who?"

Charlie nodded to the door being held open by Adam Stone.

"Happy New Year, Private Stone."

"No longer. I am now civilian Adam Stone."

"Well, I'll be. You did go and do it then?" Rand shook his hand. "I thought you were planning on a career in the army."

"I was, until . . ."

"Until?" Ruby unwound the long scarf from around her neck.

"That's what I want to talk to you about."

"I see." She smiled at the nervous young man. "Care to join me in the schoolroom? Bring some coffee." This was getting interesting. First Jed Black had wanted to talk with her and now Adam Stone. If it was about the same kind of thing, there was getting to be a regular pattern here.

She took the cup he offered her, sat down on one of the school benches, and waited.

He paced one way and then the other, obviously trying to decide how to say something.

"Mr. Stone, if this has to do with Milly, well, I heartily approve."

"Do you really?"

"How could you doubt?"

"Well, now, I don't have a job, but I will have as soon as I get home. So I want to take Milly with me, but . . ."

Ruby held up a hand. Never had she heard this many words at one time from this particular young man.

"You want to take Milly home with you to where?"

"Indiana. I thought we could be married in Dickinson. That way some of you could be there."

"Have you discussed this with Milly yet?"

"No. I wanted your permission first."

"Well, you have my permission and my blessing. I don't know what I am going to do without her around here, but that is my problem, not yours. When are you going to ask her?"

"Right now. Can I use this room?"

"It's not very romantic, but it's fine with me. Do you know where she is?"

"Up cleaning rooms."

"Does she know you're here?"

"I don't think so."

"Good. I'll send her in." Feeling like a matchmaker at work, she went to find Milly.

She heard the girl singing in one of the rooms and stepped in, making her face sober, a real act of will. "Milly, there's been a spill in the schoolroom. Would you go clean it up, please?"

"Of course. I'm done here anyway." Milly took her mop and bucket and cleaning rags and headed out the door.

Ruby followed behind, wishing she could be a mouse in a corner of the schoolroom.

Hearing Milly squeal Adam's name made it all worthwhile.

"What's going on?" Daisy started through the swinging door.

"No!" Ruby spoke louder than she'd planned but put a finger to her lips when Daisy halted. "Adam Stone was waiting for Milly in the schoolroom. I told her to go in there and clean up a spill."

Cimarron laughed out loud, the others giggled, some hiding behind their hands. Rand's eyebrows tickled his hairline, but his grin joined all of theirs.

— ❧ —

Rand, Ruby, and Opal traveled on the train the next day to Dickinson with the two to be married. A local pastor performed the ceremony, and afterward he promised Ruby he would come to Little Missouri one Sunday to lead a church service.

"I can't believe this is happening." Milly hadn't let go of Adam's hand since they got on the train.

"It has happened. You are now Mrs. Adam Stone." Opal hugged her friend. "I'm going to miss you so much."

"You sure you wouldn't just as soon stay out here and work

in Medora? There'll be a lot of work there." Rand ushered them into the hotel where he had ordered three rooms. "Now you all go upstairs for a bit, and we'll eat in about an hour."

Ruby and Opal followed behind the newlyweds, Opal giggling at the many shades of pink that galloped across Milly's face.

"She's really married." Opal leaned back against the closed door. "So fast. Who will go fishing with me now? And riding?"

"I know. Who'd have ever thought it would be like this?" Ruby bounced a little on the side of the bed. "I thought Cimarron would be the first."

"You look nice."

"Thank you." Ruby stroked down the fine fabric of her brick-red traveling gown. "I get to wear this so seldom. One of these days we are going to have to make some new dresses, some nice dresses, not just waists and skirts for work."

"I'd like some britches."

"Opal."

"Well, I can wish, can't I? Riding, fishing, working in the garden—they all would be so much easier with britches."

"I was thinking more along the lines of a nice blue dress with black trim."

"Green."

"If you like. We better be getting back down there."

Rand had ordered a special table for them all with a nice supper and even gave a toast to the blushing couple.

"May God bless you, make you prosperous, and keep you close to Him all the days of your lives." Rand raised his coffee cup.

Ruby stared at him in amazement. What other depths did she have to learn about this man?

CHAPTER FORTY

"Listening to you read is a deep pleasure."

"Thank you, Mr. Hegland." Pearl set her closed book on the table to be taken back to the schoolroom later. "I have always loved to both read and to be read to. All of us together like this feels like a family." She glanced around at those gathered. Cimarron and Jed always sat side by side now, Ruby and Opal, and somehow Daisy and Charlie ended up close together. Some of the other guests joined them at times, and sometimes men gathered around tables in the schoolroom, no longer referred to as the cardroom, to play a friendly game of cards. But only if they agreed to get along without spittoons.

Daisy passed around a plate of chocolate cookies, and Cimarron poured the hot cocoa. Sometimes they had hot apple cider.

"I finished *A Tale of Two Cities*," Carl said to Pearl.

"And?" She liked the feel of him leaning close to talk with her, as if he really enjoyed her company, not just the evening.

"Ja, I liked it. Makes one realize how fortunate we are in America. We are free to vote and raise up our own leaders. No monarchy and privileged royalty."

"But you must admit we have a class system here in America too."

"Not necessarily. If someone makes enough money, they can do about what they want."

Pearl thought of her father. He was wealthy, but that still

didn't open all doors to the society he desired. Did Mr. Hegland know who her father really was?

"Do you honestly believe that?"

"Yes." His eyes crinkled slightly at the edges.

Do I use my family as an example? No, I better not. "So what would you like to read next?"

"Changing the subject?"

"My mother said politics and religion were two subjects not to be discussed in polite company."

"You mentioned a stepmother at one time."

"Yes, my mother died when I was twelve. But Amalia, my stepmother, was—is a most loving woman. If I had trusted her more, I think we should have been friends far sooner. I suppose I have started thinking of her as my mother lately."

"That is good, as it should be. And you have brothers and sisters?"

She nodded. "Jorge Junior is twelve. Anna, who is six, and Arnet, age seven, are my half sister and half brother. I miss them."

"Will you go back?"

"I guess God alone knows that. To visit perhaps one day, but not to live in my father's house again." *Not if I can help it.* "And you, Mr. Hegland?" Strange that they should be having this conversation after all these months. Books had been a much safer topic. Now she got him talking at least.

"Read the next chapter tomorrow night?" Ruby set her cup in the dishpan, as did the others as they left the room.

"Of course. And perhaps one night we can play a few rubbers of whist?"

"Or poker?"

Was that Opal who whispered that? Where, when did she learn to play poker?

— ❧ —

On Monday the Robertson girls were missing from school. Tuesday, the Bensons, and on Wednesday Opal woke with a sore throat.

"My eyes hurt. I'm hot."

Ruby laid a hand on her sister's forehead. "Yes, you are."

Ruby held the lamp close. "And you have red spots. I wonder if that is what is keeping all the other children home from school."

"Looks like measles to me," Daisy announced. "When one gets them, they all get them." She glanced around at the others gathered in the kitchen now that breakfast was over. "You all had measles? I had them when I was about seven. My mother had her hands full with three children sick at one time."

Charlie, Ruby, and Cimarron all nodded. Pearl shrugged. "I think so. I remember having a rash or spots and being miserable." But she couldn't ask her mother, and her father probably wouldn't remember anyway.

Atticus, who had started school again after Christmas, Robert, and their little sister, June, were the only ones to make it to school, so Pearl spent the day drilling on the alphabet, the sounds of letters, and writing the letters on slates and blackboard. By the end of the day, Atticus could write his name.

He stared at his slate. "That is my name?"

"It most certainly is."

"A-t-t-i-c-u-s." He slowly spelled out his last name too, forming each letter as he pronounced it.

Pearl swallowed the heat of tears in her throat. To think she'd been almost afraid of him those first days. And there truly was a good mind behind that rough exterior. If only she dared offer to cut his hair, but the thought of what might be living in that wild tangle made her hesitate.

When he scratched his head, pulled something out, and squashed it between thumb and finger, she knew. Head lice. How Ruby fought to keep lice and vermin out of the hotel.

"Atticus, would you like to get rid of those itchy things in your head?"

"Ever one has 'em."

"No, not everyone. If you three would like, we can take care of that right now." *But how do I tell their mother she must do the same at home?* She took in a deep breath. In for a penny, in for a pound, as the old saying went.

"You three keep working, and I'll be right back."

When she told Ruby the situation, Ruby nodded. "Of course. Let me get some extra water hot, and we'll do what we can. Their clothes need to be boiled too."

"Oh land, that's right. Perhaps I'm taking on too much. What if their mother gets really offended?"

"I doubt it. That poor woman will most likely be grateful beyond measure. Just that someone is taking an interest in her children makes her smile stretch from ear to ear."

"What do you think, Charlie?"

"I say any help you can give them is good. I'll bring in extra water."

An hour later the two boys had short haircuts, the hair burned along with its extra burden, and all three heads were ready to be doused with kerosene.

"I know this is going to burn, so you must not get any in your eyes." Pearl felt like itching her own scalp, her arms, everywhere. She scrubbed the vile-smelling liquid into their hair and wrapped a towel around each head. "Now you sit there for a few minutes, and then we'll wash it out."

Little June started to cry. "It hurts."

"I know, but only for a few minutes."

"What do we do for clothes for them?" Ruby poured more water into the boiler heating on the stove.

"You know that box that came the other day? It had clothes in the bottom, under the books. Perhaps some will fit."

"Atticus can have an old shirt and pants of mine. We're about the same size." Charlie returned in a minute with pants and shirt. "Going to have to dry their long johns some way, or they'll freeze going home."

"What if we keep them overnight?"

"I could use their horse to ride out and tell their folks."

"Good. All right, you three, we have clean clothes for you to put on, so we'll set up a washtub in the pantry, and after we wash the kerosene out of your hair, you'll take a bath."

"But it's winter," Atticus mumbled from under his towel turban. "Catch our death of cold."

"You're going to stay here overnight. Charlie will let your mother know."

"Stay here?" June squealed.

Pearl smiled when the young girl peeped out from under her towel, her delight setting her to wiggle. "Yes, stay here."

"We'll fix up pallets, and you can sleep in the schoolroom," Ruby said.

"With Milly gone and Opal to bed, things sure are quiet around here." Daisy changed flatirons. "Think I'll go on up and see how Opal is doing."

They had moved Opal down to what they now called the Red Room—though they still stumbled at times and referred to it as Belle's room—so she would be close enough to call if she needed something. Mostly she slept in the darkened room, with Ruby spending as much time beside her as possible.

Which wasn't much, busy as they were.

Charlie bundled up and headed out to the shed. At least it wasn't far out to the Grady farm. When the horses were needed again for spring work, the children would walk to school.

With the bath water hot, Pearl took June by the hand and helped her undress and get into the tub.

"I ain't never had such a big tub." The little girl sank in water up to her shoulders. "And it smells good." She lifted some soap-suds to her nose, then up to Pearl. "Smell."

Pearl had used the rose-petal soap that Cimarron made during the summer. "I know." *Forgive me, Lord, for taking so much for granted*. Even though they had washed the kerosene from the children's heads earlier, the smell still stung one's nose.

Pearl soaped the child's hair again, at the same time looking to see if any nits survived. The whole treatment should be done again in a week or so. Otherwise the child's head would have to be shaved. That was far the easiest method of delousing, but it took a toll on the child's self-esteem.

"Come now, let's get you out and your brother in."

"I don't never get to be first."

"First in what?"

"In the bath, lessen I go takes a bath in the river. We do that sometimes, clothes and all. Scrub with soap and play in the water."

Pearl took all of June's clothes and dumped them in the boiler steaming on the stove, scraping more soap into the boiler from one of the bars of lye soap they'd made one day in the fall. They always kept a can for grease, saving every bit to make soap.

"All right, here's your towel. Let's get you out and dressed, so you can sit by the stove and dry your hair."

"I can't braid it."

"Oh, someone will."

Pearl poured in more hot water and motioned Robert in. "As soon as you're in the tub, I will get your clothes so they can be washed. You have to really scrub your head again to get rid of the kerosene smell."

Robert looked at her like a frightened rabbit caught in the lantern light. "What can I wear then?"

"Those clothes I showed you from the box. They're for you."

"To take home?"

"To take home."

Atticus was last and no more willing, but when Pearl refused to back down, holding out clean clothes for him too, he finally entered the pantry. A couple minutes later, he tossed his dirty clothes out the door.

"Now that's a miracle if I ever saw one." Cimarron gave the boiling clothes another stir. "I just hope this can help that family. Poor is hard enough without dirty too."

Pearl thought about that as she tucked the two younger children into bed that night. She'd never known poor. She'd never known dirty. Her skin felt like something was still crawling on it when she recalled the morning. While she knew the saying "Cleanliness is next to godliness" was not scriptural, it wasn't a bad precept to live by.

She thought back to the story hour, as they'd taken to calling that evening time. She had read with a little girl sitting on her lap, a boy at her feet, and Carl behind at her shoulder, where she could sense every move he made.

— ✣ —

"What's that on your neck?" June asked the next morning during school.

Pearl's hand flew to her collar. Sure enough, the collar had slid down. "I-I have a scar there from when I was a child." She'd never said the words in public before. They stuttered and scraped over the gravel in her throat like a body drug along the riverbank. *I didn't starch my collar enough.*

"Does it hurt?"

"No, not now." She tried to tug the material back up, but it wouldn't stay. *I have to go put a different waist on.*

"I am sorry you got hurt." June brushed down her dress with a gentle hand. "Thank you for my new dress."

"You are welcome."

That afternoon she let the three go home early because a storm looked to be heading toward them. June had not been horrified at the sign of the scar. Of course she'd not seen the entire ugly mass, pinched and bubbly like cooking oatmeal. No one had seen it since she grew old enough to take her own bath and dress herself.

She rubbed the outline of the shape with one finger. Surely no one could love someone with a disfigurement like that. Her father hadn't. Could any man—ever? *Would Carl Hegland go to all the trouble to make a desk like that for someone he didn't care about?* The thought brought a warmth to her entire being. But caring and loving were two different things, weren't they?

CHAPTER FORTY-ONE

Even though February was the shortest month of the year, sometimes it seemed like the longest.

Rand saddled Buck and laced some things in a roll behind the saddle.

"Why don't you just marry the girl and get her out here so you don't have to keep ridin' into town?" Beans handed him a deerskin-wrapped package.

"What's this?"

"You just give it to her. You'll see."

Rand shook his head at his friend's shenanigans. "See you tomorrow."

"Don't hurry home. Ain't nothin' goin' on here anyways."

"Need anything from Johnny Nelson's?"

"Plug a terbaccy if yer feelin' generous."

"If he has any." Leastways the snow was frozen hard enough that Buck didn't sink through. They'd kept a trail clear this year, mostly because he used it so often.

Beans was right. It was time to ask her—again. Only this time he knew how to do it right, and if she didn't feel the same way he did when they were together, then he'd been misreading all the signs and he deserved no better than he got.

She'd leaned against him of her own accord. She smiled at him for no good reason. She sought him out when she used to just want to scream at him. He could tell by the way her jaw had tightened and her voice got real clear. She was not a screamer, but you sure knew you'd been screamed at. All in such perfect ladylike tones, albeit with flashing eyes.

The snow-covered roof of the Chateau, with tendrils of chimney smoke etched against the blue, was always visible now as he came around the last bend and before he could see Dove House, other than the two matching chimney smoke trails.

He nudged Buck into a gentle lope. The northern sky looked pregnant with more snow.

After unsaddling Buck in the shed, Rand stomped his boots on the porch and used the round broom by the back door to sweep snow off his boots and pant legs. North wind was kicking up. Good thing he'd not waited until later.

"Where's everyone?" He stood by the door to take off coat and hat. He'd never heard this place so quiet.

"In here." Cimarron called from the storeroom.

Rand followed her voice.

"Hey, cowboy." She turned from her seat at the sewing machine. "Ruby is upstairs with Opal, who has the measles, like most every kid in the territory, or at least this part of it. Daisy is feelin' puny, so Ruby sent her up for a nap. Pearl is in the schoolroom without children because they are all home with the measles. She's been doing the ironing but wanted to finish a letter to go out on the eastbound train."

"Is Opal really sick?"

"She's better now, but still needs to stay in a dark room, and that frustrates her out of her skin."

"She's feelin' better then."

"You had the measles?"

"Yep. One winter we all had the measles one after the other. Ma was beginning to think we'd have permanent spots."

"Go on up. They're in the Red Room."

"Red Room?"

"Belle's room, but don't you say that. It's a surefire way to light her fuse. What you got in that package?"

"Don't know. Beans sent it along for Ruby."

"And you didn't peek?"

"Would you?"

"A' course."

"How's Jed?"

Cimarron turned red as woolen long johns. "He bought us a piece of land just south of town."

"On the river?"

"No, but a creek runs through it. It's just beyond that first hill."

"Ah, that will be a good place to live." He waved with the package. "See ya. Oh, got a room free?"

"Got a bed in that four bunker empty."

"Good. I'll throw my roll on it." Rand jingled his way up the stairs, took off his spurs, tossed his bedroll on the empty bunk, and returned to knock on the door of the Red Room. What kind of fit would Belle have if she knew about this?

"Come in." It was Ruby's voice.

"Rand!" The joy in Opal's voice matched the smile on her sister's face.

"Hey, with a welcome like that, maybe I better go out and come in again."

"I hope you brought some good stories along, because I'm about storied out." Ruby stood and stretched her shoulders.

"I brought you something." He handed her the package.

"What is it?"

"How should I know? It's from Beans." *And he said I should just marry you and bring you home. What do you think of that?* He knew what *he* thought of it. His whole insides leaped at the sight of her. He watched her stroke the soft deer hide. Would her hands be soft on his face? At the catch of her breath, he tore his gaze from her face to look at the gift.

Beans had outdone himself this time. The dim room did not do the necklace justice, so Ruby moved toward the window where a chink in the curtains let in a beam of light. Beans had braided horsehair to make the chain between beads formed of horn and burnished to a gleam. On the large ones he'd etched a looping design like the scrimshaw Rand had seen once, made by the Eskimos in Alaska.

Ruby held the necklace flat across the back of her hand so the dark horsehair gleamed and the beads shone against it. "Such intricate work. How does he have the patience for this?"

"I don't know. I wouldn't." He inhaled, a scent of roses and summer floating past. She glanced up and met his gaze, a slow smile lighting her face.

"Tell him thank you for me."

"I will."

Ruby Torvald, I love you. He wanted to shout it from the tops of the bluffs, holler it down the valleys, whisper it for her ears alone.

He swallowed.

"Ruby, let me see," Opal called from the bed.

"Come over here then but don't look into the light."

Opal stopped and breathed a sigh. "Ooh, how lovely. Beans made this?"

Opal, much as I love you, why don't you go take a nap? "Yep. He's made earbobs too. Don't see how his old beat-up fingers can get around all this fine work, but they do."

"All right, Opal, back to bed. Rand, if you will be so kind as to tell her a story or two while I go check on things below, I'd be most obliged. You are staying, aren't you?" At his nod, she added, "Good." She tapped Opal, now back in bed, on the end of her nose. "And you, missy, if you behave, you can come down tonight for the story hour."

"Pearl has been reading the story to me, so I didn't get behind," Opal confided to Rand.

Ruby started to scold her for calling the teacher by her first name, but sometimes keeping Opal in line on the manners thing grew too burdensome.

—⁕—

"Ruby," Rand asked after supper, "could I talk with you a bit?" *If I wait any longer, I'll be worse than a landslide—all rocks and dust and destruction.*

"In the schoolroom?"

"Good a place as any."

Ruby led the way, lamp in hand. She set the lamp on the desk, the pool of light burnishing the wood golden. She nearly bumped into him when she turned around, but he didn't step back.

"Ruby, Miss Torvald . . ." *Why can't I speak beautiful words?* "I love you."

"Oh." She breathed the word.

Her eyes took on even more of a shimmer. He could drown in them.

"Is there any chance that you have come to feel the same way?"

"By the same way, do you mean does my heart leap when I hear your voice? My knees go soft as limp dough when I stand next to you?"

"You want to reach out and touch my hand?" He took both of hers in his, his thumbs stroking the backs, soft like the kisses of Cat's whiskers.

"Or lean my head against your chest so I can hear if your heart is thudding like mine?"

"Is this love?" he whispered into her sweet-smelling hair.

"I'm afraid so." Ruby nestled against him.

"Ah, Ruby, I've wanted to say this for so long now."

She tipped her head back to see his face. "Then why didn't you?"

"Well, after that last time, I was scared you'd say no again."

"No to what?"

"I want you to marry me."

"Oh, Rand." She might as well have stepped back a mile, the gorge widened between them so immediately. "I can't leave Dove House. I promised Far—"

"To take care of the girls?"

"Yes."

"I know that, so I figured we could live both places. And besides, the only one left is Daisy. Ruby, we can make this work. I know we can."

"Would you give up living on the ranch for here?"

"No, as I said, we can do both. I'm not asking you to give up Dove House. Do you hear me?" He took her by the shoulders and pulled her against his chest once more where he didn't have to look into her stricken eyes. "I'm not asking you to give up Dove House." He kept each word gentle but distinct. "We can manage. I know we can."

"I just don't see how."

I'm not giving up. Not this time. "Do you truly love me like you said you do?"

"Yes."

"Then trust me. We will work this out." *And I sure hope and pray it will be sooner rather than later.*

CHAPTER FORTY-TWO

Blizzards come when you least expect them.

Pearl stared out the schoolroom window. How could it be gray and cloudy one minute and pure white the next? Never had she seen such swift weather changes. Had there been an inkling, she would have dismissed the children an hour or more ago so they could get home safely.

"Whiteout, Miss Hossfuss. I daren't take Robert and June out in that." Atticus stood slightly behind her and off to her right.

"I know, Atticus. Everyone will spend the night here. I'm just utterly amazed at how swiftly it changes."

"Pa says whiteouts come like a roaring train. Only safe place is home."

"Yes, well, we are all safe here. I'll go tell them we'll have extra mouths for supper." She turned to the rest of the pupils. "Keep on with your work, and I'll be right back. Opal, would you please bring in another lamp?" She'd already lit the two in reflective sconces on the walls, but still it was hard to read.

Pearl headed for the kitchen where Ruby was removing loaves of bread from the oven. "Ah, it smells heavenly in here."

"I know. How about snacks of fresh bread and jam for the children? If you're coming to tell me they'll be spending the night, I already figured that out. That's the fastest I've seen a blizzard hit since I came here." She tipped the loaves out onto their sides, then righted them so she could butter the crusts.

"I'm so grateful the children weren't caught out in that," Pearl said, her voice shaking. "If something happened to them, I'd . . ." She trailed off.

"There are stories of people losing their way in a blizzard, even just going between a barn and a house. Charlie strung a rope out to the shed so we can take care of the horses out there. Good thing we have some grain and hay left."

"I'll think of games and such to keep the children all busy."

"We'll turn this into a party, make it an evening to remember."

"What about the men working in Medora?" Pearl wanted to say Mr. Hegland, but she refrained, although she could feel heat rising in her neck.

"If you mean Carl, I'm sure they are all holed up at the Chateau. They might not have much food left, but they are warm and dry. Please God that no one was caught out on the roads."

The wind caught the door out of Charlie's hand and slammed it against the wall. Snow drifted across the floor before he could get it closed again. "Talk about a northerner. What a vicious one this is." He brushed the snow off his shoulders and dusted off his bowler hat. "You lose track of all direction in that whirling white world out there. Good thing I had that rope up since the baby storm we had last week." He crossed to the stove and rubbed his hands together over the heat.

"I better get back in the schoolroom," Pearl said. "Think we'll have a spelling contest."

"Spelling bee?" Charlie asked.

"That what they call it out here?"

"That's what we called it where I come from."

"Send them out in a couple of minutes for bread and jam," Ruby said. "Some relays would be good to run some energy off too."

For the next hour Dove House rang with shouts of children, the twelve sounding more like twenty-four. But when Pearl brought out the book for story time, they collapsed on the floor around her as fast as if someone yelled "drop dead."

"Sure was good bread and jam," little June said.

"Shush, let her read," Robert barked.

"I was just . . ."

Pearl smiled down at June and drew her closer to her side. "You make sure you tell Miss Torvald that. Good manners are always appreciated."

Robert glared at his little sister but crossed his legs and rested his elbows on his knees, cheeks propped on his fists.

Pearl smiled at each one of them. How precious these children had become to her. Even more so than those in Chicago, maybe because there were fewer here and they were all together on church Sundays and for the Christmas program. They had become part of her daily life, whereas in Chicago, she left the school and went home to a far different life. Would she rather attend a soiree than the sing-along they'd have after supper? The question didn't bear asking.

"Where did we leave off yesterday?"

"Where the bookmark is." Ada Mae made the others giggle.

"Where he woke up tied down by ropes."

"Very good." Pearl opened to the proper page and began reading the story of a rope-bound man named Gulliver.

"Oh, don't stop," someone said when she came to the end of the chapter.

"Please keep reading."

Pearl rolled her eyes, making them laugh. "I suppose, just this once, we can go on."

— ✵ —

After supper and the dishes were done, everyone gathered around the piano and sang till Pearl ran out of tunes, many of which she'd been playing hit or miss anyway.

"I sure miss Belle," Opal said, then added quickly, "not that you don't play good, er, well, Miss Hossfuss, but Belle knew every song imaginable."

"And a few more," Charlie said under his breath.

"All right. You may play games for a bit while we make up beds," Pearl instructed. "Opal, how about hearts and old maid?"

"One of each? Six is a good number."

"Good. In the schoolroom, two circles, make them even." While the children went off to play cards, Pearl and Daisy made up pallets in the Red Room for the girls and in the schoolroom for the boys.

"We could probably put them all into beds, but if the men come back in the middle of the night, they might not be too happy to find a child where they want to be." Daisy reached for another quilt off the top shelf. "Good thing we got extras now."

Pearl stopped in the doorway to watch the two groups play. When Opal shuffled the deck and held the cards between her cupped palms so they whirred back together, Pearl asked, "Where did you learn to shuffle like that?"

"Belle taught me. Faster that way and easier on the cards." She dealt another hand, flipping out cards as well as any card player Pearl had seen. *I wonder if Ruby knows this? Surely she does. Pearl, keep your nose out of other people's business.*

The blizzard blew out by morning, leaving a dazzling white world and two feet of new snow. One drift came over the railing of the Dove House front porch.

— ❧ —

One evening after the Marquis de Mores returned and Dove House was full, Ruby turned around and asked, "Anyone seen Opal?"

"Not since supper." Charlie looked up from the chair he was repairing. One man too many had rocked on the back legs, and this time he ended up on the floor, to the merriment of those who saw him crash. All the others heard the ruckus.

"She should be doing her homework." Pearl wiped the soap off her hands. "I gave everyone plenty to do."

"Most likely reading." Daisy patted Charlie's shoulder as she went by.

Pearl and Ruby exchanged raised eyebrow looks. Was another romance blossoming under their very noses?

Cimarron and Jed came through the swinging door laughing together over a private joke.

"I got news for you folks." Jed paused, one hand on Cimarron's shoulder.

"You started your house?"

"In the snow?" He shot Daisy a patient look.

Ruby kept her gaze on her coffee cup. She knew the surprise. *I'm so glad for them and so sad for me. Please, Rand, be patient.*

"We are . . ." He paused for a long moment.

"Just tell 'em," Cimarron prompted.

"We are . . . getting married on Sunday over to Dickinson."

"Well, I'll be. I was beginning to think you forgot all about that." Charlie set the chair down on all four legs and extended his hand. "Congratulations."

Ruby shared a tremulous smile with Cimarron and gave a slight nod that said "I told you one day there would be a man who looked beyond your former life." Not that she'd have chosen Jed, but God in His mercy did strange things at times.

Where's Opal? She'll hate having missed this news. Ruby left the others laughing and offering advice and went in search of her little sister. She heard a burst of laughter from the cardroom as she climbed the stairs. Surely Opal wouldn't be reading up in their room, cold as it was. She wasn't.

She wasn't in the Red Room, or the storeroom, or the kitchen, or the dining room. Where could she be?

Thinking to ask if any of the card players had seen her, Ruby stopped to straighten a tablecloth, then approached the card-room—cum—schoolroom double doors. She heard the laugh before she saw her sister.

"That's mine, gentlemen." Opal leaned forward and raked the pot toward her.

Piece by piece, because her mind would not absorb more than a bit at a time, Ruby watched Opal, cigarillo dangling from her reddened lips, turn to laugh at the marquis.

"Young lady, you cleaned us out."

"I warned you."

"I know, but"—he looked around at the other players—"but we did not believe you." Two of the others were not laughing. Two were.

Opal pulled the cigarillo from her mouth. "I had a good teacher."

Ruby forced herself from her shocked stare and said, "And who was your teacher?" Her words sliced through the smoke and laughter.

"Ruby!" Opal's eyes widened. She glanced at the cigarillo, to the pile of money in front of her, and back to her sister.

"Give it all back."

"Non, non, she cannot do that. She won fair and square." De

Mores skidded his chair back, the squeal of wood on wood loud in the now silent room.

"Say good night, Opal."

"Good night, gentlemen." Opal straightened her shoulders, smiled to each of her opponents, and started to turn.

The marquis swept her winnings into his hat and handed it to her. "You played fair and square."

Opal took the broad-brimmed black felt in the curve of her arm and marched from the room.

"Enjoy your evening, gentlemen." *It will most likely be your last.* Ruby pulled the doors closed as she exited.

Ruby knew without asking again who had been Opal's teacher, she just wasn't sure how or when. Had Belle been in the building, she would be dead by now. Or at least badly wounded. Ruby stopped in the middle of the dining room to take a breath. Opal playing cards with the men. Her fun and funny little sister playing the cardsharp and pretending to smoke a cigarillo. Why on earth had they stayed? *If I'd gone back to New York immediately, this would never have happened. If I had booted Belle out immediately or anytime soon thereafter, this would not have happened.*

She hung on to the back of a chair, her knees too weak to hold her. *Opal, how could you?*

Did the others know? Had everyone been keeping this secret from her?

When she could find the strength, she marched up the stairs to the room she shared with her little sister.

She stopped before going in, took a deep breath, sucked in another, and stepped through the door.

Opal sat on the bed, one knee bent across the quilt, the other foot still on the floor, counting the money.

Counting the money! Where is her remorse? "How long has this been going on?" Ruby kept her tone conversational with only the greatest effort.

"First time. Guess I had beginner's luck."

"And the last time. You will not keep the money."

"But, Ruby, I don't have any money."

"What do you need money for?" Her voice had gone up a few notes. She took another deep breath. *I will not yell and scream. I will not.*

"Like the marquis said, I won it fair and square."

"You will not keep the money, you will not gamble again, and you will never touch a cigarillo again. Do-you-hear-me?" Flint steel could not have cut the words more cleanly.

Opal's bottom lip came out, her eyes narrowed. "I hear you."

"Good. Then I suggest you take that money back down and return it to the *gentlemen*." Her emphasis on the final word said what she actually thought. True gentlemen would not allow an eleven-year-old girl to play cards with them.

"They won't take it back. You heard them."

"Then pour it down the privy."

"Ruby! There's a lot of money here."

"The better the lesson."

"I'll give it away."

"Fine."

"Can I go downstairs now?"

"No. I have yet to decide what your punishment will be."

"Isn't giving away the money enough?"

"I have *no* idea what to do with you!" Ruby fought the tears that threatened. How could she do this? Had she not been strict enough? *Why, Opal, why?*

"Why, Opal?"

"Why what?"

"Why would you do something like this?"

"It started out as a joke, and then I was having a good time, and, well . . ." Her sigh matched her sister's. "I didn't hurt nothing."

"Anything."

Opal gave her one of those looks and, after stuffing the money in a pouch, stalked down the stairs in front of her steaming sister. Everyone was still in the kitchen when they burst through the door.

"Opal, honeybun, did you hear our news?" Cimarron said eagerly.

"No."

"We're gettin' married on Sunday."

"That's good." Opal turned to glance back at Ruby, plunked the pouch in Cimarron's hands, and gave her a hug. "You can use this better than me." She turned, brushed by Ruby, and mounted the stairs.

"We'll talk about this later." Ruby smiled at the consternation on Cimarron's face. "But that is yours to keep. Do not try to give it back to her."

Ruby pulled paper out of the back of the counter in the dining room, sat down at a table, and uncorked the ink.

Dear Belle,
  I have changed my mind. If you can give me eighteen thousand dollars, Dove House is yours.
      Sincerely,
      Ruby Torvald.

All right, Belle, you win. You get Dove House, but you don't get Opal.

CHAPTER FORTY-THREE

"You did what?" Pearl asked, aghast.

"I wrote to Belle and offered her Dove House for eighteen thousand dollars. If she doesn't want it, I'll sell it to the highest bidder."

Pearl stared at Ruby, sitting so calmly at the kitchen table. With the weather nice for the first time in days, they had the place to themselves.

"Now that I've had time to think about it, I'm going to suggest to Charlie that he look after Daisy. I think I've been seeing some romance there lately. If Belle takes my offer, I shall ask her to give us two weeks to finish school and move out."

"Where will you go?"

"Well, Rand has asked me to marry him." Ruby went silent for a long moment, blinking several times. She cleared her throat. "But I've seriously thought of taking Opal right out of this demented place and back to New York."

"You'd be a governess again?"

"I don't know. I just know that this hotel is not the place for my little sister. And it never has been. What in the world made me think that if I was careful enough of her, she would not be colored by what went on around here?"

Pearl shook her head. "I don't think you'd be happy in New York society again. You've had too much freedom." *And Opal? She'd set the tongues to flapping the minute she opened her mouth, no matter how hard you have tried, my dear friend.*

"I just know I have to get her out of here."

"Have you talked with Rand yet?"

"No, he's not been to town. You know what? I could cheer-fully strangle Belle."

"You knew what she was."

"But I was hoping, praying for her to change."

"Some people can't, not unless God gets them and shakes them good. He's the only one who can do the real changing."

"And He did a lot of that here."

Yes, a lot of changes. Pearl thought back to the night before. After story hour, they'd gathered for singing again. Carl's voice from right behind her had set the tingles to running up and down her back. She caught herself leaning just the slightest backward to feel his presence. *I think I am besotted with that man. Intrigued at the least, but surely it is more than that. I know when he walks into a room without even seeing him. How can that be?*

"Ruby, can I ask you a question?"

"Of course. You know you can ask me anything."

"How did you know when you were in love with Rand?"

Ruby held her cup with both hands and stared over the edge, her eyes speaking of dreams and deep joy. "When I knew I no longer wanted to kill him."

Pearl burst out laughing. "Now that's some definition."

"Not what you expected?"

"No. Not at all."

"For so long he irritated me beyond belief. Then I found myself thinking about him. He'd do something that was so kind and generous, and then he'd set out deliberately to make me mad again." She shook her head, a half smile playing tag with the dreams in her eyes. "Then one day, he touched my hand, and I thought he'd burnt it. I could hardly breathe."

"This love thing sounds like a real pleasure."

"Why are you asking?"

"I-I think I care deeply for Carl Hegland." There, she'd said it. Not the actual word but close.

"I hear a *but* in your voice."

"But I don't know if he cares for me."

"Of course, men go around making desks for any old friend

or acquaintance. For Christmas even."

"Well, I think he cares, but . . ." Her head felt too heavy to hold up any longer. "But does he love me enough to see beyond whose daughter I am?"

"Does he know you love him?"

"I'm pretty sure, but he's never said anything."

"Ask him."

"Ruby Torvald, what is the matter with you? I know, you've been on the frontier too long. Ask him. Nice women don't do that."

"Nice women don't do what?" Opal stopped in the doorway. "Is this another one of those conversations I'll know more about when I get older?"

"Something like that." Ruby extended an arm and, beckoning Opal to come on over, put it around her waist and drew her in. Since they'd been on a guarded truce ever since *that* night, she took any opportunity to be more motherly. Up until now Opal had resisted.

"We're talking about life." Pearl lifted the plate of cookies for Opal to have one. "Did you have a good time out there? Your cheeks are red as holly berries."

"We did. I sure miss Milly though." She pulled away. "I'm going to practice on the piano. You have any more sheet music?"

"Just the books and sheets that are out there. I've ordered some more."

"Thanks." Opal snagged another cookie and ambled into the dining room whistling.

Ruby huffed, started to rise, then sank back in the chair. "What am I going to do? She's as tall as I am, and sometimes when I try to talk to her, she seems to disappear inside herself. Where is the Opal I used to know?"

Pearl knew enough to keep silent when she had nothing to say.

Rand didn't make it to town that week. Ruby kept watching for him, but each day closed with a sigh. How was she to talk this over with him if he never came to town? Perhaps he changed his mind. That thought occurred more than once. Other than Pearl, who'd been sworn to secrecy, she told no one of her letter.

— ❧ —

One week to the day after Ruby had mailed the letter, Belle rode into town, got off the train, and along with her escort, strolled in the front door of Dove House.

"I come for my home back."

"I see. Have a seat." Ruby pulled paper and pen from behind the counter and took her place at the table. "All right, this is what I offer. Eighteen thousand today, and you take over in two weeks, which makes that date, the fifth of April."

"I thought you would be out immediately."

"I can't do that. I'm sure you would not want school meeting here after you own the place. We should go to May for school, but we will close after the first week of April. I will pay you fifty dollars' rent for each week for a total of one hundred dollars." Ruby saw light flare in Belle's eyes. "If this is not satisfactory for you, I will approach some others who have asked me to let them know should I decide to sell."

Belle stared at her, eyes hooded, nodding slightly. "Why are you selling now when things are going so good?"

"It is always best to sell at the top." Ruby had no idea where those words came from, but they sounded great.

"So you are proposing that I give you all the money today and I move back in two weeks. Dove House is now mine. Correct?"

"Yes. I will write the bill of sale right now, and you can catch the afternoon train out."

"We'll stay here tonight."

Ruby now understood the term, *curled lip*. Belle did it well. "Sorry, we're full up. No room at the inn." She crossed her ankles to keep her legs from shaking. *Lord, am I doing the right thing? Will Opal ever speak to me again?*

"Where will you go?"

"I haven't decided yet." *Besides, it is none of your business.*

Belle leaned back in her chair and studied Ruby.

Ruby smiled in return. A slight smile, edged in ice. She waited, knowing how Cat must feel at the edge of a mousehole. Imperious was easy when she was still mad enough to spit. No, not mad, but deep down, burning, get-even angry.

"It's a deal." Belle leaned forward.

Ruby bristled inside at the word deal. But she dipped her pen in the ink and wrote out a bill of sale.

> I, Ruby Torvald, sole proprietor of Dove House located in Little Missouri, Dakotah Territory, on this day of March 23, 1884, sell this building and the contents therein to Belle . . .

"What is your last name?"

"White." Belle mumbled into her hand.

Ruby hid a smile and went back to writing.

> . . . White for the sum of $18,000.00. If there is any contact by Belle White of the people employed by Dove House before April 5, 1884, this contract shall be null and void, and the purchaser, Belle White, shall forfeit the money paid. Purchaser has agreed to accept one hundred dollars as rent and will allow the current occupants of Dove House to remain until April 5, 1884.

Ruby signed the paper with a flourish. "You sign there." She pointed to a line she had drawn. "Do you want your partner to sign too?"

"No, Dove House is mine. All mine." Belle read the contract. "What about . . ." She glared at Ruby. "Aw . . ." She muttered an expletive then signed with no further words. Leaning over, she pulled a bag out of her reticule, plunked it on the table, and drew out one stack of bills, then another and another. "Eighteen thousand. Count it."

Ruby counted out six thousand dollars in hundred-dollar bills in each stack, then tied them back together. Quickly she made a duplicate bill of sale, signed and dated it, and handed it to Belle to sign again.

"Do you have a place I can contact you?"

"No. No need. I'll be here on the fifth." Belle rose. "And you better not be". She took her paper and, escort in tow, marched out the door.

Ruby collapsed in her chair. Over. Two years of the hardest work she'd ever done, and it was over. Or would be soon. Now to tell the others.

She broke the news to Opal as they were getting ready for bed.

"What! How come you didn't tell me first?"

"Because I felt I needed to make this deal without anyone else knowing."

"Why? Where will we go? I love it here." She turned her back to Ruby. "I'm not going back to New York. You can't make me."

"Rand has asked me to marry him."

"What!" Opal flew into Ruby's arms. "And you didn't tell me?"

"I haven't said yes yet, and he hasn't been to town for weeks." *Perhaps he's changed his mind.* "Please, Opal, it has been a long day. Just go to sleep. We will talk more tomorrow."

Ruby went to sleep with that thought and woke with the same. *People do change their minds. Please, God, don't let him change his mind. Not now when I can be free.*

— 🪳 —

"So we'd live on the ranch?" Opal asked the next morning. Ruby nodded.

"And I'd have Bay all the time." Opal was thinking out loud. "What about Charlie and all the rest?"

"I've been thinking of something. But you must let me announce this first. No sharing secrets, do you understand?"

"Yes. But you better do it soon."

"Tonight."

— 🪳 —

"Sure wondered why Belle was in town," Charlie said after she told them all.

"Do we have to work for her?" Fear lurked in Daisy's eyes.

"No, you can work wherever you want. You won't be going back. There'll be plenty of work in Medora. Besides, I've got an idea going, but I have to ponder it some more."

Daisy breathed a sigh of relief. "Good."

"Far as I know, Belle will keep things as they are, other than I'm sure the saloon will reopen, and the gambling be on a larger scale than ever."

"Most likely."

"She won't have any of her former girls." Cimarron smiled up at Jed.

"Not a chance. Even if we have to live in a tent before I get us a house built," Jed promised. "I've lived in a lot worse places 'n that."

"Most everything stays with the hotel unless you have personal things you want to keep."

"I surely don't want those flatirons." Daisy grinned when everyone laughed with her.

"What about you, Miss Hossfuss?" Daisy asked.

"I'm not sure. I think they will renew my contract for the fall, but that depends on finding a place for the school. I imagine I will find somewhere else to room."

"What about this summer?" Opal spoke up for the first time.

"I don't know."

Opal glanced at Ruby, but Ruby shook her head just the slightest. "I'm thinking that part of our money could be used to build a school. What do you think, Opal?"

Opal appeared to ponder, then shrugged. "Why not?"

Ruby's smile held extra love for her sister. "We have two weeks, and in the meantime, we'll give all our guests the same care we always have. If anyone asks, just say we are sure no one will be put out in the street." *Except Opal and me. And we can be on the train east that afternoon . . . if Rand changed his mind.*

"Can I see the money?" Opal asked that night.

"Of course, but you must not show anyone where I've hid it."

"I won't."

Ruby dug down to the bottom of her trunk and pulled out the bag of bills, setting the three packs on the bed between them.

"That's a lot of money. What will we buy?"

"We'll save some, and perhaps we can buy more cows for Rand."

"Yes, he'll like that."

I sure hope so.

— ❧ —

"A new month." Ruby turned over the page on the calendar on the kitchen wall. April 1, 1884. She got the haunch of smoked venison from the cellar and began slicing pieces off to mix with the eggs for breakfast. The hens were starting to lay again now that the warmer weather had come. And Mr. Johnson's cow had a new calf. *If I were staying here, I'd buy a cow or two of my own.*

"Good mornin'." Cimarron came down the stairs, Jed right behind her. "What do you want me to do first?"

"Slice those cold potatoes. Then make the biscuits. Daisy can start the bread. Think we'll fire up the wash outside again."

"That'll sure make a difference in here. If Belle were smart, she'll build a washroom out back."

"I have a feeling Belle isn't going to keep things quite as clean as we have."

"Or have as good of food." Cimarron smirked.

"If she serves food at all. I keep thinking that someone is going to have to feed all these men."

"I have been too. Maybe Jed and me ought to buy two tents—set up one in town to cook in and the other out to our place."

Ruby noted the pride in her voice. Ever since the wedding, Cimarron seemed softer, so happy even her hair glowed.

With the early rush out the door by seven, they kept things hot for the latecomers. Charlie lit the fire, and Daisy threw the tablecloths and napkins into the wash water.

"Storm coming up," Daisy said when she came in for more. "Guess I'll have to hang these on the porch."

"I better go get ready for my children." Pearl set her coffee cup in the dishpan. She pushed on through the swinging door to the dining room. "Looks like we'll need lamps today, it's so dark."

"I'll light them for you." Opal returned to the kitchen for a spill. "Hope they all get here before the rain does."

They could hear thunder grumbling in the distance.

"I'll go help Daisy wring out those tablecloths." Ruby dashed outside. The wind whipped around the corner of Dove House and wrapped her skirt right to her legs. "You want some help wringing those?" She had to shout to be heard.

"Yes, just got a couple more."

"Mornin' Miss Torvald." The Robertson girls bailed off the horses and let them loose in the pasture before running for the building.

The three Gradys trotted up, and while the two younger went to the porch, Atticus let the horse loose.

"Mornin', Miss Torvald, Daisy."

"Now that is one changed young man from that first day he came here."

"Sure is." They twisted the last cloth and tossed it in the basket.

"You think I should start another batch?"

"No. Looks like it's going to rain so hard it'll put the fire out. Come on in. We'll start again later." Ruby left Daisy to hang the clothes on the lines Charlie had stretched on the back and side porches.

"April the first and our first rainstorm of the season. You think that's a sign?" Ruby asked.

"Of what?" Cimarron gave the cake batter another couple of licks.

"Of a rainy season?"

"Doubt it. But right now that river is high enough. We don't need more water."

The thunder crashed closer this time.

A tree limb thumped on the porch roof and blew on by.

Ruby took her dust rag into the dining room and started cleaning the counter and the storage shelves behind it, wiping the dust away and sorting through the things she wanted to keep. She had several boxes packed in the storeroom. There wouldn't be much to take. About the only things here were the buksbom—her father's carved box—and the ledgers. She fingered the necklace Beans had made for her.

Lightning cracked so close she flinched, and the thunder crashed within seconds.

Frissons of fear ran up and down her back. *You know better than to be afraid of thunder and lightning after all these years.*

"That was a close one," Daisy said.

Another crack shook the entire building, so close it sounded like an explosion. Ears ringing, Ruby ran into the kitchen. Was that smoke? Before she got three feet another crash resounded. The building shook as more crashing rocked the air.

"Smoke! Cimarron, get the children out. Fire!"

CHAPTER FORTY-FOUR

"Oh, God, rain. Please send rain. Open your heavens and pour."

Smoke and flames tore at the roof. Ruby leaped onto the porch and ran back in to grab her ledgers and buksbom.

"Get out of here!" Charlie yelled at her. "Anyone still in bed?"

"No." Smoke poured down the staircase. She could hear the flames now, roaring like fury released. She and Charlie both ran back outside, coughing from the smoke.

"Pearl has the children up the street. I'm going to help her with them. You can't save anything in there." Cimarron ran around the east side of the house. The huge cottonwood tree that used to shade Dove House now lay crashed over and against it. People came running with buckets, then stood shaking their heads.

Ruby, with buksbom and ledgers clutched to her chest, glanced down to see all three cats dash past her and head for the pasture.

"Let's get those horses out of the shed in case it goes too," Charlie yelled to some bystanders. "Daisy, let the chickens out!"

Ruby wandered on around the flaming building, now burning on the front too. The men from the Chateau ran across the railroad bridge, but like the others stood watching.

Carl ran up to Ruby. "Pearl, where's Pearl?"

"Over there with the children."

Since the wind was blowing from the west, no one started watering down the other houses, not even Nelson's store.

When the rain came, it sizzled and steamed in the heat, but the fire raged on. With a mighty roar and shudder, Dove House crashed into a pile of blazing rubble.

"I'm sorry, Miss Torvald," Joseph Wainwright, the superintendent on the Chateau, said when he came to stand beside her. "Lightning sure can be destructive when it hits just right."

"I know." Ruby wiped at the tears she realized were not raindrops pouring down her face. Her hair hung on her shoulders, and her teeth chattered, she was so cold.

"We need to get the children out of the rain."

"Mrs. McGeeney has taken them into her house."

"The Chateau is dry if you want to come over there, all of you who work here . . . er . . . worked here."

"Thank you."

Charlie and Daisy joined her, then Jed and Cimarron.

"Well, Belle got herself a pile of rubble." Charlie slicked his hair back and set his bowler in place.

"You mean she already paid you?" Cimarron leaned close to Ruby.

"Yes. She did." *Lord if this was some sort of retribution, you didn't have to go this far.* "But the money burned in the fire." This new shock made her stumble.

"Oh, my God," Charlie muttered.

Ruby fought the darkness that encroached her mind. *God above, our inheritance is ashes.*

As the rain lessened, other folks arrived, and those with schoolchildren claimed them at the McGeeney place. Everyone expressed their sorrow with invitations to come stay with them if need be.

Carl, his arm around Pearl, who was still shaking, joined them on the porch of Nelson's store.

Ruby stepped outside again at the sound of someone yelling. Rand was swimming Buck across the river, waving his hat when he saw her.

"Rand, we're all right!" she yelled and waved as she ran toward him, sloshing through mud puddles, grabbing her sodden skirt to get it out of the way.

He leaped off his horse, and she flung herself into his waiting arms. "No one was even injured. We're all right." He shut off her cries with a kiss that left both of them reeling. Rand leaned into the heaving Buck for support and kept Ruby tight against him.

"I thought sure, I mean, in spite of the storm we could see flames and smoke." He kissed her again and wiped the hair from her face. "I thought, I mean you could have been . . . Oh, God, I am so grateful!" He shouted the words at the heavens, then looked down at her again. "You lost Dove House."

"No." She looked at him with a shrug. "Belle did."

"What?"

"She bought Dove House. I've been wanting to tell you, but you didn't come to town, and I didn't have time to drive out there, plus the snow. She was to take over on April the fifth."

"You sold Dove House."

"And the money is now ashes." She nodded toward the steaming remains. "I hid the money in my trunk in my room." She looked up at him. "I was going to buy you more cows."

"Cows?" He kissed her again.

"What am I going to do?" she asked when she could breathe again.

"You're coming out to the ranch."

"That wouldn't be proper."

"It would be if we were married." He kissed her slowly and gently this time.

— ❧ —

That afternoon two couples took the train to Dickinson, were married by the local pastor, and even though they were all a bit damp, the vows could not have been more heartfelt.

"But I wasn't sure you loved me." Pearl leaned against her husband's shoulder later that evening.

"What else did I have to do?" Carl rested his head against her hair. Hair that after a shampoo and bath smelled faintly of roses, no longer smoke. "I thought the desk said it all. I will build you another one, even better."

"All you had to do was say those three little words."

"Ja, and make a fool of myself. The Hossfuss daughter. Everyone in Chicago—"

"We're not in Chicago."

"Thank God, because there I would not say three little words. I would not say any words to you. I would not know you."

"So isn't it much better we are in Little Missouri?"

"Nei, dear heart, we will be in Medora as soon as we can build a house. In the meantime, we could get a tent?"

"Like the cobbler's children who have no shoes, shall the carpenter's wife have no house?" She ran her fingers across his cheek, finding the courage for the words that she'd wanted to ask since he saw her in her dressing gown. "Do you think I am ugly?"

He drew her eyebrows with a fingertip, down her nose and to her lips, where he kissed her again. When his fingers felt the pucker of the scar on her neck, he watched her eyes. "You are beautiful, my Pearl, shimmery, with a glow that shines within and without."

"You think so?" Her eyes filled with tears.

"I said so, didn't I?"

Pearl snuggled under his chin. For a man of few words, he managed to say the most important ones. And one other thing, Carl Hegland was never boring.

Learn the art of comforting a grieving friend from someone who has been there.

R Revell

More from Lauraine Snelling!

Each of these winning and bestselling series offers all the romance, history, and family drama you come to love from Lauraine!

RED RIVER OF THE NORTH

Faced with the forbidding prairies of North Dakota, the Bjorklund family must rely on their strength and faith to build a homestead in the untamed Red River Valley.

Laboring from dawn till dark, breaking and cutting sod, planting and harvesting what little they can, the family experiences tragedy, loss, but also joy, hope, and a love that continues strong through all the rough times.

1. An Untamed Land   *3. A Land to Call Home*   *5. Tender Mercies*
2. A New Day Rising   *4. The Reapers' Song*   *6. Blessing in Disguise*

RETURN TO RED RIVER

Returning a generation later to the Red River Valley and the Bjorklund farm, this series follows the family as the adult children look to their own future. With a story as timeless as the prairie, the series shows the struggle the family faces when the dreams of the children clash with those of their parents.

1. A Dream to Follow   *2. Believing the Dream*   *3. More Than a Dream*

The Leader in Christian Fiction!

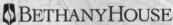

Unbeatable Historical Fiction
from Lynn Austin and Tracie Peterson!

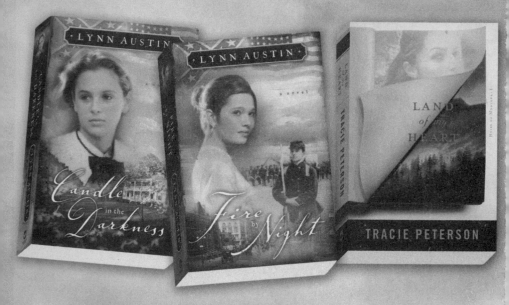

An Unforgettable Look at the Civil War

Candle in the Darkness, Lynn Austin's first novel in her REFINER'S FIRE series, was honored with the 2003 Christy Award for North American Historical Fiction. *Fire By Night* follows up with another compelling story of the Civil War as told from the perspective of characters both intriguing and lifelike.

REFINER'S FIRE by Lynn Austin
Candle in the Darkness • Fire By Night

Bestselling Author Tracie Peterson's Unforgettable New Saga

From her own Big Sky home, Tracie Peterson paints a one-of-a-kind portrait of 1860s Montana and the strong, spirited men and women who dared to call it home.

Dianne Chadwick is one of those homesteaders, but she has no idea what to expect—or even if she'll make it through the arduous wagon ride east. Protecting her is Cole Selby, a guide who acts as though his heart is as hard as the mountains. Can Dianne prove otherwise?

Land of My Heart by Tracie Peterson

The Leader in Christian Fiction!

❖ BETHANY HOUSE